Valley of the Vines

A NOVEL BY *Joy Packer*

VALLEY

of the

VINES

J. B. LIPPINCOTT COMPANY
PHILADELPHIA AND NEW YORK
1956

Contents

CONTENTS

Valley of the Vines

Author's Note

All the characters in *Valley of the Vines* are entirely fictitious, with the exception of the cellar ghost—*the spook*—who belongs to Natte Valleij Wine Farm of the Paarl Valley and who has been borrowed for my Dieu Donné of Constantia with the kind permission of his present owners, Mr. and Mrs. Dudley Kiernander.

JOY PACKER

Bishop's Court,
  Cape Peninsula
1955

THE WIND

In all the world there could be nowhere more beautiful than the Valley of the Vines. Nobody ever disputed that.

The blue velvet mountains enfolded the vineyards, but not too closely, for this was a spacious valley, and the wine-growing foothills looked away across the Cape Flats to False Bay, cupped by the dreaming Hottentots Hollands, pale as smoke.

The sun rose over the Hottentots Hollands and shone down on the coloured fishermen dragging their nets in the mild Indian Ocean; it went its way over the Flats, hiding its face for an instant in shame at the hidden shanty settlements behind the mimosa-covered dunes; gazed benignly upon the Constantia Valley—the Valley of the Vines—ripening the young grapes and the fruit orchards, and continued over the mountain-tops to its splendid immolation in the cold Atlantic at Hout Bay. From the Valley you could see its glow across the Constantia Gap— a lingering gold riding the saddle between the peaks in pagan glory.

Hout Bay people were very proud of those spectacular sunsets. When they invited Valley people to dinner they said, "Come in time for the sunset." And the Valley people were always a little late, because it was really too much—all that magnificence, and the Hout Bay people owning it, owning the Sentinel spur falling sheer into the sea westward of the fishing harbour, and the gilded dunes and the long beach, and the mountain bush, dotted with chalets, that was worth a fortune these days—worth nearly as much as Constantia land!

"And of course we don't get the wind here," they said—these poets and artists who lived in Hout Bay. "We don't get the southeaster like you do." They looked with pity at the people of the Valley.

9

But the people of the Valley only smiled. They were sure that there was nowhere in the Cape—or anywhere else—so desirable as Constantia, even if the summer wind did come raging up from the sea to ruffle the bushy vineyards and toss the poplars and tease the great old oaks that grew and met overhead in green tunnels, or stood sentinel outside historic homesteads like Alphen or Dieu Donné.

Roxane, who was eleven years old, liked the wind. She played her own special games with it. But then Roxane was a queer little thing, half French and wholly fanciful.

She was Grannie Constance de Valois's war-orphan, and she had come to Dieu Donné in 1939 at the age of five with one of the first batches of sea-vacuees from threatened England. It was generally assumed in the Valley that Grannie Con had known Roxane's mother somewhere or another—a young French widow who was teaching in a London convent school at the outbreak of war and who was soon caught up in the frightening machinery of the Secret Service. The child's possessions had been few when she arrived—a scanty wardrobe, easily contained in one small trunk, a miniature of her mother and a rosary that had belonged to her, a porcelain image of the Virgin and Holy Child, a Teddy bear with one eye, and a charmingly illustrated volume of French fairy-tales.

When it became known that Roxane's mother had been parachuted into Occupied France to help the maquis, had been captured, tortured and killed, Grannie Con had adopted the little girl legally, given her the de Valois name and brought her up in the Protestant religion.

Roxane was happy among the vineyards of Dieu Donné; but hazy glimmerings of another life—of Maman and the parks and towers of London—still hovered in remote corners of her mind, and these grew clearer, rather than fainter, as the years passed and imagination built its pictures upon the shadowy foundation of almost forgotten fact.

So, when she played her game with the southeaster, she made believe it was a great magic bird with power to spirit her away to the places she most longed to see—London . . . Paris. . . . She ran to meet the wind with Wolf, her young Alsatian, at her heels. She turned her back on it and leaned against it, letting it hold her on its mighty breath—a thin waif with black hair streaming forward across high cheekbones and rapture in her long, golden eyes. She invoked the wind.

Wind, wind, hold me up! Take me on your wings and blow me over the sea to England—to France!

No-oh-no-oh-no-oh, boomed the wind, and let her go. And the young dog barked and threw his head about and jumped up at her. You can't go, he said. Thinus gave you to me and you are mine!

Marthinus Vos, Grannie Con's nephew by marriage and the manager of Dieu Donné, came up out of the vineyards and laughed at Roxane.

"Hullo, Roxie; taking Wolf for a run? Fine stiff ears he's getting." He rocked the dog's head between his hands, and Roxane heard his kind, slow voice over the wind. "Good boy, Wolf—take care of her!"

"He is good, he is good! And he's mine, my very own! Thank you for giving me Wolf, Thinus!"

She scampered away with her dog, and Thinus looked after them with his half-smile, touched the black shield over the empty socket of his left eye. He and the child had something in common. The war that had tossed him into the Valley—a young disabled soldier—had tossed her into it too, a leaf in the storm, torn from the parent tree and swept far afield to Constantia in the Cape, thousands of miles from her home.

She scrambled over a low parapet into the flower-garden where an ancient coloured man stooped among the roses—old as Grannie Con, old as God. A felt hat covered his grizzled head, and his cotton tartan shirt flowed over his patched trousers.

"What are you doing, Klaasie?"

He answered her in the *taal*, the bastard Afrikaans of the Cape coloureds.

"Chopping off the dead heads, Miss Roxie."

Oh, the poor roses! Off with their heads! She clasped her hands over mouth, remembering the Dreadful Thing. Everybody had told her that Maman had gone to heaven—everybody except Merle. And Merle knew better. Merle had said, "Listen, you! Your maman was a spy—a spy in France—and the Germans caught her and chopped off her head . . . or maybe they just shot her."

Snip-snip went the gardener's secateurs, and the faded flowers thudded softly into the raffia basket. Somewhere in France a rose had fallen. . . .

Listen to me—to my voice and my music! cried the wind.

Roxane stood still. She heard the organ swell in the oaks, the cymbals clash in the magnolias and the violins weep in the willows, while down in the reeds by the stream rose a wavering song, sweet as the sound of the bamboo flute little brown Ben had made for himself.

And see my dance!

She knew where to look. There, on the white walls of Dieu Donné with the slatted teak shutters pinned back against them like elephants' ears, on the moulded central gable above the fanlight, you could see the shadow-ballet of the leaves. Against the stoep a bank of massed blue hydrangeas muttered and sighed with the nodding and swaying of the branches. There was the same pierrot dance on the white walls of the big gabled cellar at right angles to the house. Roxane skipped a little nearer to watch it—but not too near, because, truth to tell, she was afraid of the cellar.

It was then that she saw Merle.

Merle was Grannie Con's grand-daughter, the last of the de Valois line, and the heir to Dieu Donné. Her father, Dirk de Valois, had been killed in the Western Desert. One day all this would be Merle's—the house, the cellar, the lands; Thinus too, if she liked. But she didn't like. Merle was always mean to Thinus.

A strange car near the cellar told Roxane that Merle had been showing somebody round. There were often people visiting Dieu Donné, especially in the wine-making season, and Merle hated showing them round.

"If I'm to act as guide I ought to be paid," she'd complain. Merle didn't like doing something for nothing. "All that patter —'Yes, Mrs. Snooks, Dieu Donné was built in seventeen hundred, soon after Governor van der Stel planted the first grapes in Constantia. He gave a grant to his friend, Pierre de Valois, a Huguenot wine-grower from the Rhône. There have been de Valois here ever since.' "

The visitors followed Merle out of the cellar and a coloured boy put a firkin of wine in the boot of their car. As they drove away Merle stood smiling, with her hair a golden halo round her head and her thin dress blowing against her soft curves and her long legs. But Roxane knew that her smile was on her mouth but not in her eyes, for her eyes were blue marbles, and marbles do not smile.

Merle caught sight of Roxane. "Come here, you!" she called imperiously.

When sixteen calls, eleven listens. "Yes," said Roxane, hanging back from the cellar doors. She could smell the fermenting juice, sickly and sour, and, even over the wind, she could hear the bubbling and gurgling in the huge cement fermentation tanks, and the bang-bang of the crusher as the boys shovelled the grapes down a chute into its gaping mouth. At this season the cellar lived a shocking, greedy life of its own. It became a witch's cauldron.

"It's the red," said Merle. "They've started making Constantia red."

She pushed the child forward into the odorous gloom, and Roxane stood goggling.

Into the crusher they went—the fat bunches of red grapes— and out belched thin little skeletons as the crusher stamped the skin and the flesh to pulp, and down the gutters ran rivers of blood. . . .

"No, no!"

She hid her eyes with her hands and ran into the bright, gusty light with Merle's laughter following her.

"Little funk! The yeast is making spume in the tanks, with huge frothy waves, popping and bursting!"

But Roxane didn't care. She feared the tanks more than the crusher. If you fell into a tank among the *doppies*—the skins— and the wine, you died—in a second—and Merle had threatened to throw her in if she were naughty.

Even the monster oak vats were the tombs of men. She had seen the boys creep through the trap-doors into the empty vats to clean and sulphur them, and Merle had said:

"If a boy goes in too soon he may die of the fumes—*snap*, like that!"

And it was true. A slave had died so, two hundred years ago. His ghost haunted the cellar still. When Dieu Donné was in danger the ghost walked and the coloured people wailed that the spook had come. *"Die spoek! Die spoek! Hy het gekom!"*

"Hey, Roxie, what's your hurry?"

It was Thinus again, Thinus going to the cellar, and Wolf was with him. But now the dog jumped round the child. She stopped, and said in her grown-up voice:

"It's the red. They've started the red!"

"Good," he said. And strolled on towards the cellar, towards Merle, who was his cousin. Quite suddenly the wind was hushed, and Roxane saw Merle waiting in a slanting beam of evening light with that nimbus round her head and her dress gossamer-thin. Thinus put his hand under her bare dimpled elbow to turn her about, and she shook it away and stamped her foot in rage.

"Take your damned claw off me!"

It was a claw. Two fingers and a thumb make a claw. Thinus had a claw—poor Thinus with one eye and two fingers from his left hand lost somewhere in the rocky heights of Abyssinia.

Roxane went slowly round to the back of the house. It was pinioned by its two side gables, held as the folded wings of a bird holds its warm body, and the deep thatch was as dusky as Grannie Con's best *hanepoot* grapes.

Outside the back door a little coloured boy gathered acorns and put them in a sack which trailed after him in the dust.

"What are you doing, Ben?"

"Collecting acorns to sell Baas Thinus for de pigs."

He had skinny stove-pipe legs and skinny brown arms, and the wind lifted his thick blue-black hair and tossed it into his eyes and away again. His eyes were enormous—wet, black and shiny as the body of a seal, a seal on blue-white sand, damp too.

"What will you buy with the money?"

"When I have saved enough I will buy a guitar."

"But I love your bamboo flute."

"A guitar is better—he will buy a guitar and play for us to dance!"

Saartjie, the child who lived with Ben's mother, Lizzie, had come from nowhere to join them. Saartjie always came out of nowhere and went back into nowhere; it was her magic. Now she began to thump her feet in the dust and posture, and wriggle her behind and her shoulders like a jitterbug. Now she was a mad thing. And Ben dropped his sack of acorns and took her hands and they leaped about and shrieked and laughed and sang. The boy was dark as the teak doors of Dieu Donné when they were newly oiled and Saartjie was pale as milky coffee, and Ben's mouth and nose were wide and gay while hers were button-small, but their eyes were the same—no, not wet seal after all, but liquorice after you've licked it, moist black liquorice, neither bitter nor sweet, with a flavour none could describe and none forget.

Roxane wanted to take their hands and dance with them. But Merle would be cross. Merle said, "You shouldn't play with little niggers, but if you must, don't touch them! The brown comes off!"

It wasn't true, it wasn't true! The stain did *not* come off! She began to sing with them. *"Daar kom die Alabama—die Alla-*baa-*ma*——" And she pulled Wolf on to his hind legs and held his front paws and danced with him. You mustn't dance with little niggers, but a dog was all right . . . good doggie, Wolf, good partner! Now the two coloured children had begun to fight playfully—putting their hands on each other's shoulders and butting their heads together like small buck.

Up the Valley the silver-trees rippled against the dark pine plantations and beyond the berg the sky was apricot and gold.

"Miss Roxie, it's nearly suppertime!"

Lizzie stood on the back stoep outside the kitchen door and called through the fly-wire. She was small and quick as a fly herself and her frizzy hair was pepper and salt. Roxane thought Lizzie was Grannie Con's shadow—a shadow got loose, living its own life in Grannie Con's kitchen. But there was plenty of substance in this shadow that was Lizzie, if not in volume then in value. Lizzie was as supple as a small *sjambok*—a rhino-hide whip; she could lay about her with a crack and a flick, and Joshua, her husband, and Saartjie, her niece, fled when Lizzie was cross. Even the white members of the household kept out of her way then—Grannie Con, Merle and Roxane; and Thinus stayed in his cottage. Only Ben did not worry, for Ben was the child of her old age and he could do no wrong.

"You spoil him," Grannie Con had often told her. And Lizzie had smiled and said, "My Oumissus spoilt Master Dirk too—an' for de same reason. Me an' my Oumissus, we borned our sons too late."

"Too late and too few, Lizzie. Our only sons. And mine lies dead in the desert, and there is only his daughter left for Dieu Donné—no one but Miss Merle. . . ."

And Lizzie, who was full of comfort when she was not cross, would console her Oumissus. "Miss Merle will marry an' give us chillun for Doo Don—if de good Lord wills." Lizzie never left the Lord out of her speculations; He had surprised her too often for that. But her heart grieved for her Oumissus. She did not trus' Miss Merle—she was like her ma, that one, hard and col' as de icebox.

She stood now, hands on hips, and watched the capering children.

"Miss Roxie!" she called again. "Nearly time for supper!"

"What's for supper, Lizzie?"

Roxane pushed open the fly-wire door and sniffed round the kitchen with Wolf at her heels, sniffing too.

"Aches, an' summer puddin' with mulberries."

"What sort of eggs?"

"Scammelt aches."

"Goody-goody! I love scrambled eggs and summer pudding."

There were some mulberries over, in a white pudding-bowl. Roxane picked one out and ate it, and licked the purple juice off her fingers.

"Pasop!" warned Lizzie. "Dose t'ings stain."

The two coloured children had crept into the kitchen, and they too dipped their fingers into the bowl, their eyes shining with greed and mischief as they bolted the fruit as fast as they could.

"Out, out, out!" scolded Lizzie in a high voice, suddenly impatient with all of them. "*Voetsak*, dog! *Voetsak*, you little brown skellums! Off you go an' wash yourself, Miss Roxie—Lizzie's busy."

They cavorted into the wind—the brown children to their acorn picking, while Roxane chased round to the front of the house.

There, at the top of the steps, was Grannie Con—sturdy and solid as a stone statue of Queen Victoria, her white hair smooth against her skull under its net, her heavy black dress scarcely stirred by the gusts that sprang up onto the stoep and puffed in her face.

Tap-tap-tap, peck-peck-peck, sounded her voice.

"Go and get ready, Roxane! Get ready for supper!"

But the child stood still. This was the beginning; it was always the beginning. "Get ready for supper!" After supper came the dark. She lingered, seeking the last gold in the sky above the Hout Bay Gap, praying deep inside herself: "Let night not come —just this once let night not come."

For, ever since Merle had told her the Dreadful Thing, night had been horror and grief and a snake crawling into your chest —heavy and cold, coil upon coil—moving down into your stomach and up into your throat, flickering and stinging behind your eyes. Night was the prayer that was never answered. Even the Holy Mother in the niche above your bed, in her robe of midnight blue, spangled with stars, and her Babe in her arms, could only look at you with love and pity and shake her gentle head.

"Holy Mother of Jesus, let it not be true . . . let them not have killed Maman . . . let her not have been a spy, not have been caught, not have been killed by the Germans! Let me wake and find it isn't true! Holy Mother, let me wake. . . ."

The pain was inside you, bigger than you; it was the snake uncoiled in your heart and your body and your neck, bursting you, shaking you as you clung to the pillow that was not

Maman. It was fire streaming from your eyes and a sobbing that brought Lizzie from her kitchen to rock you in her arms.

"Let her not be killed. . . . Lizzie, Lizzie, let it not be true."

Choked words and stormy weeping, and Lizzie talking—no longer shrill.

"Your mammy is a star, Miss Roxie—up in de heavens. She is a star like one of dose stars on de Virgin Mary's dress. . . ."

Your hot wet face and swollen eyes were pressed against Lizzie's breast, her hand patting your heaving shoulders as bit by bit, coil by coil, the snake slid away and melted into the night. . . . The Virgin in her starry robe leaned over you, and laid you down and smoothed your hair and said, "Sleep now, sleep, chile," and her voice was Lizzie's and her hand was brown. Brown, but it left no stain.

CHAPTER 2

THE WEDDING

There was to be a wedding at Dieu Donné.

Roxane's eyes begged: Merle, Merle, ask me to be one of your bridesmaids, please, Merle!

Roxane was fifteen with long skipping legs and little high breasts pushing at her blouse; she was gypsy-dark with her summer tan and cloudy hair. Merle ignored her pleading eyes.

"I want a blond wedding," she said. "All blondes." And that cut Roxane out.

Grannie Con spoke her mind. "Blond fiddlesticks—the simpering creatures! Roxane should be one of your flower-girls."

"A bride has a right to pick her own attendants."

"You are a cruel thing. You play cat and mouse with the child. You always have—mercy knows why!"

But Merle just tossed her curly head and laughed in her careless way. She chose two tall bridesmaids of her own age and two flower-girls from among Roxane's friends. "And I must have Aletta Krige's Jannie," she said. "As my page."

"A boy of four is dangerous," said Grannie Con. "They let you down."

"Boys of any age let you down—and at least Jannie Krige looks like an angel straight from heaven."

Miriam, the Malay dressmaker, with two assistants, came daily to cut and fit and sew. And Lizzie grumbled. "Dese Malays is a nuisance! Dey can't eat dis and dey won't eat dat because dey is Moslems. Better Miriam comes in Ramadan when dey is fasting!"

Miriam had a strange Eastern face and she wore flimsy cyclamen head-scarves on her black hair, petunia lipstick on her pouting mouth and kohl round her eyes. Her fingers were nimble, for she came of a family of tailors and seamstresses.

It was November, the blue month, when jacarandas, hydrangeas and agapanthus lilies cast their blue-mauve spell on the gardens of the Cape, and this was to be a blue wedding except for Merle, the snowy bride.

The Valley loved a wedding. It pulsed with pleasurable interest, and over the tea-cups and cocktail glasses heads bobbed and nodded.

"Do you know Guy Masterson—the bridegroom-to-be?"

"A brilliant young architect—but one of those moderns——"

"Grannie Con gave Merle five acres of Dieu Donné land as a wedding present, and Guy has built a charming cottage, not a bit modern."

"The old lady insisted on that. A cottage to conform to the character of the Valley, she said."

"And why not? She paid for it!"

Bzz-bzz-bzz went the Constantia chorus. They—the great anonymous THEY—knew everything.

"My dear, have you heard? They say the sparks are flying over at Dieu Donné!"

The click of a cup put down, an attentive breath drawn deep.

"Grannie Con wants Merle to keep the de Valois surname, and Merle tossed her head and said, 'Masterson is good enough for me,' and back came the old lady, 'It may be good enough for you, but it's not good enough for Dieu Donné!' "

"But that's her phobia. Dieu Donné and de Valois let no man put asunder."

"Of course, my dear. When she married Stephanus Vos he had to take her de Valois name and hang up his hat in *her* hall! He changed his religion too. The Vos family are all Dutch Reformed, but when Stephanus married Constance de Valois of Dieu Donné he went over to Anglican to suit her book."

"So he sold himself body and soul to Dieu Donné."

"But he loved her. No one can ever deny that he loved her."

"Victoria loved the Prince Consort—but *she* remained Queen!"

It was true that there had been deep devotion between Grannie Con and her husband, but only one child had come of the marriage—Merle's father, Dirk Vos de Valois, who had been killed in World War Two. And Merle's mother, pretty, brassy Bella (born van der Walt of the Valley), had quickly married again. She had married Dirk for Dieu Donné, they said, and Solly Caine of Johannesburg for his money. Love? Oh, no! The van der Walts, they said, drew a sharp distinction between love and marriage. The composite tongue was forked and flickering.

The day before the wedding Merle's mother and step-father arrived from Johannesburg.

Roxane saw old Joshua in his peaked cap and long white chauffeur's coat waiting with the station-wagon. His frizzy hair was grey, but his face was bland and moon-like, and if his wife, Lizzie, beat him, as he always swore she did, it was evident from his girth that she also fed him well from Grannie Con's larder.

"I'm waiting for Miss Merle," he said. "We is going in to Cape Town to fets Miss Merle's mammy and de Yentleman from Yo'burg. We doesn't know dis Yent from Yo'burg here, Miss Roxie, but I can say dis—Miss Bella was his wife before Baas Dirk was cold in his desert grave. Dey's coming on de Blue Train."

That was a train worth meeting, fast and expensive, rushing from the Golden City on the veld, through the mountains and down to the sea, a thousand miles in a day and a night.

The Blue Train for a blue wedding. Roxane gulped down one of the wads of emptiness that so often stuck in her throat these days. All those billowing yards of mist-blue organza in the sewing room, and Miriam, the Malay, putting the final touches to dresses for a bride and her retinue—but not for Roxane.

Merle's mother had not been to Dieu Donné since Dirk's death. She stepped delicately out of the station-wagon and kissed the air somewhere near Grannie Con's withered face.

"So this is Roxane?" she said. "How do you do, Roxane. Solly, come and meet Grannie Con!"

The Yent from Yo'burg was as plump and pink as a nice red *steenbras*. He steamed in the mild November heat, and Roxane thought that, like the fish he resembled, he would always be bright and shiny and never quite dry. The hand he offered Grannie Con was cold and damp as he said in his liquid voice:

"Delighted to meet you, Mrs. de Valois—and to see Dieu Donné, the famous, incomparable jewel of Constantia!"

He flapped his fins in the direction of the Valley and the vineyards and his pleasant, protruding glance embraced the lawns, gardens and old homestead in its grove of oaks.

Grannie Con smiled against her will.

"The house has been repainted for the wedding, and the teak doors and shutters oiled. We have done the cellar too, and the adjacent cottage where my manager lives—Marthinus Vos, my dear departed husband's nephew."

"It all looks very nice," said Merle's mother, but she wasn't looking at the house at all. "My case, Solly—the little case with my face in it."

"I have it," said Merle.

"And the hat-box with my wedding hat? Surely we didn't leave *that* on the platform?"

"It's here, Miss Bella."

"Oh, thank you, Joshua. I'm sorry to be a pest, Grannie Con, but you know how vague I am, always losing or forgetting things."

The old lady's face hardened. Yes, Bella, you forgot my son, Dirk, fast enough! But overriding the thought was Solly's voice.

"My Bella never loses anything that isn't insured, not she!" He turned to Roxane. "And you, little lady, I suppose you are all thrills for tomorrow—chief bridesmaid, no doubt?"

Merle's mother stopped at the head of the steps and made a

shshing movement with fingers dipped in blood. Roxane looked down and swallowed the lump that had risen in her throat.

"N-no—Merle wanted fair bridesmaids—all blondes."

"The 'All Blondes'? Sounds like a football team! Here, what's this in your ear?" He leaned over her in consternation, and there was a thin rustle as he withdrew a pound note from under the soft dark hair. "What a funny place to keep your money!"

Roxane giggled at his startled expression, but Merle's mother was not amused. "Throws it about," she said to the air with a shrug. "Picks it out of the sky and flings it around!"

"Stars too," he remarked with a glance at her hands. "Hard, glittering little stars—worth a fortune."

Lizzie cooked them a beautiful dinner that night—the night before the wedding.

Guy Masterson was there with his quick ways and his red hair and that unbelieving look in his eyes, and a sort of trembling impatience all over him. He talked in little rushes with his words scurrying after his swift-winged thoughts, never quite catching up with them. Thinus sat opposite Guy and Merle, and he could have wished that just this once he was blind in two eyes instead of one. For he loved Merle, his cousin, who was fairer than the roses on the round polished table, brighter than the silver and more intoxicating than the wine, and tonight she seemed to waver in the candle-light, she who was always so hard and sure.

Merle's mother said, "Oh, by the way, I've asked the Kriftis to the wedding."

"But I don't care for Mr. Krifti," said Grannie Con.

Bella Caine shrugged her shoulders. "His wife, Louise, is my first cousin and we saw a lot of them recently when they were still in Johannesburg. Besides, it would hurt old Auntie Marthe van der Walt if you left out her daughter and her husband. After all, they are your neighbours in the Valley—new arrivals—and one should be hospitable."

Bella had aimed two shrewd blows. Grannie Con bristled. Hospitality was a tradition of Dieu Donné, and she was fond of old Auntie Marthe in a somewhat carping way. They were both of them survivals of an almost extinct generation. But none the less Auntie Marthe's son-in-law got in Grannie Con's hair. He was up to no good in her Valley of the Vines.

"Very well, Bella," she said tartly. "If you have invited Louise and the curious man she has married, that is the end of that. But I don't remember seeing his name on our list."

She rose to carve the exquisitely browned goose which Joshua set before her. She prided herself upon her carving only second to her hospitality.

"Kriff made a fortune in Johannesburg speculating in land," said Solly Caine, helping himself to green peas. "He'll do the same here, mark my words. You could sell him Dieu Donné for a fancy price, I should say. He's bent on living in Constantia, in a genuine historic homestead. To him it would be the final symbol of success, financial, social and cultural, the crown for his superb collection of Africana. But, in any case, I'm sure he'd willingly relieve you of a good slice of the estate."

Merle uttered a slightly hysterical giggle as Grannie Con set down her carvers. The old lady's face had closed down with the mouth long and narrow between the upper and nether mill-stones of nose and chin."

"Sell a slice of Dieu Donné? Cut it up as if it were this goose! You don't know me very well, Mr. Caine."

"More's the pity," said that gallant gentleman, unabashed.

Bella Caine frowned at her husband. How like Solly to plunge in and go on floundering! Sometimes she fancied he did these things out of devilment. She changed the subject deliberately, and allowed her porcelain-blue eyes to return to Roxane's young sensitive face as they had done many times that evening.

"There is some resemblance in this child that haunts me," she said. "I can't place it and yet it's there, like a name on the tip of one's tongue. Where have I seen her before, Grannie Con?"

"The world is full of likenesses." Grannie Con's tone was dry as paper. "Queen Victoria and myself, for instance."

Guy was looking at Roxane with new interest, really seeing her for the first time. "She's not unlike that eighteenth-century portrait of Sarah de Valois in the *voorkamer*. They have the same alabaster flesh tints. But on second thought she reminds me of an Italian Renaissance Madonna——"

Merle cut in with a quick laugh. "Guy has Italy on the brain! He's always finding somewhere or somebody to remind him of Italy. Ever since the Italian peasants hid him when he escaped in the war he's been mad on Italy."

"I escaped in the middle of the grape harvest," smiled Guy. "I lived on nothing but grapes and tomatoes for six weeks!"

Grannie Con threw him a gracious smile. "There is wonderful nourishment in grapes."

"And in rice," said Solly. "When one thinks of the millions in China who exist on rice alone——"

Rice, thought Roxane—tomorrow we'll be throwing rice and confetti. If only I could have been a bridesmaid! Perhaps a miracle will happen to make me one? Miracles *do* happen!

Grannie Con was saying grace when the telephone rang and Joshua came to call Miss Merle. It was a humdrum and belated little miracle. But it served its purpose. One of the bridesmaids had mumps.

"Grannie Con, will I do?"

The old lady set a grey satin-straw hat straight on her smooth grey hair and turned from the ageing reflection in the old-fashioned dressing-table mirror to the small blue cloud that had danced into her bedroom.

"Wait, my lorgnettes!"

The cloud came into focus—love-in-a-mist, young and appealing. Fifteen, on the threshold. Long-ago memories pierced Grannie Con's heart, little thorns drawing tiny drops of blood. At fifteen there is no armour.

"Miriam took it in on me, tacked it, so it can easily be let out again for Marigold."

"It's charming on you. Marigold would have looked a lump."

Roxane's blue slippers pirouetted on the yellow-wood floor. She was so happy in her first long dress, even if it *was* only lent for today; she felt light as a bird.

From every side of the Peninsula cars streamed into the Valley. They came over Constantia Nek from Hout Bay, and over Kloof Nek from Camps Bay; they followed each other nose-to-tail from Cape Town above the magnificent sweep of Table Bay past the buck and wildebeest grazing in the Devil's Peak Nature Reserve; they poured through the southern suburbs to Wynberg, where they met up with the cars from Simon's Town and Muizenberg. The traffic police were on guard at the corner where the road forks into the green acres of the vines. They were very military in their khaki uniforms, but friendly and smiling today, not roaring up on their motor-cycle combinations with stop-watches and frowns to say, "But you must know that there is a thirty-mile-an-hour speed limit in the Peninsula. Name and address, please?"

Dieu Donné stood at the head of the Valley to receive her guests, glimmering white among her leafy oaks, wearing her vineyards like a bridal train spread fanwise down the slopes before her. But today the green, bushy vines were untended, for on this occasion the people of Dieu Donné were receiving a holiday and a bonus.

It was, in a way, less Merle's wedding than Dieu Donné's. And the babies that came of it would be pledged to honour their heritage.

The coloured folk turned out in their Sunday best; the little boys with ties and blazers and shoes, and the little girls in candy-coloured frocks and frilly hats. And, as the bride and bride-groom left the stone church among the pines to drive home for the reception, all the brown hands waved happily and a clamour of voices called after them in the *taal*, "Good luck—God bless you!"

Then Merle and Guy were back at Dieu Donné standing on the lawn in the angle of the homestead and the cellar, and every-one was filing past and whispering pleasant things they hardly heard.

"Isn't he an angel—the little page?" smiled the women to one another. But soon the angel was bored and broke loose, and Roxane saw him playing hide and seek among the tea-tables till—*crash*, as a damask cloth was clutched and tugged and a small boy buried beneath sandwiches, savouries, china, glass and silver. Wolf, the Alsatian, wondering at all the strange things that were coming to pass, sniffed under the debris and dragged forth a weeping child by the seat of his blue satin pants.

"It's Jannie, of course!" cried Aletta Krige, and smacked her son more out of habit than indignation. "Wherever there's trouble it's Jannie!"

The big dog gobbled up the sandwiches, and Roxane said to the page, "Stop crying and look! The bride is going to cut the cake!"

So Merle was cutting the cake with its decoration of marzipan grapes and tiny wedding bells. "Little slave-bells," murmured Solly Caine, with a glance at the big copper slave-bell in its high white arch. Then Guy was saying in his quick, almost stammering way, "My wife and I thank you—I have been dying to say *my wife and I.* . . ." Glasses were raised in the sun. "To Guy and Merle!"

"Delicious champagne!" Old Auntie Marthe van der Walt licked her lips. "Certainly, waiter, I will take another glass."

"So will I," said Mr. Krifti.

Auntie Marthe sometimes wondered how her daughter, Louise, had come to marry Mr. Krifti. He was a queer fellow. But then, he was also very rich and Louise, like her cousin, Bella Caine, had a proper respect for the value of money. Louise liked to say that the van der Walts were full of pride but empty of purse. So now Mr. Krifti and Mr. Caine had come into the family to put the matter right. And why not, pray?

Auntie Marthe glanced down at the flowered chiffon gown she had worn to every smart wedding for the past ten years, and she didn't think much of it, nor did she fancy her shabby fur stole, known in the Valley as "Auntie Marthe's old cat." Still, she stood herself a new hat every now and again! She tossed her snowy head so that the loose skin on her neck rippled and the feathers on her large picture-hat shuddered with a purple palsy.

Mr. Krifti had a long, lugubrious face which fell into pallid folds as if the Almighty had been wasteful with flesh and sparing of blood in fashioning the features of this, His creature. But, in his morning coat and striped trousers, Auntie Marthe found her son-in-law rather elegant. He might have been mistaken for an eminent surgeon, she thought, or perhaps a very superior undertaker. Actually, he was spoken of as a financier and she had recently sold him a considerable portion of van der Walt land adjoining Dieu Donné. In the Valley people were always selling off sections of their property to relatives, so that family clans were dotted all over Constantia.

Beside her husband sat Louise, refusing all the tasty morsels she was offered. "Studying your figure?" asked her mother, helping herself to a cream puff.

"Yes, Mother," said Louise, and thought, If she says that again I'll throw a bun at her!

In fact, Louise Krifti made an agreeable picture in her fashionable dress and sparkling jewels. Auntie Marthe thought that she would "carry" Mr. Krifti in Valley society. Oh, yes, no doubt about that! With Louise's background and her husband's fortune, a fine house and an impeccable cook they would be acceptable anywhere. She heard her son-in-law's odd muffled voice as if his tongue were uncomfortable, too much of it, like the skin of his sagging face.

"I would like to make old Mrs. de Valois an offer for this place. Dieu Donné would suit Louise and me admirably."

"Make Grannie Con an offer for Dieu Donné!" Even Louise, long past surprise at anything her husband might do or say, raised her eyebrows.

Old Auntie Marthe was shaking with laughter. "My dear Kriff, the very idea is blasphemy! You certainly don't know our Valley —or its doyenne!"

He had drawn a chaplet of amber beads from his pocket and was running them gently through one small Oriental hand—a curious habit of his. "We will wait," he said. "We will wait and see."

The press photographers moved among the tables taking notes and pictures. "There!" said one of the social reporters to the photographer. "Get that group if you can! That's the famous English novelist Adrian Fairmead and his wife and son. They are staying with the bridegroom's parents, and rumour has it they are going to settle at the Cape."

She made her way towards the tall figure of the novelist. He walked rather stiffly—like a crane, she thought. The social reporter was one of Adrian Fairmead's most ardent fans.

"Dare we hope," she said, "that you and Mrs. Fairmead are really going to live in the Peninsula?"

"It is possible," he said with his somewhat sardonic smile. "But I shan't write a book settling the problems of Africa, if that's what you want to know."

"You'll be the exception," she laughed. "Everybody writes books on Africa."

His wife had joined them. Straight out of *Vogue*, decided the reporter. Fortyish, sophisticated, with a quaint face and challenging grey eyes. And what a figure, no tire, no hips! And here was the son, a head-in-air young fellow with his mother's aggressive eyes, but hers were weary and his were gay and eager for life.

"Yes," Mrs. Fairmead said in answer to the reporter's question. "We sail for England tomorrow. It's too sad. I'm mad about the Cape—infatuated with it! . . . Yes, our son, Hal, sails on the same ship, but not in our class—the little snob. He insists on travelling second class—so unsociable." She had a clear English voice, high and over-emphatic, as if she were speaking her lines on the stage.

"I suppose you have to get back and do your military service?" the reporter asked Hal.

"Yes," agreed the young man briefly. He hated talking about himself to strangers, although he had to admit that Miss Social Column looked rather jolly and pretty when she wasn't being too business-like.

"And then?" she persisted. "Will you be a writer, like your father?"

He laughed down at her at that, and she saw that his face was alight with humour and self-mockery. "My father is a very fine writer! But I might have a go at journalism. I'd like to be a war-correspondent."

Mrs. Fairmead broke in. "The happy pair have gone in to change. A lovely bride, but then, it's symptomatic. All brides are lovely. And the angel-page, what a cherub!"

"Your cherub is going to be sick any moment, if you ask me," said the reporter. "Little Jannie Krige has eaten everything in sight and was knocking back his mother's champagne when last I saw him!"

A few moments later Hal Fairmead observed the little dark bridesmaid bending over the "cherub," who was a curious shade of green. He slipped away from his parents and Miss Social Column to the shadow of the great oak where the young girl stood with her arm about the child.

"Can I help?"

She looked up in swift surprise, and recognized Hal Fairmead although she had not met him, for the appearance of the best-selling novelist and his wife and son had caused quite enough flutter to be a subject of conversation among the other guests.

"Oh, yes, please! Would you carry him indoors? I daren't, because he may be sick any moment and my dress is only borrowed——"

"And my suit doesn't matter," he laughed, lifting the child with gentleness and saying, "Now hang on, old chap, and keep your mouth shut for the next few seconds."

Roxane led them quickly up the wide stone steps into the cool old house, through the lofty *voorkamer* with its aroma of bees-wax and lavender, and across the *agterkamer*, which comprised the afterpart of the large inner hall, and into a bedroom with a bathroom beyond it.

"There," said Hal. And held the cherub's head where it would do no harm. Jannie Krige wasted no time.

"Miss Social Column wasn't far wrong," Hal grinned presently. "It was certainly a case of 'all this, and heaven too'—the heaven being champagne!"

"Champagne! Jannie?"

"Miss Social Column spotted him guzzling his mother's, and I should say he'd had a sip of father's too!"

Roxane finished sponging Jannie Krige's angel face and Hal carried him into her room and laid him on the bed.

"It's a hot day, but we'll cover him," he said. "He's chilly."

Roxane drew a light blanket over the little boy, who fell asleep instantly with two of Hal's fingers firmly clasped in his hand.

"He's fine now," said Hal, "but I expect we ought to report to his parents."

"Yes," she agreed. "But give me a moment to comb my hair. This forget-me-not nonsense is all askew. I'm going to take it off."

She shook her hair free of the wreath, and while she tidied herself, Hal looked round the room.

It was austere, and somehow a little touching with the heavy, old-fashioned furniture and a heap of school-books open on the desk suggesting unfinished homework. French doors gave on to an orchard still starry with blossoms. A bear with one eye sprawled on the bed next to Jannie Krige, and on a small bed-side table was a rosary, a miniature of a young woman with the same tilted golden eyes as the girl's, and a slender volume of Rostand's *Cyrano de Bergerac* in the original French. In a wall-niche was a statuette of the Madonna and Child. The brush which Roxane was using was part of an ivory toilet set engraved with the name "Anne."

"You must be Anne," he said. "Anne who?"

"No, I'm Roxane de Valois. My mother's name was Anne."

"Is this your mother?" He picked up the miniature with his free hand. The cherub still grasped the other. "It must be—it's so like you; the same delicate bone structure. It's an unusual face with strength in it as well as beauty."

Her heart quickened. He's not just looking, she thought with astonishment; he is really *seeing* her! I would like to tell him about Maman—the way I feel I must go back where she came from and learn everything I can about her—how I want to *find* her!

"Maman was French—but the pity of it is I can't honestly re-member her. You see, I was only his age"—she indicated the cherub—"when I was parted from her; when she sent me here to Grannie Con as a sea-vacuee in the war. I just have a sort of vague memory of someone who laughed a lot and who hugged me when I hurt myself. I have a picture of her in my imagination, of course, because I think about her a tremendous lot, but it's built on such a few things, mostly on the things that belonged to her. There was very little, but they sent them here—after—after . . ."

"After what, Roxane?" he asked very gently.

"My friends mostly call me Roxie," she said.

"I would like to be your friend, but I would rather call you Roxane. It's a lovely name."

She glanced at the little volume on which her rosary lay.

"Roxane was the girl Cyrano de Bergerac loved. I expect that's where Maman got the name from. The rosary was hers too. She was Roman Catholic, but Grannie Con brought me up as a Protestant when she adopted me formally and gave me her family name—after . . ."

Again she hesitated, and again he repeated, "After what? Tell me what happened, Roxane. I think you want to tell me."

"Yes," she said. "I like to talk to you about her. You seem to understand somehow."

She was sitting on the dressing-table stool with her back to the mirror. Her sharp little chin was cupped in her hands as she said, "They killed my mother." She spoke as if the words had no meaning, as if she had said them so often to herself that they were empty now—parrot-words drained of pain and horror.

Hal looked at her with a feeling of shock. Why did this child make such a grim statement? *Killed*—the terrible active verb! Had Anne been an air-raid victim? What?

She had let her hands fall into her lap and the fingers twisted a small lawn handkerchief trimmed with lace.

"My father died before I was born, and Maman was teaching in London, in a convent school, when the war came. Then she got a job in the Secret Service. They parachuted her into Occupied France—her own country—to help the maquis. The enemy caught her . . . and . . . tortured her . . . in the end they shot her. She was Anne Williams. You may have heard of her."

"*Anne Williams!*" he exclaimed softly. "Why, Anne Williams is a legend—like Odette!"

"Only Odette's story had a happy ending."

"You must be very proud, Roxane, very proud indeed."

She nodded, and tears pricked her eyes at the way in which he had spoken.

The cherub stirred, and Hal carefully disengaged his fingers. "He is coming to. Should we find his mother?"

"You needn't. Here she is!" Aletta Krige's round, attractive face and plump figure appeared in the open doorway. "I heard that Roxie and Hal Fairmead had been seen kidnapping Jannie. What's he been up to?"

"Over-eating—and over-drinking," said Roxane. "Champagne!"

Aletta threw back her fair head and laughed. "So that's where my bubbly went! Jannie, you're a little horror, full of original sin!"

Jannie opened one eye and cocked it at his mother with a most disarming smile.

Aletta turned to Hal.

"I've been talking to Mrs. Fairmead. She's just worked out your entire future to her satisfaction. You're to be a wine-farmer in Constantia."

He raised one amused eyebrow. "When did she decide on that?"

"Five minutes ago. She has practically bought a large piece of land adjoining Dieu Donné from Mr. Krifti. The happy bride-groom, Guy Masterson, is to plan the house your parents will build when they settle in the Valley, and then you will learn about wine-farming here from Thinus Vos—Grannie Con's manager—and after that a farm will be found for you. Like the idea?"

He grinned. "Organizing my life is Mother's hobby. But it's up to me to disorganize it every time she tries, and that gives her a chance to think up some new idea. It's a sort of game."

"You must come to our *braaivleis* this evening," said Aletta. "Thinus could lend him slacks and a shirt and sweater, couldn't he, Roxie? My Karl's clothes wouldn't fit him. Karl is a giant. A *braaivleis* is a sort of barbecue, Hal. We cook our steaks and chops out of doors on the embers—and there'll be a coon band, just three or four coons, and we'll dance."

"I'd love it," he said. "But I have to get back to Cape Town afterwards."

"There'll be others from Cape Town. They can take you back. Roxie, you see Thinus fixes him up! And now you had better hurry out, and I'll follow you with this chap presently. I can hear the Constantia Coons tuning up, and that means Guy and Merle must be nearly ready to go."

On the fringe of the lawn Hal and Roxane saw the Constantia
Coons, some thirty strong, in their harlequin satin New Year
costumes. Violins, concertinas, guitars, banjos and other name-
less instruments shook the soft summer air with the music of
Africa—wild, sad, haunting and gay. The coons sang and danced,
every fibre of them yielding to the rhythm of *liedjie,* or jazz, and
the younger boys frisked merrily up and down the flanks of the
band.

"Oh," breathed Roxane. "Don't they make you long to dance?"

Under her ivory skin Hal sensed the blood capering through
her veins. Her eyes were dancing and her blue slippers tapped
the gravel underfoot. "We must stay here. Merle and Guy will
come out of the house any time now."

They had joined the cheerful, laughing throng at the foot of
the wide pink steps. In the warmth and press of the crowd she
was close to Hal and his nearness sent strange, unfamiliar vibra-
tions quivering through every particle of her being.

"Here they come! Here they come!"

Merle paused on the stoep to throw a ruched blue garter into
the crowd. There was a sudden surge as everyone looked up and
moved forward in response to the gesture. Roxane felt herself
flung against Hal as he jumped and caught the blue frippery. She
was crushed to him, a slim wand of a girl less high than his heart.

"Look out, Roxane!" He put a protective arm about her as he
slipped the garter into his pocket. "My souvenir of Dieu Donné."

Roxane was silent, holding her breath, feeling her cheeks burn
and the backs of her knees jelly-weak. Don't speak, don't move,
don't break this spell! Let it be just like this for another instant,
an hour, forever. . . . He is so close to me I can hear his heart
beat. . . .

Thinus had lifted Merle over the low door into Guy's waiting
sports car, somebody else had flung two suitcases into the boot
and shut it down, and then Guy was leaning forward to engage
the gear, and the next moment they were gone with a roar and
a rush and a shower of rice and confetti, and an old shoe waggling behind them like a happy dog's tail. The coons pranced
down the farm road after them, singing "Henrietta's Wedding,"
and soon their bright satin costumes were lost in the green of the

vineyards, screened by slender poplars and tall flowering gums.

The crowd dispersed. Hal's arm fell from Roxane's shoulder. She was no longer part of him, and for her that movement of separation was like the song of a bird broken off suddenly and for no reason, as is the way of bird-song—an end of something hardly begun.

Already the cars were rolling home, into the western dazzle of the Hout Bay Gap, down the Ladies' Mile towards Muizenberg, and round the long dragon-back of Table Mountain to Cape Town. And at last only Roxane, Hal and Thinus were left with Grannie Con and Merle's mother and the Yent from Yo'burg. They stood on the lawn among the empty glasses and used plates, the stacked dead bottles and scattered confetti—little stars and moons and paper hearts crushed underfoot.

"Come over to my place," Thinus suggested to Hal. "And I'll rig you up with some rough togs for this evening."

When they had gone Roxane cast a mournful glance at the blue organza that must be let out once more to fit Marigold-with-mumps.

"I must take it off; it's mine no more."

But Solly Caine said, with his gargling laugh, "It's yours, Cinderella! I have talked with the mother of Marigold-with-mumps, and it's all arranged. You keep this dress, and Marigold gets another."

"Mine!" She whirled round in a pirouette of pure rapture. She flung her arms round his neck and hugged Solly Caine. "How can I ever thank you?"

"You have done so," he said. "Keep your gift for happiness, keep it all your life, child! It's worth more than blue dresses, more than anything in the world!"

Grannie Con said to her son's widow, Solly Caine's wife:

"The last Dieu Donné wedding was yours, Bella—yours and Dirk's. I must say you made a lovely bride—as lovely as Merle." The words came reluctantly, as if some need for truth forced them from her.

"And the one before that was yours," said Bella. "And the next, no doubt, will be when Merle has a grown-up daughter. So the years fly past."

But Grannie Con's cold, frail hand stroked Roxane's hair.

"The next Dieu Donné wedding will be this child's. Roxane belongs here. Dieu Donné is her home, and she has taken my name."

CHAPTER 3

"I'M IN LOVE"

The full moon trailed the long black shadows of Hal and Roxane across the Kriges' lawn. But for the contour of her head, softened by her short wavy hair, the shadows masqueraded as those of two lads with arms linked, one tall and supple, one small and very slight, a mere stripling. For they both wore slacks.

They paused at the low white parapet dividing the Kriges' garden from the moon-silvered vineyards. Away across the Flats they could see the shining Indian Ocean and the jagged range of the Hottentots Hollands enfolding False Bay. The mountains seemed carved from some luminous substance, a backdrop to a magic scene. The lights of the fishing villages winked and sparkled in the distance, while behind Hal and Roxane there loomed the berg, flanked with its ghostly plantations. The *swish-swish* of feet sounded from the stoep where a dozen or more couples danced to the music of a four-piece coon band.

Hal looked up at the brilliant sky. "Until the band stops how can we hear the song of the stars?"

As if to test his words, the coons up at the house laid aside their instruments for refreshments and beer. In the interval that followed, Hal and Roxane listened to the night. There were drifts of talk and laughter from the stoep and the dark shadows of the garden; the scraping of crickets accompanied a fanfare of frogs from a lily pond, and farther down the Valley guitars and banjos thrummed and a dog barked.

"The stars aren't singing," she said, her face lifted and pale.

"But coons are, away over there! What goes on?"

He pointed to a glow in a fold of the vineyards by the willow-fringed stream. The aroma of wood-smoke came to their nostrils mingled with the fragrance of moonflowers and tobacco plants.

"It's the *volkies' braaivleis*," she said. "Grannie Con has given them wine and a sheep to celebrate the wedding."

"Let's go and watch them."

"We can borrow Thinus's car, if you can drive it. He won't mind. He's awfully good-natured."

A few minutes later they were standing under a big nut-tree on the edge of a clearing outside the coloured village. Lamps burned in the white, box-like houses, a few with little stoeps, and old people sat on those stoeps or on their doorsteps to watch the younger ones dancing in the glow of the great log-fire. The feast was over, but here and there a few stray curs snarled at one another over the possession of a juicy bone.

The coon band played with mad abandon to match the intoxicated exuberance of many of the dancers. Men seized any partners they could find, girls, boys, even withered crones or a babe snatched from its giggling mother's arms and clasped aloft, its little black head bobbing drowsily over some jitterbugging shoulder.

"They certainly go to it!" grinned Hal. "The only people I've ever seen go wild like this are sailors. Every now and again the music seems to throw a switch and bring on convulsions! Look at those two, the handsome boy and that pretty high-yaller girl; they've gone crazy!"

She laughed. "That's Ben and Saartjie. Ben is the son of our butler and cook, Joshua and Lizzie. He plays a guitar in the Constantia Coon Troupe. He saved up for it for years, starting when he was only a little chap and he used to gather acorns and sell them to Thinus for the pigs, or pine-cones for our fires. He can imitate any bird's call, and the mate always answers. The girl is Lizzie's niece, Saartjie. She lives with them. Her mother was a bad girl, so Lizzie took Saartjie in and brought her up respectably."

"Lizzie must be very kind."

"She is, when she's not cross. The coloured people are good to spare babies as a rule. They are used to them."

His eyes smiled down at her. "Are there so many spare babies about?"

She nodded. "These folk are very irresponsible and unmoral."

It was her grown-up voice, and her little air of superiority amused him.

"I don't suppose they have many other diversions—nothing much to look forward to—or work for," he suggested.

"They live for the day. Grannie Con says they are lucky in that. She lives for the past and the future—what has been at Dieu Donné and what is to be, and often the day, with all its lovely things, seems to pass her by."

His arm encircled her waist, and the touch of him set her trembling. "The day, with all its lovely things," he repeated. The tone of his voice melted her heart. She closed her eyes so that she should *see* his voice, velvet, but on a steel frame. If you fought against that voice it could be hard. . . .

"You're shivering, Roxane! Shall we go back and do a bit more dancing ourselves to warm up?"

When he had parked Thinus's car under the oaks near the Kriges' house and switched off the headlights, Hal drew her to him.

"Tell me something, how old are you? Maybe seventeen?"

She made a little sound that might have been assent. Please, Hal, think me seventeen! If I tell you I'm fifteen you'll despise me for a kid, and I couldn't bear that. I don't feel like a kid, I feel like a woman, at least I guess that's how I feel. . . .

"And you—how old are you?" she whispered.

"Eighteen."

Of course, eighteen. He was going to be a soldier, called up for his National Service in England.

"Have you ever been kissed, Roxane?"

"South Africans are always kissing each other. It's a habit—the oddest people kiss." The trembling was inside her now, a swarm of gossamer wings.

"I'm not South African, and kissing isn't one of my habits." Again he echoed the words she had spoken earlier: "The day, with all its lovely things, and you, one of them, the loveliest."

As he said it the trembling was outside her too, it was everywhere. All the myriad stars were dancing round the sky to their own strange music—the music of the spheres, perhaps. Hal's mouth was soft, soft as his voice, but his arms were strong and hard. . . . Roxane was falling through space into some sweet oblivion of her own when Hal's elbow came to rest on the steering-wheel and the horn.

Thinus's car brayed loud and long, rending the startled night with its klaxon cry. As if in answer to its call, the owner and his partner came towards it from the shadow of the trees. Roxane, weak with love and laughter, saw the astonished faces of Thinus and Aletta at the window.

"We borrowed the car—to go and see the Dieu Donné *braaivleis*," she explained. "We knew Thinus wouldn't mind."

"We've been looking for you," said Aletta. "There's soup at the house, and Hal's lift wants to get back to town."

Her expression was full of merriment in the moonlight; Aletta, who played with her children like a cat with its kittens and who wanted a large family and was clearly about to have another contribution in the not too far distant future.

"Then we heard Hal here howling for help," added Thinus. "You all right, Hal, man?"

"I sometimes sing," said Hal.

Over at the house hot soup steamed in the big tureen. Karl Krige, blond and bearded like one of his own Boer ancestors, ladled it into cups and handed it out with a joke to each of his guests. Karl's friends loved the contradiction between his patriarchal backveld appearance—so much in keeping with his wife's fruitful charms—and his sensitive sophistication; for Karl, like Grannie Con of Dieu Donné, was a true product of the Valley which was still the stronghold of Cape culture and tradition.

Roxane heard Hal talking to the young man who was to give him a lift back to Cape Town. "I must just go and shift out of these things of Thinus's and get into my own clothes; shan't be a minute."

So I won't see him alone again, she thought. I can't bear it! He'll go back to Cape Town and tomorrow he'll sail for England. I may never meet him again. . . .

Before he left Hal drew her on one side for a moment. He held her hands in his. "Come on board for lunch tomorrow—please, Roxane!"

"I can't," she gulped. "I have to go to school. I'm not really seventeen, Hal, only fifteen, and working for an exam."

She saw dismay darken his eyes, and she wanted to laugh and cry, both at once. Don't be sorry, Hal! I'm glad you kissed me. All my life I'll be glad!

"Then this is goodbye," he said. She felt the tightened clasp of his hands, and saw the half-smile and the one lifted eyebrow that seemed to say, Forget me, Roxane; I'm sorry. The next instant he was gone and she was standing with Thinus at her side.

"Come along, Roxie; we must be off. Tomorrow is a working day!"

Sitting next to him in the car that had brayed like an ass, she held on her lap the shirt, slacks and sweater Thinus had lent Hal. They were still warm and she longed to bury her face in them, like a dog who is unhappy without its master's old coat to make it feel at home.

"Got your key?" asked Thinus, outside the French doors to her bedroom.

He took it from her and fitted it into the lock. The moon had set, but the apple-blossom glimmered in the starlight.

"Enjoy yourself, little squirrel?"

She turned suddenly and buried her face in his broad chest.

"I'm in love, Thinus . . . I'm in love . . . it hurts. . . ."

His mutilated hand moved softly through her hair.

"That makes two of us, Roxie. Looks like we'll have to console each other. My girl has gone off with a red-headed man and your boy sails away tomorrow. . . . I'll tell you what, when you grow up, you and I will get married, and live happily ever after. . . ."

In the following year Mr. Krifti sold Adrian Fairmead a substantial plot of land adjoining Dieu Donné, and, at his suggestion, Guy Masterson planned the house that was to be built on it. It was extraordinary how much land and influence Mr. Krifti had acquired at the Cape. His interests stretched far and wide, but their core was Constantia.

Already, at his instigation and financed by one of his many companies, a new residential estate had sprung up on the southern ridge, and, where once the grapes had ripened in the sun, raw new houses raised their heads. To Grannie Con they were a pox upon her Valley, scabs that had come to stay and for which she blamed Mr. Krifti—Mr. Krifti, that abominable man who had actually had the audacity to make her an offer for Dieu Donné!

The Fairmeads named their new home Farway, and the Valley welcomed them with open arms. And although Grannie Con could not approve of the house her grand-daughter's husband had designed for them, with that idiotic tower-studio standing up among the vineyards like a sore finger, she genuinely liked her new neighbours. Roxane, of course, was enraptured. Hal, she knew, had been drafted to Malaya on his military service, but when that was over he would surely join his parents and settle down in Constantia to learn wine-farming. That was what his mother wanted him to do, and Roxane had the impression that Mrs. Fairmead was accustomed to getting her own way.

The prospect of Hal coming to Farway was constantly in her mind, although she never referred to it, not even to Thinus. The night of Merle's wedding when Roxane had buried her face against his chest and said, "I'm in love—it hurts" had been tacitly forgotten by both of them. He too had been heart-sick that night, wanting Merle, but his passion for his cousin had died, while Roxane's infatuation for Hal was still nursed in the living warmth of her memory of him. And she unconsciously stimulated its growth by every means within her reach.

Secretly recalling him had become one of her "games"—like building up her picture of Maman. In bed at night, before falling asleep, she had acquired the habit of reliving their brief encounter, but with her own modifications. That horn, for instance. It did not bray. . . .

One evening, when she was returning from one of the walks she loved to take with only Wolf for company and protection, she met Hal's father. She saw him in the avenue of poplars bordering Farway. An old war wound had left him slightly lame and he moved rather stiffly with his head down and a trifle on one side—like a secretary-bird, she thought, picking his way delicately through the long grass in search of a snake or some small prey.

He looked in surprise at the trim little figure in shorts with a light knapsack on her back.

"Been climbing alone?" he asked.

"With my dog," she smiled. "We often go up the berg, and I take my tea and find some lovely place to be alone. Sometimes I take a book, maybe one of yours."

He laughed, charmed by the mischief in her eyes. She was beautiful round the eyes, he observed.

"You've discovered the joys of solitude and meditation rather young," he said. "I would have expected you to prefer tennis."

"I like tennis too," she said. "And I'm not really very young. I'm seventeen."

"Still at school?"

She shook her head. "Not strictly speaking. I go to the Technical College in Cape Town. I'm doing a secretarial course."

"Can you type?"

"Very well." Her confidence amused him, but she went on quickly. "I've typed since I was quite a little girl. I taught myself, the proper way, touch-typing."

"You might have time to do a bit of typing for me," he suggested. "A short story or two?"

Her hands clasped ecstatically. "I'd hardly dare!" she breathed.

"My writing is quite legible. It would be easy to show you the system of hieroglyphics that rules my corrections."

As he spoke he flexed his long fingers that were at times subject to writer's cramp. His hands were like Hal's, strong and sensitive. Roxane would always remember Jannie Krige asleep on her bed with Hal's fingers clasped in his grubby little paw.

"Could you show me one of the stories?"

"Now, if you've time."

So she was following him up the spiral staircase leading to his tower-studio. He heard her catch her breath as she stood in the angled bow-window and looked out across the glowing green vineyards to the distant sea and the mountains beyond.

"Yes," he said. "It's an inspiration."

"This Valley, I love it so much! No wonder Grannie Con can't bear Mr. Krifti cutting it up; trying to turn it into another suburb of Cape Town."

"To Grannie Con land is a heritage," he said. "To Mr. Krifti it is just another investment."

She turned back into the room, its walls lined to the ceiling with his books, many of them rare volumes that would rejoice the heart of a student or a historian. His manuscripts lay on his big walnut desk and she touched one reverently. Yes, the flowing hand was easy to read.

That was the beginning. In the months that followed Roxane became Adrian Fairmead's typist, and after a while Mrs. Fairmead asked her to type copies of Hal's letters from Malaya.

"I want to send Hal's letters to our daughter who is married to a diplomat at UNO. They are good letters, you must admit, and if I part with the originals to Hilda I'll never get them back!"

Roxane agreed that they were "good letters." When she took them home to type she read them again and again. She saw him fighting those strange hide-and-seek battles in the steaming green hell of jungle forests, she smelt the sweet perfume of the rubber trees in flower and learned the dangers of a planter's life in the lonely heat of the plains with the shadow of death never far off. When Hal wrote of people, you knew them. They came alive. So did he. His letters were himself. Humour and humanity shone through them. They increased Roxane's knowledge of him, and with it her infatuation for him.

During their second summer in the Valley the Fairmeads constructed a swimming-pool and their neighbours from Dieu Donné used it freely.

One evening, when Merle and Thinus and Roxane had been swimming, Mrs. Fairmead joined them at the pool. She came towards them with quick, supple grace and the high carriage of the head so characteristic of her son.

"I'm furious!" she announced in her high, clear voice. "That son of ours has let us down flat!" But if there was exasperation in her tone there was also pride in her grey eyes.

Merle took off her cap and shook out her blond curls.

"What's his crime, Lavinia?"

"He was no sooner discharged than he landed himself a job as war-correspondent for the *Weekly Post*. It'll be a roving assignment, but still in the Far East. And we were absolutely counting on his joining us here in a few weeks' time."

Thinus said in his slow, gentle fashion, "But surely that was very enterprising of him? I didn't realize he wrote."

"It seems he has been keeping some sort of a diary, with his Commanding Officer's permission, of course. And he sent it off to the *Weekly Post*, who are publishing it under the title of 'Jungle Journal.' On the strength of it they've offered him this job and he's jumped at it."

Roxane said nothing. She began to dry her hair, and thus she covered her face and the tears of bitter disappointment smarting in her eyes. She did not know that Thinus could see the muscles of her throat contract and that he had made a move of swift, instinctive pity towards her. Silly little squirrel, could it be that she still cared about a boy she had met only once?

Jungle Journal enjoyed remarkable success.

Adrian Fairmead read his son's work with parental pride and the critical eye of an experienced writer. He found Hal's style sparkling with life, tough and brutal in parts, but enriched by a natural kindliness and touched here and there with tenderness.

"He has the makings," he said to his wife. "Some of this stuff is crude and unbalanced, but he has that *extra thing*. It's there, Vee, it shines through."

She knew what he meant. "That extra thing" was the expression they used between themselves to define the intangible quality which sets exceptional talent apart from adequate skill. Its root lay in human understanding and blossomed in a sensitive interpretation of life.

In time Hal's reports from the Far East were published in South African papers as well as in the English *Weekly Post*, and before long the American hallmark of publication in the *New Yorker* had set its seal upon more than one of his short stories.

He'll never come out here and be a farmer, thought Roxane, as she read the columns under his name. And her heart was sore.

One autumn day Lavinia Fairmead told Roxane of their plan to go to Hollywood for the filming of Adrian's best-selling novel, *Ballerina*.

"We are going to visit our daughter in Washington first, and then we'll spend a few months in Hollywood while they make the film. I've written to Hal to suggest that *Weekly Post* transfer him to Hollywood for a while!"

"It's a different sort of jungle," said Adrian. "But just as ferocious, I'm told."

"A film of *Ballerina!*" cried Roxane. "But that would be wonderful! It's my favourite of all your books. Who would they get to play the part of Olga?"

"They talk of Alexa Rome," said Lavinia.

"Alexa Rome. She's marvellous! I saw her in *Legend* and *The Little Mermaid*. She'd be a lovely Olga!"

Adrian's eyes were thoughtful behind his strong glasses.

"Olga was a woman—too much a woman," he said. "In both *Legend* and *Little Mermaid* Alexa played the part of a creature of another element, and I grant you she was sublime. But Olga, my ballerina, is a woman of flesh and blood with a soul, and a heart to break when her lover leaves her. That's something else again. And I wonder if Alexa Rome has it in her to play the part of a human being with all its ecstasy and suffering."

Roxane considered. "Why not?" she asked at length. "Alexa, like Olga, must be a woman as well as a dancer, a woman with a soul, and a heart to break. . . ."

The corners of his mouth drew down in his cynical smile. He flexed his long fingers and looked along them as if down a gun-barrel.

"Not necessarily," he said. "The way to the top is hard for a prima ballerina, hard on body and soul. Sometimes the soul dies on the way up . . . the woman is destroyed, and only the dancer it left."

Roxane shivered and the goose-pimples rose on her arms. Would you feel it, she wondered, if the silver cord snapped and the shining soul fell away to lose itself in obscurity? Would you feel a sudden emptiness, a shocking sense of loss, the ultimate despair? Or did you dance on, on and up to the top, unknowing, believing yourself still whole, believing yourself to be a woman with a soul, and a heart to break?

Lavinia said drily, "Alexa Rome is a great artist and a born actress. Whether she plays the part of Olga or the Little Mermaid she will make you believe in it and she will draw your tears."

CHAPTER 4

THE OMEN

Although Roxane nursed the image of her French mother and often tried to envisage English John Williams who had died before her birth, in spite of her dreams of France and a somewhat fantastic London built on *Peter Pan in Kensington Gardens*, she regarded the Valley as her natural background and Grannie Con as the supreme authority, father and mother rolled into one. She thought of herself as South African and of the de Valois family as her own. The graft had taken.

Moreover, Roxane knew that she was closer to Grannie Con's heart than the old lady's own grand-daughter, but Merle's rights of legitimate heredity were invulnerable, and it never occurred to any of them to dispute the fact that one day Dieu Donné would be Merle's. But in the meantime it belonged to Grannie Con, and therefore to Roxane it was home.

Roxane loved Dieu Donné with the ardent intensity she brought to the business of living. Everything in it was known and dear to her. She often studied the sombre Dutch and Flemish portraits of Grannie Con's ancestors, and one in particular attracted her. It was a portrait of dark-eyed Sarah de Valois painted at the age of seventeen shortly after her marriage nearly two centuries ago. Roxane liked to imagine Sarah packing her fine bridal linen into the carved camphor-wood chest, or hanging her stiff crinolines in the great armoire with its gabled top and swollen base and the silver hinges wrought by some long-ago

Malay craftsman. And at times she was moved by a tender vision of the young Sarah rocking her first infant in the heavy teak cradle that now held logs by the library fireplace. She had seen Sarah's name in the monster leather family Bible with its records of births, deaths and marriages, and she had found herself wishing that her birth too might have been inscribed among those of the de Valois' of Dieu Donné. Grannie Con had given her the de Valois name, but the blood was Merle's.

As a child she had often examined the pictures in the Bible and admired the illuminated text, but to read it was beyond her capacity, for it was all in the Dutch of Holland, very different from the Afrikaans she learned at school. The Bible rested on a lectern between the gilded outspread wings of an eagle. Over it hung a rough impressionist study of Dirk Vos de Valois, Grannie Con's dead son. His was a poet's face, thought Roxane, with the winged black brows and mobile lips. The eyes were dark and sad. Merle was not like her father; she took after her mother's people, the van der Walts, who were blue-eyed and golden-haired. Or perhaps she took her fairness from the Vos family. The true de Valois' were dark and pale, like Grannie Con.

Roxane seldom thought ahead to the day when Grannie Con would lie up there on the side of the berg with her forefathers and her Vos husband, who would share her grave as he had shared her home; to the time when all this would be Merle's and she, Roxane, cast out. For she did not really believe that Grannie Con could ever die. Grannie Con and the Valley were her world, and, because she was young, the disintegration of her world was a possibility she was unable to entertain.

Yet, in her nineteenth year, this little world of hers began to quake as the greater world about her had quaked in her early childhood, and the first long menacing chasms yawned at her feet.

Everything really dated from the time Lizzie's niece, Saartjie, saw the ghost.

Saartjie had been promoted to the position of cook-general in the manager's cottage, and in consequence Thinus was taking more than his usual quota of meals at the homestead.

"You could stun an ox with her omelettes," he informed Grannie Con mournfully.

"She'll learn," said the old lady, who could afford to be philosophical about Saartjie's culinary shortcomings since she was not called upon to endure them. "I'll get Lizzie to give her some more lessons."

They were sitting on the stoep after dinner. It was a hot January night and the dark of the moon. All day a gusty berg-wind had puffed down from the mountain, disturbing the air without cooling it. The oaks were hunched black against the stars, and the light from the *voorkamer* shone softly through the carved teak fanlight and the open upper half of the front door, the traditional "stable door" of many old Dutch homes.

Beyond the trees they could just discern the silhouette of Farway's tower, but the novelist's lamp had not burned there for some time. The Fairmeads were in Hollywood and their house stood empty save for the native boy, Elias, and two Rhodesian ridge-backs. Roxane liked the heavy toffee-coloured lion-dogs and often exercised them when she took Wolf for a walk. Wolf regarded them with suspicious patronage. He had seen the fat puppies grow into massive maturity and come to respect them. He twitched now as he lay dreaming beside Grannie Con's chair and from time to time he whimpered.

"We'll be doing our fruit-picking early this year," remarked Thinus. "And, touching wood, we'll have a bumper harvest."

"We could do with it," said Grannie Con. "Since the *vlamsiekte* got into the vines and the Government stopped Constantia farmers grafting for sale we've lost thousands a year."

She was crocheting nimbly at a length of lace for a church bazaar—somebody's white elephant, thought Roxane with an inward smile—but every now and again the gnarled old hands let their work fall resentfully. Grannie Con would much rather have been crocheting a baby's jacket, blue for a boy. But Merle scoffed at the idea. All in good time, she said. Was she deliberately putting it off, sinfully cheating Dieu Donné of an heir? Young people these days were entirely irresponsible. Only yesterday old Auntie Marthe van der Walt had told her about boys and girls in this very Valley who thought nothing of tossing back half a dozen gins or brandies before dinner and turning up their uncivilized noses at good red or white Constantia wine. "They drink to get drunk," Auntie Marthe had whispered, "like a coloured boy with his tot!" South Africa ought to be a wine-drinking country, but this liking for hard liquor was death to the palate—and to the wine-farmer.

Grannie Con had other worries too. Of late her bad leg had been troubling her more frequently and a course of hospital treatment had done little good. Pain and two sticks always close at hand were the constant stimulants of fears she refused to acknowledge.

From the kitchen they could hear Lizzie's radio tuned in to Lourenço Marque's echoing dance-music that set Roxane's feet itching.

"Lizzie plays that thing too loud," grumbled Grannie Con.

But Roxane laughed and tapped her toes on the stoep. Because she was happy she wanted to dance, and she was happy at news she had received that afternoon by airmail from America. Mrs. Fairmead had written to thank her for exercising the lion-dogs and to give her news of Hollywood—and Hal.

". . . You will be glad for my sake"—Lavinia had written—"when I tell you that *Weekly Post* is sending Hal to Hollywood to write about the making of the picture *Ballerina!* The editor thought that for the son to write about the filming of the father's best-known novel was in itself a human angle scoop. Later he will come back to South Africa with us for a few weeks at least and get some copy about the Union, which is so persistently —if not always pleasantly—in the news.

"Adrian has fallen for his leading lady. Alexa has something, not beauty exactly, but a haunting quality. We believe she is an ideal choice for Olga."

If there was anything in the letter that might have troubled Roxane, she was unaware of it. She knew only that quite soon she would see Hal again.

"Give Thinus some more coffee, Roxie! You know he always takes two cups. You've been in dreamland all evening."

"Sorry, Thinus. Give me your cup."

But Thinus did not think she looked sorry. There was something about Roxie tonight, a way of moving and of smiling that was new. She had fixed her hair in a different fashion, showing her ears, neat little ears like those mother-of-pearl shells you picked up along the beaches, and her eyes, those clear slanting eyes, were abrim with some exciting secret. What was she up to? She could be a sly little squirrel when she wanted to. Probably she was leading a new boy-friend up the garden path. She picked them up and brushed them off without a care, boys in the Valley or from the Naval Base at Simon's Town, young officers in the Union Defence Force or students from the University, but none of them lasted. She couldn't make up her mind to "go steady" with any one of them. Well, he could understand that. Marriage was a grave undertaking. He'd never been able to face it himself—but now, with Saartjie's lethal cooking fresh in his memory, he was beginning to think that a wife in the house might be a blessing after all.

It was just then, as Roxane put down the coffee-pot, that they heard the scream.

It was a long-drawn yell as terrifying at it was terror-stricken. Wolf rose, bristling and growling, and Roxane covered the ears Thinus had so recently admired. Grannie Con dropped her crochet and gripped the arms of her chair. The hot summer night was torn with the blood-curdling shrieks that drew rapidly nearer, ending at last in strangulated gulps and gasps, as Saartjie stumbled up the steps to fling herself, moaning and sobbing, at Grannie Con's feet.

Roxane switched on the stoep light and Thinus dragged the coloured girl to her knees and spoke to her roughly in the *taal*.

"Shut up now, and tell us what is wrong! You can't be hurt or you wouldn't have come tearing round the house like a baboon with buckshot in his backside!"

But she only gave at the hinges and fell wailing to the ground.

Lizzie and Joshua had come rushing from the kitchen to see what the noise was about. All to no purpose, Lizzie tried to lift her niece.

"Her laiks is as flop as wet macaroni! Dear Lord, what is de matter?"

"Joshua, get a fire-bucket full of water!" said Thinus. "We'll give her a sousing. That'll do the trick."

But, as Joshua appeared with two fire-buckets, Saartjie raised her ashen face and rolling eyes.

"It was de spook," she muttered. "Never I seen de spook before."

Joshua's moon-face paled, and a high keening cry broke from Lizzie's lips. "Lord have mercy . . . have mercy. . . ."

Long ago, before the news of Dirk de Valois's death had been brought to Dieu Donné, Lizzie herself had seen the cellar-ghost and much evil had befallen the Valley after that dread manifestation.

Grannie Con looked sternly down at Saartjie, who was still clinging to her skirt and moaning.

"Calm yourself, girl!" she commanded. "And tell us where you saw this spook."

She did not mock Saartjie or say, "There is no spook." She knew better than that.

Gradually the tale was drawn from the shaking girl.

It appeared that Saartjie had tidied Thinus's cottage for the night, and was, as usual, on her way home to her aunt's dwelling. She had gone past the open cellar door, and out of curiosity had peeked in.

"An' dere, way in de back of de great dark cellar, I sees somet'ing crawling out from one of dose trap-doors in a big cask. Just for a moment I t'ink it's Ben playing a trick. Den he slip out an' stand up dere in de shadows of de big casks—a little kerel, but not like Ben . . . pale . . . so pale! He comes after me—an' I scream an' scream and run an' run till I gets here——"

"What makes you say he came after you?" asked Thinus. "You surely didn't stop to look back."

"I fall down. I trip an' fall 'cause my laiks won't hold me up . . . an' when l looks back, dere he is among de oaks, de only pale t'ing in all dat awful dark!"

Roxane found herself shivering in the hot, oppressive night.

The slave who had gone into the vat to clean it and died

instantly from the fumes of the wine it had held was a well-known legend of the estate. And he was not the only one who had died thus in the careless days of old. Other farms had their spooks too.

The warm wind from the berg blew suddenly in fierce, erratic gusts that set the leaves whispering in the trees. All nature seemed seized with some fearful agitation. They could hear the *cree-keet, cree-keet* of the crickets, the clacking of frogs, and the barking of dogs down in the coloured village. Somewhere Lizzie's Ben was imitating the calls of night-birds, and little feathered females, easily deluded, were responding to the magic of his pipe.

Into this night symphony fell Lizzie's voice with a note of doom.

"I saw de spook so, Oumissus! Dat time he come after me from de kellar, he come so's Saartjie says. She is telling de trut'. May de good Lord help us all!"

"Put her to bed, Lizzie," said Grannie Con. "And you may give her a small tot."

"That's a mistake," murmured Thinus to Roxane. "They'll all be seeing spooks if there's a tot attached to it!"

The old cook took her niece by the shoulders and led her away while Joshua removed the coffee-tray.

"I will ring when you can lock up, Joshua."

Grannie Con's tone was calm and reassuring, but, as the old butler disappeared into the house, she turned to Thinus.

"I don't like it."

"She's a silly girl, that one. She could have imagined it. The boys all chase Saartjie. If the spook wasn't Ben it was one of the others."

"You know as well as I do that it was not one of the boys."

He rose and stood beside her and laid his hand on her shoulder.

"Don't worry, Grannie Con. We should have the best harvest in years this summer. Don't look for trouble. This superstition of the spook is witch-doctor stuff. We mustn't encourage it."

She lifted her wrinkled face and he kissed her cheek gently.

As he went down the steps back to his cottage, Roxane said, "He's right. We mustn't give in to the legend."

But Grannie Con only shook her smooth white head.

"When the clouds roll over Table Mountain the southeaster will blow, Roxie. We don't wonder about it, or ask each other whether the white horses are rising in the Bay. We look at the cloud—*and we know*."

CHAPTER 5

CALAMITY

February passed and the grapes ripened in the hot sun.

The spring rains had been just sufficient and Thinus watched the crops with hope and pleasure. Given a little luck this should be a vintage year. The export grapes too were fattening to perfection. He was glad because he knew that the estate had been running at a heavy loss since the war and the *vlamsiekte*.

It was on a Friday evening early in March that he said with satisfaction, "Next week we begin picking."

Although the season of picking, packing and pressing was the busiest on the farm, it was Roxane's favourite. She loved to watch the nimble-fingered coloured *volkies* pick the grapes and stack them in the big deep baskets deftly and gently without spoiling them. Only the coloureds really understood the vines; they were born and bred to the care of grapes, the free descendants of freed Dieu Donné slaves. But Grannie Con grumbled that too many of them left the land these days to seek work in the towns. They had changed since her time, just as the Valley itself had changed, with new roads running through it, new houses clustering on its ridges and new people like Mr. Krifti buying up land and selling it off in small lots.

Grannie Con disliked change as much as she disliked Mr. Krifti, for in her eyes the tall sallow man with the flabby features and Oriental hands that were forever playing with a string of beads stood for the new era in Constantia—the era of dwindling vineyards and increasing housing estates. "Confound mine enemy," she prayed in the little grey stone church on that first

Sunday in March, and the face of Mr. Krifti with its colourless fish-eyes rose before her. "And grant us a good harvest that we may preserve our heritage in this, Thy loveliest valley. . . ."

Beside her in the front pew Roxane's dark head was bowed.

"Let him come back—please let him come back. Let him remember me and want me as I remember and want him . . . Holy Mother, you have the heart of a woman, intercede for me, I beg."

Mr. Krifti, sitting between his wife, Louise, and his mother-in-law, Auntie Marthe van der Walt, observed the tender nape of Roxane's neck and the soft tendrils of hair and sighed for that which gold cannot buy, the sweet, perishable gift of youth.

The congregation rose to sing a hymn, and the song swelled in the back of the church where the coloured people stood in all humility. They shame us, thought Grannie Con, with a hostile glance at the empty seat next to hers. Merle and Guy were as Godless as all their set, the young sophisticates of the Peninsula.

"It's the coloured folk who praise their Maker loudest," she had said once to Thinus. "They who have least to thank Him for!"

"But most to pray for—" he had grinned. Thinus did his own worshipping at the Dutch Reformed Church, which was always well attended.

It was during the sermon that everybody first became aware of the gathering gloom—a strange unseasonable darkness cutting off the sunlight that filtered through the stained-glass windows in rainbow shafts. By the time the service was over the entire Valley was overcast by immense black clouds.

The coloured children, in their Sunday best, began to race each other for home and shelter. The little girls were afraid of the storm that might spoil their frilly hats and light dresses, but some of their elders were more widely concerned and thought in terms of a ruined harvest as well as a ruined hat.

As Roxane helped Grannie Con out of the car at Dieu Donné, Thinus came to meet them. He had already changed out of his formal blue suit into farm clothes. There was a frown between his fair eyebrows, and he ran his maimed hand through his thick crisp hair as he always did when he was disturbed.

"I don't like the look of it—or the sound of it!" he said.

The first mutterings of thunder had begun to rumble over the berg and occasional flashes of lightning forked down the ravines.

In the big kitchen old Lizzie basted the joint. "Turn on de light," she commanded Joshua. "It's gorn dark as de grave in here."

Now a curious stillness gripped the Valley. The berg drew closer and loomed indigo over the homestead of Dieu Donné. The plantations stood out in extraordinary clarity, every tree separate and individual. Overhead the storm-clouds massed for some monstrous invasion. The chill scent of rain saturated the air, and the cooing of the doves had become suddenly loud and echoing like voices heard through fog. But it was not till Joshua had set a fruit pie before Grannie Con that the outer gloom was slashed by a blinding flash and a clap of thunder that ripped the clouds apart and released their burden on the Valley in a mighty deluge.

"De crack of doom!" The old butler's eyes rolled upwards in his round face, showing the startled yellowish whites. "De las' trump!"

Thinus sprang to his feet. "It's a cloudburst! And now, of all times, now when the grapes are ready for picking!"

In a few moments he was out in the downpour and on his way to the vineyards, and presently Roxane and Grannie Con had followed him.

The cloudburst had singled out the Valley from the rest of the Peninsula. It had fallen like the hand of a vengeful fate upon the fruitful vines.

Within an hour every gutter and culvert in the new built-up areas on the ridges had been transformed into a raging torrent discharging flood-water, silt and debris into the low-lying lands. The Liesbeek River had overflowed its banks and the farmers mustered their forces against the encroaching flood. At Dieu Donné the old slave-bell clanged its summons, calling all hands to help in a vital emergency. As the first dramatic deluge settled into steady rain, Thinus and Brink, the foreman, gave their orders. Every irrigation furrow must be cleared of silt and sand-bags filled to dam the break in the river-bank. Men, women and children must do their share.

To the children it was a joyous occasion, like fire-fighting, only playing with water was more fun and less dangerous than playing with fire. They were banded under the leadership of Lizzie's quick, intelligent Ben. Sixteen-year-old Ben was the Pied Piper of the Valley, the coon with the magic pipe and the haunting guitar, and wherever he went the children scampered after him, dancing and clowning. So now they did as he told them, eagerly helping to shovel sand into the sacks and dig silt from the water-channels. They laughed and shouted and splashed, they slithered in the mud and wet clay and made their own Roman holiday of the disaster.

Grannie Con leaned on her sticks and stared at the havoc with a stony countenance. The rain pelted onto her oilskins and into her withered face. When Roxane tried to protect her from the weather she snapped at her.

"Don't hold that thing over my head! I'm not a sultan with an umbrella bearer, and in any case you're dripping it down my neck."

The need to use two sticks when she walked made it impossible for her to carry an umbrella for herself and it irritated her to be reminded of her increasing infirmity.

This cloudburst is an Act of God, thought Roxane. It won't be covered by insurance.

She said, "I suppose this counts as an Act of God?"

"An Act of God, yes, made immeasurbly worse by the acts of men like Mr. Krifti and his confederates." Grannie Con waved a furious stick at the silt pulsing into the vineyards. "That, all that ullage—comes rushing down on us from the fine new residential estates on the ridge—from Mr. Krifti's latest Constantia investments! Rain that used to seep into the soil up there is borne down to us now to swell our river and wash out our lands. Cut up our green belt and let it bleed to death! What does Mr. Krifti care? He'll find a way to profit from this calamity. You wait and see!"

Towards nightfall the storm abated and Thinus returned to the homestead, weary but not without hope. He found Grannie Con and Roxane in the library, where a fire of logs and pine-cones blazed in the hearth. A fire in March—it was crazy! He sat down heavily on a low *bankie* and held out his palms to the warmth of the flames, and then, as if the sight of his disfigured left hand offended him, he withdrew it and let it fall between his knees.

"I'm afraid most of the export grapes have had it," he said. "They are sodden and battered. Everybody is in the same boat—Karl Krige, the van der Walts, all our neighbours. But the rain is letting up a bit, and when the wind changes to the southeast we'll get sunny drying weather and there's no reason why we shouldn't save our wine crop."

Grannie Con's lips were compressed. It was her obstinate face.

"I see," she remarked acidly. "And in the meantime our best table grapes must be crushed into poor liquor!"

"Ja," he said. "That's it. And now we must pray hard for the sun and the wind to dry out the rest of the harvest."

He took a log from the teak cradle and put it carefully on the fire. Then he rolled a cigarette.

"Pray like the devil!" he said.

Days passed, and the bright weather the farmers prayed for did not come. The unseasonable mists clung to the berg and a light mizzle kept the grapes damp and subject to mildew. Without sun to ripen and mature them their sugar content would be inadequate for wine-making.

There were special services of intercession in the little grey stone church, and now, among the coloured folk, the story of Saartjie and the spook was revived. The spook had appeared at Doo Don to warn the Valley that the hand of the Lord was turned against it. Quick to mirth and joy, the coloured people were equally quick to despair, and superstition was bred in their bones. They were sunk in gloom.

Thinus and Grannie Con went daily into the vineyards to examine the grapes for one or another of the dread fungus diseases. Often the old lady had to stop because the pain in her bad leg made further movement impossible. Once she slipped on a slimy patch of clay and fell, bruising it so severely that she was compelled to remain indoors for several days. This enforced inactivity was mental torture to her, for grave decisions must soon be taken.

The problem of Dieu Donné was, in some measure, that of every farm in the Valley: whether to pick and sell the grapes at a heavy loss for the making of inferior liquor, or whether to hold on for the sun that might still mature them. But to hold on meant risking fungus disease. Each farmer solved this problem according to his personal judgment and temperament. For Dieu Donné it was most acute. Dieu Donné made its own wine, and the ruin of the harvest meant the loss of a whole vintage.

Thinus came into the library, where Grannie Con lay on the couch. His face was grave.

"We have to make a decision, Oumissus." When he was worried about the estate he often used the *volkies'* name for her. "Do we cut our losses and pick now, or do we hang on for a change in the weather? Can we afford to go on gambling on the sun that doesn't come?"

Grannie Con's expression hardened. "I can't afford *not* to gamble, Thinus! This weather is all wrong for March. The wind *must* change!"

He thrust his hands deep into the pockets of his corduroys and looked down at her, a tough young man with a troubled face.

"Oumissus, you know the risk we are taking?"

She put down her shocking crochet-work and stared back at him defiantly. "I was born and bred on a wine-farm, Thinus. I was making wine here at Dieu Donné when you were making water in your napkins. Yes, my dear nephew, I know the risk we are taking."

Two days later he came to her once more. She was white and drawn with constant pain. Merle was visiting her, and Roxane sat behind the gleaming tea-tray.

"Tea for you, Thinus?"

"Ja, Roxie. And make it mighty hot and strong!"

He sat on the footstool beside the couch and Grannie Con saw his profile, blind and masked by the black eye-shield. So he didn't want to look at her, a sick old woman about to receive some very bad news.

"Oumissus," he said gruffly, "we have lost our gamble."

"The fungus disease! Which one?"

"The Black Spot."

Roxane saw the old lady flinch, and Merle started. All of them knew what the Black Spot meant—a harvest ruined and the growth of next year's vines threatened.

At last Grannie Con spoke. "We took a chance, all or nothing."

Still Thinus did not look at her. "Ja, Oumissus," he said. "And it's nothing."

Mockingly, when it was too late, the boisterous southeaster romped up the Valley from the sun-bright sea and blew away the lingering mists. The children skipped and frolicked on their way to school. Today they would fly their gay paper kites above the stripped vineyards.

Roxane was on her way to see Merle when she met Mr. Krifti. He stopped to speak to her.

"And how is Mrs. de Valois? I fear this trouble has hit her hard."

"It has hit most people round here," said Roxane with the cold, touching dignity of the young and loyal.

"Of course." His lugubrious features fell into mournful folds of sympathy and he gazed at the vineyards with the air of an undertaker measuring a corpse for a coffin. "I have been able to help out a number of farmers, Roxane. A little loan to tide them over."

"So we have heard."

He looked down at her, fine-drawn and unapproachable. An idealist, he thought with a curious stab of envy and regret. Only young love would move this girl's heart; she was not one who would be susceptible to the lure of luxury and wealth. A new sadness in her eyes, and that quaint pride of bearing, added to her charms for him. She had both the strength and frailty of a sapling bowing to the storm.

"One likes to help where one can," he persisted in his soft thick voice. "I have already told Mrs. de Valois that if I can be of any assistance—financially, or in any other way—she has only to call on me. And I mean it."

"I will remind her."

"I heard that she had hurt her leg during the flood. I hope it is none the worse."

Her hands interlaced suddenly and tightly.

"We are very troubled about it, Mr. Krifti . . ." She broke off and turned away.

"I am so very sorry. Please give your grandmother my regards, and don't forget my message. Anything I can do, at any time."

As she walked down the avenue of slender Chilean poplars it seemed to her that the silvery trees rocked themselves to and fro in the southeaster that had come too late like tall woebegone women beside themselves with grief.

She found Merle cutting flowers in the garden.

"Merle," she said. "I'm frightened about Grannie Con. Dr. Steyn is calling in a second opinion this afternoon."

Merle frowned. "What do you expect *me* to do about it?"

"Come back with me now and see her. She's very ill, Merle, and afraid too, though she tries to hide it. Lizzie told me that this morning she asked for the old family Bible, and then demanded to be left alone. When Lizzie went back to her Grannie Con was crying. . . . I have never seen her cry. . . ."

"Come then," said Merle. "We'll get out the car."

At Dieu Donné they heard from Joshua that Dr. Steyn and the specialist were with Grannie Con.

"Dey been wit' de Oumissus a long time." Joshua shook his grizzled head mournfully. "What will dey do, Miss Merle?"

"We must hope, Joshua," said Merle, her blue eyes blank. Was the burden of her heritage about to fall upon her? she wondered, with a tremor of fear.

It seemed an eternity to Roxane before the family doctor and the specialist joined them in the library.

"Please help yourselves to a drink—cigarettes," Merle said when the introductions had been made.

Dr. Steyn poured himself a brandy and soda, but the specialist refused. He went straight to the point, addressing himself to Merle.

"I am very sorry, Mrs. Masterson," he said gravely. "I am afraid my opinion can only come as a great shock to you all, but there is really no alternative. . . ."

Roxane buried her face in her hands as he confirmed their fears.

"There is no time to lose," he concluded. "Your grandmother should go into hospital tonight. Dr. Steyn will make the necessary arrangements. We will operate tomorrow."

"Has she been told?" Merle's tone was incredulous. Grannie Con! They couldn't really do this to Grannie Con!

"Yes," said Dr. Steyn. "And she has taken the news as one might expect, like a Spartan."

The specialist added, "After the pain she has endured this decision has probably come as a sort of relief. She will be better without that limb. Nature paves the way for a blow such as this."

Yes, thought Roxane. Nature paves the way with unbearable pain! In her own distress she had only one idea, to go to Grannie Con.

"Will you come with me to see her?" she asked Merle as the medical men took their leave.

Merle hesitated. "I'd rather not, Roxie . . . I shouldn't know what to say, or do. . . . You go—and if she wants me you can call me. . . ."

So Roxane went alone into the big lofty bedroom.

She stood at the foot of the old four-poster. A cage over the injured leg formed a sinister hump under the bedclothes. The face on the pillows was shrunken with suffering, but at the sight of Roxane the dull eyes brightened and the pale lips forced a wry smile.

"So they've told you, child?"

Roxane nodded, fighting back the emotion that threatened to overwhelm her.

The last of the daylight slanted through the open west-facing window and fell upon a bowl of roses glowing on the chest of drawers. Its reflections caught the crystal tear-drops of the antique chandelier and brought to vivid life the photograph of Dirk de Valois on the table next to the bed. Oh, Dirk, Dirk, if only you were here to help your mother now! thought Roxane.

The old woman's face relaxed into an expression of rare sweetness, and she put out her hand. The girl seized the cold bony fingers and pressed them to her lips. She fell on her knees beside the bed.

"Grannie Con—they *can't*——"

"Yes, Roxie, they can. I have known for a long time that this would happen." As she spoke she felt the warm tears fall on her prisoned fingers, and with her free hand she gently stroked the soft hair. "No, child, it's not as bad as all that. I am an old woman. Think of the young soldiers in the war. . . ."

"*You . . . you . . .* trying to comfort *me*. . . ." Roxane looked up, her tear-stained face quivering with love and grief and pity. "Is there anything I can do? Tell me how I can help you!"

Grannie Con's fingers began to clutch the sheet and twist it, and her head moved from side to side as if to escape some hateful conclusion. Then the spasm passed and she opened her eyes and fixed Roxane with a calm but imperious gaze.

"Yes, child, there is."

"What is it? I will do anything you ask."

Now a fierce and angry light filled the old eyes. Bring me a sword that I may fall upon it! they seemed to say.

"Telephone to Mr. Krifti, Roxane. Tell him to come here—*at once!* Tell him it is urgent that I should talk to him."

In the agony of mind and body that followed Grannie Con's operation a queer, persistent confusion clouded her brain, a confusion so deeply rooted that it never entirely cleared.

A limb was a vineyard, and the homestead of Dieu Donné was the heart. You, like your beloved Valley, were being dismembered bit by bit, and Mr. Krifti was your executioner. Today it was the right leg, tomorrow it would be the left, and the day after that he would sharpen his merciless knife and prepare to cut out your heart. A bloodless, shrivelled old heart it might be, dry as a raisin, but warm and palpitating yet, and you would hear him washing his hands with invisible soap before performing the operation. "You won't miss it once you are used to being without it, Mrs. de Valois! You will really be much better without your heart."

And that would be the end. He would have what he wanted most in the world, Dieu Donné, the core of the Valley. First the limbs, then the heart; first the vineyards, then the homestead.

They brought her back in a wheel-chair, little Queen Victoria near the end of her reign, but regal still.

"Well," she said to Thinus and Roxane, her face incredibly old and determined, "if this is how it has got to be, the sooner I learn to manage on wheels the better. By next spring I'll be getting round again, and quicker than before. Dieu Donné and I will pull through our troubles."

But Lizzie, while she helped Roxane to care for Grannie Con with patience and forebearance foreign to her peppery nature, was not content.

"Troubles always come in t'rees, Miss Roxie," she said. "Two we has had wit' dat terrible cloudburs' and de Oumissus losing her laik—but de Lord knows dere is more on de way."

The third calamity came towards the end of the winter and struck straight at Lizzie's heart.

An epidemic of measles ran through the Valley, and among those who went down with it was Ben.

"It's measles, Miss Roxie," said Saartjie, who had thrown off the spell of the spook long since. She was laughing and her black eyes danced. "I told Ben he is too old to go catching a child's sickness!"

Roxane smiled in sympathy. She guessed that Saartjie had good reason to know that her young coon lover was a child no more.

But, when the Pied Piper of the Valley recovered, the children no longer followed the magic of his pipe, nor did Saartjie sing her *liedjies* to the music of his guitar. For Ben had entered the silent world of the deaf.

Seeing the boy, brooding and lonely, Roxane's heart ached for him. How long did the memory of a song last, or a snatch of melody? How soon would a loved voice fade from the records of the mind? Never perhaps. Hal's voice, heard for so short a time, still sounded in her ears. She thought she would remember it always. Let it be like that for Ben; let him keep his *liedjies* and his bird-calls and hear them when others do not; let him never lose the music that is part of him!

But Ben was thinking that now it would be hard to get well-paid jobs and make money to give to Saartjie the presents she liked and take her to the bioscope. He was thinking that now he had lost his hearing he would also lose his girl.

CHAPTER 6

"I'VE NEWS FOR YOU!"

September is a lovely month in the Peninsula, a month of hope and promise.

The sap is rising in the trees, the wattle spreads its yellow mantle over the sordid shanty-settlements of the Cape Flats, hiding the tragic evidence of families rendered homeless by the winter floods; the low-lying meadows are starred with wild flowers and creamy arums, and every breeze carries the heady fragrance of water-hyacinths from the *vleis*. On the mountainside proteas put forth their sticky chalices and pin-cushions, and the *keurboom* toss fragrant pale-pink plumes in the wind.

In Constantia the clipped vines rise, darkly notched, gnarled and naked, from a blue mist of lupins, and mounds of dry prunings lie in the sun. Along the Ladies' Mile the coloured and Malay children waylay motorists with bunches of spring-carrots and armfuls of lilies and harlequin poppies. The squirrels scamper among the young leaves of the oaks, birds flirt on the wing and doves strut after their mates in the formal pavane of their courtship.

At Dieu Donné Roxane tried to keep her mind on the farm accounts, but spring was in her blood with all its restless messages. Something is going to happen, she thought, something wonderful. I feel it in my bones!

The office in which she sat was a careless, untidy little room that had been roughly thrown on to the side of the main house. It looked across a paved courtyard to the side door of the cellar, and at an angle to it was a cool, dark den in which lived a big wine-barrel, the boys' tots. The vineyard workers, summoned by the five o'clock tolling of the old slave-bell, lounged in the shade of two fine nut-trees and waited their turn to dip the tin beaker into the tub of harsh red wine that was to them both food and drink and their main reason for labouring among the vines.

Roxane watched them idly, a mass of unanswered correspondence lying in the wicker tray on her desk. She turned as she heard Thinus's unhurried step cross the library to the office, and his voice with its deep sing-song inflection.

"Roxie man, I've news for you! It's usually old Auntie Marthe who brings the gossip to Dieu Donné, but today it's Thinus Vos."

He carried a copy of the *Cape Argus* open at the social page and, as he sat on the edge of her desk, he held it up and began to read. From her position Roxane could see only his broad back and powerful neck emerging from his town suit and collar—the suit rather too tight for his muscular frame and the collar a little frayed. I must get that collar fixed for him, she reflected; he needs somebody to look after him. He must have been in Cape Town to have the evening paper already. . . . And then the sense of what he was reading dripped into her consciousness, cold, cold, little drops of ice. . . .

" 'September the fourteenth. From our Hollywood Correspondent. SECRET MARRIAGE REVEALED. The marriage of the famous ballerina Alexa Rome to war-correspondent Hallam Fairmead, son of novelist Adrian Fairmead, took place here in August. Until today it had been kept a secret. The cat jumped out of the bag this evening when flim director Rollo Ramski threw a party to celebrate the completion of his best-ever picture, *Ballerina*, which stars Alexa Rome. Says Ramski, "Hal Fairmead came to Hollywood to meet his parents after three years in the Far East. His paper commissioned him to write about Alexa in the screening of his father's famous novel, *Ballerina*, and Hal fell in love with his subject. The young couple will spend a holiday in South Africa in the beautiful vine-growing Constantia Valley with Mr. and Mrs. Adrian Fairmead. After Christmas they will return to London, where Alexa will go into rehearsal for her next ballet season." ' "

Thinus paused to allow his bombshell to take full effect.

Outside, the boys were returning to work in the vineyards, for their day's labour was from dawn to dusk.

"Well?" He faced about, making a full turn because Roxane was on his blind side. "What do you think of that?"

Hal . . . Hal married? No, no, no! It mustn't be true! Lavinia

Fairmead would have warned her, would have written something, given some hint . . . no, no, no. . . . She felt sick and faint and her palms were cold and damp.

Thinus was rolling a cigarette, using his maimed left hand to do so. He liked to force it to accomplish small tricky feats.

"Roll one for me," she said. Her mouth was dry, and in her own ears her voice seemed to come from far away, from somebody not even in the room with them. To get out, to find an excuse to get out, that was all that mattered now, to be alone. . . .

Thinus was looking at her with that little frown between his fair brows as he lit her cigarette.

"Roxie, I'm sorry, but surely after all this time——"

She made herself laugh.

"Dear Thinus, you flatter my fidelity! It's four years since I saw Hal Fairmead, the first boy who ever really kissed me!"

She picked up the newspaper he had put down.

"I was just amazed—flabbergasted. I heard from his mother only the other day and there was no suggestion——" Thinus, for God's sake, leave me before I give myself away. I can't act much longer—go, *go!*

As if in answer to her unspoken plea, he slid off the corner of the desk.

"I must get along, Roxie. I have to see Brink. He's out there now locking up the tot-room. I'll just catch him."

She nodded. Inside her a moving staircase was going down, down, down, bearing a host of dreams and foolish schoolgirl hopes, bearing them into darkness and limbo, and leaving an emptiness that was death. And now she must get away, quick, quick, to her special place, before this numbness, this death, woke into active living pain.

She called Wolf. "Walkies, boy, walkies." The big old Alsatian began to behave like a puppy, wagging his hindquarters, twisting his head and grimacing, making little sounds of joyous anticipation.

She slipped out of the house, no one must see her or stop her, and presently she was following the course of the stream up the berg and into a *kloof* where the red disas grew in the inaccessible shadow of waterfalls and grottoes.

The last rays of the sun still slanted over the shoulder of the mountain and the air was chill with approaching evening. The stream rampaged over the smooth boulders in full spate from the spring rains, but for once she walked blindly, unheeding the little lovely things about her, the feathery grasses, the giant ferns, the cool smell of water, the birds and dragon-flies darting among the flowers and shrubs that were her usual delight. She went to her "secret place" as a woman goes to her lover in distress, not for rapture but for consolation.

The dog ran ahead of her, this way and that, and came back to her side. He knew this track and watercourse so well, yet every sortie into the bush yielded new thrills and enchantments.

At last, where the waterfall foamed down the mossy rock-face with broken rainbows dancing in the spray, Roxane stopped and flung herself onto the springy turf. She buried her face in her hands and rocked her body to and fro.

Fool, crazy little fool! You meet a boy when you are still a kid—fifteen years old; you fall in love—deep, deep, so that he is yours forever and always has been. Every word he spoke to you, every look he gave you, every touch became part of you. The memory of him grew inside you, strong and deep-rooted; you followed him through talking to his parents about him, reading his letters to his mother and his published writings; you clung to your foolish passion like a vine to a trellis. Drag down the vine from the trellis and see if it dies! . . . Maybe it will live, crawling along the ground, no longer proud, a broken, untidy thing fit only to be uprooted and thrown away. . . . Wolf, Wolf, why do you come and put your long nose under my hands, pushing them away so that you may lick at the tears on my cheeks, understanding without knowing?

You fool. Roxane—you believed in love-at-first-sight—fool, fool! And what was it? Calf-love . . . they laugh at it, but do they remember the pain of it?

The rainbows had ceased their dancing, the sun hovered on the shoulder of the berg and was gone. Only the glow was left, the unearthly golden glow of the Hout Bay Gap.

An old, primitive impulse threw the girl face-downwards onto the bosom of the earth, her hands clawed at the grass and her nails filled with the loamy soil beneath. It was warm, strangely warm, below the surface. Perhaps that was the warmth of death, the kind blindness of the ground. It would be good to die, to be without this bursting, sinking pain. Once more she felt the dog's damp muzzle thrust itself between her cheek and the grass, forcing her head up. Through swollen lids she saw his eyes, golden as her own, dumbly anxious.

She sat up slowly and patted at her hair, and stared down at her earthy hands—gardener's hands. She made a faint attempt to smile.

"It's all right, Wolf, old boy," she said aloud. "It's over now; all finished. It was calf-love, you see; just something to laugh at later on. . . ."

She stood up and shook out her skirt, she dipped her handkerchief into the ice-cold mountain stream, and, as she washed her face and bathed her eyes, she knew that she was washing away the last traces of a hope that had been without foundation. To Hal she had been a kid worth a kiss on a moonlight night. To her he had been first love. It was over now; all done.

For a few moments she stood quite still in the sanctuary of nature that had long since become her own.

Help me, said her heart, help me to grow up!

And she wondered why this simple prayer was breathed to the trees and the waterfall, to the arums, pale as tapers in the dusk, to the fading sky and the great old mountain, rather than to the well-loved figure of the Madonna in the niche above her bed.

So the Fairmeads, with their son and their new daughter-in-law, came back to the Valley early in October, and all the Peninsula was agog. They forgot that Adrian had recently been their Number One Lion, and tumbled over themselves and each other in their eagerness to welcome a real live film-star actress-ballerina into their small exclusive society.

But Alexa had no wish to be absorbed into any part of the Peninsula merry-go-round.

"I only want to rest, rest, *rest*," she told Lavinia. "Fend them off, Vee! I can't be pushed around any more. I must be *me*, not the world's sweetheart, just *me*. I must relax."

Lavinia thought that sometimes Alexa had the look of lady-halfway-into-fox with that narrow, wedge-shaped face and the wide-set eyes that were so wary and impersonal, except when she was acting.

"You can't expect us all to go into purdah on your account, darling!" The light, clear voice held a certain relentless persistence. "People here are kind and sociable, Alexa. It is only natural that they should want to meet you and entertain you."

The sun shone on the terrace and sparkled on the swimming-pool below it. They could hear Hal splashing in the Lido-blue water.

Alexa merely shrugged her beautiful disciplined shoulders and strolled down among the flower-beds and lawns towards a grove of sweet-scented acacias. Some way off she paused and turned her head with a toss of her silver-gold mane. She called out, "Give me a few days, anyway!"

Lavinia looked after her with displeasure. Alexa was like that. She divorced herself casually from her surroundings and obligations and disappeared, or she sat apart and silent with her hands lightly folded and her eyes hidden behind her dark glasses, utterly relaxed, as inhuman and half-asleep as an old cart-horse standing in the sun.

Hal came up from the pool, his tanned body still wet and gleaming; a body so firmly muscled that it seemed carved in fine-grained wood. His mother restrained an impulse to touch him, to stroke those strong shining shoulders. When you could no longer touch your children you lost them. Your son grew into manhood where maternal kisses were forbidden. No more cries of "Kiss it well!"; no more burying of the face in a soft breast; no more rushing into arms opened in a loving embrace. Reserve took the place of spontaneity; the child clinging to its mother's skirt gave way to the defensive schoolboy still vulnerable to affection, and he in turn hardened into the young man standing fierce guard over his hard-won independence. And, after a while, another woman took your place—a woman with the right to hold him in her arms. . . . To touch was to possess, the spirit yielded with the body.

"Where is my wife?" Hal rubbed his rumpled brown hair with a bathing towel, his grey eyes sparkled with health and the arrogance of the dominant male. He was immensely proud of Alexa, and whenever he said "my wife" he wanted to shout with triumph and laugh at the absurdity of their courtship. "Not marriage," she had protested, "only love." And he had answered, "Marriage or nothing—you must make an honest man of me, Lexa!"

"She was here a minute ago," said Lavinia. "But it would seem that she *warnz to bee alawn.* . . ."

"Poor girl, she needs a little solitude after being driven round the set of *Ballerina* for months."

"But, darling, one can't always do exactly what one wants."

She was lying on a wicker *chaise-longue*, and Hal pushed her sandalled feet gently to one side and sat down in profile to her. Unable to resist, she put out her hand and ran her finger-tips gently down the long livid scar across his cheekbone—the mark of a Malay *kris*. It tightened his smile, made his right profile appear grim and forbidding. It had a dangerous look, rather exciting, like the sabre slashes of the nineteenth-century duellists.

He was saying thoughtfully, "Look, Vee, I can't help noticing that you haven't really got Alexa right."

A sharp little spurt of flame licked over her heart, and there was an edge on her voice as she said, "Why ever should you fancy that?"

"You criticize her. Inwardly you are always criticizing her."

She felt and resented his loyalty to his wife.

"Is she beyond criticism?"

He hated the laugh with which she spoke, the touch of malice.

"Alexa is different," he defended. "She is a very great artist. You can't apply the ordinary rules to somebody with her genius."

She said coldly, "Life will apply the ordinary rules, even if I don't."

He persisted in what he had to say. "Couldn't you make an effort to understand her needing to be left in peace? She hates being paraded."

"Paraded!" The word stung Lavinia. "I have never suggested parading Alexa. But one has certain duties to the community in which one has settled, and I must admit there are a few neighbours I would like to ask here to meet my son and his famous wife."

"Who, for instance?"

"To begin with, there are the young Mastersons. Guy designed this house."

"And we stayed with his people four years ago. I remember Guy very well—and going to his wedding at Dieu Donné over there——" He made a gesture towards the old homestead gleaming among the oaks further up the Valley.

"Guy's parents are in Europe at present," said Lavinia, "but the young couple live in that pretty thatched cottage only a stone's throw away from Farway. Then I'd like to have Merle Masterson's grandmother, old Grannie Constance de Valois, who is a terrific character, a dyed-in-the-wool traditionalist, and her ward, Roxane de Valois." She paused with a slightly puzzled expression. "As a matter of fact, I can't think why Roxane hasn't been over here to see us yet. We've been here four days already. She does a lot of typing for Adrian and she used to be in and out of the house all the time. While we were away she exercised these chaps for me——" She indicated the two heavy ridgebacks asleep in the sun. "I can't make it out."

"Roxane de Valois——" Hal's face softened as he turned to his mother with a smile. "Would she be the little dark bridesmaid with the lovely eyes, the girl whose mother was shot by the Nazis as a spy somewhere in France?"

"You remember her then?"

"Very well. She was awfully sweet. I suppose she is quite grown up now, engaged perhaps?"

"She's about nineteen. The boys fall for her, but Roxane is an aloof little person in some ways. She plays tennis and dances and swims with the various young men who belong in her set, but she doesn't commit herself to anybody in particular."

"Well, now, who else did you want to ask to your little party?"

"Grannie Con's farm manager, Thinus Vos." She spelt the name, and added, "You pronounce it Teenis Foss. He is an Afrikaner from the Free State, and like most Free Staters, he is a Nationalist who would like to see this country a republic. But he has certain political weaknesses. He doesn't hate the British. On the contrary. And to a true full-blooded Nat, tolerance is like decay in a sound tooth. Thinus has tolerance." She paused and added, "Then we would have to invite old Auntie Marthe van der Walt. Nothing goes on in the Valley without her knowing all about it."

"So she has to know Alexa and me and report on us?"

"Most certainly. And naturally we must include her daughter, Louise, and Louise's husband, Mr. Krifti. Kriff sold us this site. He is influential round here, a queer fish with more money than friends, and a magnificent collection of Africana. Collecting things of historic value and importance is a *thing* out here. Kriff would like to crown his collection with Dieu Donné, and he once had the temerity to make Grannie Con an offer for it. I'd like to have been a fly on the wall that day!"

"I gather she didn't entertain the offer?"

Lavinia laughed. "Grannie Con *is* Dieu Donné. She sits up there in her wheel-chair, planning to keep her beloved property all in one piece as it has been for the past two and a half centuries, fighting against fearful odds for the past while the future is eating it up as fast as a puppy gobbling up a plate of raw meat."

"Grannie Con moves my heart. Is that the lot?"

"That's all. You see, I only want the people who are genuinely tied up with our new home, with Farway. These few are. Each of them has contributed in some way or another to our lives as settlers in a new country. And they should interest you as a journalist. This Valley, with its clan-system and its conflicts, has much to offer you."

"Perhaps," he agreed thoughtfully. "But to Alexa it offers only peace and seclusion. We don't want to break the spell."

He felt, rather than saw, her stiffen. Being with her had become dangerous since his marriage. For a few moments it would seem as if they were back on the old easy footing, and then, suddenly, for no real reason, he would find himself struggling in the quicksands of some feminine, only half-comprehended resentment.

She said coldly, "Your wife owes me a certain degree of courtesy as my guest." She broke off and caught her lip between her teeth, aware that her hostility had come out into the open, breaking the bonds she had set upon it.

Hal rose and looked down at her, his eyes narrow in the way she had come to fear.

"If that's the way you feel about it . . ."

"That is exactly the way I feel."

"Then arrange your party. I will do my best to produce Alexa when you wish. Just let me know when you expect us to be on view."

Again she was aware of the hot flame of indignation, fast becoming familiar. How Alexa had altered and possessed him! It was fantastic that Hal, at twenty-two, should find himself married to a famous ballerina! It was too much for an experienced man of the world to take on with much hope of success, let alone Hal! That was why she, Lavinia, had fought this entanglement from the very moment she had first realized what was in the wind. And she had lost, for Hal was as stubborn as the devil, and Adrian had been very little help. She had beseeched him to put his foot down. "How can I?" he had said in that exasperatingly reasonable manner he so often used towards her. "Hal is of age. He has been soldiering for two years and has already made a name for himself as a war-correspondent. As for Alexa, she is getting a fabulous salary. So what can I do?"

And now, where would it end, this absurd marriage?

She sat up, resting her chin on her hands. She wanted to plead with Hal; to say, "Don't let's quarrel! Please, darling, don't let this young woman come between us in this way!" But she said instead, in a tone so bitter that she hardly recognized her own voice:

"Thanks for your co-operation." (Idiotic to talk to one's own son like that!) "But you would do well to remember that *you* have a future and a career as well as Alexa! You are a journalist by profession, and you can't stop meeting people and observing life simply because your wife happens to be in an anti-social frame of mind."

He did not answer her, just put his bathing towel round his neck, and turned away in the direction of the garden, following the path Alexa had taken.

CHAPTER 7

BALLERINA

Old Auntie Marthe van der Walt put on her most outrageous hat and the long gloves she had worn to a dance at Government House at the turn of the century; she found her chased-silver card-case, long unused, and stepped into the back of her ancient Chevrolet.

Accompanied by her daughter, Louise Krifti, and driven by Joel, her wizened little coloured man-of-all-work, dressed in his white coat and cap, she rattled off across the Valley to Farway.

"Calling is completely out of date," protested Louise to her determined mother. "These days you simply ring up the new-comers and invite them in to drinks. Then, if they like the look of you and your home, and you like the look of them, they will come to a meal later on."

"These Fairmeads are English," replied her inflexible mother. "They know what's what. English people do."

"English people have forgotten what's what—as you put it— long ago. You forget that, since your day, England has been through a social revolution. The new settlers come here to get out of their sinks and their taxes. They may say they adore the Cape climate and they can't stand the English cold, but what they really can't stand is the new English way of life."

"Poor souls!" Old Auntie Marthe was incapable of envisaging the changed England, but Louise was always drumming it into her head that the gracious days were done. "It all sounds too awful! For women of gentle birth to be compelled to cook and scrub! I don't wonder they come out here in search of a civilized existence!"

Elias, the Fairmeads' native house-boy, symbolized this "civilized existence." An odd symbol, perhaps, but not out of place in the home of the descendants of a race of Empire-builders.

Elias was Nubian black, and, as he opened the door, his amiable smile revealed a striking frill of snowy protruding teeth. Too cannibal! thought Auntie Marthe; the whites of his intelligent eyes were buttercup yellow, and his voice was as deep and resonant as a lion's purr. The starched tunic of a house-servant seemed only to emphasize the aboriginal force that moved within it. He received their cards on a silver salver.

"I am sorry my Madam is out," he rumbled in his careful English, so different from the high, quick Cape coloured intonation.

But Auntie Marthe was not easily put off. The bright plumage on her cartwheel hat quivered as she leaned forward to put a confidential question. Elias watched it, fascinated; it was a headdress worthy of a Bantu chief; only a monkey's tail was needed to perfect it.

"Your old Madam may be out," said Auntie Marthe, and Louise suppressed a smile; Lavinia Fairmead would not care about that "*old* Madam." "But is your new *young* Madam in?"

Elias was unsophisticated where social tarradiddles were concerned, and Auntie Marthe's rheumy, inquisitive eye had a way of extracting the truth.

"Young Madam is in the garden by the swimming-pool. Young Madam is asleep."

"We won't disturb her," said Louise hastily. "We wouldn't dream of it."

"Nonsense! She can't still be taking a siesta at four in the afternoon. She'll be wanting her tea. I could do with a cup myself."

"*Mother——*"

"Young Madam don't drink no tea," explained Elias. "Young Madam sleep and sleep in the sun." He was accustomed to long leisurely palavers under the thorn trees in his native veld and he was still under the spell of Auntie Marthe's plumed and princely headgear.

"Which way is the pool, boy?"

"If you go," said Louise to her mother, "I shall sit in the car and wait for you."

"By all means," agreed old Marthe. "But I intend to stroll round and make myself known to this young woman." She addressed the hypnotized Negro. "You need not come with me. Just point out the way."

As he did so Louise shrugged her shoulders and went to the car. Really, the old lady was becoming insupportable, her curiosity was remorseless!

Old Joel opened the car door for her, his eyes bulging.

"Natives all over de Walley, Miss Louise! In my young days dere was never a native in de place. Now dey is everywhere wit' deir fancy pullowers, deir big buck-nigger hats, an' deir yellow shoes. It's bad, Miss Louise!"

"It's your own fault," she said crossly. "The coloured people all go into the new factories, so what can you expect? Are we to do our own housework—like the English?"

He removed his peaked cap to scratch his head, and his little wizened face wore a pained expression. Joel, like Joshua of Dieu Donné, belonged to the old school. He was part and parcel of the Valley, the descendant of slaves, the privileged and trusted servant of one of the leading Constantia families.

"What you say is true, Miss Louise. One of my daughters is working in a factory. De girls don't want to go into service no more. Dey get more money in de factory an' more free time. I tell her it's better to have a good home an' her keep, but she t'row her head in de air and laugh at me."

"Then blame yourselves if the natives take your places in European households!" But to herself Louise added, Or blame the industrial revolution that is turning our country upside down. She took her cigarette case and offered it to the old man. "Take one, Joel. You can hide it when the Oumissus comes in sight."

"T'ank you, Miss Louise. I will put it in my pocket, because I can see my Oumissus coming roun' the corner now."

Well, thought Louise, she must have received a very quick flea in the ear! But her mother's bizarre countenance was glowing with warmth and secret amusement.

Elias stood politely in the porch to see them off, the brilliant, desirable feathers nodding and waving on the old She-Elephant's hat as the car moved away. In his own country the term She-Elephant was one of homage and respect.

"My dear!" Auntie Marthe's tone was hushed. "My dear, when I tell you what I saw! She was lying on one of those inflated mattress affairs on the verge of the pool, *sound* asleep, covered from head to foot in grease and practically nothing else; a moochie the size of a postage stamp and a brassière that certainly didn't serve its purpose!"

"A *bikini*, you mean?"

"I wouldn't know," declared Auntie Marthe, who liked to use a little up-to-date slang every now and again. "But I thought to myself, Just imagine if a gardener were to come on her like that —or even that big house-boy—well, *anything* might happen! It's not right."

"What does she look like?"

"Filleted, Louise. Flat as a pancake; looks more like twelve years old than twenty-three; a tiny body and face and a mass of whitish hair."

"Platinum—probably bleached."

"I wouldn't know about that either, but I dare say. You modern girls never leave nature alone. I didn't see her eyes. She had dark glasses on, and she didn't stir while I watched her, not a muscle. She was dead to the world."

"Animals do that," said Louise. "When they scent danger they freeze."

"She wasn't freezing, she was cooking. It's hot for October this year." Auntie Marthe leaned forward and spoke to the back of Joel's head.

"To Dieu Donné, Joel. We'll be sure of a cup of tea *there!*"

"Yes, Oumissus."

Louise groaned. Then she too gave an order.

"Drop me at my house on the way." To her mother she said, "You and Grannie Con will enjoy yourselves more without me."

"Poor old Con," said Auntie Marthe. "Tied to that dreadful chair, immobilized for good. Somebody has to get around and bring her a little gossip from time to time."

"Darling, she'll never be without a little gossip, so long as you are in the Valley!" But Louise was smiling, and a certain tenderness softened her cold, carven features. "I hate to think how she'd manage without you."

Old Auntie Marthe took a compact from her handbag and dabbed her aristocratic van der Walt nose with powder, and added a touch of scarlet to lips tucked and puckered with the erosion of the years. Visiting Grannie Con always made her feel very young and spry.

"It isn't really a party," Lavinia had explained in issuing her invitations. "Alexa hates parties, but we did want a few of our nearest neighbours to come in for a sundowner quite informally."

So there they were.

Old Auntie Marthe and the Kriftis were the first to arrive, and as Elias showed them through the hall and out onto the terrace he observed with keen disappointment that the She-Elephant was not wearing her plumage. Without it she lost something of her majesty. In fact, however, Auntie Marthe was preening herself on the new floral toque she had bought specially for this enthralling occasion, an intimate party to meet the famous Alexa.

"At my age," she said to her daughter, "one is never wholly informal. One wears a hat—and gloves."

Louise wore neither. Her smooth black hair with its wings of premature grey was well shaped and groomed, and her printed-silk dress was plainly and expensively cut. Her husband looked at her with satisfaction. She was always exactly right. Mr. Krifti regarded Louise as one of his best investments.

The Mastersons came next. Guy had developed assurance in the past few years; he had caught up with many of his own leaping thoughts, but there was still that peculiar urgency about him, a tendency to stammer at times. He enjoyed coming to Farway. It was his first really successful house, triumphantly contemporary, and lavishly graced by the Fairmeads' beautiful and distinctive possessions.

Merle, in her mid-twenties, was at the height of her fair good looks, and well aware of it. But she was also conscious of the flaming sex-jealousy of her red-headed husband. An unguarded word or look of hers was to Guy like a match thrown into dry summer grass. In a moment there was a blaze. He ought to wear one of those forestry warnings, VURR SEISON—FIRE-SEASON. It was always the fire-season with Guy. But his intense jealousy still excited and flattered her.

To each of her guests in turn Lavinia said the right thing, making them feel that they were the only people she wanted to see— until the next body came into the magnetic field.

"Auntie Marthe—what a heavenly hat! Dear Louise and Kriff, lovely to see you. . . ."

How did she do it? wondered Adrian. No man could bring himself to put on such an act, unless, of course, he happened to be *one of those*. . . . There she went again.

"Guy, my dear, you must be very sweet to Merle—no woman could be so much *en beauté* without good reason! Adrian darling, get Auntie Marthe a sweet sherry, and Louise likes hers dry— and, Hal, Merle takes gin and tonic with ice and lemon. Kriff, you men must help yourselves . . . no, *don't* ask me where Alexa is—my daughter-in-law cannot resist making an entrance. She always sees that she is just late enough to bring it off!"

That was unwise, and unnecessary, thought Adrian, aware of his son's eyes hardening as every nerve in his system tensed in silent defense of Alexa.

But it was Grannie Con who "brought off" the entrance at that moment.

Lizzie's deaf Ben, dressed in a smart white suit, guided her wheel-chair onto the terrace, flanked on either side by Roxane and Thinus like a bodyguard.

Lavinia hurried forward to meet them. Why did these South African young men always wear their suits a size too small? But Roxane looked charming in her primrose cotton dress with the tucked bodice and white collar and cuffs, fresh as the spring. Surely Grannie Con's hat was the same she had worn to Merle's wedding four years ago! But then shopping at her immense age and with her severe disability must be an ordeal to be avoided at all costs.

"Darling Grannie Con, how wonderful of you to come!" she cried. "We hardly dared hope—knowing how seldom you go out these days—but we did so want you to meet Alexa. . . . Where *is* Alexa, Hal? Grannie Con—Roxane and Thinus—you remember Hal—at Merle's wedding, only he was quite a youngster then."

How foolishly the English introduce people, thought Adrian, always in a vague or slightly hysterical fashion. We should take lessons from the Americans, wear labels if necessary.

He said to Grannie Con, "Now tell me what you would like— sherry, gin, or perhaps a glass of sweet Constantia?"

But, even as he attended to his guest of honour, those peculiar antennae of the born and practised novelist were probing the air for drama, seeking the cause of some almost imperceptible tension, and finding it—to his surprise—in the taut little face of Roxane.

Hal was speaking to her now, looking down at her with mischief in his eyes and that attractive crooked smile curtailed a little on the right side of his mouth by the long vertical scar on his cheek. One eyebrow was characteristically raised, and he seemed to be teasing her about something. Thinus was with them, and Adrian heard his deep chuckle as he said, "No, I've sold that old car. I have one with better manners now." The girl's smile was strained and she was pale and scared-looking, the hand grasping her white bag was trembling, and he wondered if she could be ill. But as he took Grannie Con her glass of sweet wine he was reassured. Roxane had mastered the bad moment, she was saying something to Hal, laughing with the others. Yet the impression of extreme distress lingered in Adrian's mind to haunt him later. He heard his wife's high, light voice.

"Darling, here are Karl and Aletta——"

The Kriges had been included in the party at the last moment because, as Lavinia pointed out, they were neighbours, and if you had a dozen people to drinks you might as well pop in a couple more.

Roxane had both dreaded and desired the moment of meeting Hal again. She had hoped that by some miracle his actual presence would banish her picture of him and disillusion her. It must—it *must* be so! Let him be different from the way she remembered him, no longer lovable, but if that was not to be, then please, please let her be strong and cold so that no one should guess what she might be feeling! She had kept away from Farway in case, by going there, she should meet Hal alone and betray herself by word or look. She knew that it would be best for her to meet him again in the presence of others, sustained by her pride. But now, at the first glimpse of him, at the way he moved and smiled, at the touch of his hand and the sound of his voice, her flimsy defences shook and crumbled and her heart was leaping in her breast like a fish breaking surface.

His eyes, smoke-grey and bright with mockery, laughed at her from under the narrow brows, one of which was raised to lend his face an engaging lack of symmetry accentuated still further by the long taut scar. The scar was new to her. She longed to feel the thin thread of it against her own soft cheek.

"Why, Roxane de Valois! You've grown up; you are even prettier than when you swept me off my feet the first time we met—the only time."

It was so easy, the way he said it, so unimportant and trivial. He threw away that summer day, that night of the singing stars —he reduced an embrace that had stolen all her heart to a little joke between them, a joke shared by Thinus because his car had brayed like an ass. And here came Karl and Aletta Krige, and they were greeting Hal and reminding him of Merle's wedding and their *braaivleis*.

"We hoped you'd come to our Valley and grow vines." Karl's deep voice matched his massive appearance and full fair beard. But Hal only shook his head and smiled. "Not yet. But one day, maybe, when Alexa gives up dancing."

Roxane saw his eyes change and melt and brighten, as if a torch had been lit in their depths. Hal was looking towards the garden.

She turned to follow his gaze. A fragile form approached the terrace from the lawn—ethereal—immortal.

"Oh, there you are at last, Alexa!" called Lavinia. "Whatever have you been doing down by the swimming-pool at this time of day?"

Lavinia had difficulty in controlling her indignation. She would—Alexa would—come onto the stage from the one direction that made no sense at all! Why on earth should she be messing about the garden with guests waiting to meet her?

"I love the pool," said Alexa, unperturbed.

She crossed the grass and came up the steps onto the crazy paving, unhurried, exquisitely balanced, her bare feet clad in flat, green sandals, her smooth sun-browned shoulders rising from a leaf-green dress of some filmy material, her pale hair touched with evening gold, an aura about her small pointed face.

The artist in Guy Masterson cried out within him at sight of her—the spirit of the trees! And Merle thought, with odd relief, But she isn't beautiful; I was afraid she might be beautiful!

So her eyes are brown, noted old Auntie Marthe. A curious contrast with that light hair. . . . Mr. Krifti, standing beside his mother-in-law, wondered what they paid Alexa Rome to make a film. If her earnings were assessed for income tax in conjunction with her husband's in the English fashion, it must create an absurd situation. They would do much better to live in sin. Louise Krifti found herself longing intensely for an evening at Covent Garden. She adored ballet—*Lac des Cygnes, Spectre de la Rose.* . . .

Grannie Con shook her head. They were a law unto themselves, these artists, and that nice young man, Hal Fairmead, was surely unequal to all that this marriage might involve. Karl and Aletta Krige thought the same thing at the same time. The big man glanced at his Junoesque wife. She'll never give him children, said the look that passed between them.

Thinus saw the pain and sudden pallor in Roxane's face, and, as his eyes sought the cause and found it in the delicate alien figure among them, he was filled with sudden pity and a strange stab of enmity. Roxie, my squirrel, when they cut you, you bleed. But this fairy-creature is not made of flesh and feeling! How can she be a man's wife—his mate?

Deaf Ben, behind the wheel-chair of the cripple, caught his

breath at sight of the little ballerina. He sensed in her the rhythm that was part of his own Saartjie. But Saartjie danced with all herself all the time, waggling hips, shoulders and buttocks, while this one was quiet, all in one piece. But you could tell that the dancing was in her just like you knew there was electricity in the thin silver wire. His fingers plucked the strings of an invisible guitar while ghost *liedjies* drifted through the silence that would never laugh or sing again.

Roxane watched Alexa mount the steps with lovely timing, as if to secret music, and her heart turned over. No wonder Hal loved this woman who was like no other. She was more than beautiful, she was a song. She was looking at Hal and smiling, and her hands made a small unconscious gesture towards him so that they spoke to one another wordlessly in the language of lovers. And the brightness was still in his eyes. So now Roxane knew what they meant when they said, "She is the light of his eyes"; they meant that without the beloved image there was nothing, only darkness, blindness. She knew—how well she knew! So this was Alexa—his love! So this was how it felt when your heart broke, when it was torn from its moorings in your breast to sink somewhere deep in the pit of your stomach. . . .

For the second time Adrian Fairmead was aware of Roxane. What was hurting the child so badly? Her shoes, perhaps, and perhaps not. He was at her side, saying quietly:

"Nobody has given you a drink, Roxie. What will you have?"

"Something soft, please—tomato-juice, lemon, anything——"

"Come along and choose."

Follow me, child, and presently that look will leave your eyes, and the overtone, the near tremor, will disappear from your voice. That is life, Roxie. So often we must do our suffering in public. But as we grow older we grow armour too, and you have none as yet. But why should you be suffering? Why?

Grannie Con watched Auntie Marthe dart at Alexa like a fish at a fly, and she smiled as the cool, dark eyes of the dancer recoiled from the raddled countenance thrust into hers with avid curiosity. And then Grannie Con noticed Roxane go with her host to the table at the end of the terrace where a varied assortment of drinks was set out. A nice man, that English novelist.

Intellectually intolerant, they said, but why not, after all? He was a scholar. Sad about his limp. But that was life; war for men and childbirth for women. There were five men here at this moment, and three of them carried the scars of war. Adrian Fairmead's was the souvenir of World War One, Thinus had made his sacrifices in World War Two, and Hal's cheek bore the signature of jungle warfare that went on and on, like Mau Mau in Africa. Mr. Krifti's wounds were not visible, Mr. Krifti did not take his body into battle. As for childbirth—there were three young women this evening who still had to travel that road one day. Merle, who was biding her time. Alexa—what of Alexa? And Roxane, dear Roxane, who would love her babies with all the selfless, pent-up devotion that was now bestowed on an old woman and a dog. Louise Krifti, of course, had had sense enough not to risk reproducing her husband!

Ah, here was Mr. Krifti! Grannie Con's back straightened, and her fingers involuntarily touched the police whistle that hung round her neck on a velvet cord. Mentally, she blew a shrill blast to sound the Alert and summon her wits. Come hither, all ye senses, the invader is in sight, the enemy is on his way!

Adrian Fairmead smiled as he saw the tall man go over to the old lady's chair. Kriff had left his beads at home today and his fingers were restless without them. It was an odd habit—Levantine really—that trick of fondling a chaplet of amber or ivory. Where did Kriff come from? The shores of the eastern Mediterranean, perhaps, or some Asian or Arabian desert? Adrian observed that Mr. Krifti was drawn to Grannie Con as if by some compulsion outside himself. She was looking up at him with her glance sharp and hostile. They understood one another, those two. There was between them the intimate, distorted relationship of natural antagonists. They shared secrets.

Alexa and Guy had gravitated together with the intuitive recognition of one artist for another. But Lavinia was too conscientious a hostess to allow her little lioness to become interested in any one person. Alexa must be shared out, offered to each in turn, a nibble at a time. And now it was Thinus's turn to help himself. What, in heaven's name, would those two find in common? Adrian realized that he must go to the rescue before his wife was appalled by a pool of silence falling into her party.

Old Auntie Marthe had had two sherries and a nice bite at Alexa, so she felt free to give her attention to Merle.

"You are too thin, my dear—*much* too thin from your grandmother's point of view, I should say!" Her inquisitive old eyes raked the young woman's girlish figure. No great-grandchild there for old Con to gloat over!

Merle took her meaning and laughed. "We want to go travelling when Guy has made enough money for a trip oversea —Italy, Europe. . . . The babies must wait."

"Don't leave it too long. You have a duty to Dieu Donné, you know."

"Dieu Donné!" It came out like a cry. And Merle's lip curled in an ugly canine way. Almost a snarl, thought Auntie Marthe, surprised.

Louise Krifti was saying to Roxane, "I should be so interested to see our host's library, or wherever it is that he writes."

"He writes in his tower-room. I could take you up."

"Let's go and ask him if he minds," suggested Louise.

They wandered over to Grannie Con's wheel-chair. The old lady was holding court. She had insisted that Lavinia sit beside her.

"Stop flitting about, my dear. Sit down and talk to me. You must sit because it gives me a crick in my neck to look up."

Adrian too had drawn up a chair, and Mr. Krifti had fetched one for Auntie Marthe. Guy and Hal and the Kriges had strolled into the garden to choose a suitable site for a tennis court.

Ben helped Elias to serve the small savouries. "These eats," said Auntie Marthe, helping herself to a perlemoen patty. "Delicious! Try one, Con! You needn't consider your figure at your age."

Grannie Con pursed up her lips. "I never eat between meals."

"Then you are not a good South African," laughed Lavinia.

"Mr. Fairmead . . ." The soft, tentative voice was Roxane's. "Mrs. Krifti is keen to see your crow's nest. May I take her up?"

"Certainly. But wait, I will take her myself."

"Me too," clamoured Auntie Marthe. "And Thinus."

Adrian said doubtfully, "It's a spiral staircase—rather steep."

"*I* should worry!" Auntie Marthe's floral toque bobbed defiantly. "I'm as nimble as a spring chicken."

Grannie Con looked after them wistfully, but her tone was caustic as she addressed Mr. Krifti. "Your mother-in-law has a childish passion for showing off."

"Yes," he agreed. "I find it rather endearing. She has an insatiable interest in life for a woman of her years—whatever they may be. Tell me, do you still dislike this house—Guy's masterpiece?"

"I find it raw, Mr. Krifti, like immature wine."

"You are right. It has no real bouquet yet, no soul."

"A house does not evolve a bouquet, or a soul, in a couple of years. That takes centuries." She spoke with a certain disdain.

"Many generations must live and die and love in a home before it can breed its ghosts," he agreed. "A ghost is an intangible asset, Mrs. de Valois, not to be measured in material terms."

"Yet you have set your price upon our Dieu Donné ghosts; you have made me an offer for my home—and all that goes with it."

He bowed his narrow head with the strands of thinning greasy hair.

"Van der Walts would understand the ghosts of Dieu Donné," he said. "Louise would not be out of place in Dieu Donné, Mrs. de Valois."

"Perhaps not," she answered, staring out across the lovely Valley of the Vines. "Van der Walt women have married de Valois men in the past. But the name of Krifti would ring oddly in the homestead. Krifti is not a name that is known in Constantia."

"It will be," he said quietly, with the smile that was without mirth.

Up in the octagonal tower-room Adrian Fairmead showed his guests his magnificent library. His large untidy desk stood in the alcove of the main window, commanding the entire spread of the landscape.

Louise drew two or three volumes from the shelves, handling them with reverent care. "These must be very precious to you, Adrian. Kriff would give his ears for some of these first editions."

"Kriff knows what's what," put in old Marthe with satisfaction.

Over by the window Thinus and Roxane stood apart, looking

across the vineyards already melting into the dusk. Eastward, False Bay and the Hottentots Hollands were topaz in the reflection of the sunset.

Roxane was speaking in a low voice, brittle with urgency.

"Thinus, you asked me to go home to Tweefontein with you for a few days when you visit your old folks next week. I said I wasn't sure if Grannie Con could spare me."

"She can. I've asked her."

The evening gold seemed trapped in the thick feathery gold of his eyelashes. What a shame that his left eye must always be shuttered by the black mask!

"Then take me with you!" Her voice broke suddenly, and he saw her throat working. He put his hand over hers and his slow, deliberate tone steadied her.

"My old folks want you to come. It's two years since you went to Tweefontein last—a long time. And I'll tell you what, we are going in Merle's big car. She wants to go to Johannesburg to see her mother, and Guy can't get away, so I've promised to share the driving with her as far as Kimberley, and she can stay with us at Tweefontein for a day or two and then go on to Jo'burg. On her way back she'll pick us up again. It all works out perfectly."

While he spoke, she recovered herself and presently she smiled up at him. "You are a darling, old Thinus; I love you."

"That makes two of us," he said. And, for the second time in her life, those words of his deepened a sense of loss within her and left her sad and empty.

CHAPTER 8

NIGHT DRIVE

But to escape from the storm in her own heart was not as easy as Roxane had hoped.

By some ironic chance Merle had invited Hal and Alexa to go with them to Johannesburg.

"Thinus's parents, Oom Jacob and Tant' Petronella, will put us all up for a night at Tweefontein—that's their farm near Kimberley—and my mother and step-father have a big house in Johannesburg and will be delighted to welcome you. We won't want more than a suitcase each and we can take five passengers comfortably in my car."

Hal had accepted with enthusiasm. He was eager to see the City of Diamonds and the City of Gold, and then he had turned to his wife with sudden misgiving.

"It would be a wonderful opportunity of seeing the country with people who really know about it," he had said. "You'd like to come, wouldn't you?"

"Arrange what you like, darling," Alexa had said with her air of sublime indifference and acquiescence. "Anything you want."

"We'll drive through the night," Merle had suggested. "It'll be full moon. The tires don't get hot and we'll simply eat up the miles through the Karroo. It'll give us an extra day."

It was late afternoon when Merle picked up Thinus and Roxane at Dieu Donné. The day was mild and the fresh sparkle of spring mingled with the langour of summer in the air. As they drove over to Farway in the big American tourer, Roxane thought, I've walked into a trap—trying to get free of Hal, I've tangled myself up worse than ever! Seeing him with Alexa, so obviously in love, was going to hurt, hurt, hurt. . . .

But, when they arrived at Farway, Hal was waiting for them alone.

"Alexa is not coming after all," he said. "She isn't feeling very well, and she thinks she may be car-sick."

A spurt of joy flamed in Roxane and died. What difference did it make? Whether Alexa was with them or not, she still possessed Hal.

It was sunset when they reached the top of du Toit's Kloof high in the mountains above the plain of Paarl. Merle stopped the car.

"Here is where we have a sundowner and sandwiches. You must admit this view is worth looking at!"

She produced tumblers, gin and lime ready mixed, and a packet of avocado sandwiches. "There's beer if anybody wants it," she added, "and tomato-juice for Roxie. She loves the stuff."

Below them the pine and poplar windbreaks between vineyards and orchards were tipped with gold, and far away they could see Table Mountain and the sea. Here and there they caught glimpses of old homesteads like Dieu Donné, and under the Paarl Rock dreamed the little white town of Paarl—the Pearl—among its avenues and gardens.

Hal would have to confess that this was a fine and prosperous sight, thought Thinus, who regarded the Englishman—in his professional capacity—with some mistrust. Foreign journalists were dangerous animals who bit the hand that fed them. He had said as much to Merle when she had told him that Hal was coming with them because he wanted "copy."

"More harm has been done to the good name of our country by ill-informed, irresponsible journalists than by anything else in recent years," he had said.

She had only laughed at him with that canine lift of the lip that meant she was going to be nasty. "You forget our Government," she had retorted.

There she was now, oblivious of the view, snarling into a little looking-glass while she smeared her mouth with lipstick. So Roxie was fishing out a compact too. Women were like birds that way; one made a move towards a powder-puff and instantly the rest began fluttering in the same direction.

"It's quite breath-taking," said Hal. "In a way it reminds me of the Midi, the wine-growing country round Avignon. Some of those early Huguenots must have felt quite at home when they saw the pattern of their African wilderness."

"My Huguenot ancestors came from the Rhône Valley," said Merle. "When Guy takes me to Europe one of these days we want to explore the country they came from."

Yes, Merle, my ancestors came from France too, thought Roxane; my mother died for France. But aloud she said, "The Huguenots gave their homes the names of exile, like Dieu Donné. And there is Bien Donné too, Bonfoi, La Gratitude, Rhône, Provence, Picardie. . . ."

"Names that move the heart," said Hal. "There is faith and

hope in them; belief in the future and nostalgia for the lost homeland."

His eyes were drawn to the girl who had risen to stand a little apart on the rocky slope of the mountain.

The evening breeze blew her fine dark hair away from her up-turned face, a thin haunting face, hollowed under the cheek-bones and waxen round the almond eyes that held in their depths the look of a visionary. Her silk blouse whipped against her small round breasts and her slight waist, and, as he watched her, he was curiously touched by her look of youth and loneliness. She seemed to have withdrawn herself from her companions spiritually as well as physically, and suddenly the circumstances of her sad childhood came back to him. She too had known exile, she too had been uprooted by intolerance and conflict, but she had been fortunate. She had fallen into loving hands. She was no longer homeless. The suffering slant-eyed faces and wasted bodies of children he had seen in the Far East, abandoned, lost or orphaned under violent and tragic circumstances, rose to his mind. Why must it always be in the nature of man to hate and kill and persecute his fellows?

Thinus's voice interrupted Hal's reflections.

"Most of the Huguenots were settled in this area, but their grants of land were deliberately scattered. The Dutch East India Company did not intend to have a French community grow up here with its own language and church and customs, a minority that might one day make trouble. It intended that they should be absorbed. And they were. Within a few generations they had intermarried with the Dutch colonists and they had lost their language and their identity."

"That's the only thing to do with new settlers," said Merle. "Absorb them."

Thinus's slow smile spread across his face.

"Not all settlers are easily absorbed. The British, for instance, remain plain British all their lives, and so do their descendants."

Hal grinned. "That little island has a powerful pull on the loyalty of its people, but as a rule they love it most when they are away from it."

"Love of one's birthplace, what a scourge it can be!" said

Merle impatiently. "It's an instinct, blind and unreasoning. Take Grannie Con, for example. The Cape is full of lovely and historic wine-growing valleys, but her soul is set on Constantia because Dieu Donné is the home of her ancestors. She could make a fortune by cutting it up and selling it off piecemeal, instead of which she slaves to keep it intact. Sacrificing yourself for your country or your home is a sentimental luxury no one can afford these days."

The birds had fallen silent and the summer shrilling of the crickets had begun. From way down below came the evening sounds of the coloured villages and the town of Paarl. A little train puffed across the plain trailing its plume of smoke. The scene was pastoral and peaceful.

When they resumed their journey Merle turned the driving over to Hal. "I can't bear the half-light," she said, "and Thinus isn't too good at it either with his old blind eye. So you take on now, and Thinus can have her later when we get into the Karroo. Roxie, you stay in the back. I loathe swinging about in the back of a car."

Here and there they passed great desolate burned-out patches of bush or mountain forest.

"It happens every summer," Thinus explained. "When the country is parched and the southeasters begin to blow we get the fire-season. Sometimes these awful fires begin by accident, but quite often it is done on purpose by fire-bugs."

"But why? It seems such a pointless crime."

Thinus shrugged his broad shoulders. "There are various reasons why they do it, and none of them makes much sense. Sometimes they hope to be paid as fire-beaters, or the Communists tell them that it will make another nuisance for the Government and the white man, or they get full of drink or dagga—you'd know dagga as hashish—and they have the devil in them. Or maybe on a farm someone raises a fire because he has a grudge against the farmer—or if it's a wine-farm it may even be that he knows he'll get an extra tot for fire-beating!"

"What's the punishment?"

"Prison if it's deliberate, lashes perhaps; and a heavy fine if it's carelessness."

"The penalty would be the same for black or white?"

These journalists! Thinus turned right round to look at Hal.

"The fine for a white man would be heavier, because he could afford it better. So be very careful—*voorkom bosbrande,* guard against bush-fires, as the forestry notices will tell you all over the country in both official languages."

Hal realized that in spite of Thinus's agreeable expression he had irritated this farmer whose people were to be his hosts. How easily, how unknowingly one could put a foot wrong, how secret each individual person remained with the mind locked in the casket of the flesh. Yet, when Alexa had tried to tell him that, he had denied it. He saw her again as she had been this morning, sitting on the end of his bed with a blue satin gown flung over her diaphanous nightdress.

"Darling, would you mind very much if I rat from this trip?"

"Very much indeed." And a sinking of the heart.

"When we made the plan I simply didn't realize the distance— a thousand miles by car, and always with people! I'm sorry."

"But why only now; why didn't it strike you sooner?" Slow anger beginning to smoulder inside him.

"I'm really very sorry."

But she had not been very sorry. She had spoken so calmly, with her hands resting lightly in her lap. Her little pointed face had been covered with cold cream, and she had told him that she meant to let him down as casually as if she had said, "I'm going to take my bath now."

"You'll get better copy without me there as a distraction. Nobody will miss me."

"Alexa! How can you say that—you? We'll all miss you, and I most of all! I hate being without you, even for an hour, a minute! You know that."

She had smoothed his ruffled hair with her cool little hand, but her next words had not smoothed his ruffled temper.

"That's just it. You try to possess me entirely, Hal. I cannot, I will not, be possessed by anyone. I am me, I belong only to myself. A few days apart will do us no harm."

A sort of fear had shaken him. She was no longer his wife, she was Alexa Rome, the prima ballerina, Alexa high on the blocked toes of her ballet shoes flitting across the stage, evading the too ardent embrace, sublimating love and desire with a gesture, the averted cheek, the lovely backward curve of the neck.

He had made a foolish move then. He had caught those slender expressive arms, the little arms so often arched above her head in dancing like the frail handle of a delicate basket of Dresden china blossoms.

"But this is *marriage*—to be married to somebody you love is to possess and be possessed, to glory in the knowledge of that possessing."

She had shaken her pale hair at him in a movement of withdrawal.

"How young you are sometimes! Human beings are always separate and apart. We are all lonely. In the last analysis we must live and die alone."

"Those are words, parrot words! Not truths!" He had spoken passionately with all his heart leaping up through his voice. "Love breaks through loneliness, whether it is of the spirit or the body! How can there be loneliness where there is love, Alexa?"

He had closed his eyes tightly, fighting back the emotions he was afraid to betray. And it seemed to him that she left his side in a series of perfect pirouettes, the fine disciplined form whirling away in the brisk mechanical manner of the ballet—a lovely puppet. . . . Yet when he opened his eyes she was still there, a young, very small, slight woman with a grave unpainted face and pitying eyes.

"Darling, there were tears on your cheeks—you mustn't! It's all right between us. It's just that I can't be held too closely. I am as I am. Only my work may impose demands that must never be disobeyed. . . ."

The full moon was rising when Merle said to Hal:

"Let's stop there, about half a mile on, and we'll have our picnic supper."

The car radio was on and there was dance-music coming from some studio hundreds of miles away to join with the crickets and the night-birds on the sandy banks of the dry willow-fringed watercourse Merle had chosen as their picnic-spot.

The Cape mountains had fallen behind them and they were on the first plateau of Southern Africa. The endless stunted bush of the Karroo spread to the far horizon, broken by the dark silhouette of hills whose summits might have been levelled by the sweep of some mighty knife. They were entering an empty mysterious world, the sea-bed of millenniums ago. Hamlets and habitations were few in this arid waste where only sheep could thrive with the little animals of the bush—skunks and meerkats. The great dome of the sky was heavy with its blazing constellations, lesser stars powdered the Milky Way and the spread-eagled Southern Cross dreamed in the hammock of the night. It could fall, thought Roxane, I could catch it in my hands, I could wear it like Grannie Con's brooch with the slanting struts in gold tipped by four big diamonds and one tiny one. She breathed deeply of the pure cool air.

"This isn't a real picnic," said Merle. "Cooking things over a fire and all that—because we have to press on. It's just a snack."

Her idea of a snack was generous: cold chicken and home-made sausage, cold new potatoes, lettuce and tomato salad, savoury cheese patties, bread and butter and biscuits, cake and fruit and coffee and a bottle of Dieu Donné's best red wine.

Hal talked well and listened well. He had made up his mind that he must stop thinking inwards. It was his business to think outwards, to look and learn and ask and find out about this great troubled land. And South Africans were always willing to talk about their country, to defend its way of life. Even Thinus Vos, the quiet, war-battered Afrikaner, volunteered his views in his thoughtful, deliberate way that allowed of very little compromise. He was moderate enough, but like most of his countrymen he had implicit faith in the future of the Union and in the success of the unique experiment of preserving a small white hegemony in one remote corner of the Dark Continent.

"A white way of life, a white civilization. This is a white man's country and we will keep it so. Many of your British colonies are not, and where the white man does not mean to make his home, he must abandon the greater part of his rights.

That word *home* is important, Hal, man. Our critics forget how important it is, what it means to us here. . . ."

Home. Yes, it was a word that went down into the depths of human feeling. And the way Thinus said it was simple and sincere. Hal realized then that the emotion this Afrikaner felt for his country was not only powerful but intensely personal, and that it was stimulated now by the fact that they were travelling north into the land opened up by his ancestors and their treks in the face of suffering, hardship and grave danger little more than a century ago. The history of his people was very young. One forgot that.

As if to emphasize the thought, Thinus said, "You folk take your country for granted. And no wonder. It was bequeathed to you over a thousand years ago. The relationship between you is Darby and Joan. But our country—beyond the early borders of the old Cape Colony—was given to us by our grandfathers and our grandmothers at the cost of lives and blood. It is still young and beautiful, and dangerous; and perhaps you might say that we are *in love* with our land."

He hesitated and smiled, and Hal waited, wondering if the key to a nation's outlook was being gently but firmly placed in his hand.

Thinus went on, "You have fought for your little island all over the world, and for centuries you have added to her possessions. You added us. Parts of South Africa came to you through guile and the enterprise of men like Cecil Rhodes; other parts, like the twin Boer Republics, were taken by conquest. Now your Empire is shrinking and breaking away——"

"That is natural enough," Hal put in quickly. "It is the outcome of our policy—to educate our backward dependencies towards self-government. But we hope to keep them as our friends, within the Commonwealth."

"That may be," replied Thinus cautiously. "But whatever happens, the core will always be there. You have a song to that effect—'There'll always be an England.' We can't be sure of as much here. We have conflicts within our boundaries that you have not."

Merle's clear voice cut in. "And it's our own silly fault half the time. If the Afrikaners and British South Africans won't get together we can be sure of one thing, the Union of South Africa will soon be Bantustan from end to end!"

Obstinancy crept into Thinus's voice: "Our country is our heritage—and we will keep it."

Hal said, "It is not easy to predict the future here; even you South Africans can't do that with any certainty, not beyond the next fifty years. But it seems to me that you are up against forces that will not be held back. Emancipation is a strong tide, and it flows fast after wars. The abolitionists won their cause, so did the suffragettes, and this force you are trying to control and direct—this movement towards equality—will go on! In the end you will be compelled to find some compromise. The days of Herrenvolk in the world are over—no matter how wise or enlightened those Herrenvolk may be."

Thinus's profile was towards him, masked by the black shield, and suddenly Hal had the feeling that he was talking to a deaf side as well as a blind one. The lines of communication had been cut.

It was past midnight and Thinus was at the wheel. Merle sat beside him but away from him with her curly fair head on a cushion wedged between the window and the back of the seat. She was asleep. And so quietly and smoothly did the big car devour the long straight National Road through the semi-desert of the Karroo that she was seldom jerked into wakefulness. The radio had bidden them goodnight, and there was no more conversation between them.

"Sleepy?" Hal asked the girl next to him on the back seat.

"Very."

"If a shoulder is any good to you, you're welcome."

She laughed drowsily, curled her slim legs up on the seat and let her head rest against his shoulder. Presently he slipped his arm round her so that her cheek came against his chest.

"Comfy?"

"Mmn——"

Holding her thus gave him respite from the sense of apartness and frustration that had haunted him all day. How soft and dark her hair was, like a child's, like Lexa's might have been if Hollywood had not seen fit to turn it into cellophane. The clean fresh scent of it stirred a memory in him. Of course, he had held Roxane in his arms before—in that old car of Thinus's that moonstruck night in Constantia. He had tipped up her little chin and kissed her lips. She had been very young then—too young— but her response had been that of a woman in love. He could feel the tender curves of her body in the close, drowsy intimacy of the back seat—was she asleep?

Thinus swerved very slightly to avoid a small night animal running in the glare of the headlights, and the movement threw Roxane's light weight upon her companion. Desire woke in Hal hand in hand with a furious resentment that it was not Alexa he held against his heart. His lips moved in Roxane's hair. She *was* asleep—sound asleep. . . . Don't wake, Roxane! . . . Lexa, I want you . . . why didn't you come with me? Damn you, Lexa! . . . darling Lexa. . . .

Thinus glanced at the speedometer. Eighty—eight-five—ninety miles an hour. How sweetly the engine purred! They always ran best at night.

The Karroo had flattened and the road unwound to the north through the open veld. Thinus's blind side was towards Merle, so that he seemed blinkered and alone, cut off from the others. Strange that being near Merle no longer wounded him. She was no more to him than a cousin now, a first cousin once re-moved, but removed many times by the very quality of her half-contemptuous affection. The stars faded and the limitless land-scape spread chill and ghostly to a ridge of distant hills. Here and there a tin-roofed farmhouse stood among its guardian gums and the tall steel windmills posted like skeleton sentinels against the perpetual enemy, drought. Thinus observed that the level of the dams was low, the spring rains had not yet fallen south of the Transvaal; and some way off he picked out a herd of springbok making its way to the willow-fringed water's edge. Springbok often grazed and watered with the cattle.

By sunrise they would be home at Tweefontein. Thinus won-dered why his pa had sent for him now. Usually he took his holiday in the winter when things were slack at Dieu Donné. But his Oubaas had some special reason for wishing to see him at once.

The pink flush of dawn stole over the tawny grasslands. Blue-grey guinea-fowl scuttled through the verge and widow-birds trailed their long tails across the dewy grass, red and gold finches rose in clouds from the spruits. Thinus felt his heart lift as he turned off the National Road to by-pass Kimberley and cross the border into the Orange Free State. Ja, the Cape was soft and beautiful, but this open country moved him still more deeply. He had been brought up in the veld and he never returned to it without a feeling of liberation. He had not been out of Africa like Guy Masterson and so many of his wartime comrades who had seen the Italian campaign. He had been wounded too soon for that, and sometimes he regretted his ignorance of Europe and foreign parts, but, on the whole, he had no great desire to travel. His homeland was good enough for him.

Merle yawned and stretched, cat-like. Roxane half expected to see her arch her neck, tuck down her chin and begin licking tentatively at her collar bone. The early morning light made a halo of her ruffled golden curls and her fair skin was pink with recent sleep. She turned round.

"Wake up, you two! We are nearly there."

"We've been awake for hours," laughed Roxane, "watching the day break. You've missed all sorts of things—springbok, guinea-fowl. . . ."

Merle took a compact from her bag and began doing things to her face and hair.

"There's Tweefontein!" said Roxane. "Up on the rise, Hal, there, among the trees! Wherever you see trees on the veld you may be sure there is a homestead."

She had often spent winter holidays at Tweefontein with Oom Jacobus and Tante Petronella, but two years had passed since her last visit and she was happy and excited at the prospect of seeing the old people again.

"*Maak die hek oop, asseblief*, Roxie," called Thinus, drawing up at a cattle-gate in the wire fence. Afrikaans was the language of his home and unconsciously he had fallen back into his mother-tongue, first in thought and now in speech.

Hal and Roxane sprang out, glad to stretch their legs as they pulled aside the rough wire contrivance to let the car go through.

"Now we are on Tweefontein lands," she said. "Two more gates to breakfast and a bath!"

Hal heard the lowing of the cattle driven to the pasture by a black piccaninny, naked save for his tiny hide apron; he saw the goats nibbling the spring shrubs on the slopes of the nearby *koppie*, and a span of sixteen oxen ploughing on the skyline. He saw an avenue of blue-gums leading up to a white single-storied house with a green galvanized-iron roof. The blades of a wind-mill turned slowly in the morning breeze, flashing as they caught the sun, and he heard Merle say:

"I'm as hungry as a wolf; step on it, Thinus!"

Up at the house Tante Petronella shouted to her native house-boy in Afrikaans.

"Tell Sixpence to crack the eggs into the pan and make the coffee! Here come our guests!"

She stood on her stoep and watched the cloud of red dust on the farm road and the sun-glitter of the big tourer. Oom Jacobus joined her and put his arm about her shoulder. He was a gaunt old giant with a snowy patriarchal beard that in its day had been as yellow as ripe wheat.

"I am happy," she said, her broad, motherly face aglow. "Our youngest son is coming home, even if it is only for a few days."

Oom Jacob shook his head gravely.

"Our youngest son is well past his thirtieth year, Mammie, and it is high time he brought us home a bride."

CHAPTER 9

UP-COUNTRY RELATIONS

The travellers ate a hearty breakfast, after which Merle and Roxane decided to rest while Thinus and Hal went round the lands with Oom Jacob in his vintage Ford.

Tante Petronella showed them to their room.

"I am sorry you girls must share, but we had this room ready for Mr. Fairmead and his wife, and Thinus was going to sleep on the stoep. Now it seems a better plan to divide up this way and let Thinus have his own room. After all, it's only for a night."

Merle said, as she opened her suitcase, "These stage people are very spoilt, Tant' Pet. Alexa decided not to come at the very last moment. They only consider their own convenience." She added to Roxane, "I'll take first bath, Roxie, and leave the water for you. We mustn't hog it, because the chaps will want a bath when they come in, and I know this cistern, there isn't too much hot water."

As Merle went to the bathroom Tante Pet said drily, "Stage people are not the only ones who are spoilt. Marriage hasn't altered our Merle very much—*I'll take first bath!* But you, Roxie —how you have grown! Last time you were here you were a schoolgirl, all legs and eyes!"

"I am nineteen, Tannie Pet."

"A woman of marriageable age. When I was nineteen I was married and expecting my first-born . . . a long time ago. Now Thinus, our youngest, is over thirty and we are getting old. We would like to see him married——"

"Married! Thinus. . . ."

"Why not? There is one who would take him tomorrow."

"The widow—Cornelia Bothma?"

"Why not?" repeated Tante Pet.

"But if he married Cornelia he might leave Dieu Donné——"

"Would you mind so much?"

"I don't know how we'd get on without him! Grannie Con or any of us. . . . Thinus isn't just the manager, he is part of the family—of our lives."

The old woman's face softened, and she lumbered heavily across the room and put an impulsive arm about the girl.

"You are fond of Thinus, Roxie?"

"He is like my brother."

Tante Pet sighed. Poor child. Nobody of her own, only old Con and Thinus to be her family.

"I must go and attend to my housekeeping," she said. "We will all meet again at eleven o'clock for morning tea."

"That gives us two hours for a sleep," said Roxane. "After

that Hal and Merle and I are going into Kimberley. He wants to see how diamonds are mined, and the native compound and all the rest of it. We won't be back till this evening."

"Will Thinus go with you?" Tante Pet paused at the door.

Roxane smiled. "No, not Thinus, darling. We'll leave him to you and Oom Jacob."

Oom Jacob had much to say to his son, but he was not a man to come swiftly to the point. He liked to take his time, to talk peacefully of this and that, to *gesels* about the cattle and the crops and the new borehole he had recently put down. He liked to smoke his pipe and let the thoughts wander quietly into his mind and the words could follow them, as words should, halting now and again if it were better so. When a man's thoughts went uphill and the path was steep it was as well to stop and get a second wind. Sometimes Tante Pet grew impatient with him and tried to hustle his thinking and his speaking, for women were clucking hens, more noise than sense, and silence was obnoxious to them.

The two girls and the Englishman had gone to Kimberley, the native house-boy had removed the tea-things, and the mid-morning sun warmed the enclosed stoep at the side of the house.

Tante Pet sat in her rocker with her mending basket beside her while Thinus and his father, comfortably settled in two worn leather easy-chairs, exchanged news of Tweefontein and Dieu Donné. They spoke in Afrikaans—not the *taal* of the coloured people of the Cape, but a language with its own refinements and touches of grace, yet well suited to agricultural matters.

There was always a touch of disapproval in Oom Jacob's voice when he talked of Dieu Donné, for, in his eyes, the atmosphere of a wine-farm could only be ungodly. Yet he had to confess that old Constance de Valois had been a good and faithful wife to his brother Stephanus, God rest his soul, though it was a pity she had borne him only one son late in life—and that one killed in battle, leaving none but this bird-witted Merle to inherit the old place. But no doubt the Almighty had His own good reasons for striking a blow at de Valois pride and the Dieu Donné estate which existed by the manufacture of intoxicants. What did the Good Book say? *Who hath woe? who hath sorrow? who hath contentions? who hath babbling? who hath wounds without cause? who hath redness of eyes? They that tarry long at the wine. . . . At the last it biteth like a serpent, and stingeth like an adder.*

"That new young Friesland bull—you must have paid well for that beast, Pa."

Thinus's voice jerked the old man back to the affairs of Twee-fontein.

"Eight hundred pounds," he admitted. "But we did very nicely out of the wool boom, and I am ploughing my profits back into the land—except for certain sums—certain special sums. . . ."

Slowly and deliberately Oom Jacob plugged his meerschaum pipe, pressing the Rhodesian tobacco down with a horny thumb and covering it with a cap like a miniature tea-strainer. Oom Jacob knew better than to risk a veld fire in his flowing beard. In the ensuing silence, which Tante Pet suffered with uncharacter-istic patience, they could hear the tiny tinkle of the seeds in her round polished darner as she turned it this way and that with the worn heels of her husband's large hand-knitted socks spread over it. Her babies had all loved that darner. Each in their turn they had used it as a rattle, often in the past little Thinus had shaken it in his tiny hands, delight in his eyes—two strong little hands, two bright eyes, and look at him now! For shame that men must fight one another!

Oom Jacob cleared his throat and Thinus waited. Whatever the Oubaas had on his mind to tell him, here it came.

"We have a good Government," began Oom Jacob, who believed in the integrity of the Nationalist Party almost as devoutly as he believed in that of the Dutch Reformed Church. "But good or bad, no Government is going to deprive me and mine of more of my fortune than I can help. Neither in taxes nor in death duties." Tante Pet nodded her smooth white head, and Thinus made a gesture of assent. This was good sound talk. "So—after long consideration—I have decided to give a certain sum out and out to each of my children, and I will make over to them a further amount in shares—the dividends to be paid to

me so long as I live and after that to your ma. That last is a
gentleman's agreement, but I must trust my children if I am,
in effect, to undress myself for their future benefit."

"We are getting on," said Tante Pet, "and the time has come
to put our house in order."

"When I go," went on Oom Jacob, "this farm will be divided
between my three sons, and it is possible that one or another
may find the means of buying or leasing his brother's share, but
that will no longer concern me." He chuckled comfortably. Oom
Jacob had no fear of death and no distaste for contemplating
his own demise. He was a man of orderly habits, and a family
man above all. He took his sons into his confidence as a matter
of course. Nor did it enter his head that any discussion of his
passing might upset his Ouvrou. On the contrary, he was as
matter of fact about anticipating her exit as he was about his
own. "Whichever of you lives in this house will take care of
your ma till she joins me on the *koppie*," he added.

Thinus rolled and lit a cigarette, and Tante Pet let her mending fall into her capacious lap and removed her spectacles to look
at her husband. What now?

Casually, without undue emphasis, the old man mentioned the
actual sum each of his children was to receive "out and out"
and immediately.

Thinus uttered an exclamation of astonishment, and Tante
Pet began to laugh softly so that her rolls of matronly fat
quivered with pleasure and satisfaction.

"We thought that might surprise you."

"Ja, it does," said her son. "I don't know how to thank you,
Pa."

Oom Jacob swept aside the notion of thanks. He said, "You
will therefore be in a position to marry. You can now think
seriously about getting a wife."

"Ja," agreed the young man slowly. "I can do that."

Tante Pet said, with her eyes once more on her darning, "Have
you anyone in mind?"

"I may have," he answered cautiously. "At my time of life a
man considers these things."

Oom Jacob was staring out at the veld with those hard blue eyes that were such a striking feature of the Vos family. He waved a vast hand at the middle distance.

"Cornelia Bothma would take you tomorrow, and we would welcome her." Tante Pet opened her mouth to say something, but he silenced her with a frown and a gesture. "The Bothma lands run with the lands of Tweefontein, and since Jan Bothma died his widow has managed that farm very capably. She is young, as gentle and pretty as a Jersey heifer, and she has a little son by Bothma, so you may be sure you are not marrying a barren woman. Ask her, my boy, and you will have our blessing."

"Pa, you go too fast."

"A man does not go too fast in clinching a sound bargain. But think about it by all means. You were never one for hasty decisions."

"You have given me much to think about and to be grateful for," said Thinus. "I am going to take a stroll by myself and let these things sink in."

Thinus turned his steps towards the *koppie* at the back of the house. The noonday heat had the curious stillness of that hour as if even the birds were taking a siesta. A few goats nibbled at the young spring leaf or bush or shrub, and two piccaninnies squatted in a patch of shade and played some game with pebbles. The skin of their brown naked bodies and swollen bellies was hard and dusty like chocolate that has been left too long in a drawer. Halfway up the *koppie* a rocky outcrop overhung a flat clearing. There were caves in the rock, the homes of *dassies*—squat dun-coloured rock-rabbits with aggressive protruding teeth and the bodies of guinea-pigs.

The clearing was sacred ground, the last resting-place of the Vos family.

Thinus sat on a rustic seat under a big thorn tree and contemplated the graves of his progenitors. Oupa and Ouma Vos were dust of this Free State dust, their names were inscribed on rough stone slabs hewn from the natural stone of the *koppie*, and climbing roses and honeysuckle trailed their fragrance over this simple burial ground. Children lay here, little ones who had scarcely survived infancy, and the ashes of great-uncles and aunts had been scattered over this earth.

Thinus knew no fear of this place. Since early childhood it had been his refuge when he had felt the need to be alone with some grief or problem. His pa and ma were getting old. Soon they too would be here, still part of the farm they loved. A fine farm. Five thousand morgen of arable land, and the share that would come to Thinus was that which bounded with Cornelia Bothma's land. Pa was a sly one, Pa had arranged it that way with definite intent; almost as if he hoped to lure the young man away from the call of his heart. But the Oubaas does not know the call of my heart, thought Thinus, he only knows my love of the land and my liking for the widow.

Indeed Thinus had all the Afrikaner's strong feeling for land. He did not desire land as Mr. Krifti did, for its value as a speculation or for the minerals that might lie below the surface; he loved it for itself, for the look and the feel of it, for the cattle it grazed and the crops it grew, for the sound of it under his horse's hooves and the smell of it with the sun hot on the grass. Especially he loved Tweefontein, and the Bothma farm was a natural extension of this one.

But of late he had learned that he did not want to marry Cornelia Bothma, much as she pleased him in many ways. She was blond and soft and dimpled, but she could be stupid and obstinate in her bovine way. No, his heart had turned elsewhere and he knew himself to be deeply and truly in love for the first time in his life. Merle—Cornelia—once the thought of those two had made his head spin, but there had been no tenderness in his feeling for them, and he knew that love without tenderness was lust.

But Thinus was afraid of this new love he had so recently discovered, afraid to reveal it lest it alter or harm the blessed security of a relationship that had become part of his entire being. How could he change her feeling for him from one of habit and affection to the swift passionate flame which burns between a man and a woman ready to mate? He had watched her grow and taken her for granted as if she were his little sister, and then suddenly he had found that she was no longer a child but the woman he wanted for his wife. When had he first made that momentous discovery? He thought now that it had come to him on the night Saartjie saw the spook. Many things had been begun that night.

He slipped off his black eye-shield and put it into the pocket of his bush-shirt. He raised his face to the sun and felt its warmth fill the empty socket. This was a thing he seldom did with anyone except Roxie, to bare his disfigurement, but she had run into his cottage once and found him so, and she had not been shocked. He ran his awkward fingers over the stubbly fair hair ridged by the thin elastic band. It was freedom to be without that patch, like being naked.

The dust-devils of the veld whirled suddenly over the graves of his grandparents, little spirals of fine red sand dancing in the windless heat. Watching them, he felt a spasm of revulsion. Man! Why had he chosen to come *here*? Why had he walked into the stronghold of his Calvinistic Dutch Reformed dead to examine his young new love for the daughter of a Papist? Already the old folk were breathing hard under the earth, thrusting up their protests in these weird spurts of outraged dust! His Oupa, that stern uncompromising old man, and Ouma, his devout wife, were writhing in their graves. If he brought little Roxie home to Tweefontein they would surely rise and march down the *koppie* to reject her. Even his pa and ma, who loved her, would look sadly upon her. What do we know about her? they would say. Yes, it is true that her mother was a brave woman, but a Roman Catholic, and the child herself has been brought up in the Anglican faith. Now Cornelia Bothma is a good member of our Reformed Church. . . .

I can do what my heart dictates, he told himself. I am my own master. But he remembered hearing that there had been years of bad blood between his father and his Uncle Stephanus, because when Stephanus had married Constance de Valois he had given up his own church to worship in hers. Still, Stephanus had been happy with his Anglican wife. He had defied the narrow outlook of the Vos family and had chosen his own course. Thinus intended to do the same. And surely he could depend upon

Grannie Con to be his ally. This thought comforted him and strengthened his resolve.

That evening, when Tante Pet asked Hal what he thought of Kimberley, the young man hesitated.

Merle laughed. "Hal wasn't much impressed with the hotel where we had lunch—in fact the City of Diamonds struck him as being a bit unsophisticated!"

"Not quite that," he said. "It just doesn't seem to have grown up, though perhaps that's what makes it interesting. It has an atmosphere of the past—of Cecil John Rhodes and his associates and the birth of de Beers."

"Oom Jacob could tell you a great deal about those old days," said Tante Pet. "He was born and bred in these parts, and he has seen the growth of Kimberley, and whatever you may think, my boy, it has grown!"

Oom Jacob was not at all loth to talk of the early days, and Roxane watched Hal while the old gentleman held forth. She could see him noting the picturesque biblical phraseology of Thinus's father, and she smiled to herself, for she knew that Oom Jacob saw in life only a reflection of the Good Book— mild or lurid as the case might be. It was the only book he ever read, and he read it aloud to his wife and family and servants whenever he could induce them to listen.

They were sitting on the enclosed stoep, and, although the afterglow of the sunset was fading, nobody made a move to draw the curtains and shut out the darkening veld.

"I haven't asked anyone to supper this evening," said Tante Pet after a while. "We thought you would all be too tired from the night drive and your day in Kimberley, but tomorrow Cornelia Bothma is coming in, and one or two others."

"I'm sorry, Tant' Pet," put in Merle quickly, "but Hal and I must be on the road tomorrow morning. Mother is expecting us in time for dinner."

"What about Roxie, Merle? Roxie has never been to Jo'burg. Why don't you take her along with you?"

Thinus glanced at his mother with a frown. What was Ma up to? She had her *slim* look, that suppressed slyness tucked away in the corners of her eyes and lips. He didn't want Roxie rushing off to Jo'burg with Merle and Hal. He wasn't any too sure that she wasn't still a bit under the spell of this good-looking *rooinek*.

"Then on your way back you must all spend a few days with us here. Oom Jacob and Thinus can fix up some shooting for our English guest."

"It sounds wonderful!" Hal's enthusiasm warmed the heart of his hostess. "And do come to Johannesburg, Roxane! You could give me some woman's-angle impressions of the City of Gold seen for the first time."

"Much evil has been born in the City of Gold," declared Oom Jacob sonorously. "The three years' war between your people and mine—the conquest of Boer by Briton and all the hatred that came of it—was conceived on the day that gold was discovered under the Ridge of White Waters. Jo'burg is a bad city, my boy, full of strife and greed. It is the Temple of the Calf of Gold, and one day it will be consumed in flame and ground to powder, and in it every man will slay his brother, his companion and his neighbour. It is the City of Satan in our midst. But you must see it, for all that. It is a vital part of South Africa, just as the evil within us is a part of our mortality."

In his host Hal saw the spirit of the Old Testament when the wrath and rude justice of Jehovah ruled the tribes. And he found himself wondering whether Oom Jacob had also studied that last small portion of the Bible given over to the teachings of the Son, in which mercy, tolerance and love supplanted the gospel of life for life, eye for eye and tooth for tooth.

"You'd better come along, Roxie," said Merle. "It won't make any difference to Mother now that Alexa has dropped out."

The sound of the big brass gong drowned Roxane's reply, but Thinus noticed the heightened colour in her cheeks and the sparkle in her eyes, and he knew that for a few days he had lost her. His sudden keen disappointment was tinged with a sharp pang of mistrust.

That night, as Merle switched out their bedside light, she said to Roxane, "Did you see through that manœuvre of Tant' Pet's?"

"What manœuvre?" Roxane asked sleepily.

"Palming you off on Hal and me for Johannesburg."

Roxane's eyes snapped open, and her heart performed one of its sickening somersaults. Then a wave af anger caught her hot and hard.

"Palming me off! Why do you always have to hurt people, Merle? You do it on purpose to see them wince! You should have left the light on; it would have been more amusing!"

"I say! Very temperamental, aren't we?" Merle sat up in bed. "What's eating you?"

But Roxane only turned over and buried her face in the pillow. Merle, Merle, you've never felt not wanted. . . .

"Oh, for heaven's sake, I didn't mean to upset you, Roxie. As a matter of fact I'm glad you're coming. Guy is so jealous of man, woman, child or dog where I'm concerned that I doubt if he'd like having me go off to Johannesburg on my own with Hal. You must admit Hal has something—or haven't you noticed?"

The dark head against the lavender-scented pillow did not move. Framed in the open window the stars twinkled and a breeze rustled the trees that sheltered the house. Merle yawned and lay down with her hands under her head.

"I only wanted to say that in my opinion Tant' Pet 'palmed you off' on us—no offence intended—in order to give Thinus a clear run with the widow, Cornelia Bothma. But maybe you aren't any more interested in Thinus than you are in Hal. Goodnight—and pleasant dreams."

CHAPTER 10

TEMPLE OF THE CALF OF GOLD

They were on the outskirts of Johannesburg when Merle took the wheel from Hal.

After the day's journey through the open veld, with its dusty dorps drowsing in the sun, its ugly reef-towns in the shadow of the pastel mine-dumps, and its glimpses of sordid outlying shanty locations, both Roxane and Hal were astounded at the spreading splendour of the city itself. Its fantastic cubist skyline soared into the pure rarefied air of six thousand feet above sea-level. It was the season of the jacarandas, and the magnificent residential suburbs on the ridges surrounding Johannesburg were laced with avenues of blue-mauve blossom, while parks and gardens blazed with exotic splashes of colour.

"This is the place to live!" Merle's eyes were brilliant with an excitement Roxane had seldom seen in them. "I adore Johannesburg! It is symbolic of our day and age—violent and thrilling. It's exaggerated and intensely alive—and swift-moving."

Roxane was sitting in the wide front seat between Merle and Hal. She said, "And by comparison you find the Valley slow—dead?"

"Dead as mutton. And there sits poor old Grannie Con at Dieu Donné with one foot—no, one whole leg!—already in the grave, refusing to see that her beloved vineyards are doomed; that one day soon Constantia will be part of greater Cape Town, of that sluggish hungry old city that is stretching out like an octopus to devour the beautiful green Peninsula."

"Merle, don't! The way you say it, as if you enjoyed the prospect, frightens me!"

Merle laughed and said to Hal, "A lot of things frighten Roxie. It was fun to scare her when she was a kid, to watch the way she went white and clasped her hands like a thin little praying-mantis."

Roxane was silent, remembering the ways in which Merle had terrified her: "Your maman was a spy—they tortured her—tortured, and then killed." It had always amused Merle to inflict pain, in the small ways as well as the greater ones. Yet she had never torn the wings off flies; perhaps that wasn't worth while, flies didn't clasp tiny hands, or look up with shocked eyes, or cry out.

Merle turned up a long drive of pale pink beauhinias, and drew up in front of an attractive house built in the Spanish style.

A native boy took their baggage and another drove the car round to the garage.

"That's a new house-boy," remarked Merle. "My mother isn't good with servants. She never keeps them very long."

Solly Caine and Merle's mother were waiting for them in a lounge that reminded Hal of Hollywood. It was a combination of gay comfort with originality, and yet it was impersonal, the work of some fashionable modern interior decorator. Immense sliding glass doors opened on to a paved patio in a grove of orange-trees. Beyond was the veld and in the distance they could see the spires and towers of the City of Gold. But Hal noticed that the panes of plate-glass were all protected by wrought-iron grills of a scroll pattern too narrow to allow the passage of a human body.

The scent of orange flowers pervaded the room, and a huge Persian cat sat on the sill and washed its face languidly.

"At the last minute Alexa was unable to join us," explained Merle, when she had introduced Hal to her mother and step-father. "So we brought Roxie along instead."

Bella Caine gave her unexpected guest the searching blank blue stare that had remained in Roxane's memory across the years. There was neither warmth nor welcome in the look, and suddenly the girl's heart contracted, and she thought, She hates me! But why, *why* should Merle's mother hate her? The idea was crazy, pure fantasy, and now Bella's lips were smiling as she said, "I am so about your wife, Hal. I can call you Hal, can't I? But it's nice that Roxane has come to visit us."

The next moment the Yent from Yo'burg had taken both Roxane's hands in his.

"Christopher Columbus, child! You've grown into a lovely young woman! But you haven't grown into your eyes, they are still three sizes too big for your pretty face!"

He was balder and plumper than she had remembered him, but he still shone with kindliness and the clean damp gleam of a big red *steenbras* straight from the sea. And his delight at seeing her again was so spontaneous that it obliterated the chill of his wife's greeting.

"Where's Poody?" asked Merle. "He's always round to greet me." She turned to Hal. "Mother has an adorable chocolate poodle, a big one, very clever, and the perfect watchdog."

Bella Caine's brow was furrowed under the metallic hair.

"He has been missing since yesterday. I can't recall exactly when I saw him last, you know how vague I am about details, but he didn't sleep in my room last night and I'm worried about him."

Solly's gargling laugh made light of her concern.

"My Bella idolizes Poody. He never answers her back, and he tells her she's wonderful every time he looks at her. But even Poody has his outside interests. There's a neat little dachsy across the road, and girls will be girls, and then boys will be boys."

"I don't believe it's that," she insisted. "And, even if it had been, he'd have been back by now."

"Like a good husband; push him around as much as you like, then let him off the lead, but trust him to come crawling home."

Bella ignored him. "You girls will want to rest and change," she said. "Dinner is at eight, but come down a bit earlier for a cocktail. Solly mixes a delicious dry martini."

After dinner they had coffee in the open air. Bella had a mink stole about her shoulders and the girls wore wraps, for the spring night was fresh. A pergola, heavy with wistaria, covered the little patio, and across a low creeper-covered parapet they could see the orange-trees against the dark, empty veld, and farther away the loom and light of the city. Along the horizon lightning flashed intermittently as if some other-world power were sending out signals, repeating urgent but incomprehensible messages again and again.

"Tomorrow I have arranged for you to go down a mine," said Solly to Hal. "And Roxie too, if she likes. Merle hates it. She gets claustrophobia nearly as badly underground as she does in the Valley. And in the evening the mine natives are doing their war-dances."

"I'll do some shopping in the morning," said Merle. "You can get anything you like here; not like sleepy old Cape Town."

Solly drew contentedly on a Havana cigar and sipped his French brandy. They had eaten an excellent dinner and he felt mellow and at peace with his fellow-man.

Presently he said. "On Saturday night my Bella is playing

poker, so I've booked four seats for the theatre, and afterwards we'll go to the Blue Danube Night Club and dance a while. They have a good gypsy band and a first-class Hungarian chef. It's lucky Roxie came along or I might have been odd man out at my own party!"

Roxane's eyes glowed with pleasure, then her face fell.

"But I haven't an evening dress with me. I was expecting a farm holiday. This Johannesburg visit only materialized at the last moment."

"Then I shall give myself the pleasure of buying you one." Solly disregarded the little gasp of exasperation from the vicinity of the mink stole. He was strong and defiant this evening, and it really was good to see how charming his little friend from Dieu Donné had grown.

Roxane uttered a gasp. "But you did that before, Solly! Maybe you don't remember, but I do; my very first long dress, and *you* gave it to me."

"I get into the right habits easily. Just ask my Bella. And when she plays poker with her fast friends old Solly Caine is off the lead, just like Poody."

Through pale smoke-rings he was watching Roxane. He certainly had not forgotten giving her the blue bridesmaid gown when she was still little more than a child. He was not a man who forgot the gifts he made, although he had long since ceased to expect that the recipients might remember them, and now, as he looked at the eager upturned face, he recalled the young girl whirling round in a rapturous pirouette on the high stone stoep. Something about Grannie Con's war-orphan had touched him deeply, her genius for happiness perhaps, the joy and gratitude for small mercies that welled and bubbled in the bitter waters of misfortune and sweetened them. Once again he found himself falling under her peculiar spell. To make her happy was to be enriched. Her pleasure reflected back and warmed the giver. The years with his Bella had not accustomed Solly Caine to appreciation. She took what he had to offer as no more than her due, and her daughter too exacted material tribute to her beauty as a matter of course.

When Bella and the girls had gone to bed, Solly and Hal sat

talking far into the night. The host found his guest good company, keenly interested in the Union and its problems. His observation was acute and sensitive. And he showed imagination, an ability to get into the mind of somebody else. At last Solly said reluctantly:

"Well, I suppose I must allow you a few hours' sleep, as tomorrow may be quite a heavy day for you. But before we go upstairs I must just make sure that everything is securely locked and bolted."

"The decorative grilles," smiled Hal. "Are they really *necessary* as well?"

Solly hesitated, and Hal was immediately aware of a slight change of atmosphere. In the little moment of silence between them the South African was putting up his defences, for Hal's question had touched indirectly upon the particular problem of the Union, the danger the white man perpetually feared from the black, and his unwillingness to admit it to a stranger. The South Africans lived in constant fear of the future, they sought anxiously for allies, and yet they were divided within their own European ranks.

"Every city has its criminals," said Solly Cain, after a pause. "And every sensible household takes precautions against them. You have only to read your English Sunday papers to realize that the world is in a continual state of violence. You in England have boy gangsters who shoot up policemen, and in America they have killers who beat up their victims because they 'like the sight of blood,' while here we have faction fights between the tribesmen on the mines. You have your burglars, your murderers and your rapers and we have ours. There isn't much to choose between them."

He locked away the liqueur brandy and the whisky and hid the key.

"And I've no doubt our servants and yours, if you can get them, have much the same weaknesses," he added lightly. "I regret to say our native boys are very fond of helping themselves to my liquor, so I do my best to put temptation out of reach."

He went out into the garden with Hal and took a last look round for the missing poodle, calling and whistling. But only

the big Persian cat came out of the gloom to rub itself against
his legs.

"I wish that damn dog would come back," he said. "I make
light of it to Bella, but I'm not happy. There are three things
we don't like losing here—a knife, a firearm and a watchdog.
When cars and wives disappear it's less serious. After all, cars are
insured."

The next evening, when Merle's mother had seen her house-
party off for the theatre, she went into Roxane's room.

Guiltily she closed the door after her.

Ah, yes, there it was!

Under the bedside lamp lay a rosary and next to it a miniature.

Bella picked up the rosary and ran it through her fingers. The
beads clicked against her rings. Did Roxane count her blessings
on these as Krifti no doubt counted bonds on his? And what were
Roxane's blessings? The affection of Grannie Con, that doting
old fool who loved this cuckoo in the nest more than her own
grandchild! And what else? Her strange elusive charm, the come-
hither that could make an ass out of a hard-headed business man
like Solly. What the devil did he want to buy her a dress for?
Bella could have lent her one—those things on the bias fit anybody. . . .

Bella dropped the rosary with an exclamation of distaste and
heard the little cross strike on the polished wood. It wasn't the
rosary that interested her in any case.

She took the miniature and carried it over to the dressing-
table.

She turned on the strong lights on either side of the mirror
and began to examine the tiny portrait with curiosity and care.
Astounding really, this resemblance between mother and daughter! Especially the brow and eyes. Unforgettable those eyes,
almond-shaped and tipped up a trifle at the outer corners. Clear
amber, clear as a cat's. But there was nothing in a cat's eyes, and
every emotion was reflected in Roxane's. Her heart swam about
under the surface of those shining eyes like a damn-fool goldfish
in a sunny pool waiting to be hooked by any child with a piece
of string and a bent pin. Not good eyes for secrets. Yet the

mother had kept her secrets well, even under torture. What had they done to this young woman whose image gazed so calmly from the narrow gilt frame? This face must have looked very different when they made her pay the price of her silence in those ways they had. . . . Bella shuddered. In the end it had been a shot in the back of the head, that pretty head set on the long slender neck. The daughter had the same graceful tilt of the head. Only the mouth was unlike her mother's. The mother's was determined and uncompromising, while Roxane's was full and gaily curved, almost voluptuous. That would be her father's mouth, of course, the father she had never known.

A gust of wind blew the curtain behind Bella Caine, and she looked up only to meet her own reflection in the mirror. There was no one else in the room, but what she saw frightened her. She heard the sound of splintered glass as the miniature crashed onto the plate-glass surface of the dressing-table. And then the diamond-studded fingers of Merle's mother hid her face from her own gaze.

Roxane's new dress of crisp dawn-gold moiré had been chosen for her by Solly Caine himself. "It's you, it has the colour and texture of the rose they have named Peace, the rose of illusion." And she had not needed the look in Hal's eyes to tell her that it suited her.

As they entered the Blue Danube Night Club the gypsy band was wailing an old nostalgic melody, "I've got *eeyooo* urn-der my *skin*. . . ."

"Let's dance," said Hal.

She was in his arms, she was part of him, he was the singing heart in her breast and the young bright blood in her veins.

"Don't let's talk," he murmured. "You dance like an angel."

But all too soon it was over and the band leader with the sad, clay-coloured face was plucking at the strings of his violin in a little fall of minor notes, his sign-off.

Merle looked up at Hal as he guided Roxane to Solly Caine's table.

"You can certainly dance," she said. "I suppose Alexa gives you lessons?"

Up went that one expressive eyebrow and his glance was full of laughter.

"Alexa is intolerant about ballroom dancing. She finds it—shocking."

Solly Caine's chuckle gurgled like a straw blown into a gold-fish bowl. "So it is too! We were watching some of the cheek-to-cheekers! How could this small-floor stuff be any use to a prima ballerina who is used to having the whole stage to her-self? Ah, here comes our crayfish cocktail, and the champagne!"

It was after midnight when the gypsy violinist came over to their table to play to Mr. Solly Caine's attractive lady guests. A lock of blue-black hair fell across his brow as he leaned towards them. His melancholy Slavonic eyes were heavy-lidded and sombre as his bow drew a passionate Romany love-song from the strings. Roxane's bones melted and she felt the tears pricking behind her eyes. Why, oh, why, was the music of love so sad, so full of heartbreak? She looked down at her empty coffee-cup and under the table her fingers were interlaced as if she wrung her hands.

When he had done, the violinist bowed and Solly Caine slipped a pound note into his willing palm.

Roxane laughed a little shakily. "Why, Solly, you should have taken that note out of his ear!"

"Maybe you are right, Roxie. Will you dance with me?"

His chill, damp hand took hers lightly. "Your sort gets hurt," he said. "You pay for the genius for happiness with the capacity for suffering. I saw that gypsy fellow pull your heart right out of your body with his love-song."

"You see too much, Solly."

"You must grow yourself a nice thick hide, like old Solly Caine, a hide like a whipping boy's, to dull the flick of life's *sjambok*."

Odd: his perception, and his bitterness.

Some time between half-past one and two o'clock Solly turned his racy-looking English car into the last curve of the drive. As he did so he frowned up at the façade of his house, where a single light beamed in an upstairs window. "That's queer! My Bella isn't often home before the milk when she goes poker playing. If she's winning she wants more, and if she's losing she wants it back."

"Well, that's her light," said Merle from the back of the car.

But, even as she spoke, the light vanished, and the pretty house stared at them with blind eyes in the starlight.

The tires gripped on the brick courtyard as Solly stopped at the front door.

"Here's the key, Hal. You take the girls in while I put the car to bed."

Merle said, "Give me the key, Hal. I know how it works." She fitted it into the lock. "That's careless of Mother! She's left the door unlocked."

As they went into the house she switched on the hall light. Upstairs, the landing was in darkness, and slanting up to that heavy shadow was the graceful camber of the carved oak staircase.

"Wait!" Merle's whisper was as tense as the sudden grasp of her fingers on Hal's arm. "*I can smell nigger!*"

In the warmth of the house, closed for the night, it came to them. It crawled down the stairs like a living creature, the pungent emanation of native skin, heightened by sweat and fear.

Roxane's heart was pounding. It made footsteps in her ears, and through the thump-thump she heard Hal's voice, very low and quiet.

"Is there a back stair, Merle?"

"No. He is trapped. He has to get out this way or break his neck jumping from a window."

Her whisper was steady. She's a cool one, thought Hal. He said:

"Telephone the police, quick! And you, Roxane, get me that poker from the fireplace."

He stood guard at the foot of the stairs, looking upwards into the shadows. There was a point above the top step where they were massed in a dense warm threat, and from that menacing thickness came breathing and the odour that had first arrested Merle.

As Merle dialled the emergency number, she said to Hal, "Be careful, they carry knives."

Roxane put the poker into his hand and he said, "Turn up the landing light, it must be that switch on your right."

She did as he told her.

For the rest of her life the next few minutes were burned into Roxane's memory.

The sudden light flooded the stair. On the landing, facing them with his back to the white wall, was a huge black figure. The great hands were braced flat against the wall at an angle to the powerful frame. They might have been nailed there. The head was back, showing the bull neck, a sharp breath hissed through the wide flaring nostrils, and the strong white teeth were bared barbarically in the thick-lipped mouth. For a moment the intruder maintained his attitude of defiant crucifixion, and then, with a loud whistling cry, he hurled himself forwards and downwards.

Roxane saw the flash of a naked blade in the black fist, and Hal's upraised arm as he swung the poker. She heard a groan, and then Hal was falling back with the knife buried in his chest and a red stain spreading on his white shirt front. And now his blood spilled over her trembling hands and her new dress as she knelt beside him.

The receiver crashed from Merle's fingers, struck from them by the dark figure rushing past her into the night as Solly Caine opened the front door.

Solly stared after him, eyes protruding, fins flapping, mouth agape. Ever afterwards Merle declared that her step-father had stood at the door to usher the burglar out.

When Hal regained consciousness in the hospital ward there were screens round his bed and he was dimly aware of a young Afrikaans nurse standing beside him. Her cold competent fingers were on his pulse.

"In a few minutes he will be round," she said in Afrikaans to the big C.I.D. sergeant who waited patiently at his bedside.

Hal was in an aeroplane, flying blind through thick fog, but every now and again the mists dispersed for a moment and he came to earth painfully. To move was impossible, to breathe was agony, and he was glad to let himself return to the high drumming darkness of semi-consciousness. Every now and again a rent in the clouds showed him strange dark images shot with scarlet, and somewhere among them the white face of a girl leaned over him—Roxane. He sank back into the mists that wreathed and thickened and shredded again.

"Take this. It will strengthen you."

The sister's voice came to him over some long-distance line. The word "strengthen" sounded foreign—perhaps she was telephoning from Germany. . . . He felt his head being raised. It was torture. But the stuff she was holding to his lips was strong. Now he could see the man in uniform standing over him, some sort of policeman.

"Now, sir, if you think you can remember what happened." This voice was foreign too, but it had drawn appreciably nearer. It tugged at his wavering mind, drawing him back into the present. Ah, yes. . . .

Hal made a supreme effort.

When his statement had been signed he turned his throbbing head on the pillow.

"But, Roxane, why did I think she was here with me?"

The sister smiled. She had a glowing healthy face and eyebrows like a black bar across her forehead. Hal was fascinated by her eyebrows. She looked very strong, yet her touch was gentle.

"Your girl-friend came here with you. She is resting at present. You are lucky that the knife struck a rib."

So Roxane was here. He fell back into the drifting clouds—to sleep.

When the C.I.D. sergeant took Roxane back home she found Solly and Merle waiting up with Constable Beyers, a sturdy young Afrikaner. Exhaustion and a sense of elation made her feel light-headed. Hal would get well. The doctor had said so.

Solly was smoking a cigar and he was wearing a maroon-coloured dressing-gown over his white shirt and black trousers, while Merle was still in the metallic-blue evening gown that showed up the brilliance of her eyes. She seemed excited rather than tired, as if under the influence of some strong stimulant. She thrives on thrills, thought Roxane, that's why she hates the

Valley. At the same time she recognized her own mood as being extraordinary. Her brain and body no longer existed. She was nothing now, nothing but a highly sensitive recording instrument. She hardly felt Solly Caine's arm about her as he led her to a chair.

"Sit down, child. You're all in. And you are going to have a brandy and soda whether you like it or not."

While the sergeant and the constable conferred with Solly, Merle sat on the arm of Roxane's chair and talked to her. Her voice had sharpened and heightened, and Roxane had the impression that Merle's whole nervous system had been keyed up by the events of the night.

"Mother came in with a fat cheque in her bag, pleased as punch, but when she heard what had happened she immediately went into hysterics. I think she was more worried when Solly told her that her beloved poodle had been found dead under the compost heap than when he said Hal had been stabbed! It's pretty sure our gardener, Zulu, was the theif. Zulu is a huge fellow, and that burglar certainly seemed like a giant to me! And the new house-boy was probably an accomplice. They must have poisoned Poody to make sure he wouldn't give the alarm. We came home just ten minutes too soon for Zulu. Really rather bad luck on him."

Curious, but she meant it; bad luck on him; violence and betrayal had failed by a small margin of time. Merle, this is a new side of you! Roxane said, "But your poor mother——"

"When my poor mother pulled herself together her first intelligible words concerned the insurance policy on her jewels! The burglar got away with all those she wasn't actually wearing, and a wad of notes." She lit a cigarette. "Drink that stuff, Roxie. It will buck you up, and there's no need to pull faces about it, it's quite a decent brandy."

Solly joined them.

"There's nothing further to keep you girls up. Go and get some rest. The house-boy has cleared out, the cook has been questioned and he has identified the knife as Zulu's. The whole thing is pretty well cut and dried. Constable Beyers will be on guard here tonight, so there is no reason for us to feel any anxiety. The sad part is that poor Hal should have been injured in this wretched affair. And even that might have been worse."

Merle followed Roxane up to her room.

"I'm too het up to sleep," she said. "I'll get a sleeping-pill from Solly presently. What about you?"

"I'm out," said Roxane. The dark smudges round her eyes and her pallor bore out her words. To be alone was all she wanted. She began to pull her wilted dress over her head.

Merle took it from her. "What a shame! It's completely spoilt. We can take it to the Lightning Cleaners tomorrow, but I doubt if they'll get rid of these ghastly marks without shrinking the material."

Solly's words came back to Roxane. "It's you . . . sweet as the rose called Peace, the rose of illusion." And here it was, ruined and stained with blood violently shed. She sank onto the stool in front of the dressing-table. Suddenly she stiffened and cried out.

"Oh, Merle, the thief has been here too! Look—he has broken this!"

She held out the broken miniature of Anne Williams, and Merle took it from her and stared in a puzzled way at the web of splintered glass raying from a spider point near the lips of the little portrait.

"What a curious thing for him to break! As a matter of fact, we did just glance in here to see if there were any traces of him, but somehow we didn't notice this. There were no drawers open, nothing out of place, so we assumed it was all right. He must have come here to the dressing-table to hunt for jewels."

"But this wasn't on the dressing-table when I left! It was by my bed. I always have it by my bed—wherever I happen to be."

Merle put the miniature back on the bedside table and switched on the pink-shaded lamp. As she did so the rosary, with its small gold cross, gleamed softly. She touched it with her indolent finger-tips.

"You'd expect him to pinch this for his girl. All natives love beads, any old beads, and he could easily have thrown away the cross. But our friend, Zulu, wasn't after junk. He was a wise one. He only went for things of *real* value."

CHAPTER II

MR. KRIFTI SOWS THE SEED

While Merle was away up-country Mr. Krifti took the opportunity to call on Guy Masterson in his Cape Town office and put a little proposition to him. It could hardly be termed a hard proposition as yet; in fact, it was more a matter of sowing the seed, dropping a few hints and suggestions.

Mr. Krifti smiled to himself as he rang the bell outside Guy's office. It was really quite a formidable stroke of good fortune that young Masterson should be a brilliant and extremely ambitious young architect as well as the husband of old Grannie Constance de Valois's heir. But it often happened that way in Mr. Krifti's experience. If you wanted something sufficiently and kept your eyes and ears open and your wits about you, fate strengthened your hand.

"Please come in, Mr. Krifti. Will you wait in the office? Mr. Masterson should be back any minute."

Mr. Krifti thought that Guy was fortunate in having such a cheerful fresh-faced blonde about him. His own secretary was dark and dreary, but she was efficient and she could keep her own counsel, and those assets were worth more to him than a happy smile and a schoolgirl complexion.

Guy Masterson's office was on the top floor of a fine modern building soaring above the old-fashioned stores and chambers of Adderley Street. Mr. Krifti looked down upon the budding trees of the Botanical Gardens and the oaks of Government Avenue and admired their tremulous spring green against the violet buttress of Table Mountain. Westwards, towards Signal Hill, he could see the old Malay Quarter crouched defensively in the sunshine, as irrevocably condemned as if sentence had already been passed. One day it would be swept away, and the Oriental dwellers in the flat-roofed, pastel-pink houses would have to find some new district in which to carry out their ancient Moslem traditions.

There might be pickings when that time came. One must always look ahead.

Mr. Krifti strolled over to the drawing-board attached to the longest wall in the room. The plans for a private residence were pinned on to it. As he examined them his fingers teased the chaplet he had taken from his pocket. Yes, there was Guy's inimitable style; the simplicity, the sense of breadth and freedom brilliantly combined with practical economy of space; a house easily workable, the ideal home of the future. Mr. Krifti recognized talent when he saw it, but Guy's gift was more. It was genius, and Mr. Krifti revered genius. Let's see, where was this house situated? In the hollow of the Southern Cross Estate which was impinging ever more deeply upon the vineyards of old Constantia. The beads of his chaplet slid faster through his narrow fingers. Soon, soon the vineyards would disappear altogether and only a few historic homesteads and perhaps some acres of table grapes would remain to evoke the memory of the days when the wines of Constantia were offered at the banquets of kings and emperors. And he, Mr. Krifti, would possess the finest relic of the past, he would live in Dieu Donné and cultivate the shrunken vineyards. Dieu Donné would be the crowning glory of his notable collection of Africana.

"Kriff! I hope you haven't waited long! My lunch-date took an unconscionable time a-feeding!"

There was Guy, slightly stammering as usual, always catching himself up physically and running ahead of himself mentally.

"Time to burn. No hurry." Mr. Krifti indicated the plan of the house pinned to the board. "What is this worth? A little matter of ten or twelve thousand?"

Guy told him.

He shrugged his sloping shoulders and thrust out his moist underlip. "Chicken feed, my dear boy. Now I have a real proposition to put to you, something with meat in it."

He sat down facing the young architect across the mahogany desk.

"Make no mistake, this city is of world importance. In peacetime the Cape is the gateway to Africa, in wartime it is also the door to the East. The great reclamations on the foreshore are only a hint of expansion to come. Industrial areas are springing up along the road to the north, and the Peninsula is still the heart of tourism. Forget these private houses and small commissions, except as hobbies—little gems for your own enchantment—and go out for the big things."

Guy moved restlessly. He was never a patient listener, nor was he susceptible to professional flattery, for although he often doubted himself in other directions, he never doubted his architectural ability. Yes, he had the vision and the faith. It was only the scope he lacked. The world was not yet ready for the pattern of 2000 A.D., and Guy Masterson was. He began to doodle on the blotter while the import of Mr. Krifti's words sank into his brain. Again and again the face of Merle slipped from the point of a soft lead drawing pencil, Merle's lips, her eyes, her ears, here, there and everywhere, but never in the normal juxtaposition of one to the other.

"You must go for the big things!" reiterated Mr. Krifti. He drew a map of the Constantia Valley from a briefcase beside him and spread it on the desk, covering Merle's nose which had doodled itself into her collar-bone. "Here you can see how the new arterial road through the southern suburbs is going to run. It will bend right past your own front gate and follow the natural boundaries of the Dieu Donné property."

He took a red pencil from the inkstand and described a ring round Guy's cottage and some forty morgen of Dieu Donné vineyards adjoining it.

"Look at this! Here we have a magnificent site facing the morning sun—an ideal position for a luxury hotel. We could put up a splendid building with quarters for native staff, tennis courts, swimming-pool, a tourist bureau, an exclusive shopping-centre and a home-farm."

"But——"

Mr. Krifti silenced Guy with a gesture.

"It would be the finest hotel in Southern Africa, and *you* could be the architect. Mind, I don't say you *will* be, but if you co-operate with my company, you *could* be the man responsible for designing Hotel Constantia. There is fame and fortune in this project, and, if we like what you give us here, there will be vast openings in our big new industrial enterprises. You will have a free hand. You will be able to put into effect your conception of the future."

Mr. Krifti knew that at last his words had registered, that they were flooding the mental and spiritual system of this ambitious young architect with light and power. He could almost see the dreams flashing across the cerebral screen, hotels, shopping-centres, factories, hospitals, towns, cities. . . .

"My company would buy your cottage for a start," he said.

Guy burst out laughing.

"Our cottage, Kriff! Five acres? How can that help you when you are thinking in terms of forty or fifty morgen?"

"Your cottage is a charming little enclave in the area I want. It would make a delightful manager's house."

"But, hell, Kriff! Your project would be the ruin of Dieu Donné! A damn great tourist centre right on Grannie Con's doorstep! Some hundred or more native boys let loose on the Valley, and you know what they are! They must have drink and women. And where are they to get it there except through the coloured people? There'll be drink stolen to supply them, and coloured girls selling themselves to the natives. There's enough vice in our lovely Valley already with drunkenness, dagga-peddling and immorality. Our people aren't saints! Good heavens, Grannie Con would think it was the beginning of the end!"

"So it would be." Mr. Krifti's tongue was padded with velvet and coated with honey. "But the end of Grannie Con's world is the beginning of Guy Masterson's. Her ancestors have set their seal upon the Valley, and the homestead of Dieu Donné will always be preserved intact with its cellars and its records and a limited acreage. It will be the souvenir of old Constantia. But this is a new age, and the time has come for you, Guy Masterson, to write *your* signature across the Valley!"

Guy felt his scalp tingle. What the hell was Kriff getting at? Was he taking him up a high mountain to offer him the cities of the world? Fame, fortune, jewels and furs for his beautiful

Merle, the travels they longed to take—Italy, Greece. . . . Damn
the fellow! He expressed himself in a tortuous fashion. That was
the Oriental streak, the flowery phrase, the flattery that hid
some deadly purpose, the basket of fruit with the asp under the
leaves. "Time for you to write *your* signature," Kriff had said.
Sure, Guy intended to sign "Masterson" indelibly across his city
and his time—but would he really be proud to write his name
over Grannie Con's glowing green-belt in concrete and glass,
erasing Dieu Donné's finest vineyards in the process?

"You need sanction for a scheme such as you suggest," he said,
suddenly irritable because he was nervous, feeling his independence threatened; perhaps more, his personal integrity.

"My dear boy, if you consider it sensibly, our project will
bring prosperity to the Valley—of a new kind, admittedly."
(*Our* project! Was he already being included in the deal?)
"But in any case I have never had any trouble over permission
for my company's schemes. It is just a matter of approaching the
right person in the right way." As he was doing now, no doubt!
All the labyrinthine ways of graft must be well known to Kriff
—through the palm, through the mind and ambition of man;
through his past perhaps, for bribery and blackmail were the
male and female of the same sinister species.

Guy said, "I still don't see where our cottage comes into all
this?"

"It would be the bridgehead to my little hinterland——"

The young architect sprang to his feet and tapped the map of
the Valley with a nervous forefinger.

"You talk in riddles, Kriff! Let's put the cards on the table—
whatever they may be!"

Mr. Krifti raised straggling eyebrows.

"Surely that map speaks for itself."

"Look, Kriff, you believe that if you get this cottage of ours
and this five acres that puts a wedge into what you are pleased to
call your hinterland, you will be able to persuade Grannie Con
to sell you these forty morgen. But, let me tell you, you haven't
a hope in hell! The old lady has an obsession about Dieu Donné
land. You'll never get so much as a footing in your—hinterland!

You must be out of your mind to imagine that Grannie Con would sell you even one of those vineyards, much less some forty morgen. She'd sooner die! Surely you must know that?"

Mr. Krifti folded the map and put it carefully back in the briefcase.

"I hold a bond on those vineyards and orchards," he said gently. "Forty morgen. When I require them I will call up the bond. The interest has fallen badly behind. . . ."

Guy found himself shivering as the tall man left his office.

What subtle bribery was this?

Kriff was offering him a stupendous contract worth many thousands and considerable publicity, with prospects of more to come, if he would persuade Merle to part with her cottage and, by so doing, breach the defences of Dieu Donné to the enemy. And he had made it fairly clear that contracts with the Krifti group were dependent upon his willingness to play the Krifti game. If Merle refused to sell her five acres and her home, the bonded land would be rendered practically valueless for Mr. Krifti's purpose. Merle could hold out on Grannie Con's antagonist. She could deny him access to his—hinterland.

What would Merle say? What would she do?

His telephone rang, and he heard his secretary answer it on the other side of the glass partition between her office and his. He took up the receiver and his buzzer sounded.

"Mr. Masterson—Johannesburg on the line."

And then Merle was talking to him, her voice filling the room as if she were in it. Merle always shouted on the telephone, and this instrument was like a loudspeaker in any case! And today her voice was more than ever high-pitched, even shrill. It was a long conversation and the blond secretary in the next room longed to listen in. She could hear Mr. Masterson's expressions of dismay and horror. What on earth was up?

When at last he rang off, Guy summoned her.

"Listen, Maud, there's been a burglary in my wife's home in Johannesburg, and Mr. Hal Fairmead has been stabbed. . . . No, the danger is past; he was very lucky, the point of the blade was deflected from the heart by a rib. But Mrs. Masterson wants me to break the news to his family before the papers get hold of the story. What are my other engagements today?"

"Only Mr. Burghers, about the bank building in Wynberg." Her eyes were wide and alarmed. "I hope Mrs. Masterson is all right——"

He looked up and grinned suddenly. "My wife adores excitement, in any form; it nourishes her system! My mother-in-law lost some jewels, but they were well insured, and Mr. Caine had a wad of banknotes stolen, but I've no doubt there are plenty more where those came from. The only casualty was Mr. Fairmead, poor chap. Now bring me the bank-building file, and as soon as I've seen Burghers I'll get off to Farway."

He was doodling on the blotter again, a hand clasping a knife. Merle had said, "Hal wants no fuss. He will be out of hospital quite soon and then he'll come back here to our place for a few days, and, as soon as he's fit, he'll fly home. Roxie and I are sticking to our plan of driving back and picking up Thinus on the way. But don't forget, Hal doesn't want Alexa rushing up-country to his deathbed, and a lot of headlines about it. In any case, he's *not* on his deathbed; he'll be quite well in a week or ten days."

Guy was at Farway before the evening paper or the radio news could announce their respective versions of the affair.

No fuss was made. Hal's parents received the news in a way that Guy privately considered "very English." And Alexa made no suggestion of flying to her wounded husband's side. She merely said, "Thank God he's safe!" And then, in one single drooping movement, the upper part of her little body wilted sideways over the arm of her chair. She drooped, green-pale as a moonflower, in a small semblance of death.

"She's fainted!"

In a moment Adrian Fairmead was at her side. And Lavinia was thinking, Adrian is a little in love with her too; oh, Hal, my poor boy, Hal. . . .

CHAPTER 12

"ALEXA WANTS IT THAT WAY"

Hal made a swift recovery from his wound and returned to the Cape by air. Very soon he was well enough to ride and swim and climb the surrounding mountains, but when he pleaded with Alexa to join him she had other occupations.

"Lexa, will you never ride or swim or walk with me?"

She sang in her light contralto, " 'Madam, will you *walk?* Madam, will you *talk?* Madam, will you *walk*—and *talk*—with me . . . ?' Hal, love, I can't. Simon is coming to practice the 'rose adagio' from *Sleeping Beauty*."

"Blast *Sleeping Beauty*, and Simon too!"

She laughed and tugged gently at the lobes of his ears, but he shook her hands away like an irritable dog.

"You have your work, and I have mine," she explained patiently. "You must get copy for your articles, and I must keep in trim. I dare not let up. Get the girl next door to be your playmate. Take her riding and walking. She knows the Peninsula inside out, and she'd love to be with you. I have a notion she's a little bit swept up——"

"As if you'd care!"

He caught her to him and stared down into her small pointed face. How dark and secret brown eyes could be! There was no knowing what lay beneath them.

"Why should I care? You are in love with me, Hal."

"Yes. God help me!"

During his short absence up-country the entire situation at Farway had changed.

Lavinia had watched with dismay and resentment the infiltration of her daughter-in-law's "extraordinary companions." For Alexa, who had stubbornly refused to enter into the social life of the Peninsula, had been quickly and joyously absorbed into the local world of ballet. She was at home with these slim, small women and athletic, long-haired young men who spoke her own language and treated her with the respect due to a divinity. In particular Lavinia objected to Simonoff, the danseur noble of South Africa ballet, who asked nothing more than to partner Alexa in any rôle she cared to practise. Lavinia referred to him as "that dancing poodle." Hal tried to laugh her out of her dislike.

"Alexa has to exercise with a partner, Mother. Even she is incapable of automatic levitation!"

"And where do you come in?" she asked. "It strikes me your wife has very little time left over for you."

"Unfortunately I'm not a—dancing poodle. I'm just a clumsy great Dane."

"Yes," she said wickedly. "That's about it. You are the great Dane with his kennel in the yard, the *outside* dog!"

Adrian remonstrated privately with his wife.

"It's not right, Lavinia! Your venomous remarks fly round like poisoned darts. Are you trying to break up his marriage?"

"Do you see any hope of it succeeding?"

"Not if you insist on your campaign of sabotage."

Suddenly her face crumpled, and he saw that she was ashamed.

"I'm sorry, Adrian. But I can't bear seeing Hal excluded the way he is. And it's not fair on Roxane either. Alexa throws him into that child's arms—and she's young and susceptible."

Adrian frowned. He had his own misgivings about the amount his son was seeing of Roxane, not for Hal's sake, but for the girl's.

"Hal has eyes for no one but Alexa," he said slowly.

"Nor has Simonoff," she added sharply.

"He means nothing to her. But professionally she needs him. You must make an effort to understand her, Lavinia. Our daughter-in-law has it in her to be one of the very few great ones of ballet, a prima ballerina assoluta like Pavlova or Karsavina or Fonteyn. She has the face and the figure, the endurance and the sensitivity, pathos, humour, intelligence, all that it needs to make a truly great artist. And she has ambition too, but she has made one false step. She has fallen in love with a young man not of the ballet. She is trying to reconcile her career—and Hal. It's not easy for her."

"Split personality," Lavinia said, with a laugh and a sob. "Are you asking me to pity Alexa?"

"Perhaps I am."

"It wouldn't surprise me to discover that you were in love with her too—Pygmalion and Galatea!"

Adrian said, "I could shake you today!" But he knew that there was a grain of truth in the accusation. Alexa was indeed his Galatea. It was her sensitive interpretation of Olga in *Ballerina* —the dancer torn between love and her career—which would give life and substance to his heroine for millions of film-goers. His feeling for his son's wife was a compound of compassion, affection and profound admiration for her artistic ability. He enjoyed watching her practise with her fellow-dancers, a jewel set in paste. With them she was vibrant; darting, gliding, hovering, a creature of light and air. But when they had gone she rested throughout her entire being. She put herself "out of play."

Hal, too, knew that habit of hers.

He would see his wife move out of the orbit of family life and conversation and sit apart, her eyes hidden by her dark glasses, her hands in her lap, one resting limply in the furled palm of the other, and he sensed that in this mood of suspended animation she was invulnerable. Even his mother's ringing comments could not pierce her or draw blood. Alexa simply was not there.

It's her training, he told himself, the necessity to relax, to make yourself oblivious of your surroundings. But sometimes the frequency of this withdrawal alarmed him. She was so seldom willing to take time off to be with him and he wanted her; God, how he wanted her! Once, when he had remonstrated with her, she had said, "Have you considered my programme when my work is in full swing?" And she had given him a rough schedule of the hours devoted to practice, rehearsal and performance. There seemed no time left.

He had said, "Our life together will work out all right. It *must*—because we both sincerely want it to! Isn't that what matters; the intention to adjust ourselves; and loving each other, needing each other?"

But did she need him? Or was he, with his demanding physical love and his efforts to explore her heart and mind and to understand the professional side of her life that was foreign to him, a liability in her eyes? Alexa was very much a real person, an indefatigable worker, a woman of ideas and intelligence, a supreme artist; and yet at times she was so remote, so other-world, that he might have been married to Hans Andersen's Little Mermaid. When we have our own home, he thought, then it will all come right, as it was that time in Florida when she put her work aside and there was nobody and nothing to come between us. It had been so simple; just a man and a woman and their love.

So now, more and more, he followed Alexa's laughing advice and took "the girl next door" on his excursions.

He galloped with Roxane across the sandy Flats and along the broad fire-paths of the Tokay plantations. He drove with her to the lovely little fishing harbour of Hout Bay and at low tide they collected mussels in the clear rock pools and brought them back to Farway, where Lavinia's native cook-boy made *moules marinières* on a recipe from the South of France. Sometimes they went surfing or climbed the mountains.

But Roxane did not take Hal to her secret place by the waterfall. She took no one there, not even Thinus.

Hal soon discovered that his young companion's interests were wide, and that many of them were serious. She went with him to the House of Assembly and acted as his interpreter when the speakers declaimed in impassioned Afrikaans. She showed him over the soup-kitchens and clinics among the squalid *pondokkies* of the Flats where native and coloured families lived below the bread-line in temporary homes knocked out of old packing-cases and biscuit-tins, where sanitation depended upon the scavenging of pigs, and law and order on the authority of vigilantes appointed from among themselves by the pitiful communities of the distressed areas.

She took him to the biggest teaching hospital at the Cape.

"One of the house-men is a friend of mine," she explained. "You'll be interested in the non-European wards. We like British journalists to get some idea of what is being done for the benefit of our brown people."

Her eyes were dancing; teasing him. All that afternoon she was gay and mischievous, and Hal found himself wondering if the young house-surgeon meant anything to her. For it was abundantly clear that he was attracted by her. The notion displeased Hal, which, he admitted to himself, was absurd.

She took him to the Home for Crippled Children—a splendid modern hospital which, like so much non-European welfare, depended largely upon the charity of the citizens of the Cape and the *pro deo* labours of the medical staff. The dark eyes in coloured, Indian, Malay and native faces followed them round the big light wards. How sad those eyes were till the coy, shy smile broke, and then how irrepressibly merry!

"They will sing to you," said Roxane. "They sing beautifully."

He stood with closed eyes to listen, shutting out the picture of wasted limbs and little twisted bodies stretched on the tubercular frames. The clear sweet child voices escaped the fetters of disease and rose unaccompanied and pure as bird-song. They sang hymns and *liedjies* in Afrikaans and English, and they sang of freedom and happiness. In the darkness behind his closed lids Hal forgot that the singers were child prisoners condemned to months and years of suffering by the twin evils of heredity and malnutrition. And when they had finished, and he saw their great black eyes waiting for the praise they knew they would receive, he found it hard to speak. The words came gruffly as he thanked them, and Roxane slipped her hand through his arm and pressed it impulsively.

"I know," she said. "It gets one that way."

On his own account Hal studied the industrialization of the Union of South Africa and the problems arising from it.

He met and interviewed thinkers, administrators and business men who were able to give him an over-all view of the particular difficulties of this southernmost corner of the African Continent —white Africa. He was taken over the great new factory areas and began to realize the rapid rate of industrial expansion. Housing schemes could not keep up with it, and the Government was hard pressed to control the influx of labour from the Native Territories.

Hal spoke to the secretary of the Minister for Native Affairs, and it was arranged that he should visit these Native Territories of the Transkei and see for himself the remarkable achievements of the administration. The tour was planned for November.

But although he listened and observed and collected fat and useful files of notes there were times when he was neither happy nor single-minded in researches that a few months earlier would have held him spellbound.

Hal's powers of concentration had been impaired of late and he could not trace the cause. Was it physical, due perhaps to his injury in Johannesburg? Or did the trouble lie deeper? Sometimes at night he woke with a sense of unreasoning dread. In the bed beside his, Alexa breathed so quietly that he would wonder for an agonizing moment if she were really there and living, and the room would throb with the anxious pumping of his heart. He must not wake her, yet he longed to touch her and feel her safe and alive in his arms. But the space between their beds would widen until it seemed a mighty chasm, wider than the Valley, so wide that if he called to her she would not hear his voice. Then fear would possess him entirely, and he would burst into cold sweats. "I am still sick," he would tell himself, and press his hand on the recently healed scar over his heart in an effort to quell the intolerable pain that went so much deeper.

It was Guy Fawkes Day—one of those sensuous November afternoons between the last spring storms and the first summer southeasters.

Roxane had put away her ledgers and changed into a fresh cotton dress. She sang as she pulled on her walking shoes. During the past few weeks she had lived from day to day, paying no heed to the future. She laughed as she rocked Wolf's head between her hands in the way Thinus did. "Walkies, boy, walkies!"

She had gone out through the French doors of her bedroom before she saw Grannie Con's wheel-chair among the apple-trees. This was an encounter she had wished to avoid.

"Where are you off to?" asked the old lady.

It crossed Roxane's mind to prevaricate. Then she shrugged her shoulders and told the truth. "For a walk up the berg."

"Alone?"

"With Hal."

"And his wife?"

"His wife is probably dancing the *pas de deux* all over Farway with Simonoff. Does it matter in any case?"

Down the years Roxane and Grannie Con had had their differences and the old lady recognized the dangerous note in the girl's voice and the quick lift of her head. But she was not one to baulk an issue.

"I think it does," she said, snipping off her words. "When is the young man taking his wife back to England?"

"Early in the New Year, I believe."

"Not soon enough."

"What are you getting at, Grannie Con?" Roxane's temper was rising.

"You are seeing too much of Hal, far too much. No good can come of it."

Roxane's face flamed and her hands clenched. So they were beginning to talk; the period of silent disapproval was over!

"There is such a thing as friendship," she said hotly.

"Fiddlesticks!" snapped Grannie Con. "I may be an old woman but I haven't lost my memory. When a pretty girl and an attractive man begin to live in each other's pockets friendship soon changes its complexion." Her voice softened. "I don't want to see you hurt, Roxie. Hal is a married man."

"Has Auntie Marthe been putting ideas into your head?" The old ones—the old ones! They always thought the worst! They had as many eyes as a spider, they spun their webs of gossip round you, they watched you flutter and struggle, and then they devoured you! Her clasped hands and the pink in her cheeks told Grannie Con more than the fury in her tone as she went on. "Because, if she has, I can tell you she's barking up the wrong tree. Hal Fairmead likes to ride and walk with me because I know every ride and walk there is round here—and maybe he even enjoys my company! And that's the beginning and the end of it where he's concerned."

"And where you're concerned?" pressed Grannie Con, greatly daring.

The girl winced. "*Please*, please just ask Auntie Marthe to keep her inquisitive nose out of my affairs! I must go now; I'm late already."

Beat the sack and chastise the donkey, thought Grannie Con, as she watched the slight figure hurry away. Auntie Marthe had been brought into this to serve as the sack. In effect Roxane had begged Grannie Con to mind her own business. But this is my business. . . . If you knew what I know, my girl. . . .

A tall figure had joined the smaller one, and they were swinging up the orchard path, matching their steps as two people do who are accustomed to being together. There was harmony between them, the base and the treble of the same score.

All day long the coloured children had trailed their guys through the vineyards of Constantia, and now, as Hal and Roxane turned towards the berg, they met one of these little parties prancing down towards Dieu Donné. The threadbare pants of the boys were padded and little rope tails wagged gaily from their protruding backsides. Their faces were smeared with clownish paint and whitewash, and the little girls had ribbons in their hair. Between them they dragged the guy in his soapbox on wheels, a ragged scarecrow, topped by an ancient stovepipe hat.

As the children caught sight of the young man and the girl their bare feet broke into a dance and they chanted some calypso in the *taal*. "Penny for de guy! Penny for de guy!" they cried, and Hal threw the fawn-like leader half a crown.

"That was a generous contribution," laughed Roxane. "They don't expect more than sixpence at best!"

They stood to watch the children disappearing among the apple-trees, shouting and cavorting with glee. Behind them their battered, tattered victim nodded and swayed in his home-made tumbril as he jolted towards nightfall and a noisy *auto-da-fé*.

"When they've collected all the money they can they'll go to the Greek or the Indian and buy fireworks. There'll be great doings tonight."

"They are merry little monkeys. They know how to enjoy themselves."

"Just wait till New Year and the Coon Carnival——"

"I can't," Hal chipped in. "We won't be here at New Year. We are flying back to England next week."

There was a whirling in Roxane's chest, a whirling and a sinking, and a weakness in her legs.

"But why?" she faltered. "I thought . . ."

"Yes." His voice hardened. "I know. You thought we were staying till the New Year, that I was going to tour the Native Territories. Well, now all that will have to wait till we, till I, come back some day."

"It's such a sudden decision . . . why, Hal . . . ?"

"Because Alexa wants it that way."

Why? He had been through all that this morning with his mother. His father had accepted it; Lavinia had fought it.

Roxane saw the tightening of his jaw and the weariness round his eyes. He hasn't slept, she thought. What was wrong? Had Alexa quarrelled with Lavinia? It was quite possible. And then a sudden fear struck her as she recalled her little passage at arms with Grannie Con. Could it be that Alexa suspected that there was "something between" Hal and herself? Oh, if only there were!

But Hal said, "Alexa feels that she must get back to London. She is afraid that she is losing touch—here, so far from her working milieu. . . ."

How lame it sounded! It was the excuse they had decided to offer—the only one that made any sense at all.

The truth was still too new in him to be contemplated without horror. He would never forget Alexa as she had been last night— her white silence at dinner, and her outburst afterwards in their bedroom.

"I went to Merle's doctor this afternoon. I didn't want to tell you. I've been afraid lately, yet I couldn't believe it was *that*! How could I guess? There'd been no nausea, none of the usual signs . . . but he said it happened like that sometimes—rarely—and it had happen to me, of all people, *me*!" The note of hysteria still rang in his ears. "Oh, God, Hal, I begged him to help me— implored him . . . but he said the law was the law and I was a healthy young woman, and, in any case, in his opinion it was too late. . . ."

There had been her terrible tearless weeping, racking her little body as he held her to him shocked and appalled.

"You should have told me. I'd have gone with you. Lexa, you said nothing. Together we could have accepted this verdict, been glad of it; couldn't you be glad, Lexa?" Then it had come, the accusation. "I'm trapped, you've got me in a trap! You must get me out, we must fly home, tomorrow, soon, *soon*, so that I can find someone. . . ."

He had tried to reason with her. "But, Lexa, we can afford a child, God knows, and the best nurse in the world. And if you miss one season's ballet, what of it?"

She had turned on him, her strange little face gone wild and vixen. "You fool! What do you know about a dancer's life and a dancer's body? How can I throw a year of my youth to the dogs and let the others spring up over me? Great ballerinas don't have homes and families like other women, they don't saddle themselves with husbands or let their bodies be distorted and slackened by childbirth . . . !"

Roxane saw Hal draw a sharp breath and press his hand down on the wound over his heart. Did it still hurt him? She had not seen that gesture before. His face was sallow and the long scar down his cheek had whitened over the strained muscles. Her own deep distress at losing him was shot through with anxiety.

"Hal, are you ill?"

He shook his head and quickened his pace.

Neither of them noticed the path they were taking until the song of the waterfall threaded the silence that had fallen between them.

They heard Wolf and two ridge-backs jostling each other among the bushes, and barking as they flushed a bird, or as a squirrel scampered into the branches overhead.

I've brought him here, to my secret place! thought Roxane. But it doesn't matter now. This is the end. This is goodbye. Perhaps she had followed Wolf without thinking, or perhaps she had simply obeyed the old instinct that always led her here to her sanctuary in moments of grief or joy, or when she felt the need for solitude.

She said, "I come here sometimes to be alone. I have never brought anybody to this place before. It has a sort of peace."

"Thank you," he said quietly. The colour had returned to his face and he was able to smile down at her.

"Just stay still, and listen to the silence."

Flowering trees nodded delicately against the sky, the tips of the silvers glinted like tiny knives and the pale sweet-scented mountain-mimosa bloomed among the darker green of pines. Giant ferns and orchids grew in the cool shade of the waterfall, and the air was alive with wings, birds, butterflies and frail, hovering dragon-flies. There was the clean sound of water foaming over rock, the fluted call of a warbler and the lazy *zoom* of a bumble bee. Hal felt the tumult within him subside. He breathed deeply and took comfort from the presence of his companion.

I don't know your trouble, thought Roxane, but Alexa is part of it. And you will never speak of it because your loyalties won't let you. If you were less loyal I should be less in love with you. Do you ever dream that I want you with every bit of me, or have I kept that secret? I've tried to, but it isn't easy. Alone with you here it isn't easy. Of course, I should have avoided you. In the beginning I tried, when I asked Thinus to take me to Tweefontein, and see where that got me! And ever since then I've been gathering memories of you like a squirrel hoards acorns against the cold and hunger of winter. And the cold and hunger is on the way . . . you are going. . . .

She sat on a sun-warmed boulder and he stood beside her, his face averted. But the misery of the night was fading, and presently there was only this lovely quiet place and the girl leaning forward with her thin brown hands clasped about her knees.

"I'm going to miss you," she said.

The sun was caught in her hair, rippling with the rainbow lights of a prism. He let his hand touch it, soft, silky and fresh. He remembered the texture of it under his lips, not spongy like Lexa's, not cellophane. This girl was natural, uncomplicated, she was herself. So often Alexa was somebody else. It struck him then that he would miss Roxane too. He lifted her chin to look at her, and it seemed to him that there was great sadness and resignation in her face. A forgotten illusion returned to him. And he said:

"That time in Johannesburg, at the hospital when I was near bleeding to death—well, I had a queer dream. . . ."

"What was it?" The leap in thought did not surprise her.

"It went back to our first meeting, to the day of Merle's wedding."

"Yes?"

He smiled now. "It sounds absurd, but I dreamed that I was the little sick boy in your room, and you were the Madonna up in the niche above your bed. . . . She had your face, Roxane, she had your gentle eyes. . . ."

She took that for granted too.

"My Madonna changes, Hal. When I was a child, and crying and frightened in the night, old Lizzie used to come and comfort me. And then the Madonna had Lizzie's eyes, or maybe Lizzie had hers. My Madonna is kind——"

"Yes, but I am not acquainted with her as you are. Remember, I have only seen her that once!"

She paused. Then she said, "That night, the time you speak of, I was praying to her all the time. That was why she came to you."

He looked at her in wonder. Did she believe in magic, in miracles and the mystic power of the Saints? He was touched that she should have prayed for him.

"Are you a Roman Catholic?" he asked her.

"My mother was. The rosary I always keep beside my bed, and the little statue of the Virgin and the Holy Child, belonged to her. But Grannie Con had me at Dieu Donné from a tiny child and she brought me up in the Protestant faith." She smiled. "But I dare say I have a few Catholic habits because I often like to say my prayers to the Holy Mother. There are some things it's easier to talk about to another woman, requests she'd understand."

"What are your requests? What do you ask of life, Roxane?"

You! responded her heart. I want the one thing that is forbidden—your love. Aloud she said, "Oh, lots of things! I want to go to Europe, to London, where we lived before the war, and to France, my mother's country; and to Germany, where she—was killed . . . a sort of personal pilgrimage."

"I understand. But after your pilgrimage?"

She shook her head. The mischief was in her eyes.

"Never mind about afterwards!"

"Tell me! I want to know."

"You'd be very disappointed. There's nothing exciting or glamorous about my object in life. No great ambitions, not even noble ideals."

"Tell me!"

"Very well, then. Here it is. All I ask of life, one day, is a home of my own, with a garden and a nursery, and the vineyards and the sea to look at."

"A husband must have some place in that picture?"

She was laughing. "He is absolutely essential! Without him there could be no nursery!"

"Roxane—you move my heart with your simplicity."

Suddenly his hands were on either side of her waist, strong hands lifting her down from the mountain rock, and she was in his arms, closely held, his lips on hers.

All the leaves on all the trees were trembling, the grass beneath their feet was quivering, the last rays of the setting sun caught and burnished them with filaments of light, and the stream sang a new song.

"This is goodbye," he said at last. "Dear Roxane, this is goodbye."

She opened her eyes and saw the tenderness come into his face, banishing that other look, the dangerous look; and she thought, He knows I love him . . . he knows . . . but what does it matter now when everything is over and this is goodbye?

"Then, Hal—goodbye——"

The sad little word lingered in the air, parting her lips, so that he must kiss her again and hold her to him and comfort her.

Say you love me Hal . . . but no, you will never say that, because you love Alexa—only Alexa. . . .

CHAPTER 13

ULTIMATUM

During the busy summer months that followed the departure of Hal and Alexa there was little time for anyone at Dieu Donné to brood over personal worries. Yet most members of the household had reason to dread wakefulness in the small dark hours when consciousness opens the door to a Bluebeard's chamber of hidden anxieties.

Grannie Con knew that a certain deadline was approaching, and, at thought of it, her missing leg leapt and tingled, that phantom limb created by her raw-edged nerves. Morning would often find her drawn and old and beaten, haunted by the image of Mr. Krifti strolling up the path between the poplars.

Her grand-daughter, Merle, woke sometimes to hear Guy twisting and turning in the bed next to hers.

"What is it, Guy? Can't you sleep?"

"The plans for that new hotel of Kriff's keep churning round in my head. Give me one of those sleeping-pills, Merle. . . . I'm not happy about what we're doing . . . it seems like . . . selling the past——"

"Don't be so damned melodramatic, darling! *Selling the past indeed!* Think of the future! Fame, wealth, travel—that trip to Italy. . . . And in any case you know I'm not signing that deed of transfer till Kriff is actually in possession of his bonded land."

And then she was in his arms, warm and desirable, and there was forgetfulness.

On nights when the southeaster rattled the windows of Joshua and Lizzie's cottage, Lizzie would tiptoe into the little room where her deaf son slept. If his bed happened to be empty she peered out into the night with anxious, sleepless eyes.

Yes, there was a fire, there in the Hout Bay Gap, and Ben would be up in the mountains helping to fight it. There was never a bush-fire within cycling radius but what Ben smelt it out and volunteered as a beater. He would miss days of safe well-paid work at Dieu Donné to chase after the excitement and terror of these summer fires that were the curse of the Cape. And his deafness made him rash, for he could hear neither the roar of the flames nor the orders of the head beaters. "Good Lord, keep him safe," prayed Lizzie. And added, "An' make Saartjie a good girl. . . ." For Lizzie often worried lest Saartjie go the way her flighty mother had gone. Saartjie had been buying finery of late that no girl in her situation could afford, and Lizzie, who set respectability above all other virtues, found Saartjie's behaviour as irritating as a burr in her underwear.

Roxane too was restless. It was mid-March, the moon was nearly at the full, and she lay listening to the dry summer wind rampaging up the Valley. The grandfather clock in the *voorkamer* struck the half-hour, half-past one, and sleep was a mirage far off. The cream wall opposite her window had become a shadow-show of dancing leaves silhouetted by the light of the moon. What a wonderful tempestuous ballet it made, the ballet of the southeaster! The ballet . . . the ballet . . . there was music in the wind, a great rushing, bellowing symphony, and the dark tossing trees were dancers . . . that one there—that wild, graceful, slender bough—was the prima ballerina . . . it was Alexa . . . Alexa. . . .

She threw back the bedclothes and ran to the window to draw the curtains and shut out the shadow ballet, but she could not do so. The moon-magic of the night held her spellbound.

In the orchard she saw the ripe apples fall to the ground, whipped from their branches by the raging wind. A cat went hunting along the far side, crouched low on the ground, its fur blown back, pausing every now and again, head lifted. What prey was it seeking—a field-mouse, a young mole, a sleeping bird? Or was it in search of a mate? Any mate—cats don't care—lucky cats!

She could see the white tower of Adrian Fairmead's study rising above the trees. Normally a light might still have been burning there, for the novelist worked best at night, but Adrian and Lavinia had sailed for England a week ago and Farway was deserted.

Roxane put her hands over her ears. Be still, wind! Stop your wailing and blustering and let me think! She stared at the stars, remote and unfeeling in their firmament. Lucky stars, what do you know of love? Cover your face, Moon, you fill me with madness, you pour it into my veins like ice and fire and there is no peace.

Five months had passed since Hal had gone, and no doubt by now he had forgotten her for the second time. And she, for her part, had tried and failed to throw him out of her heart and mind. She began to scold herself. What do you want, Roxane? What do you ask of life? The same as most women: a husband, a home and babies of your own. Then get yourself a husband! If a woman can't have the man she wants, she must find herself another. That's life. Everything in life is second-best. You had no mother and Grannie Con took her place; you had no home and there was Dieu Donné. They gave you happiness. It can happen that way again.

The wind held its breath as it sometimes did, expanding its mighty lungs for the next burst of fury. And in the silence her heart said, "There is Thinus; he will give you love and companionship, a home and children. He will keep you safe from yourself and from this foolish lonely course you are following."

ONE, TWO, said the grandfather clock. Thinus would be in the cellar now, taking over from Max Immelmann, the wine-maker. For this was the birth-period of the new vintage. Every two hours night and day for the next few weeks the mammoth thermometer must be plunged into the fermenting-tanks, and, if it registered too much, the juice must be run through the coolers, and if too little a proportion of yeast must be added swiftly. Nothing could be left to chance at this stage. This was a hard and sleepless time for Thinus and Max Immelmann and Brink, the foreman, who all stood their shifts.

Roxane jumped down from the window-sill and slipped off her nightgown. She took slacks and sandals and shirt from her wardrobe, and, just for a moment, before pulling them on, she saw her own slim girl's form in the pallid gleam of the mirror, virginal but ripe for love. Yet one day that body might wither, unfulfilled, if she persisted in this lunacy that held her with relentless, invisible bonds.

She opened the French doors and went out into the moonlight. She ran into the wind as she had so often done as a child, her hair streaming behind her. She turned her back on the wind and leaned against it. Wind, wind, blow him out of my heart and let me go free! The first dry leaves of approaching autumn whirled out of the oaks and flew past her like a cloud of tiny migrant birds, but the leaves were dead, finished. They did not desert the trees for summer lands, they would not return like birds in the spring, they could frolic for so long as the wind lasted, and then they would flutter sadly to earth and lie in soft mouldy carpets in the deep of the woods and along the paths, dead as summer, dead as first love.

She made her way slowly round the back of the cellar to the entrance and stood there outside the open solid-teak doors. All her life she had feared the cellar at this time of year when it came alive in its own sinister way, and now the old childish panic gripped her once more. But she made herself cross the threshold and go through the lane of great casks to the fermenting-room, but even before she came into that section of the cellar she could hear the unfermented wine in labour, gurgling and bubbling in the violent agitation of new life.

Her nostrils contracted against the familiar sickly odour of the yeast-treated must, and she stared into the gloom as if at some scene from Pluto's kingdom.

The cellar was in darkness save for a few naked bulbs hung at intervals from the high yellow-wood ceiling. The separator and crusher seemed to crouch in their corners, dozing after the day's labour, but the open cement tanks against the long wall seethed with their porridge of husks and juice throwing up waves of sour-smelling spume. In a sort of antechamber the closed tanks of the white wines mumbled their own bacchanalian incantations. On the parapets of the open tanks stood dark figures stirring the witch's brew with long pronged wooden poles. They seemed immensely tall with their heads almost touching the rafters, featureless in the gloom. Against the wall their grotesquely elongated shadows moved rhythmically together and apart as they plied their poles. They worked silently like somnambulists, and

Roxane saw them as the grim gondoliers of Charon paddling their Stygian craft to the nether regions.

She ventured forward and stood on tiptoe on a little wooden ladder to peer into the tank. She shuddered. Here was life and death in dreadful turmoil, the ferocious explosive life-after-death of the mangled grape exhaling fumes that would kill a man instantly were he to slip and fall into this grumbling pottage.

"Roxie! Whatever are you doing here?"

She jumped as Thinus emerged from the passage between the cellar and the wine-maker's laboratory.

In that livid light his healthy sun-tanned face was deathly. He had removed his eye-shield and the empty socket was dark and sunken over his cheekbone. His hair was rumpled from recent sleep. In his hand he held the monster thermometer.

"I couldn't sleep," she said, raising her voice against the chorus of fermenting grapes. "So I thought I'd come and keep you company for a bit."

"That's fine," he shouted. "When I've taken the patients' temperatures we'll have some coffee."

The ghostly gondoliers withdrew their oars and clambered down from the sides of the tanks, and suddenly Roxane smiled to see that after all they were only sleepy little coloured men, too weary to laugh and joke. Somehow the presence of Thinus had altered the entire character of the cellar. It was no longer the diabolical cooking-house of man's downfall, but simply the factory of Dieu Donné wines, the finest and most famous wines of Constantia.

Thinus plunged the thermometer into the tank and drew it out again. He nodded. "All going well." When he had taken all the temperatures in the "ward" he led Roxane down the passage to the wine-making laboratory. Roxane tidied the rugs and pillows on the camp-stretcher that was kept there during the pressing season, and perched on it with her legs curled up under her, while Thinus brushed his hair at the spotted old mirror over the little wash-basin in the corner. He took the black eye-shield from his pocket and slipped it back into place. Then he poured coffee from a thermos into two enamel cups and removed the grease-paper covering from a plate of sandwiches.

"Ham," he said. "Just the thing for two-thirty in the morning."

"Am I a nuisance?" she asked as she helped herself.

He grinned down at her. "A surprise, let's say."

The first sip of coffee and nibble at the sandwich stimulated her appetite. "I've been suffering from night-starvation."

"One way and another, it's quite a common complaint."

She pulled a little face at him, and it struck him that she looked quite gypsyish with her dark untidy hair and her un-painted mouth. She had many moods and many faces, this girl of his.

"I thought you were frightened of the cellar, Roxie?"

"Not with you around."

"Do I take that as a compliment, or the reverse?"

"Take it the way that makes you happiest."

He shrugged his broad shoulders and straddled a little wooden chair. "Old Dog Trust—that's Thinus Vos."

"Trust . . . ? If you think about it . . . it's a nice name. To be trustworthy. . . ."

"Ja," he agreed. "To be trustworthy is a fine thing. And some are, and some aren't." He began to roll a cigarette, and she saw a frown between his fair brows. The harsh light was reflected in his crisp straw-coloured hair as he bent his head to strike a match.

"Meaning . . . who . . . ?"

"Meaning Guy."

"Guy Masterson!"

"And that goes for Merle too."

She leaned towards him, her eyes immense. "What do you mean?"

"To go back a bit," he said, "I've been planning some altera-tions to my place, at my own expense, of course. But before saying anything to Grannie Con I thought I'd have a word with Guy and get some idea of the cost and so on——"

"I didn't know——"

"Keep your hair on, Roxie! I was going to ask your advice later. Anyway, this morning I was in town and I happened to be quite near Guy's office, so I thought I'd just look in—on the chance. I suppose I should have phoned for an appointment, but on the whole I'm not sorry things turned out as they did."

"How did they turn out? I can't wait."

"I go my own pace, so have patience. Guy was out when I went up, and that secretary girl with the nice smile showed me into his room to wait for him. There was a huge plan on his drawing-board, and while I was prowling about I stopped to look at it. Written on it was 'PLAN OF HOTEL CONSTANTIA.' It seemed like a pretty big outfit to me, about eight storeys high with staff quarters, restaurants, shopping-centres, tennis courts, swimming-pool, beauty-parlour and God knows what not all——"

"What's wrong with that? It could be anywhere—Southern Cross Estate, Hohenort."

"It could be, but it wasn't. *It was on Dieu Donné land.*"

"How can you know that, Thinus?"

"The entrance to this Hotel Constantia is on to the new arterial road that will pass along Dieu Donné boundaries, and in one corner of the plan is a landmark, a cottage; to me it looked mighty like Merle's cottage. But it was marked 'Manager's Residence.' "

"Thinus! You could easily be mistaken!"

He drew on his cigarette and rocked the little wooden chair gently back and forth.

"When Guy comes in I point to the plan and say, 'What's this?' And he turns bright red to the roots of his red hair and says to me, 'What the devil brings you here?' Then he takes a look at me and sees that he's been too quick on the draw and he starts making excuses about being over-worked and in a hurry —and just then the telephone rings. You know that phone in Guy's office?"

"Why, yes."

"Well, it's the sort that talks to the whole darn room. You can't help overhearing what the other end is saying."

"Who was the other end?"

"Krifti."

"Go on."

"And I hear that thick voice of his—'The deed of sale is complete any time Merle is ready to sign.' But Guy cuts in, 'Listen, Kriff,' he says, 'I can't talk now. I've got a client here. Thinus Vos—on business. You call me back another time.' And he hangs up in a hell of a fluster. So I get to my feet and say I'll come and see him some time when he's not got so much on his mind."

"What deed of sale could it be?"

"What could she sell? She doesn't own Dieu Donné—*yet*. All she does own is her cottage and the five acres Grannie Con gave her as a wedding present."

"I still don't see . . . if Krifti wants to build a hotel he'll need more than Merle's property, especially if it's a big scheme. And Grannie Con will never let him have so much as a square foot."

"That's what puzzles me. There's something going on that we don't know about, and I don't like it." He crushed out his cigarette as if he ground the grey lugubrious face of Mr. Krifti into the ash tray. He dismounted the little wooden chair he had been riding and took Roxane's hands, pulling her to her feet. "You're *'n mooi meisie*, Roxie," he said, "but you can't afford to lose any more beauty sleep. I'm going to take you back to the house."

For an instant the atmosphere was electric between them as they stood alone together in Max Immelmann's sorcerer's den with its test-tubes and retorts, its Bunsen burners and odours of must and sulphur. The naked light illumined their tense features and behind them the small open window framed the night—dark now, for the moon had set. In the garden a chorus of frogs had set up a coon's cacophony of their own, and in the cellar the juice of the labouring grape groaned and burbled. Roxane was suddenly aware that the wind had died down. No, she thought, no, no—not here! Her eyes, looking up at Thinus, began to laugh at him. Don't be an idiot! said those eyes. Not in this place, not now, there's a time for everything!

So Thinus released her little hands. Sure, she was right! "To everything there is a season . . . a time to plant and a time to pluck up that which is planted . . . a time to embrace and a time to refrain from embracing. . . ." Well hell, this must be the time for restraint, for this must certainly be the least romantic spot in the world for a man to ask a girl to be his wife!

His slow half-smile banished the hot urgency from his tough one-eyed pirate's face, and he ruffled her hair gently with his strong battle-scarred hand.

"You . . . you . . . my Roxie, one of these days I'm going to tell you why I am so keen to get my cottage all dolled up and altered."

She slipped out of his reach, and he heard her say:

"Why, yes, Thinus, and I'll help you with it. But now I'm sleepy—Lord, how sleepy I am!"

Mr. Krifti also had his particular sense of timing. He knew full well that there was "a time to break down, and a time to build up . . . a time to cast away stones, and a time to gather stones together . . ." and the time he chose to break down Grannie Con's resistance to his schemes was April the first, for, after his own fashion, Mr. Krifti had a certain ironic sense of humour.

He found Grannie Con in her rose garden towards the end of the day. She was in her wheel-chair among her blooms, cutting flowers for the house and pruning the bushes. She looked up in surprise as the long evening shadow of the tall man fell across her lap and darkened the sunset petals of her favourite Talisman roses.

"I am fortunate to find you, Mrs. de Valois."

"Not very, Mr. Krifti. I am seldom beyond my own boundaries these days."

Your shrinking boundaries, he thought, and smiled.

"Your roses are very fine this year," he said.

"It has been a good growing season in every way. For Dieu Donné it will be a vintage year. Four years from now, when the wine is mature in the casks, we will reap the benefit."

She spoke bravely, but her old heart was fluttering in her breast, a bird already winged by the hunter's gun and waiting now for the final shot.

"Four years is a long time."

"Is it?" she said in a low voice. "At my age it seems brief as the life-span of one of these lovely flowers, but you may be right, Mr. Krifti. Four years may be all eternity."

He had drawn a chaplet from his pocket and he began to work it through his narrow cushioned finger-tips. It was a curious chaplet, one that Grannie Con had not seen before, and he did

not, as usual, keep his hands behind his back while playing with
his beads.

"This is a new chaplet," he said. "A friend sent it to me from
Istanbul."

She took it from his outstretched hand and a little shiver passed
over her as she saw that each bead was fashioned in the shape
of a tiny skull.

"A *friend* sent it to you?"

He nodded slowly. "Even I have friends, Mrs. de Valois. And
this one knows my rather eccentric tastes. These beads are interesting to the touch."

She stared at him, fascinated, as he passed the shape of death
to and fro between his fingers.

"Much may happen in four years, we mortals never know our
fate."

It seemed to Grannie Con that the tiny skulls running through
the palm of his hand like the sands of an hour-glass spoke the
rest of his thought for him. In four years her weary, withered
flesh would be dust and her bones would be at rest on the berg—
a little old skeleton mutilated by time and the surgeon's saw, as
her beloved Dieu Donné was about to be mutilated by Mr.
Krifti's relentless design.

The cut roses lay on her lap in disarray and she made a great
effort to steady her voice and her icy hands.

"Why have you come to see me?"

"I think you must know. Three months ago you had my
letter."

"You want my vineyards." The words were almost inaudible,
the thin echo of her fear.

He made a melancholy, deprecating gesture. "I want my
money. I have received no interest on my bond for over three
months, and unfortunately I cannot afford to be a philanthropist."

"I understand."

"I warned you, Mrs. de Valois. And now the time has come
when I must call up the bond. You have a great estate here, you
will hardly miss a few morgen——"

"Forty morgen of Riesling wine grapes and my finest export
Alphonse Lavals—my pear orchards. . . ."

Under the light shawl, pins and needles were shooting through the limb that was not there. You won't miss a few morgen, you won't miss a limb! Make a cripple of Dieu Donné, Mr. Krifti, disfigure my beloved lands, cover my green carpet with your hateful settlements!

"What do you mean to do with my vineyards?" she asked him.

His shoulders rounded and shrugged forward, his heavy lips pouted.

"I have my plans, I have my plans."

"Grannie Con! It's getting cold, and you must come in!"

Roxane ran across the lawn to the rose garden.

"Mr. Krifti . . . if you want to talk to Grannie Con, come in and have a cup of tea or a *sopie* of something."

She was smiling at him, and he thought that she was growing most alluring in her own exotic way. He found in her beauty an Eastern quality, the delicacy of youth, but she was not of the East, she would never grow plump and bovine. Life coursed through her, flame-like, devouring her. But now, as she looked at the little old figure in the wheel-chair, the friendly merriment died from her eyes.

"What is it, Grannie Con? What can it be? You look ill!"

"I am not ill, Roxane, only troubled. Mr. Krifti has come here to tell me that he is compelled to call up a bond he holds on some forty morgen of my land, the vineyards and orchards adjoining Merle's cottage."

"What bond is this?"

"After the cloudburst, when I was ill, everything came at once, Roxie. I had to call on Mr. Krifti for financial help. I cannot go on paying the interest on the money I owe him. He will take his security. . . ."

"No!" cried Roxane. "No . . . no!"

Grannie Con's words and the menace of Mr. Krifti's silent acquiescence had quickened and materialized the dread that had possessed her ever since the night in the cellar when Thinus had told of his visit to Guy. So this was it! The purchase of Merle's cottage was, as they had known it must be, only the foothold on the way to the greater scheme. And where would it end, where would it end, Mr. Krifti's policy of encirclement?

Roxane's hands were tightly clasped as she stared down at the threatened vineyards. The last rags and tatters of autumn leaves clung to the trellised vines and the loosened earth was already given over to the weeds and lupins that would bind it against the winter rains. The deep thatch of Merle's cottage was visible behind the skeleton boughs of a great plane-tree, thatch as smooth as a ring-dove's feathers and as mellow as a grey squirrel's coat—and beyond it the Hottentots Hollands dreamed their topaz dreams across False Bay. And if Mr. Krifti had his way this sylvan scene would be exchanged for an enormous concrete edifice at the heart of a tourist centre of shops and beauty-parlours and charabancs. There would be a flood of native staff sniffing round the little box-like dwellings of the coloured people or haunting the woods to lie in wait for the brown girls of the Valley. Even the white girls might be in danger, for there was dagga-smoking in the Valley already, and there would be more. With dagga and drink inside him a man became an animal, full of brute power, a raper and a killer. As for the vineyards that would be left to Grannie Con, labour would be harder than ever to come by, it would be drawn off for Hotel Constantia, and Mr. Krifti and his associates would grow rich and fatten as Dieu Donné declined and died.

As she swung round to face him Mr. Krifti was shocked at Roxane's expression. Surely this was never the gentle girl he had known and admired since she was little more than a child! In the sunset light her eyes blazed jewel-gold, the pupils narrowed, hard and clear as a cat's, an angry, frightened cat's. For a moment he found himself smiling, mentally diminishing her to a small spitting kitten, back arched, fur on end, cornered and at bay.

"What does Grannie Con owe you, Mr. Krifti? Exactly what sum must we pay?" she had identified herself with the old lady in a manner that was absurd and a little pathetic.

He told her the figure, and sadly added the interest that was owed on it. He saw the heightened colour ebb from her face and her fingers interlace so that the sinews along her bare forearms stood out hard and taut.

"Oh, my God," she breathed. "Oh, my God. . . ." But her recovery was swift. "When must this money be paid?"

"It is due today, Roxane."

"How long will you give us to find it?"

"Your grandmother has already had three months' grace."

"Will you give us another month?" Surely in a month she would be able to think of some way out. . . .

He shook his head mournfully. "Quite impossible, my dear. I have been very patient as it is."

"Mr. Krifti, you must give us a little more time! How long will you give us?"

Mr. Krifti glanced from the pleading girl to the old lady whose face had settled into that mould of extreme obstinacy which he had met in her before, the mouth tight-lipped between nose and chin as if the very gums were clamped together. The girl's defiance had galvanized her into new life. How the devil had this old woman inspired such passionate loyalty in her war-orphan? Mr. Krifti was amazed by its fervour. In theory he knew something of that curious quality known as loyalty, but in practice he had seldom come across it. He himself was incapable of arousing it; it was not a commodity to be bought with cash, and he had never cared for dogs. Perhaps, he thought, loyalty is peculiar to the young, to an ardent, emotional nature such as Roxane's. There was fire in the girl! If she could lavish this intense devotion on an old effigy like Grannie Con, what would she not give as a lover, or a mother——

Roxane's voice broke in on his reflections. "You don't answer me! How long will you give us to find the sum you want?"

He cleared his throat. "The sum I am owed," he corrected.

He regarded her gravely. Where could she turn to for financial aid, this child from nowhere? What source could she hope to try that had not already been explored by the old lady? Mr. Krifti did not believe in miracles. He knew that he was perfectly safe in allowing himself the pleasure of making a concession to this charming girl, only a small one, mind you, a mere gesture. But he greatly enjoyed making magnanimous gestures that cost him nothing.

"I will give you one week, Roxane—a week from today—from

this very hour." He took a flat gold watch from his waistcoat pocket and studied it carefully. "Shall we say five-thirty on April the seventh? I will call at Dieu Donné punctually at that time."

As he put the watch away the gold chain gleamed in the fading light. He raised his soft felt hat and bade them good evening, and they looked after his long back and stooping shoulders as he went his way towards the vineyards that would soon be his.

CHAPTER 14

RENDEZVOUS

Solly Caine stamped up and down inside the barrier at Jan Smuts Airport. It was past eight-thirty and the Cape Town Skymaster should be in at any moment. The night air was cold and fresh and the stars sparkled like icicles.

He was disturbed and impatient and not a little curious to know what had induced Roxane to telephone him from Cape Town that morning. She had put the call through to his office, and an odd little conversation had ensued.

"Solly, I'm in a fix. It's something I can't explain over the telephone. Can I come and see you?"

"Come and see me? But, Roxie, it's a long way, a thousand miles! Can't you write?"

"There isn't time, Solly. This thing is terribly urgent. If I catch the evening plane, can you get me a room in a hotel, a cheap one, just for the night? And will you find time to let me talk to you?"

"Of course. . . . But can't you stay with us out at our place? Bella would——"

"No! I can't do that. Please, nobody must know that I am coming to see you; least of all Merle's mother——"

"Have you a booking by this evening's plane?"

"Thinus has got me a provisional seat. He is paying my fare."

"Then confirm it. I will meet you at the airport."

Now what in the name of Christopher Columbus could young
Roxane be in such a state about? Why the secrecy? Could that
seemingly reliable fellow, Thinus Vos, have got her into trouble?
You could never tell with those quiet blighters and she had said
he was paying her passage. The notion angered Solly. All day
long the suspicion battered at his brain. Roxie was in trouble
with a man and she was relying on his worldly knowledge to get
her out of it. Solly Caine had more than his fair share of imagination, and by the time the Skymaster had touched down on the
flarepath, he had worked himself into a fine fever. He had pul-
verized that one-eyed pirate, Vos, with trenchant bits of his
mind, and he had all but wept over a desperate Roxie. And, at
sight of her, his worst fears rose up and choked him.

She stepped off the landing ladder and came across to the
barrier carrying her little night-case and a magazine. Her camel-
hair coat hung loosely over her shoulders and she was hatless;
she looked small and forlorn and he could hardly wait to clasp
her hands in his and assure her that he was glad to see her whatever her visit might mean. He scanned the faces of her fellow-
passengers with relief. Lucky there were no acquaintances of his,
for he had told his Bella that he was keeping a business date,
and it was astonishing how things leaked out in this glorified
dorp of Johannesburg!

"I've booked you a suite at a quiet little place, quite comfortable. I thought you'd better have a sitting-room so that we
could talk without interruption."

It turned out to be a cosy old-fashioned sitting-room with a
coal fire burning in the grate. There were flowers on the mantelpiece and sandwiches on the sideboard. A decanter of red wine
had been set to warm by the fire. She looked round with
mingled pleasure and dismay. He interpreted her glance and
laughed.

"You are my guest for tonight. But why did you refuse to
stay with us at home?"

"Forgive me," she said. "I know I've made things difficult for
you, but I'll explain everything soon. You've taken such trouble,
you are very kind. . . ."

She took off her coat and flung it onto the bed. Through the open bedroom door Solly could see her going through the small unnecessary ritual of powdering her face and reddening her lips. She ran a comb through her hair, and then she was back with him and he was holding her at arm's length and gazing at her. "Let's have a look at you, Roxie. Let's see if a few months have changed you."

What he saw entranced while it did not reassure him. The hollows under the cheekbones were more deeply planed, the lips were still as generous and softly curved as he remembered them—queer how vividly her image had remained with him— and the oblique almond eyes still shone with that trusting hopefulness which he associated with her gift for happiness. But there was new strength in her expression, as if the features, cast in so frail a mould, had been fired and hardened by experience. What experience? That blasted fellow Vos, no doubt!

"You have grown up," he said. "How old are you?"

"Twenty next birthday."

"To be twenty again . . ." He sighed and waved a well-manicured fin in a movement of negation, swimming away from so disturbing a prospect. "No, my Roxie! Twenty is the age of enchantment, but it is also the age of suffering. Everything *matters* at twenty—you are cutting your wisdom teeth and growing a caul to hold your heart. At twenty the sun shines hot but the wind blows cold. God forbid that anyone should endure the agonies of twenty twice over! Are you in love, child?"

The question came so suddenly on the heels of his soliloquy that for a moment she was caught off guard and he saw the quick pain leap in her eyes. But she made no reply. She sat on the plush sofa and held her ringless hands out to the dancing firelight. Her hair fell forwards and shadowed her face. Presently she said:

"I didn't come to see you about me, Solly. I came about something really important: about Grannie Con . . . and Dieu Donné. . . ."

He lifted the decanter of red wine from its place on the hearth and filled two glasses and he set the sandwiches on the low table beside her. So she had not come on her own account.

Funny, he ought to have guessed that. She was not like his Bella or Merle who asked favours only for themselves.

"Tell me everything," he said. "Take your time."

When she had finished Solly sat silent and thoughtful. At last he said, "Shall we sum up the situation? As I see it, the main points are as follows. The calamity of the flood and her illness hit Grannie Con together and put her badly in the red, so she had to borrow from our friend, Mr. Krifti, on the security of valuable Dieu Donné land. Now she is unable to meet the interest, which means that the bond cannot be regarded as easily transferable."

"This year's harvest is excellent," put in Roxane quickly. "She hopes to recover——"

"Ssh—" He flapped a fin at her. "Don't interrupt, girl! The fact is Grannie Con can neither pay her interest nor raise the capital, so she's on a spot. That's point one. Now let's consider point two. Thinus Vos has reason to believe that Kriff intends to depreciate the value and charm of Dieu Donné by building over this green belt. And that he has Merle and Guy in his pocket."

He paused to relight his cigar and draw on it reflectively.

"Thinus may well be right, but his surmise can only be conjecture, circumstantial evidence. But, if we allow that he is right and that Merle is quite ready to despoil her heritage for material considerations, a third point occurs to me, and it is rather a sad one. It would seem that my beautiful step-daughter is right in the enemy's camp and that the preservation of her birthright isn't worth a row of beans to her." Suddenly he swung round on Roxane. "And, that being so, why should you, Roxie, be fighting tooth and nail to preserve it? What do you get out of it? You have no expectations where Dieu Donné is concerned—or—have you?"

She flushed as the full impact of his words struck her.

"How can you, Solly!" Her tone was brittle as glass. "You know very well that I have no expectations from Grannie Con, no right to anything that is hers! I am equipped to earn my own living."

"Exactly. Then why are you so deeply interested?"

A feeling of nightmare possessed her—a horror of the futility of words.

"I have no good answer for you," she said. "It's just that I love Grannie Con and Dieu Donné with all my heart . . . and perhaps that has made me foolish. Grannie Con has been mother and father to me—and Dieu Donné is the only home I have ever known. . . ."

Her voice broke and she covered her face with her hands. Can't you understand, Solly? I want her to be happy for the little time that is left to her. She mustn't know about Merle, about the things they will do to her Valley! Dieu Donné is her life and her faith, her past and her future. She has fought for it so single-mindedly, given it all she has and is. But how can I make you see these things?

She heard him say, "Have you told Grannie Con that you suspect Merle of selling out to Krifti?"

She shook her head. "It would break her heart. Merle just doesn't seem to understand what Dieu Donné means to Grannie Con——"

"Merle doesn't care! An old lady's broken heart wouldn't give my Bella's daughter a single sleepless night. My womenfolk have hard golden heads on their lovely shoulders and stones in their sweet soft breasts. They leave sentiment to fools like Solly Caine."

He rose and threw the stump of his dead cigar into the embers, and then he began laughing softly to himself.

"Security that's good enough for Mr. Krifti should be quite satisfactory to Mr. Solly Caine, and never mind the interest. I only wish I could be there to see Kriff's face when Grannie Con pays him off!"

"Solly! You're going to help!"

"Yes, Roxie. But not from the highest motives. I have one or two personal scores to settle with our friend Kriff and my darling step-daughter has never been my favourite girl. But there are two things I want to make quite clear. Firstly, my part in this affair will remain anonymous. My man of business will see to that. And secondly, you must understand, Roxie, that this situation will need to be reviewed again a year from now. I am making no gifts, I am merely helping to tide things over; no more than that. And now, tell me, does Grannie Con know that you have come all this way to appeal to me? Does anybody know?"

"Only Thinus knows. Grannie Con thinks that I am spending the night with Aletta Krige. I often baby-sit for her and sleep at her place."

"Then you must assure me that the old lady will not find out from you or Thinus, and no one else must get wind of what we are up to. This rendezvous and everything that has been said must be our secret. As for the technical details, those will be arranged."

Grannie Con's man of business rose briskly and put the signed documents into his briefcase. The bracket lamps of Dieu Donné library shone down on his bald head and little goatee beard. Good gracious, thought Grannie Con, he's getting quite white! And only yesterday I was dandling Jimmy Jordaan on my knee, and a fat suet pudding of a baby he was too; and just look at him now, a skinny little ferret nearing sixty!

She heard his sharp voice addressing Mr. Krifti.

"I think that settles everything, Mr. Krifti. The transfer of the bond will go through in the usual way, and we will see that Mrs. de Valois' cheque is paid into your account tomorrow."

Mr. Krifti's face was expressionless as he bowed his head. He gave no indication of the questions racing through his brain. Who was this client of Jordaan's who was prepared to take over the bond on forty morgen of Dieu Donné land at a purely nominal rate of interest? What had Roxane been up to in the past few days to turn the tables on him like this?

Grannie Con was as puzzled as Mr. Krifti. Jimmy Jordaan's airy explanations had done little to clarify the situation. His client insisted upon remaining anonymous, and had seen fit to waive the matter of interest for reasons connected with his income tax. Or so Jimmy suggested. Her man of business often infuriated Grannie Con with his patronizing air of "Leave it all to me, my dear, you are far too old to worry yourself with business matters. Just be grateful that you have me to depend upon!"

Usually she catechized him, proved to him that she was far from addled and in complete command of her faculties, and implied that it was a great honour for his firm to be in a position to handle the affairs of a famous estate like Dieu Donné, even if it was no longer as profitable as she might wish. On this occasion, however, she had made no effort to press him for details. There was something providential here; something she wanted to accept without risking the discovery of hidden obligations. She had no desire to know the name of her benefactor. She preferred to consider him as a fortunate investor.

So, for once, to Jimmy Jordaan's relief, his cantankerous old client accepted his somewhat nebulous statements without question or comment.

"I suppose I can't persuade you to take a *sopie* before you go, Jimmy?"

"No, thank you. I haven't altered the habit of a lifetime. I'm still a strict abstainer." He caught her disapproving eye and laughed. "Yes, I know it isn't an attitude to stress at Dieu Donné, but I must remind you that I am very fond of fruit, especially Dieu Donné grapes and pears."

She put her police whistle to her lips and blew a shrill blast to summon Joshua.

"Show Mr. Jordaan out, Joshua, and bring brandy and soda for Mr. Krifti and sherry for me."

Grannie Con never offered whisky. The price was prohibitive, and in any case it was her custom to give her guests only the wines and spirits of her estate. She felt a little light-headed now that a long-standing anxiety had been lifted from her shoulders, for a time at least. Perhaps it was a dream. She had dreamed such reprieves before, and waking had been torment.

Joshua set the tray on the table and poured his Oumissus a glass of sherry.

"No doubt you would prefer to help yourself, Mr. Krifti," she suggested.

It was not Mr. Krifti's custom to take hard liquor, but this evening he felt the need for a stimulant. He poured himself a strong medicinal tot of brandy and a dash of soda.

Grannie Con sat on the couch by the fireside. Her cashmere

shawl covered her lap, for the autumn evening was chilly. Her wheel-chair was close to her hand, but she was always glad to be out of it. She sipped her sherry with keen enjoyment and visualized Roxie's laughing face when she should hear the tale of Mr. Krifti's discomfiture. Soon Roxie and Thinus ought to be back from their ride. They were together a great deal these days; too much.

She heard Mr. Krifti's thick voice. "Does Merle know that this bond of mine has been redeemed?"

"Certainly not! Merle knows nothing whatever about this bond, from me. Why should she? It's none of her business—yet."

Not yet, perhaps, but it soon would be. Mr. Krifti found the reflection consoling. When Dieu Donné did become Merle's business he was reasonably sure that she would be ready to sell the estate in its entirety, although she was too wise to let anyone guess that such might be her intention. He would have to wait a little longer; that was all. In the meantime it suited him very well that Merle should remain in ignorance of the turn of affairs.

"In fact," Grannie Con continued, with a touch of arrogance, "I have forbidden Roxane to discuss these matters with *anyone*. My business concerns are private and confidential."

He glanced furtively at her. Triumph lit the old eyes. She was a secret one, was Grannie Con. She had found a spanner somewhere to throw into the works of Mr. Krifti. Where? The question haunted and tantalized him. Still, it could do no more than delay the eventual outcome. He drew his amber chaplet from his pocket, lapsing in this little hour of frustration into Oriental fatalism. Through his fingers was the smooth run of the beads, and in his mind the knowledge that it was only a matter of time before his plans would mature. He wondered, as he had done scores of times, what age Grannie Con might be. To know that fact would help him to assess her length of life. It would interest him greatly to see her birth certificate. *Her birth certificate?* An idea grew and took shape in Mr. Krifti's brain. So simple to discover what he wanted to know! Why had he not thought of it before?

He rose to take his leave.

"No, please," he said as she raised the whistle on its velvet cord. "Don't call Joshua. It is quite unnecessary. I assure you I can find my own way out."

Her smile of dismissal was cynical.

"If you prefer to find your own way out, Mr. Krifti, then, goodbye."

He left her staring into the fire with that curious little smile still on her lips.

Mr. Krifti took his coat from the *bankie* in the *voorkamer* and slipped it on. The weather was treacherous at this time of year.

He touched the seat, criss-crossed with hide riems, and the wood with its smooth living warmth. He dipped his hands into the big burnished copper bowl of pot-pourri and let forgotten summers linger in his palms. He was in no hurry to depart. His eyes wandered from the lofty yellow-wood ceiling to the heavy teak screen carved some three centuries ago. Heirlooms of inestimable value held his gaze: the magnificent armoire, the camphor-wood chest, porcelain from the East, antique mirrors from France, and old masters brought from Holland in the days of the Dutch East India Company. These things were not inanimate. They belonged here as the old lady herself belonged. They lived, they breathed. But they would go on, increasing in value and mellow beauty, long after the mistress of Dieu Donné was dust.

The inscrutable painted eyes of de Valois men and women pursued Mr. Krifti as he went slowly to the lectern on which the great family Bible rested between gilded heraldic wings. In here would be inscribed the de Valois records of births, deaths and marriages. In here he would find what he needed to know.

On the wall above the lectern was a modern study of Dirk de Valois's head and shoulders. It was bold, impressionist and intensely vital. The eyes were dark and deep-set like his mother's, but the mouth—there was a weakness there, the mouth was too richly curved, too emotional. It was a face capable of suffering. He was in uniform at the time the portrait was painted—shortly before his death.

Mr. Krifti addressed it silently. Strange how you and I have changed places, my friend! The misfortunes of war took you north to a soldier's fate, while I was swept south—displaced, but not without means! You found your grave in the shifting sands of the desert that gave my people birth; while I intend to end my days under these rafters that have sheltered your ancestors. . . .

Now his sensitive fingers stroked the polished leather binding of the massive Bible, they explored the brass hasps and the rough edges of the thick yellowing leaves. To *touch*—what subtle ecstasy to touch that which was beautiful and precious; seasoned wood, rich materials, amber, jade, ivory, the firm skin of a young girl, or this old Bible that had known the reverent hands of patriarchal Boers and of Huguenots driven into exile by their faith.

The Good Book fell open, its covers born in the gilt wings. Here was the page he sought.

Mr. Krifti stared down at it.

"How dare you!"

He turned at the sound of her voice. He had not heard the silent wheels or noticed the chair in the doorway between the library and the *voorkamer*. He had not realized that she had her own method of getting into it unaided.

Grannie Con sat bolt upright, her gnarled fingers clutching the arms as if by will-power alone she would lever herself up. Wrath had put new fire into her eyes, and her features, sharp with age and anger, seemed to dart forward and strike at him.

"How dare you, Mr. Krifti!"

He neither excused himself not attempted to explain his curiosity.

He did not even close the Book. But his flat, pale eyes met hers with a certain respect, and the corners of his fleshy mouth were drawn down in a strange smile that acknowledged a new intimacy between him and his aged adversary.

"A woman will go a long way to conceal her age, Mrs. de Valois, a very long way. And why not? We all have our secrets; the little vain ones, and the big heavy ones. . . ."

She did not move or speak, and his muffled voice trailed away with the shrug of his shoulders. She waited until the door had closed behind him, then she propelled herself towards the lectern.

Grannie Con reached up and felt the covered page and the lumpy wax seals stamped with her family crest—four, one at each corner. These seals held a loose leaf in place—a leaf carefully spread over the de Valois records, hiding the dates of births, deaths and marriages. On this concealing sheet of strong opaque paper were written her final instructions in her own angular, uncompromising hand.

These seals are to be broken after my death
by
Maria Merle Masterson and Roxane de Valois
signed
Constance Henrietta Vos de Valois
Dieu Donné
Constantia.

She was aware of the date at the foot of the page.

That was the day she had feared death, the day she had asked old Lizzie for the Bible and for her seal and the wax. On the following day they had crippled her.

Yes, Mr. Krifti, she thought grimly. We all have our secrets. You have yours and I have mine—and some indeed are heavy ones.

CHAPTER 15

BIRTHDAY GIFT

Twice a year, on her birthday and at Christmas, Roxane was accustomed to receiving a gift of five pounds from her English godfather, General Sir Christopher Williams.

She had no real recollection of "Uncle Chris," but his formal little notes and the regularity with which he remembered her convinced Roxane that he was kind and thoughtful, and moreover, in her own mind, she had come to associate him with the father she had never known, so her feeling for him had become strongly filial. In return for his gifts she had acquired the habit of writing him long letters about her life in the Valley. Roxane wrote as she spoke and thought, with eager spontaneity, and whenever one of her letters arrived at the little house in Chelsea the General found himself restless and disturbed, his well-behaved thoughts blown this way and that by the breath of youth and the perverse winds of memory.

Sometimes Roxane sent him snapshots, and through these he had seen a wispy child grow into a young girl whose face and figure haunted him with an ever-increasing likeness to her mother. Gradually a most revolutionary idea had taken root in his mind, one which he fully realized might disturb the habits of years and open up old wounds that he had long considered healed.

General Williams was not given to impulses, but he was surprised one day to hear himself say to his housekeeper, Mrs. Maydew, "Would you think it very foolish if I invited my South African god-daughter to spend a few months here?" He smiled wryly. "After all, I'm hardly a suitable companion for a girl of twenty—and a lively one at that, if her letters are any criterion."

Mrs. Maydew smiled her pleasant smile. She was the mother of a large family of grown-up children and young grandchildren and she was inclined to regard the General as a sort of cuckoo in her nest—a demanding alien child much older and more important than her own. Even her Lucy, who had always been so nervous till she married Ned, the policeman, had never caused her as much concern as the General. "Needs taking out of himself," she had frequently told Lucy. "Ingrowing he is—and that doesn't do no more with men than it does with toenails." And Lucy had said, "Well, what else can you expect of a man whose old woman was off her rocker for twenty years before she passed on?"

So now Mrs. Maydew did not hesitate.

"The house is big enough, sir, and we could do with a young thing about the place to liven us up. She might take you out of yourself a bit."

He thought, I've been out of myself for years—what I fear is going back—into myself again. . . .

He went to his desk and wrote the letter. From her place

above the fireplace Anne Williams watched him. It was a beautiful portrait, and the eyes were the eyes of Roxane.

—I think it is high time we met. I will pay your return fare, and my home will be yours while you are over here. We will make a plan to go to France for a few days, and perhaps together we can rediscover something of your mother—of Anne——

Roxane read the words in her special sanctuary.

The waterfall, swollen by the April rains, foamed over the rocks, bearing on its surface the thin gold of autumn—light dry leaves shaken from the branches of scrub-oaks, poplars and willows and the frail winged seeds of mountain shrubs. The giant ferns were brittle now, but the moss was rich and spongy and the earth had its moist fertile scent.

Roxane clasped her arms about the pale, slender trunk of a eucalyptus sapling, and laid her face against the smooth pliable wood that was neither warm nor cold but strong with its own life of sap and leaf, and she was happy—actively, radiantly happy. Her chance had come for the pilgrimage predestined since childhood. She was going to find Maman—Anne, her mother. No more need to scrape and save for her passage and for lodging in London and travelling to France. Uncle Chris's offer right out of the blue had taken care of all that, and what she had already put by would look after the rest. But how long could Grannie Con spare her? Three, four, five months. . . . And who would do the books in her absence? The foreman's niece had helped before. Yes, Amanda Brink could take her place in the office. Everything must be arranged without delay. "Come whenever you can—the sooner the better," her godfather had written. It would be spring in England now with bluebells and primroses in the woods—all the things she had once known and long since forgotten. London in the spring, with the blossoms like lace over Kensington Gardens, and all Peter Pan's birds on the Serpentine. . . .

Here in the glade she nursed her new-found joy as she had nursed the sadness of her parting with Hal. She heard Wolf and the Farway dogs rustling about in the bush, and suddenly she called them, her voice quick with excitement. "Home, boys, home! I have to talk to Grannie Con, and Thinus, and Amanda Brink—and see about booking a passage . . . Oh, Wolf—and you two lion-dogs—I'm on my way!"

Dieu Donné was in a flutter over Roxane's departure.

"What will you do without the child?" Auntie Marthe asked Grannie Con. And Grannie Con answered tartly:

"I'm not helpless yet, Marthe. I can manage very well. In any case it won't be for long."

Merle said to Roxane, with the lift of her lip that marred the beauty of her face, "I knew you'd break away. All your lot do sooner or later. Girls go overseas from here like natives leave their territories to go to the mines. For a period of initiation." But the younger girl only laughed, for she remembered that Merle had never been to Europe. The war and marriage had postponed her opportunities. Naturally Merle was envious.

Aletta Krige had hugged her warmly. "It's wonderful for you, Roxie! But we'll all be lost without you here. Who'll baby-sit for me, or talk the devil out of Jannie when I can't cope with him? I can't imagine Dieu Donné without you." She added slyly, "What does Thinus say?"

Roxane had smiled without answering as she buried her face in the silky curls of the latest addition to Aletta's family.

"The feel of babies——" she breathed. "The sweet milky smell of them——"

"Sour as often as it's sweet," said Aletta, and stuck to her point. "If I were you I'd marry Thinus and have some of your own. He's a good man, Roxie. That may sound a bit dull, but it's what a woman needs—a fellow she can trust."

Old Dog Trust, that's Thinus Vos—he had said it himself— rather ruefully, that night in the cellar, the night he had guessed about Krifti plotting with Merle and Guy to break up Dieu Donné. Her eyes clouded for an instant. Maybe Aletta was right, maybe marriage and that other love were not to be confused. Maybe the marriages that lasted were built on trust and not on passion. Yet she guessed that Aletta's own marriage was founded on more than trust and devotion. Big Karl Krige, with his hot blue eyes and golden beard, was her master as well as her mate, her children were conceived in ecstasy. Perhaps a woman needed to be swept off her feet and carried away upon a tempestuous tide of breathless, headlong submission. But, at the thought, it was the face of Hal that rose to taunt her—the lifted eyebrow, the scarred cheek, the grey eyes that mocked and challenged or melted in tenderness, the strong arms and lithe limbs that were not for her but for Alexa. She brushed her hand across her eyes. . . . Let me alone, Hal—let me alone!

The erratic April days flew by, linking the aftermath of summer with the first signs of winter. Sun and rain came simultaneously and the children shouted to one another that it was "a monkey's wedding." The roses were nearly over, and in Grannie Con's garden old Klaas spent hours pruning the autumn bushes.

Lizzie's deaf Ben helped Klaas about the grounds. There was always work for him at Dieu Donné, and now that the fire-season was over, the boy seemed to have settled down once more. He no longer left his work by day and his bed by night to follow the lurid thrill of fire. But sometimes it occurred to Roxane that his dark, handsome face had altered in a sinister way. Since the world had ceased to call him with many voices he had retreated from it. Once he had responded to every outside impulse with his bright intelligent eyes, but now, when Roxane tapped him lightly on the shoulder and let him read her lips as she gave him some message from Grannie Con, she had the feeling that he wore his dark skin as a mask. Looking into Ben's eyes these days was like looking into a dark room—and there was in that dark some intangible danger.

Presently Miriam, the Malay, came to Dieu Donné to make some new dresses for Roxane, and in this matter the advice of Mrs. Krifti was sought, for Louise Krifti was the arbiter of feminine elegance in the Valley. Grannie Con and Roxane had never extended their dislike of Mr. Krifti to his wife. In their eyes she remained primarily the daughter of old Auntie Marthe van der Walt, a view encouraged by her own attitude, which was curiously detached from the activities of her husband. If Louise ever guessed that Mr. Krifti had put financial pressure on the mistress of Dieu Donné she gave no sign of it, and it was tacitly understood between Grannie Con and Roxane that if she had known she would have been profoundly shocked. So now she studied patterns and materials with Roxane and together they chose the few simple clothes that would be needed for the voyage and an English summer.

Sometimes, when Saartjie had finished her chores in the manager's cottage, she came over to the big house to help Miriam sew, for the coloured girl was as clever with her needle as she was incompetent at cooking.

At last everything was ready, and Saartjie was helping Roxane to fold the dainty new dresses and blouses.

"Miss Roxie is very lucky." The coloured girl sighed. "I would give anything to go to England!"

Roxane, who was sitting on the end of the bed sorting stockings, looked up in surprise.

"Why do you want to go to England, Saartjie?"

"I want to go on the stage. I can dance, Miss Roxie—and sing too——"

"Yes, I know. But even in England it isn't easy to get a job on the stage—at least, so I believe."

The girl's pretty light-coloured face set in a mould of resentment, and the great dark eyes smouldered.

"In the Group they think a lot of me."

Suddenly Roxane found herself considering Saartjie as a person —no longer taking her for granted as Lizzie's niece and Thinus's cook-general, as much a part of the Dieu Donné scene as the doves and squirrels. She could almost pass as white, thought Roxane. On the stage she does. She had seen Saartjie dance and sing in musical comedies produced by the All-Coloured Dramatic Group when the Cape Town City Hall had been packed with a mixed audience held in thrall by the unflagging vitality of the performers. Was it so surprising, after all, if she should crave an opportunity to make a name for herself overseas—not as a member of a group representing the cultural advancement of the coloured people, but as an individual taking her chance in the white world which here in the Union so firmly excluded those of her mixed race.

"In England anyone can get to the top," Saartjie persisted.

A wave of irritation swept over Roxane.

"Not unless they are worth it! The top is a very small high place. It's hard to climb there—and harder to stay there." Alexa Rome could tell you that, she thought, and added, "It's a lonely place too." Lonely for yourself, and lonelier still for those who try to share it with you. Her mind had gone its own way. For the moment Saartjie's ambitions were of no further interest to her.

Saartjie's attention too had wandered. She knew that Miss Roxie was just putting her off the way white people always did. Of course there was room at the top—anywhere in the world except the Union. My! How they had clapped her at the last show the Group had put on! Her Eccentric Dance had had a paragraph all to itself in the *Argus*. And if that wasn't fame, what was? With her talent you didn't have to rehearse much, you just danced and the audience was at your feet. . . .

Roxane said, "A good coloured dancer can make a name for herself here——"

"In the Group," admitted Saartjie with contempt. "What's the good of that?"

She began to fold a white evening dress with deft narrow fingers. Roxane had never noticed before that the girl's hands were beautiful with long pale nails. Her neck was lovely too as she bent over her task. Her skin was darker on the nape, with a bloom on it like purple grapes. Her hair was sleek and wavy, not frizzy, and it tossed on her shoulders in long corkscrew curls. Her features were small. It ran through Roxane's mind that she had changed greatly during the past two years—ever since she had joined the Dramatic Group. She had given up speaking in the *taal* except among those she regarded as her inferiors, and her English was carefully pronounced. One doesn't trouble to know other people, thought Roxane. One doesn't trouble to go into their minds. One simply discounts their dreams.

"I'll get to England one of these days, Miss Roxie. Just wait and see!"

Roxane observed that she didn't say "yus" for "just." She had come a long way already. She recalled Saartjie and Ben as children, the boy with his reed pipe to his lips or his fingers plucking at the strings of his guitar and the girl with the restless feet and the wild laughter who danced with head and hands and breasts and buttocks—mad, provocative, part of the rhythm of Africa. Saartjie had always been a will-o'-the-wisp—now here, now there —the light that lures. The night of Merle's wedding she had danced with Ben like a crazy creature—jitterbugging round the fire outside the coloured village. That was the night Roxane and Hal had slipped away from the Kriges' *braaivleis* to watch the *volkies* celebrate—the night Roxane had fallen in love with Hal. Strange how in the end everything always came back to Hal. Would she see him in England?

Saartjie straightened her back, but when she turned to the white girl who was still sorting stockings she saw that Miss Roxie was no longer in the room. She was somewhere far away. Only her body was on the end of the bed with a lap full of nylons.

"There," she said gently. "That's the last dress packed. There's only the little things left."

Roxane looked up and smiled.

"Thank you, Saartjie. That's all for now. I'll put in the last things tomorrow morning."

It was Roxane's last night at home. Grannie Con had gone to bed and Thinus had persuaded Roxane to let him drive her over Constantia Nek to Hout Bay.

The road snaked down to the wild Atlantic coast between towering peaks, and every now and again the car plunged into a dark tunnel of oaks blotting out the brilliant stars. Soon they saw the white dunes skirting Hout Bay Mountain and then the stern profile of the Sentinel rose sheer from the western curve of the Bay illumined from time to time by the scimitar sweep of the beam from Slangkop Lighthouse.

On the cliff road Thinus stopped the car. "You'll never see anything more beautiful than this," he said. "Add it to your pictures of the Valley. Remember it—and come back to all these places you love . . . and to the people who love you, Roxie."

She felt tired and detached. "Tonight is a strange night," she said. "For the Malays it is the beginning of Ramadan—their month of fasting and prayer. Miriam told me about it. All over the Peninsula lookouts are posted to watch for the new moon."

He accepted her mood—her withdrawal from the personal. "Like fire-watchers during the fire-season—a lookout on every peak?"

She nodded. "And, as soon as it has been seen, it will be reported to the Chief Priest and the people waiting at the mosques. Miriam's father is one of the observers. He has gone to Sea Point beach with his prayer rug. The moment he and the other observers see the crescent they will begin to recite their prayers."

"Then they'll be praying now," said Thinus.

Over the eastern hump of the mountain the thin silver crescent was rising in the cold star-frosted sky.

They were silent, listening to the night—the waves crashing against the cliffs and the breeze in the dark forests behind them. She wished that her own religion imposed a period of fasting and reflection upon its followers—not just a few hours or days of abstinence—but longer—not merely giving up chocolates for Lent, but something like Ramadan—a true discipline. A premonition of great change filled her. Tomorrow she would enter upon a new period of her life—begin her own private pilgrimage. Would anything be quite the same when she returned? She heard Thinus's voice.

"Excited, my squirrel?"

"More than that—a sort of—on the brink feeling. I hope to learn something about my parents. I have always wanted to know more about them. Knowledge of one's parents—seeing them, being with them—must surely help towards knowledge of oneself. . . ."

He said slowly, "Self-knowledge is a tall order, Roxie. How many of us really know ourselves?"

"There is example. The child's contact with its father and mother teaches it the good possibilities in itself—and the bad ones. For instance, you must feel safe, Thinus, because Oom Jacob and Tante Pet are good people."

"Ja," he agreed. "That is so." In fact, he had often felt the spirit of his father stir in him—especially at Tweefontein—and the feeling had been strength. There was security and continuity in the knowledge and respect of one's own blood.

"Your mother was a brave woman—and from that little picture of her—the miniature—you are very like her," he said.

His arm was about her and he felt the shiver than ran through her as if, after all, she feared some disillusionment, and for a moment he too wondered about her beginnings. She was in truth a graft upon Dieu Donné, alien in spite of her familiarity. And that was good for Dieu Donné—and for him. The home vine must be grafted onto the alien breed if it is to resist the enemies in its own soil and reach perfection.

Reluctantly he headed the car homewards, and they drove in silence until he stopped under the oaks outside his cottage.

"Come in for a few moments, Roxie. It's early—not yet ten."

She hesitated, overcome by the physical and emotional fatigue of this last day at home. She was afraid of what he might say to her—what he might ask her. She had no answer for him.

"Come——"

He drew her into the bright living-room that led off the stoep, and she saw at once that he had made preparations for receiving her. A fire crackled in the open hearth, flowers were arranged on the stinkwood table, sandwiches were set out, and there was coffee in a thermos flask. She knew every article of furniture in this cottage he was always intending to "do up"—from the worn leather easy-chairs to the old-fashioned sideboard in which he kept his drinks. He turned on the wireless and music flowed softly into the room.

"Last time we had a snack like this together was in the cellar at dead of night. Remember?"

"Mmn——" She lay back in the armchair while he poured the coffee and put a cup beside her. "Only a few weeks ago—yet it seems as if years had passed since then. It was the night you told me about your going to Guy's office—about the plan for Hotel Constantia—Krifti's plan."

"I told you more than that. I told you *why* I had gone to see Guy. I want to make this place a decent home."

"But it is—it's just right for a bachelor! I like it as it is."

He sat on the arm of her chair, his unmarred profile towards her; he threw the cigarette he had been smoking into the fire, and he said:

"It may be all right for a bachelor, but that's not what I want. I want a real home with a wife and children. I want *you*, Roxie. You knew it then and you know it still. Maybe you have always known it—that I love you more than anything else in the world. . . . Roxie, will you marry me?"

So here it was—and she had no answer. She felt his arm about her and she closed her eyes. The tiredness overwhelmed her. She was without resistance, without any feeling at all. It wasn't the right time to tell me—that night in the cellar—she thought; and it isn't the right time now. Perhaps there is no right time for you and me, old Thinus . . . yet you are very dear to me. . . .

And then—strange this—he was kneeling at her feet and his arms were clasped about her waist. She could smell his hair as he buried his face in her breast—like dry hay, a manger sort of smell, nice—and she found her hand stroking it. Funny, he had never used greasy stuff to control the crisp sun-bleached waves. The hard heat of his lips burned through her thin blouse, and she wondered whether he could feel the pity that was in her bosom. She had been sure of his love ever since she could remember, ever since she had come to Dieu Donné as a little child. He had been so kind—her friend and her brother. . . .

She was two people now. Her tiredness had split her in half. Or maybe it had doubled her—mirrored her in some strange way, so that she could observe herself, not only her physical self but that other deep-hidden being of which she was aware as one is aware of certain birds invisible in forest or bush. Like piet-my-vrou, she thought, you hear his cry in the boughs, or the whirr of his wings, but he seldom shows himself. . . . So now she saw the young figure gathered close in Thinus's arms, and the empty heart, and she wept for them both—the man and the girl—and the girl's silent prayer was part of her. *Let me feel—let me feel! Let me suffer, if You will it, but not this emptiness.* . . .

The music had ceased and the S.A.B.C. announcer was giving the news to the quiet room.

"Here are the headlines . . ."

Thinus hardly heard it. He was aware only of Roxane—of the

firm resilience of her little breast, of his own desire and her stillness, of the cool impersonal touch of her hand on his head. Then suddenly he felt shock pass through her like the tremor that runs along a wire fence that has been struck far off by a careless stick.

The words of the announcer, and their import, penetrated his consciousness. ". . . this afternoon, in a London nursing home, actress-ballerina Alexa Rome, wife of journalist Hallam Fairmead, gave birth to a baby daughter. . . ."

He sprang to his feet and turned off the radio. She had risen too and her pallor was frightening.

"Thinus—dear Thinus—I don't know if I can marry you. When I come back perhaps I can give you my answer." Her voice shook and he saw that she too was shaking. "I don't understand myself—I don't. . . ."

"Poor little squirrel—poor little heart." He spoke in Afrikaans and drew her into his arms once more, master at last of the situation. She melted into the strength of his embrace. She was a child again, taking comfort from this man who had so much to give. She lifted her face and offered him her lips, and slow fire warmed the coldness of her nerves.

It could be all right, she thought, in the depths of her weariness. If I could forget Hal it might be all right with Thinus. Let me forget—let me learn to forget. . . .

CHAPTER 16

LONDON PREMIÈRE

Roxane fell in love with the little house in Chelsea at once.

It stood at the head of one of those short intersections off the King's Road, and over the pretty porch a white stone cat stalked a white stone dove with immortal grace of the feline hunter perpetually imprisoned in the chase. In a tiny garden, gay with flowers, a purple lilac nodded and whispered between a tall syringa and a drooping yellow laburnum. From the mullioned window of the lounge the green eyes of a fine Russian-blue cat gazed with enigmatic boredom at the desultory life of the little side-street—women with scarves over their heads pushing small market-baskets on wheels, or trundling prams with the groceries piled at the baby's feet; bearded, long-haired artists with the shrewd darting eyes of the pseudo-Bohemian, and girls in slacks and sandals, their shopping-bags over their arms. Gulls wheeled up from the river, gleaming against a sky less blue than the sky of Africa, and sparrows pecked busily in the dust and preened shabby feathers.

All about were the tidy ruins of the blitz and signs of regeneration. New cottages and flats rose from the havoc created more than ten years earlier, and merry little yellow, blue and scarlet doors opened into homes already recovered from the losses and ravages of war.

To Roxane this new and fascinating environment quickly became familiar. She was enchanted by it, and by the way in which her host and his housekeeper took her presence for granted. She came and went as she pleased.

"I want you to regard this house as your background," said General Williams. "Your are not a visitor, you are at home."

Mrs. Maydew, for her part, reported favourably on the new arrival.

"You can't help taking to her," she informed her Lucy and Lucy's Ned. "No airs, but plenty of graces. The General has bought himself some fancy new shirts and ties since she came! So it only goes to show."

Ned, the policeman, agreed that that was a sign. "Like you girls when you do your hair a new way—it always means there's a new man around."

"And yesterday morning I heard him singing in his bath— singing, mind you—*him*!"

"Well I never," said Lucy, who knew the General as a quiet man whose noisiest habit was sucking on his pipe.

"She's the spitting image of her mother—the one in the picture over the study mantelpiece." Mrs. Maydew lowered her voice. "Between you and me, I often wonder what Anne Williams was to the General—a man doesn't keep a dead woman in his study for years unless she means something in his life."

"More likely under the cellar floor," agreed the policeman, and Lucy giggled.

"Hark at him," she gasped. "Always on the job!"

"Well," said Mrs. Maydew, "I draw my own conclusions."

"Just like a woman," said Ned. "Pays no attention to the evidence."

"There ain't none in this case."

"What about Miss Roxane?" said Ned. "Must be quite like having a daughter about the house!"

It was the portrait in the study that dispelled the slight constraint between Roxane and her godfather. It was as if Anne Williams looked down on them and said, "Get to know each other! You are worthwhile people, both of you."

They spoke of her often and she became a living presence, the link between them, sharing their life.

"You see, I was only four when I was parted from her," said Roxane. "So I really can't recall her at all. I've built my own picture from everything I've heard about her—and that was so little. It's a pity one can't remember back to five years old."

"Some people can."

"Well, I can't. Nor can Merle for that matter. She had a French governess when she was four or five. She can't remember her either. I've asked her."

"It varies with different people," he agreed. "And what one has been told about early events and people gets incorporated and passes for genuine recollection." He smiled. "An imagination like yours would build heavily on a very slender foundation. In that respect you are totally unlike Anne. She was fortunate in having very little imagination. Cool foresight, yes. She needed that for her work."

General Sir Christopher Williams was in appearance the traditional English Guards officer—tall and spare with a neatly clipped moustache that had once been fair. His thinning hair was almost white. His natural habit of authority and command was intensified by the expression in his light-green eyes that could at times be both remote and remorseless. He sees right through you, thought Roxane, and out the other side. You'd want those eyes *for* you, not *against* you! They were certainly "with" his god-daughter, warmly responsive to her obvious delight in being in the constant company of somebody who had known and cared for her mother.

Although the General could talk well, he was by inclination and training a listener and observer first, and, to him, silence was seldom embarrassing. He found it companionable. When he smoked his pipe in a meditative mood Roxane often curled up in the armchair opposite him with the big Russian blue purring contentedly on her lap while she read some book that would help her to learn a little more about London or France. At other times she chattered happily about her day's adventures and explorations.

General Williams was a member of the board of directors of various concerns, many of which took him out of London, and when he attended these distant meetings he always invited Roxane to accompany him for the sake of the drive.

She enjoyed these excursions, marvelling at the mellow dignity of fine old mansions standing in their deer parks, and the opulent beauty of rhododendron shrubberies covered with blooms as exotic as tropical orchids. She was enchanted by the quaint villages and little ivy-covered churches, and by cricket matches on the village green in the long soft twilights so different from the brief dusk of Africa.

The length of her stay was never discussed. It was assumed that she would be at the little house in Chelsea for Christmas, perhaps longer. But in the back of her mind she was aware that much would depend upon the news from home. If Grannie Con should need her she would have to return.

Like most distinguished widowers of a certain age the General had a few elderly lady friends who were privileged to regard him as their special charge. And they now came forward to arrange that his young guest should meet those people who could most easily help her to see the social side of the London season. Roxane accepted with enthusiasm. It was all part of this wonderful new experience.

"How do the young men about town appeal to you?" asked the General one evening as they sat in his tiny garden.

"Am I to be polite or truthful?"

"Need you ask?"

"No. Truth, of course. Well then, they don't seem quite real to me."

"Not tough enough?"

She reflected. "Not exactly that. It's just that the whole thing is superficial. There aren't enough young men to go round, and the girls do the chasing. It's upside down. The girls buy the tickets for these big charity balls—or their mothers do—and then there's a fearful scramble to find partners, so that not very attractive young men get the idea that they are wonderful."

"In fact, you find them spoilt."

She laughed. "I suppose so."

"The London season has come back into its own since our young Queen came to the throne," he said. "The impulse towards glamour is there. But money is still short. These lads in the social swim can't afford the dinners and the night-clubs and the taxis and the tips. If the girls want escorts they must foot their share of the bill. I'm old-fashioned. The whole idea is repellent to me. But it's purely a matter of economic necessity. And one must move with the times."

"We have more fun at home—in that way," she said. "When a boy and a girl are going out together they can have a gorgeous time for next to nothing—an outdoor good time. There are such lovely places for walking and swimming and mountain climbing—and there are lots of dances too that don't cost the earth."

"If a boy and a girl have interests—and attraction—in common, they can have a wonderful time anywhere, Roxane. And it needn't be expensive either. This old city is not unrewarding to those who discover its charms from the tops of buses. Gardens and parks, museums and picture galleries don't cost much to visit—and there's the river, the life of the river. Anne and I saw a lot of London together—the cheap way."

"Was that after my father died?"

He shook his head and drew on his pipe. The blue smoke wreathed upwards in the still evening air. He was staring into space with his curious light eyes as if seeking to pluck his memories from the ether and assemble them, first in the mind and then on the tongue. He was thrifty with words, seldom using two where one would serve.

"It was when your mother first came to England to learn the language. That was before she had met your father."

"My father, Uncle Chris . . . tell me a bit about him."

But he answered her shortly.

"I hardly knew him. He was a distant connection. I am sorry, Roxane. There is very little I can tell you about him—really nothing."

She had come up against this wall before—with Grannie Con—the setting of the face, the looking away. But something in her godfather's expression put her on her guard and strengthened a conviction she had already formed.

She saw the pipe gripped between his strong yellowing teeth, and she wondered, as Mrs. Maydew had done, what Anne Williams had meant to this man.

He got up and went to his desk, drawing some tickets from a pigeon-hole.

"Oh, by the way," he said, "I forgot to tell you—I've taken tickets for the première of the film *Ballerina*. I remembered that Adrian Fairmead, the writer of the book, was a near neighbour of yours in Constantia. I thought it might amuse you."

He had changed the trend of the conversation more effectively than he knew.

"How kind of you, Uncle Chris!" Suddenly her tone had become brittle. "You remember everything. I would love to see that film. Alexa Rome stayed in the Valley for a while too."

"Have you seen her dance?"

"Only on the cinema. In *Little Mermaid* and *Legend*. She is—haunting."

"She is one of the few great ballerinas of our time. She has it in her to be another Pavlova."

"You like ballet?"

"It relaxes me completely. I acquired the ballet habit during the war—during the blitzes. There was the Polish Lunch Hour Ballet in Leicester Square. I'd often go there from work and put everything else out of my mind for that hour. The eye and the ear were entranced and the brain was left free to rest. The spirit was transported to another and more harmonious sphere."

He seldom spoke of the war—of his own work in it, or her mother's—but Roxane knew that he would do so in his own time. Some instinct warned her that she must establish herself in his confidence first. Understanding was growing rapidly between them. Presently he would tell her whatever she ought to know about Anne Williams. Sometimes she thought that he must have tested his agents as he was testing her now—studying them with the object of deciding how far they could be trusted.

She glanced up at the portrait of her mother. To look into the calm amber eyes, oblique and wide-set under narrow flaring brows, was to look into a mirror. But my mother had a different expression, she thought, and a stronger mouth and chin than mine. This was a face already matured by experience of life. It was a fine portrait—rather dark and shadowed in the old Dutch style. And then, for some odd reason, Roxane's mind flew back to Dieu Donné with its sombre family portraits, to that of her "friend," Sarah de Valois, the young eighteenth-century bride with the soft dark eyes and emotional malleable lips.

General Williams was waiting for Roxane in the study, immaculate in his dinner jacket with a white carnation in his buttonhole. The mullioned window was wide open and the summer evening smelt of London and lilac—the tang and the sweetness mingling in the air. The roar of the King's Road was the background music to life here, and Roxane had grown so used to it that she woke sometimes in the quiet hours of the night to listen to the brief silence that would be dispelled by sunrise. The long English twilights were a constant pleasure to her, although she found it rather absurd to put on an evening gown in broad daylight.

Tonight she was nervous, with wheels revolving in her chest. She was bound to see the Fairmead family at the première, even though none of them would ever notice her in the crowd or even guess that she might be there; for how should her neighbours from the Valley know that she was no longer at Dieu Donné exercising their lion-dogs in company with old Wolf? The Queen Mother and Princess Margaret were to be present at the show, and the world and his wife would witness Alexa's triumph in the name part. How proud Hal would be!

Roxane possessed no furs, but a pretty shawl covered her bare shoulders and the simply cut gown, fashioned by the skilful hands of Miriam, the Malay, emphasized the delicacy of her figure and the soft well of her throat. As she came into the room the General thought that Anne's daughter seemed carved from the same alabaster as her mother. Her eyes were brilliant with excitement in which he sensed an element of apprehension. But perhaps that was his imagination.

"My dear," he said, "you look quite lovely! I shall be very proud to be seen with you."

It was Roxane's first London première and she was unprepared for the crowds surging round the big cinema at Marble Arch.

"There's nothing like a London crowd," said the General, as he paid off the taxi and guided her through the channel kept clear by the cordon of big, good-humoured policemen. "They love a little pageantry—no matter what. Or the glimpse of a film-star, and, above all, the Royal Family. They share the lives of their favourite celebrities in a vicarious, uncritical way that is peculiarly their own. They are enjoying you now! They probably take you for one of the cast of *Ballerina*."

She laughed and shivered and clung closer to his arm, aware of the sudden warmth of mass approval—the friendly smiling faces peering forward—and for the first time in her experience she had an inkling of what the adulation of a multitude must mean to a star—the stimulus more powerful than drugs or wine or the quickened glance of a lover.

In the foyer men and women in evening dress surged round a small group under the glare of the arc-lights. Photographers waited with cameras poised and ushers urged people to take their places before the arrival of royalty.

Roxane's heart stood still as she caught a glimpse of Adrian

Fairmead's grey-crested head in that blinding light, and near it Hal's, thrown back, smiling, tense, the scar on his cheek white and satin-shiny, stretched too tightly over the fine bone structure. The murderous lamps picked out the strain and accentuated it, and she thought with distress, Hal, you've grown so much older! What has happened to change you so much? And then a bell was ringing and the General was saying, "I think we should take our seats. . . ."

As Hal followed his parents and Alexa into their places in the front row of the circle, he thought, Vee and I have no part in this. Tonight belongs to Adrian Fairmead, the author of *Ballerina*, and Alexa Rome, the star. He did not think of his wife as Alexa Fairmead. She was Alexa Rome tonight, glittering star of the fabulous film firmament of Hollywood.

The flowers banked along the balcony smelled funereal, and he wrinkled his nose in distaste. A few seats away he saw the royal party—the gracious smile of the Queen Mother, and the taut glamour of Princess Margaret. Poor gifted Princess of the lovely eyes, dedicated by destiny to the lofty career of royalty—perhaps against her will. Beside him he could feel Alexa trembling. Where was her old gift of relaxation, the mastery of muscles and nerves? He had an impulse to take her hand and hold it tight, to whisper, "Don't worry, darling, there's all the first half to go—the news and the cartoon. Then the interval, and only after that the big picture—*your* picture! And then you'll see how good you are—how miraculous—and all this tension will leave you—and there'll be nothing except the old thrill of success. . . ."

But his hand did not seek hers, and it was his father who leaned towards her and said something that made her look up at him with a sudden grateful smile. Her fingers loosened in her lap and the palm of one cold hand accepted the light weight of the other as the discipline of years reasserted itself.

At last the short yet endless preliminaries were over and the story of *Ballerina* was unfolding in colour. Hal felt the woman at his side leave him while her shell remained. Ah, Lexa, how well I know that peculiar form of desertion! You are there now, on the wide screen, more real in fiction than in life. You are Olga, the

prima ballerina who falls in love with a man not of your world—
you are striving to adjust two incompatible elements to your
exacting career—love and ambition. You are Olga, the great star,
losing your man to an ordinary girl because he cannot bear to
exist like a dog upon your doorstep. You are preparing to kill
yourself in the hour of emotional defeat because you have learned
too late that success without love is dust—the dust of the grave.

But Hal found his mind refusing the climax of the story. No,
he said to himself, dry-eyed while the audience shed its surrepti-
tious tears. No—Alexa would never die for love. Ballerinas are
not made that way. They are hard as finely tempered steel, built
and trained for endurance, dedicated to their art. Ballerinas do not
die for love.

Adrian and Alexa had left their places in the circle. They had
gone with the grey, hatchet-faced director of the film to face
their audience in person. Hal moved into the empty seat beside
his mother as the storm of applause broke after the final curtain.

Now the director was introducing the star. How ethereal and
miniature she looked away down there under the spotlight in her
low-cut white gown with its full-frilled skirt—she had the dream-
look of a Degas study. Ah, here it came, the sure-fire human story:
"—to introduce our star, Alexa Rome, who—unlike the ill-fated
heroine, Olga—has successfully combined marriage, motherhood
and a career. . . ." Prolonged applause and Alexa kissing her graceful, eloquent hands to her fickle friends—her public, her fans.
The birth of Sandra had further endeared her to them. They like
their stars human. "—and very soon we hope to see Alexa on the
stage of Covent Garden——" Thunderous applause for Alexa
—calls for the author, the father-in-law of the star. Oh, yes, it was
all a very good story, and afterwards the heads would be turning in search of him—the husband. The smile of self-mockery
was on his lips, twisting them as Adrian appeared on the stage,
incredibly distinguished with his tall, spare frame and slight
limp, with that grey-crested head and the arrogant, aquiline look
of some mythical bird of ancient Egypt.

Hal felt his mother's hand, ice-cold, grasp his. He heard the
quick catch of her breath as author, director and star received a
prolonged ovation.

"Success," murmured Hal. "Triumph, Vee! That's the lifeblood of an artist—success!"

"The sort of success she needs!" He heard the bitterness hiss through her sibilant whisper. "And Adrian sharing it—loving it!" He was shocked by a sudden awareness of her jealousy.

At last the stage was empty and the Queen Mother and Princess Margaret were leaving their places. And in that moment, while the rest of the audience waited respectfully—the lights up, the haunting theme-song from *Ballerina* still playing softly—Hal saw Roxane.

She was with a fine-looking elderly man whose face was familiar to him. They had been sitting in the row immediately behind the royal party, and, as the great cinema began to clear, they reached the aisle almost simultaneously with Hal and Lavinia. He heard his mother's exclamation.

"Why, General Williams! And Roxane—of all people, Roxane! But I'd forgotten—she's your god-daughter, of course. All the same, I thought she was still in Constantia! Have you met Hal— our son? Surely you must have. . . ."

It was Lavinia at her most effusive, the charm turned on for this moment of family success—a double—Adrian and Alexa. She was expecting congratulations, and receiving them.

Hal said, "Roxane—I can't believe it—why didn't I know you were here? Why didn't you let us know?"

She did not answer him. Instead she said, "It was wonderful— wonderful! Alexa was so lovely, so heart-breaking—she made me cry——" Her voice broke a little and he knew that the tears were in her throat again.

The pleasant shock of seeing her had struck him with unexpected force. She was here—most surprisingly here—and he must not lose her. In an instant she would be gone, lost in the crowd, and he would not know where to find her. The red neon EXIT would cut her off while he went his way to the private room where a party was being given by the makers of *Ballerina* and she went hers. He hadn't even the right to invite her to this reception. Tonight was no affair of his.

He felt her next to him, pushed against him by the press of the crowd, and he could distinguish her fresh, remembered fragrance. He had a longing to tip up her chin and look closely at her, into those stream-clear eyes that could be so laughing or so tender—or sometimes apprehensive.

"You'll come and see us," he said, quick and urgent. "We're not in the telephone directory, but ring me at my paper—the *Weekly Post*. Please, Roxane—promise!"

But she did not look up or reply, and he was not even sure that she had heard him. And the next moment they were swept apart by the necessity to go their separate ways—Hal and Lavinia to the private reception in the manager's quarters, and Roxane and her godfather into the swirling current of Oxford Street, where Alexa's fans still waited—and would continue to wait—hoping for one more glimpse of the little ballerina, their own darling, the beloved of today—for Alexa Rome.

CHAPTER 17

PARIS INTERLUDE

It was the end of June.

June in Paris! Roxane could hardly believe it. She was really here with Uncle Chris in this most beautiful city which they had studied and explored together, for Uncle Chris knew Paris as well as he knew London.

Roxane was enthralled with the wide boulevards, the parks and gardens, the restaurants with little tables and chairs out on the pavements under gay canopies. You could sit there in the fresh air, sipping coffee or a glass of wine, watching the world go by and listening to the hysterical *pip-pip* of taxis and the fussy bustle of this city that, with its dignity and frivolity, was as feminine as London was sonorously male.

She loved hearing her godfather talk his impeccable French.

"No one ever answers *you* in English," she said, smiling.

They were dining in the courtyard of a little restaurant in Montparnasse where the General was clearly a well-known and honoured client.

"You must give your grandmother—Anne's mother—the credit for that," he said. "During the time I was a language student in her home I was expressly forbidden to speak one word of English! And she took great pains with my accent. She used to say that anyone with an ear for music could talk a foreign language easily. 'It's the lilt,' she'd say, 'the tune and the tempo.'"

That morning they had stood outside the old-fashioned apartment-house in Montparnasse where Maman had lived in the days when Christopher Williams had first known her. She had been fifteen then, a pretty, precocious schoolgirl studying to be a teacher.

"Although Anne's mother took in English military and naval language students, she never had more than one at a time living here *en famille*," Uncle Chris had explained. "She declared that nothing would stop two Englishmen talking their own language to each other in moments of relaxation. 'You must *think* in French!' she told us."

He had pointed out the apartment in which Maman had lived with her widowed mother and two brothers—both of whom had been in the maquis, and killed in the same raid.

"There on the third floor," he had said, "the one with the balcony. There was very little luxury in that home, Roxane, but there was happiness."

She had felt, rather than heard, his sigh. During the past few days her affection for Uncle Chris had increased greatly. They had driven down to Newhaven and crossed by car ferry to Dieppe, and from there they had toured the Normandy coast and the towns and villages in which Anne Williams had conducted her difficult, dangerous mission. They had visited the place of her execution.

The grim temporary buildings that had once housed the victims and enemies of the Nazis had been torn down, and now a herd of dairy cows grazed the rich pasturage of the hillside. Only a rough stone cross with a simple inscription commemorated those who had died in a camp the name of which still stood for torture and degradation.

As they had stood in the silvery noonday light the chimes of the Angelus had come to them from the nearby border town—a little town anxious to obliterate all memory of the tragedies that had once been enacted upon the heights above it. Uncle Chris had bared his grey head, and Roxane recalled that he, like her mother, was a Catholic. Presently she had said, "Do you mind if I take a little walk—alone?" And he had smiled at her gratefully.

So she had left him there and climbed the hill to the little wood upon its summit, for the need to be with trees was upon her just as the need for solitude had overwhelmed Christopher Williams who had sent Anne to this place to die.

As Roxane had stood among the silver birches she had found that it was less Maman she was pitying than this man who had loved her so deeply.

Gaston, the little old waiter crippled with rheumatism, hobbled over to their table. Roxane knew that he too had played a part in the *Résistance*.

"Is everything to the taste of *mon Général?*"

"The *poussins* were perfect, Gaston—as always. And now you can bring us *café-filtre* and liqueurs—a double *fine* for me, and *crême de menthe frappée* for Mademoiselle."

Gaston bowed, but Roxane saw the puzzled glance which he shot at her from under a pair of shaggy eyebrows, and she smiled to herself, guessing that he was puzzled by her resemblance to the young woman who had so often come here with this English army officer in other years.

Tonight Uncle Chris was in an expansive mood. Being in Anne's own city and revisiting her home had brought her very near. The tide of memories had begun to flow. He was able to talk about her with new ease and freedom. The dykes of silence were breached and the spirit of the past flowed back over the empty spaces of his heart and he was Anne's once more.

"Your grandmother died when Anne was about twenty," he said. "She came to London then to learn English and to teach

French. By that time I had married, but my wife and I did all that we could to help her. Then one day she had an offer to go to South Africa as governess to a child out there, and she jumped at it. She always welcomed a new adventure. . . ."

But, watching him, Roxane wondered if Anne had not perhaps taken the South African opportunity in order to escape an entanglement with a married man. A flash of pain shot through her. She knew the pangs of forbidden love . . . and Maman had been a Catholic. If she had loved Christopher Williams there could have been no way out for either of them. . . .

Suddenly he grinned at Roxane. "And let me warn you, my dear, that it's no good asking me about her time in South Africa! I wasn't there. All I can tell you is that she came back within the year. Even with those one knows best there are the waste spaces —the gaps in our knowledge of each other. Respect them, Roxane. Never try to invade the life of another too deeply. If the war hadn't happened your mother would no doubt have continued to teach at the convent in South Kensington where she was much loved by the nuns and her pupils—but it did come. . . ."

He began to talk of Anne's work as a secret agent—its risks, its periods of boredom, its dreadful isolation.

"Anne could stand these things. She was by nature reserved— even secretive—and in spite of her beauty she could make herself inconspicuous. She had temperament rather than imagination. Too much imagination in her job would have been fatal. She was never a woman who thought with her heart—as you do, Roxane, and don't deny it!—she thought with her clear cool brain. Even where her heart was most closely concerned she took her decisions with her head."

He paused. His curious light eyes seemed fixed on some distant scene, and Roxane had the feeling that he was looking back into the past, into Anne's most personal motives for her actions as a woman rather than as an agent.

"When the war came—and she undertook the mission that she knew very well might end as it did—she decided that you must go to old Mrs. de Valois at Dieu Donné. She had known the old lady during her time in South Africa, and she admired your Grannie Con tremendously. To part with you nearly broke her heart, but she believed that she was doing the right thing to send you into safety—to the care of one who would love you. And, as I have said, she was a woman who would trample her own emotions in the dust for the sake of her convictions."

The General held his cognac to the light. It was clear, rich gold, the colour of Anne's eyes, or Roxane's. He was saddened that there was no way, save in words, that he could give this girl back the remarkable mother fate had seen fit to take from her. And words were so inadequate. He shook his head in a gesture of frustration.

Roxane's fingers played with the straw in her *crème de menthe frappée*. How pretty the green liquid was in its bed of crushed ice! If only she could make herself take courage and ask Uncle Chris what she wanted so much to know!

Darkness had fallen and a string of fairy-lights lit the court-yard. A street lamp shone garishly over the wall and its beam was reflected in the pewter pot of *café-filtre* which stood between them on the table with its gay checked cloth. The powdery black coffee steamed in the small cups, rich and aromatic.

At last she said, "Uncle Chris—how did my mother come to take the name of Williams?"

He held the fragile bowl of his brandy glass between his palms, warming it. A thin spiral of smoke rose from his cigarette resting in the ash tray. Moments passed with her question unanswered. But she did not let it go at that.

"My mother was never married," she persisted. "There was no John Williams. I think I have known that for a long time, deep down. It was *your* name she took."

"A trick of interrogation," he said. "To assume the facts." His smile was crooked, conceding her point. "Very well, then, let us admit that there was no John Williams. Your mother took my name, not in marriage, alas, but legally. It gave me a sort of right to protect her—the privilege of a pretended relationship."

"She was no more Williams than I am de Valois——"

He did not seem to hear her. He was following some train of thought of his own. "When the war came it was I who made the arrangements for you to go to South Africa. Anne knew old Mrs. de Valois, and when she sent you into her care she sent a letter with you to explain certain things. That letter is to be shown to you when you come of age."

"Do you know its contents?"

She had the curious feeling that she was no longer herself. She was "in a play." It was the sense of dual personality, of being observed and observer at one and the same time, which so often overwhelmed her in moments of emotional strain and exhaustion. But now there was no exhaustion, there was only intense excitement. The girl under observation was on the brink of vital information. The observer held her breath.

"Yes," he said slowly. "I know its contents. But you must be content to wait. You must learn the facts from her in her own way, and at the time appointed by her."

The words seemed to cost him an effort, and it was clear that whatever memories they evoked were painful to him. He turned away from Roxane and crushed out the stub of the cigarette he had not bothered to smoke. He went on:

"You know my wife was in a mental home for many years before she died. If I had been free Anne and I would have married. When my freedom came it was too late."

He summoned the little old waiter and paid the bill.

"It is strange, *mon Général*," said the little bent man in his quick slurred French. "After all these years you bring Madame back here—but she is still young—immortal, while the rest of us fall victim to the years. . . ."

General Williams said, "No, Gaston—even Madame could not have stopped the clock."

The waiter's wizened features cleared and his smile broke.

"But yes, the new generations take our place—your daughter ——"

"My god-daughter, Gaston. Tomorrow we return to England, but we will come back one day and you shall give us your delicious *poussins* again."

"Do not leave it too late. Unhappily the time of my retirement is near. One aged—during the Occupation." His bowed shoulders shrugged away the period of hardship and humiliation, the handful of years that had measured eternity to the brave.

"He is a great little fellow, that one," said the General as they walked to the car. "He was one of our most reliable contacts during the Occupation."

The matter-of-fact tone of his voice—its finality—had the quality of the old waiter's shrug. He too had put away certain memories. He had closed the door on the past, and Roxane knew that Uncle Chris had told her all he intended her to know for the present.

During the next few days they journeyed through the beautiful wine-growing valleys of the Loire and the Rhône, and seeing the emerald vineyards glowing in the sun, Roxane found her heart turning towards Dieu Donné. For the time being she asked no more questions about Maman. Instead she chattered of the Constantia Valley and of her own childhood on the lovely estate founded by a Huguenot wine-grower exiled from his native France in an era of religious persecution.

Before they returned to England her godfather told her what he proposed to do for her on her twenty-first birthday.

"I shall send you a cheque for a thousand pounds. Do what you like with it. There will be no strings attached."

It was August, the "silly season," when fashionable London migrates to France and Spain or the lakes of Italy and Austria, while the proletariat flocks to Brighton and Blackpool.

Mrs. Maydew was away on her annual fortnight's holiday and her daughter Lucy was "giving a hand" in her place.

"My Lucy can't do full time," Mrs. Maydew explained to Roxane. "Her Ned wouldn't stand for that—especially now she's expecting so soon, but she'll do the cleaning and prepare the vegetables and that, and I s'pose you won't mind doing the shopping and a little bit of cooking for the General's supper of an evening."

"I'll do my best. I'll enjoy it."

"Lucky it's now and not a few months back! My Lucy couldn't have managed the breakfasts then. She had her morning sickness something shocking. But there now, it'll be worth it when the baby comes. In our family babies is kings and queens, we're all mad on them."

Roxane did, in fact, enjoy the freedom of the kitchen and the responsibility of the market-basket. The King's Road was a constant source of interest and delight to her, from the junk-shops piled high with old furniture and miscellaneous odds and ends to the Chelsea pensioners hobbling along in the sun, very proud and smart in their scarlet coats.

But today she had one of her moods of being in a vacuum. The General had gone to Liverpool for a board meeting and would not be back till late tonight; Lucy had swayed off down the little side-street with the vulnerable majesty of her condition, and Roxane had watched her from the window of her bedroom and wondered about that other world to which the young woman would presently return—the constricted world of her own home where the neighbours lived on your doorstep and the children spilled over onto the pavements and into the gutters, independent and scruffily perky as sparrows. That was one of the charms of Chelsea—the very way in which quaint alleys, huge blocks of luxury flats and hugher tenements all impinged one upon the other. There was no fashionable quarter. The same streets and the same shops served the inhabitants of exclusive mansions and inclusive dwellings.

Roxane heard the postman whistling a popular tune as he dropped the mail into the letter-box, followed by the curt snap of the brass flap. Why were English postmen and milkmen always so good-tempered? And policemen too. It must be occupational. She ran down the little staircase. Letters from home perhaps? Let there be letters from home!

Yes, three of them. Oh, good! Suddenly the day was worth while—a singing day, dusted with gold. Although there was nobody else in the house she chose the privacy of her own bedroom in which to open her precious mail. She sat on the wide oak sill of the mullioned casement with the afternoon sun catching her bowed head in a mesh of violet and primrose light. There was a fat airmail letter from Grannie Con, and one from Thinus, and a letter-card from Merle. She would read Grannie Con's first.

Down in the garden she could see the big grey plush cat sniffing fastidiously at the herbaceous border under the sunny wall, flickering his delicate whiskers against delphiniums and dahlias, and she was seized with an almost unbearable longing for Wolf—

to touch his rough harsh coat and grip his sharp ears and rock his head as Thinus did. A late lilac-tree, heavy with dark flowers, nodded at the open window, and the home-going roar of the King's Road rose and fell. Where the sun caught the bunches of lilac they glowed with the dusky burning splendour of Flaming Tokay grapes, and the voice of the city held the thunder of the oceans beating on the rocky surf-bound shores of the Peninsula.

Of late the Valley had receded into the far distance of Roxane's thoughts, for she had thrown herself into the quest for Anne with all her ardent nature. But she knew that it only waited to possess her the more completely on her return. For a brief spell she had escaped from her personal problems into the shadow-world of her maman's past, but the hour of her own decisions could not be long postponed.

She spread out the thin blue sheets covered with Grannie Con's angular hand, and instantly the written word conjured up its pictures. Grannie Con in her wheel-chair in the wintry garden; rain lashing the bare trees and finding out new leaks in the thatch and new knots of rheumatism in the old lady's gnarled, mittened hands; a roaring fire in the library grate and Thinus sitting on the low *bankie* in front of it reading the sports news in the evening paper while Grannie Con, stiffly seated in her high-backed chair, worked at her shocking crochet lace. Joshua, grizzled and bland, coming in with the coffee-tray. . . . But wait, Joshua and Lizzie were troubled about Ben:

> . . . and we suspect that he is smoking dagga. At times he is dull and stupid as an animal, and often now he disappears for days together. I make allowances because of his deafness—but Joshua gets angry with him and we know there have been fights. Once Joshua found him carrying one of those bicycle-chains, the sort of thing skollies use. Thinus is concerned too. Thinus is very quiet these days. We both miss your chatter, and the life you used to bring into this old house, but don't cut your holiday short to come home. We can manage. Amanda Brink doesn't handle the books too badly, and she is glad of the work. Still no sign of any grandchildren for me. I don't believe Merle is trying! She talks a great deal of a trip to Europe—specially Italy.

I fancy your going has stimulated her wish for travel—and naturally babies interfere with that sort of thing. And talking of unwanted babies, I hear that Lavinia Fairmead is bringing the infant back to Farway—it seems there is no room for a child in the life of a ballerina and a travelling journalist.

Roxane smiled and sighed. She liked the caustic touch—the bite. She could hear the old rusty voice snip-snap, snip-snap.

Louise Krifti brought me the news. It is quiet and sad in the valley without Auntie Marthe—like a summer without a south-easter. All wrong somehow. And now Mr. Krifti has his knife into Auntie Marthe's estate. Buying from the heirs, cutting up. Horrible.

Roxane put down Grannie Con's letter and slit open the air-letter-card from Merle.

Guy has various important prospects ahead—one or two really big jobs—and we want to go overseas for a holiday before he takes them on. But it is difficult to leave Dieu Donné at present. Grannie Con took Auntie Marthe's death very much to heart. I dare say it frightened her, made her realize that she can't go on for ever herself. She has gone downhill since your departure. Isn't it time you stopped kicking your heels and came back or has your benevolent godparent decided to keep you permanently at his side and leave you his fortune when he dies?

Time she went back? Ever since she had heard the news of old Auntie Marthe's sudden death from a stroke she had wondered if she ought not to return. She had guessed what it must mean to Grannie Con—in personal loss and, as Merle suggested, apprehension.

"Thinus comes round to a meal with us sometimes," Merle continued. "That little slut who looks after him—Lizzie's niece Saartjie—is rehearsing again for one of those Coloured Group shows and neglects her kitchen outrageously. Why he puts up with her I can't imagine. Lavinia Fairmead has asked Aletta Krige to look out for an extra maid for her—someone used to babies—as she is bringing the new grandchild home with her. Silly of

Alexa to get caught. How can someone like *her* cope with a family. . . ."

So there was no room in Alexa's life for Hal's baby—or even in Hal's. Poor little thing, it might as well be an orphan, as she was herself. Still, it wouldn't be bad to be brought up at Farway—the next best thing to Dieu Donné.

Roxane held Thinus's letter in her hands for a few moments before opening it. Until these past weeks she had never received a letter from him, and it was curious and pleasing how simply his personality emerged—solid and sound—through time and space. Even his sturdy upright script seemed to bring his presence into the room. As she looked at it she saw the brown, powerful neck rising in a brief column from the open khaki shirt, the fine golden hairs dusted over his bare muscular forearms, the thick light lashes, dark at the roots, and the bright tangled eyebrows—one eye clear brilliant blue, the other shut away by the black shield—a window with the blind drawn. She closed her own eyes and tried to feel his dry, wiry, hay-smelling hair under her hand and the ridge above the thin elastic band. She listened for the echo of his voice—slow and deep with its Afrikaans intonation—and the laugh that was suddenly rather high. And then the intruder voice cut through the thin fabric of her dream—the warm velvet with its note of mockery—the voice of Hal teasing her peace of mind. She brushed her hand across her eyes and tore the letter open.

"Roxie darling, my little squirrel, what are you up to and when are you coming back?" Then scraps of news about the farm, about Auntie Marthe's estate and Guy's interest in it. "They say Krifti will persuade Louise to break up her portion of the property. When it comes to business matters she leaves everything to him and she has none of our real deep love of the Valley for what it is and how it looks. Of course that will mean more work for Guy. Krifti puts all he can Guy's way. Grannie Con has not been very well. She forgets things a good deal these days and worries about it. She misses you, so do we all. Wolf and I take walks and rides together. He is lonely and so am I. Come back soon. The storms have been extra bad this winter with landslides round Cape

Point, and talking of Cape Point the baboons are becoming a real menace to visitors to the Nature Reserve. Manhaar, the old Sentinel, got hold of a six-year-old boy and gave him such a shake-up that there is talk of shooting the fierce old fellow. They may even do away with the whole troop. So if you want to see those ugly old baboons again you had better hurry home!"

He said nothing about Lavinia Fairmead or Alex's baby, nor did he ask if she had seen the Fairmeads in London. Yet he must wonder. Perhaps he had the instinctive wisdom to know that certain human relationships could not be discussed at a distance. Words, without the look in the eye or the tone of the voice to modify or deepen their meaning, could part when they were intended to unite. The mood of writer and reader were divorced by time and space, and understanding was not easily achieved under such conditions. So Thinus let the delicate matters bide their time and contented himself with writing of everyday things —of Dieu Donné and its people and all that was loved and familiar.

And if I marry him, what then? said Roxane to the lilac tree with its bunches of Flaming Tokay grapes.

First the manager's cottage at Dieu Donné. Then, when Oom Jacob dies, a home on Thinus's share of Tweefontein. She pressed the backs of her hands against her lids and there was the picture! A single-storied house in the tawny veld. A stoep and a galvanized-iron roof—the heat shimmering off it or hailstones drumming on it. Clear crisp days too with frost on the grass melting in the brilliant winter sun. An avenue of dusty blue-gums, willows round the dam, cattle drinking at its fringe and wild duck flying over the water at sunset. Wide farmlands and a far horizon, horses, dogs, children with tow-coloured hair—for the fair Vos strain was vigorous—the iron clank of a windmill, and the wind blowing across the empty veld, piling up the fine red dust before it, shaking it into the house like paprika shaken into a Malay curry-pot. At night the children asleep in their nursery and she and Thinus alone with the radio to keep them company—news of the stock market, and the prices of maize and farm produce, and sport—of course sport, especially rugger. Thinus, like most South

Africans, was mad about rugger. Knitting lying on her lap—something useful, a pull-over for Thinus or a jersey for one of the
children—and her thoughts far away as she watched him roll the
inevitable cigarette with his mutilated left hand, or stoop to pat
the dog—probably an Alsatian from de Beers, like Wolf—who
would be spread in front of the fire, twitching and dreaming,
hunting in his sleep.

The backs of her fingers pressed harder against her lids, making
a mottled night behind them. So then they would go to bed, with
love reduced to routine. For him the deep, instant sleep of the
farmer—the man who has been out in the lands all day—snoring
maybe. Did Thinus snore? How little she knew him—she who
knew him so well! Or perhaps he would invite the "submission"
of his wife. Absurd word with its Victorian suggestion of
prudery. Then what? Would she, in the dark, make believe that
her lover was another—subtle and tender? But no, the lips of
Thinus could be hard and fierce. . . . If she took Thinus for her
husband and her mate, it was Thinus she must take and desire and
love. No other. He was not a man to share her with a ghost.

She found herself wondering what course her mother would
have followed in the same circumstances. What would *you* do in
my place, Maman? You who went your own brave, dangerous
way to the hillside where torture and death came to meet you.
Would you marry your dear friend—compelled by his devotion
and the strength of his will and your own heart hungry for a
home and children—and security? You never sought security, did
you, Maman? You were never afraid of the future—never really
afraid of anything. I know now that you took your lover and
bore his child. I know too that there was nothing light about your
loving—you were not that sort of person. But what lover? Is
Uncle Chris my father? Do we really belong as closely as I sometimes feel we do? Or was there some other man in your life—
someone with a terrible escape-me-never magnetism for you? If
there was, you'll understand your daughter—wanting one man,
loved by another and loving him too but without the flame—the
awful wonderful flame. . . .

Tell me! she begged deep down inside herself. Tell me what
you would have done! She waited in a void of stillness for the

answer—but when it came, it came from the small painful injury in her own heart. The mad foolish longing for Hal was a splinter that had never been totally withdrawn, that festered still and would do so till the last thin sliver of futile desire was eradicated.

She woke as from a dream and saw Thinus's letter lying on the window-sill with Grannie Con's and Merle's.

She folded them and put them away in the little bureau. As she closed the drawer, she thought, I'm a fool—the thing I mean to do is crazy—better left—but I'll do it just the same!

The light had shifted and the room was no longer bright with sunshine. Roxane looked at her watch. Past six o'clock. He would never be there at this hour—or maybe he was abroad on some assignment. It was perfectly safe to ring him up. Fate would look after her. Someone would answer the call and say:

"Mr. Hal Fairmead? Sorry, he's away—won't be back for months. . . ."

But excitement mounted in her as she went downstairs to the little hall where the telephone stood in its dark corner.

She took the directory to the light, and looked up the *Weekly Post*.

She began to dial the number.

CHAPTER 18

TEMPORARY SECRETARY

She was afraid that he might hear her quickened breathing over the telephone and guess the nervous excitement that for a paralysing moment had almost compelled her to hang up the receiver before his extension had time to reply. Then there was his voice —and the dead sound of it hooded her emotions. Her heart stopped racing and she sounded perfectly calm as she said:

"You asked me to call you up. But there's something wrong. What is it?"

Nothing is so revealing to the sympathetic ear as a familiar voice over the wire, caught off guard. It is naked, unclothed by the artifice of look and gesture. Weariness, sickness, a smile, a subterfuge, a mood of exaltation or depression are transmitted instantly by the disembodied note coming blind across the miles.

Hal said, "Just self-pity, my sweet Roxane." But the echo of humour was only a glimmer of sun through the mist. "The little world of Hallam Fairmead has gone from under his feet. Disintegrated entirely. All in the past few hours."

"Can you tell me?"

"Certainly. It isn't even drama! It's the ordinary course of events for people who live as we do—Alexa and I."

Her mouth went dry and a shiver passed icily over the nerves of her entire body. Had they split up? Could it be finished between Hal and Alexa?

"What are you trying to say?"

"Simply that my wife has just set off by air on her Australian tour. And my parents have timed things wonderfully by sailing for South Africa yesterday with my infant daughter and her Nannie. So there seemed no point in going home—no home to go to anyway, because we've let our house and I'm in a service bachelor-flat till the family is reassembled. That's why you find me here—working."

"Hal! How wretched for you—how desolate!"

"Desolate is the word. Where are you speaking from?"

"From Uncle Chris's house—General Williams. He's my godfather and I'm staying with him—here in Chelsea."

"But I rang you at his number—twice. And there was no answer——"

"We were away for a fortnight—touring in France—and I guess Mrs. Maydew, the housekeeper, must have been out when you called up."

"I meant to try again—tonight. You must have received waves of telepathy that drove you to phone! Are you doing anything special? Can you come out with me—this evening?"

"Uncle Chris is away and I'm alone. I'd love to go out with you."

"Then join me now—right here in the office. We'll have a bite somewhere——"

"How do I get to Fleet Street? Not a taxi. I haven't enough money for taxis, and anyway I like London buses."

"Are you near the King's Road?"

"A stone's throw."

"Then take the Number Eleven bus and ask the conductor to put you down near Shoe Lane. Turn up it—it's narrow, right on the corner of the black glass *Daily Express* building. We're on the fourth doorway on your left, a tall block, and my office is on the top floor. You'll see *Weekly Post* lettered on the façade."

"Must I dress up?"

"Heaven forbid! Come as you are."

She chuckled. "That's rash!" Her happiness danced along the line, striking tiny sparks, infecting his reply with new life.

"I don't care what you're wearing or how you look. I only know I'm dying to see you."

She put down the receiver with the colour high in her cheeks. Nothing mattered. Foolishness and joy were one and the same. A little madness seized her as she ran upstairs to change into a fresh summer print. No hat, no gloves or stockings. London in the August heat was as informal as the Cape Peninsula. At this season the parks and gardens were full of young people strolling under the trees—those magnificent spreading English trees—sprawling on the lawns, bathing in the Serpentine, or rowing on its silver surface between the willows, watched indifferently by the beady eyes of Peter Pan's water-fowl. That was the London life she enjoyed most.

She put out a saucer of milk for the cat and locked the little house. It was nearly seven o'clock when she climbed onto the top of the big red bus.

London was very beautiful in her eyes—more intimate than Paris. London belonged to its own people, while Paris flirted with the world. Paris was all things to all men. London was itself.

She saw with a pang that the leaves were yellowing in the shady squares and crescents and that the gay little window-boxes of Whitehall were straggly and untidy. In Trafalgar Square the pigeons whirled and planed round Nelson's Column. Only they knew the features of the great little sailor high up there looking towards the fine span of Admiralty Arch. Nelson, blind in one eye like Thinus—and not only two fingers missing but an arm— was the very symbol of this island race. At his feet the stone lions crouched, proud and protective. She wondered how snow-flakes looked when winter came and the great Norwegian Christmas tree of which she had heard stood here in the Square with its fairy-lights and the fountains playing and everything floodlit, and maybe, against the night sky, the soft feathering of falling snow. She didn't want to go back to the Valley yet. She wanted to wait for all the seasons here. But the voices of the Valley were calling, appealing to her, and she was torn two ways.

The big red bus thundered along the Strand, past the Temple and the Inns of Court, honey-coloured and darkly smudged like the coats of Siamese cats, and presently the newspaper cliffs of Fleet Street drew in on them, and the bus conductor clumped up his little stair and called to her, "Here you are, miss! Shoe Lane on your left."

She turned up the narrow lane past the black glass palace of the *Daily Express* and climbed a little way up the hill, widened and lightened higher up by the forgotten ravages of the blitz, by days and nights of menace as dead as those they had buried, as dead as yesterday's news.

She looked up at a tall narrow building and saw the words "WEEKLY POST" across its constricted façade. She paused in the doorway, half afraid, with a tightening at her throat and a wild fluttering inside her—not butterflies in the tummy, but birds, all the pigeons in Trafalgar Square! Across the road she could hear the mutter of the presses—the roll of drums heralding tomorrow's headlines. She could smell the monster bales of newsprint. But, even as she sniffed the air and listened to the life-blood of a city surging down the main artery of Fleet Street, she was aware of the feverish pulses pounding in her own ears.

A young man with a bulky manuscript under his arm brushed past her with a muffled apology. Ten minutes ago he too had paused, quaking on this same threshold, and he would quake on many others and pass out again with the sick taste of disappointment in his mouth, for he was not a young man destined to realize his high hopes of literary achievement.

Roxane patted at her hair and took a quick reassuring glance at the little mirror in her powder-compact, and then an offhand lift-boy whisked her up to the top floor.

"Mr. Fairmead, miss? You'll find his office at the end of the passage."

She heard his chair scrape back as she knocked on the door and opened it, and then he was across the room and holding both her hands.

He was in his shirt-sleeves and she had a quick impression of a thin grey shirt and grey sunken eyes and a tense, lean look about him. The scar on his cheek leapt at her, taut and gleaming white against his tan, and she thought that his face had shrunk round it, but the quality of his smile and the sudden brightening of his eyes made her catch her breath.

"Roxane! Am I glad to see you!"

"Me too——" The little break was in her voice. How well he remembered it! He wanted to take her in his arms and bury his face in her hair; he wanted her warmth and companionship, repite from the empty, aching loneliness and a sense of failure as heavy as the dead weight of a ton of newsprint. Instead he dropped her hand and said:

"Sit down for a moment while I clean up some of this mess. Then we'll be off."

"Finish what you're doing," she said. "I'll look at London."

Her knees were shaking as she went over to the window. Eastward she could see the dome of St. Paul's gleaming in the evening light; and to the west a vista of chimney-pots sloped down towards the Strand and the river. Birds eddied round them—pigeons, sparrows, even gulls. There, with her back to him, she collected herself. She heard him say:

"I'm sorry to be slow. I'm really a bit lost. My secretary is on holiday—everybody is on holiday in August—and her stand-in went to hospital yesterday with an acute appendix. In fact everything seems to have happened to me at the same time."

"Can I help? I'm quite a useful secretary myself. Your father would give me a reference."

He looked into her laughing eyes. "By heaven, you've got something there! Could you take the job for three weeks?"

Red lights of danger flashed along her nerves, but she said, "Why not?"

"Starting from tomorrow?"

"Starting from now if you like."

"You're a great girl, Roxane. I have a theory. There are two sorts of people in the world. The ones who make difficulties and the others who smooth difficulties away. You're a smoother, bless you!"

She moved over to his desk and stood beside his chair.

"Well, then——?"

"No—not now. We are going out now. There's a little place by the river where we can have dinner—just right for a hot night. It's about half an hour's drive from here. All right?"

"Lovely."

"Then I'll get my coat on and have a wash and brush up."

Green banks and lawns sloped down to the river from the little Tudor inn. A cottage garden flowered in the long twilight and neither Hal nor Roxane found anything to criticize in its ragged *fin de saison* air. Chestnut trees held up their great branches to the last pink and creamy light, a copper beech glowed like dark wine, and the green leaves of the beeches showed the first touch of gold and amber.

They could hear the *plop* of a fish rising and see the thin mist of flies over the water. Voices rose softly from rowing-boats or punts—sometimes a giggle; trills of bird-song trembled in the foliage at the river's edge.

"Our birds don't sing like yours," said Roxane. "It's no good pretending they do. They call and whistle and some of them trill, and they say things—usually in Afrikaans—like *'Piet m'vrou'* or *'Werk stadig, werk stadig.'* The Cape doves say that all day, *'Werk staaaa-dig—work slowly'*—as if anyone in Africa ever worked at any other pace!"

He grinned and caught her hand and squeezed it. "It's fun to have you here—a breath of your lovely Valley."

She withdrew her hand, smiling. "And your trees," she went on. "We think the world of our oaks and silvers and proteas,

but look at your chestnuts! And rhododendrons like orchids—
azaleas like butterflies——"

"Wait till the autumn and I'll drive you through the Chiltern
beechwoods. They'll be turning colour—at their best when I
get back from my next assignment."

I'll be gone in the autumn, she thought. But she said, "Where
is your next assignment?"

One eyebrow rose, and laughter brightened his eyes.

"Three weeks or perhaps a month from now I'm going to the
West Indies to examine that end of the—well, shall we call it
the Coloured Invasion of Great Britain?"

"Coloured Invasion?" She laughed. "You mean all the black
people in London? They make me feel quite at home!"

"They are not only in London. You will see them in all our
industrial areas. Thousands are getting jobs—other are not. If
they are not they are on the dole—and the taxpayer is beginning
to get sore about it. They come from the Caribbean mostly, but
there are a great number of Africans in this little island too."

"Your own people go and settle in the sun and get away from
their taxes, and the black people come here! That's quite a
thought, Hal. You'll be having a colour problem one of these
days."

"We have it already," he said. "There's a feeling growing in
industry that it isn't fair to engage a black man if a white man
is available, and that when there's a slump the blacks must be
the first to be thrown out—and the white men don't like having
black supervisors. Recognize the symptoms?"

His amusement was reflected in her eyes as she answered.

"The symptoms of a mild case of Colour Bar."

"And the very people who shout loudest against the Colour Bar
of your country are the ones who'd now like to see it applied
in our industries. But that's how it goes. The people who have
all the answers to everybody else's colour problems are those
with none of their own."

She said, "What I don't understand is how this island can support all these—new settlers, if that's what they really are. Surely
you have immigration laws to look after that sort of thing?"

"England is still the old mother hen, dear Roxane. Until our laws are changed the people of her dominions or dependencies have as much right here as her own citizens. The Welfare State —subscribed by English taxpayers—is their fairy godmother. And old Jamaican Joe has got wise to that in a big way. He'll earn twice as much here for half the work he'd do at home— and when he's out of a job he'll be paid to do nothing. No wonder there are so many pilgrims to the Old Country!"

"I think it may come rather hard on your own people," she suggested.

"Our own people are beginning to think so too," he agreed. "That's what makes the story. That's why my paper is sending me to the Caribbean. I shall find some picturesque character and trace his adventures from the sugar plantations or dockyards of his own country to his rise to fame in the factories of ours."

"Poor fellow," she said. "I believe I pity him!"

They had strolled down to the river and they stood looking along the quiet reach between its leafy banks.

"Hal," she said, "do you really like all this travelling? Going here, there and everywhere in search of news stories?"

"It's good training," he said, evading a direct answer. "It's all experience of life and people and places, and of writing about them and picking out the old familiar human dramas against new, constantly changing, backgrounds and conditions. You see, one day I want to settle down and really write—be a novelist. I want to own land—be a farmer as well. My mother's family were all landowners, and the love of it is in me. But not yet. I haven't *lived* enough. If a person is to write well, they must *live* first——"

"Live? You haven't lived enough? You, who wrote *Jungle Journal*, and those remarkable—those successful satirical *Californian Diaries*! You've been a soldier and a journalist, you've wandered all over the world for *Weekly Post* and you've published books that everybody reads. You have a name and a reputation. How can you say you haven't lived enough?" She broke off and bit her lip. "And . . . and . . ." she began—and stopped.

"And——?" he prompted. "And *what*, Roxane?"

Her words came in a rush. "If being married to one of the world's greatest ballerinas isn't experience of living, what is?"

His mouth was cynical, and suddenly he had a strong look of Adrian as he answered her.

"They say every young author writes his first novel about himself—an unacknowledged soul-searching autobiography. I don't propose to do that. I have no wish to dissect my soul or my marriage in print. If there are special problems involved in marrying a stage or screen star some other brave fool is welcome to exploit them on paper. What I have learned of life through marriage will have to find its way into my work indirectly—and later, much, much later, when I have learned a great deal more about life."

He took her arm and turned her away from the river towards the lighted inn.

"I'm hungry," he said. "Are you?"

The bitterness in his voice distressed her, and she was glad when they were sitting at their table in the raftered dining-room. She looked round her, absorbing the atmosphere of the old coaching inn. Black beams, uneven boarded floors, a great open hearth enhanced by the pink glow of copper and blue gleam of pewter—comfort, homeliness, and a sense of history and days gone by. These things were the curtain against which she saw Hal—this new, tense Hal with nerves too near the surface.

An English waiter with a slow country accent served them without subservience, and with less attention to what he put before them than the latest cricket scores which he discussed earnestly with Hal. So different from old Gaston of the Montparnasse restaurant where she had dined with Uncle Chris! She told Hal about Gaston and her journey with her godfather, and they talked about Anne and her work. And after a time, through Hal's remarks, Roxane began to realize how considerable had been the influence of her godfather on the outcome of the war.

"Sir Christopher Williams has a terrific reputation," he said. "When he took over the Secret Service during the war he accomplished miracles. Our paper approached him only the other day to give us his memoirs, but he swears he has never written them."

"He hasn't," she said. "He declares that he can't put the worthwhile things on paper for obvious reasons, and the rest can be done just as well, if not better, by anybody else."

"He is supposed to be rather a forbidding character."

She smiled. "Only till you get to know him. I was shy of him at first. I'm not any more. He doen't talk unless he has something to say. I dare say his job has got him into the habit of holding his tongue."

"More likely his habit of holding his tongue got him into his job! But not everybody has the knack of what is called small talk, Roxane. I'm not too good at it myself."

"Yet he isn't really too strong and silent." She puckered her forehead as she thought about him—the amount of time he had given her, his efforts to interest her. "He is frightfully keen on history and things like that. He makes it come alive when he explains it in its own setting. I was fascinated when he took me to the Tower and Greenwich Palace, and Hampton Court, and the Abbey. Oh, Hal, Westminster Abbey! I could spend weeks there learning the story of England. It's all there—the warriors and poets, the kings and queens——"

He grinned. "And bits of Scottish history too."

She laughed. "The Stone of Scone—all nicely back where it belongs. Oh, and naturally we went to St. Paul's, and I firmly believe that Nelson's spirit kept it safe in the air raids. Uncle Chris drove me down to Portsmouth too, to see the old *Victory* . . . there's so much to see and do—and my time is flying by so fast. . . ."

"When are you going back?"

"I was hoping to stay till Christmas, but there isn't a chance. I can tell by the letters from home that I'm needed at Dieu Donné. A few more weeks perhaps. . . ."

It was nearly midnight when Hal stopped the car outside the little house in Chelsea. A light was burning in the study.

"Uncle Chris is back," she said. "Will you come in?"

"Yes," he said. "Just to make sure that it *is* your Uncle Chris. We've been taken in by lights in empty houses before. Remember?"

"Johannesburg—the night you were stabbed."

"Well then, I'll come in just for a minute, Roxane. But this is really goodnight between you and me. . . ."

Loneliness engulfed him as he thought of the impersonal temporary flat in Whitehall to which he must return, and suddenly he was aware of her stillness beside him, as if she had frozen into immobility like a bird or an animal in the presence of danger. But she neither responded nor protested when he drew her into his arms and kissed her lips.

"Don't worry, darling," he whispered. "That's all for now—just one little kiss. Thank you for coming out with me. I'm glad you're here—so glad to have seen you this evening, and gladder still that I will see you tomorrow—and every day until I go. . . ."

At no time did General Williams comment upon Roxane's preoccupation with her temporary job as Hal Fairmead's secretary. Nor did he dissuade her from booking her passage for South Africa when she explained that she felt it her duty to return.

"I'm sorry, my dear," he said. "I have grown accustomed to the spirit of youth flitting about this bachelor house of mine, and it won't be easy to fall into the old dull ways. But so long as you look upon this place as your second home I shall be satisfied."

"I do, I do!" She flung her arms impulsively round his neck and hugged him. For a moment he held her close, sick with the old nostalgia for the springtime of a love that had ended in tragedy.

The General saw little of his god-daughter in the next three weeks and he may have guessed that her second-class reservation on the mailboat was her amulet against some peril at which he could only guess. Sometimes Hal came to the little house in Chelsea where the white stone cat stalked the white stone pigeon on the porch with never a move from one or a flutter from the other, and the older man observed that the young journalist seldom spoke uninvited of his famous wife, but that the infant in her grandmother's care at Farway was much in his thoughts. He noticed the new tempo in the rhythm of Roxane's demeanour, the happy lilt of her voice, the swing of her slender hips and the sparkle in her eyes. And he found it oddly disturbing that Alexa Rome's husband should have, in baby Sandra, so precious a hostage in the Valley of the Vines. These two—Roxane and this young man—are going to hurt one another, he thought, and was pierced by the thin stiletto of jealousy. Nothing he could do about it—to each his or her own wounds and scars of love. Roxane knew that Hal was married—and married to a woman of rare quality marked with the shining brand of genius—so what warning could he give her? Put a curb on your heart, my little one, for you lack the fierce independence of that other, the lonely integrity that could face the consequences of her acts, whether those consequences were life or death. . . .

To Roxane it was strange and delightful how close and easy the intimacy between Hal and herself had become in spite of their many unspoken reservations.

August was the slack month and Hal had acquired the habit of taking time off to explore London with Roxane. Just as she had been his guide in the beautiful Cape Peninsula, so now he was hers in this great city. It was to her the shell in which the soft vulnerable body of her love grew and ripened.

They went to the markets and docks and down the river by excursion steamer, and from Hal she learned about the ancient craftsmen's guilds of the City and the romance of commerce. He took her to the Houses of Parliament at Westminster and showed her the railings where the first militant suffragettes had chained themselves, and over the old teaching hospitals that had fought so bitterly against the inclusion of women medical students.

"Every door closed to your sex by prejudice and intolerance," he said. "The early suffragettes and the first women medical students were stoned and despised—and see where they are now! Doctors, barristers, even cabinet ministers!"

She laughed. "Am I to find a message in that?"

"If you like, my little South African. Remember this—you can't stem the tide of progress forever, or the emancipation of human beings. Sooner or later the dykes will burst."

On warm summer days they went to Kew Gardens, or sailed in Regent's Park, and often they dined at the inn by the riverside. Roxane accepted her limited joy in Hal's company with philosophy. Already the end of the road was in sight, but she would always be able to look back upon it. How wise Uncle Chris had been when he had said that the simple ways of enjoying London were the best. She was learning the truth of that daily.

Hal's secretary returned from her holiday, a dark, mannish young woman bronzed by the sun and sea of Cornwall, and her appearance in his office seemed to Roxane like the last milestone on the way to their final parting. But she still saw Hal constantly, for to him her companionship was his main solace against the loneliness of the present and fear for the future.

September came and washing dresses went back into the cupboards and suits came out. SALE notices vanished from shop windows and autumn garments clothed the pale wax figures. The butterfly hats of summer disappeared from smooth doll-heads that now carried the moth-toques of the new season, feathered in neutral shades, fashioned of velvet or supple felt that darkened as you brushed a hand across it.

The yellow leaves of the plane-trees cavorted along the Embankment and chrysanthemums raised their mop curls in the flower-stalls of Sloane Square and Piccadilly Circus. In the Valley now the light tread of spring would leave its flowering prints and the berg would be powdered with silver and gold.

Hal and Roxane strolled along the Embankment towards Whitehall.

"It's the oldness I love most," she said. "The sense of the past wherever one goes, whatever one does. The history of your island is always with you—all of it—from Stonehenge to the stained-glass windows in the Abbey for the heroes of the last war."

"Yes," he agreed. "I suppose it strikes you strongly. There are such big dark gaps in the history of Africa. You have the remote past, the discoveries of prehistoric missing links, and the young history of white settlement——"

"And how young it is! Scarcely older than Dieu Donné!"

They paused to watch the clumsy laden barges being towed up-river on the tide. The evening was gossamer and pale apricot —Turneresque.

Hal spoke of Africa and felt the lure of it in his blood.

"Millenniums of mystery, Roxane—then the early Portuguese mariners nibbling at the fringe, rounding the Cape on their way to the East—the establishment of a trading station by the Dutch East India Company and the first penetration of Southern Africa."

"The Dutch did that," she said. "The Boer cattlemen who supplied the ships with meat."

"The border men outside the reach of the slow-moving law. Can you picture their lives? Nomads following the grazing like the Kaffir herdsmen who were their enemies. The Boers moving north, the Kaffirs moving south. . . . The only civilizing influence in their lives the Bible, the itinerant schoolmaster, the Jewish trader with his donkey wagon and an occasional trek to Cape Town. No wonder those old frontier Boers bred an obstinate, narrow, independent race with long harsh memories!"

The brim of his soft hat cast a shadow over his eyes, the scar on his cheek reminded her that he too had experienced life outside the law.

"You try to get under the skin of others," she said. "It's your special thing—tolerance——"

He looked down at her and smiled.

"I'm a journalist—a foreign correspondent. If you want to understand another country's present problems you have to learn a little of what led to them. After all, the story of a country is the story of its people."

They turned east along the river, and Roxane said as they passed two African students, "Those men are darker than our natives—more Negroid."

The two young men carried books under their arms. They wore their dark, glossy skins like exotic masks, their hats were wide-brimmed and light in colour as if for contrast, and they moved at the unhurried pace of Africa, their long, narrow fingers hanging limp at their sides. They both wore spectacles, and Roxane wondered whether they really needed them or if they assumed them in order to enhance their academic status.

"West Africans from London University, I should guess," said Hal. "Statesmen of the future perhaps. . . ."

Opposite Charing Cross Tube Station Hal and Roxane followed Northumberland Avenue and then they took a left turn to a large block of flats facing on to Whitehall and the Thames. Dusk was falling and the air above their heads was shrill with a weird, unearthly whistling. It was the hour of the starlings.

"Listen," said Roxane, as they paused outside the entrance. "It's a mad sound—sort of shivery!"

"Wish we could get rid of them," he said. "It's like the noise of a cocktail party—you don't dare let yourself think about it or it drives you crazy."

"We have red-winged starlings in the Valley—the sprues—and when they hive in a fir-tree they make this noise. But by themselves they have a sad call—a lament in a minor key."

"Do you remember that native war-dance we saw in Johannesburg?" asked Hall. "That dance at the mine?"

She nodded.

"Then listen again! This massed starling whistling is the same as their war-cry—savage."

She looked up at him, wide-eyed.

"What a strange thing for you to remember—here, in the heart of London! But it's true."

She had been to his flat before. But this evening was different. Tomorrow he was to fly to the West Indies for his paper, and by the time he returned she would be gone.

His flat, on the eighth floor overlooking the river, was small and solidly furnished in a comfortable Edwardian style. It consisted of lounge, bedroom and bathroom. No kitchen, for these were service flats and the tenants could either take their meals in the restaurant or have them sent up to their rooms. To Roxane the atmosphere was soulless and impersonal. Hal had brought nothing of his own into this temporary abode, except one cigarette box, which had its origin somewhere in the Far East, and a framed snapshot of his wife and child. Their own elegantly appointed house in Westminster had been let furnished for six months. This was a makeshift, a mere *pied-à-terre*.

Roxane stood at the window and looked down at the thinning

trees and the first lights stitching the web of dusk in patterns reflected on darkening water. A city on a river—how beautiful it was! Something to keep—this picture—something to take back to the Valley.

"After the Caribbean, what?" she asked. Behind her she heard the clink of glasses as he took whisky and gin from the cabinet. "Where will you go?"

"Sorry I've no tomato-juice, you'll have to make it gin and tonic. . . ." He poured it out, not waiting for a reply. "After the Caribbean—rather interesting. Back here, and then in October Nigeria, the Gold Coast and down Africa through the Congo, Kenya, the new Rhodesian Federation, and to the Union for Christmas."

"You'll be at Farway for Christmas?"

She did not guess how the little break in her voice betrayed her.

"I've just heard. My paper has been very decent to give me this chance. But we hoped it might be that way. You see, Alexa's company is visiting South Africa after the Australian and New Zealand tour. If our plan works out as it should we'll all be at the Cape for Christmas."

"That's why your mother took Sandra?"

"Partly."

Because she had suddenly closed her eyes she heard the tone of his voice very clearly—as if a thread had been drawn in the texture, tightening the fabric.

"That will be lovely for your parents . . . for all of you."

He did not answer. He stood next to her and stared down at the Thames. He wanted to talk to her—to tell her everything—to say, "I dread it, I dread Christmas! Alexa and I must go one way or the other then—we can't go on as we are doing. We must come together then—really come together—or . . . ."

She had moved away from him, and now she held the framed snapshot in her hand.

"Alexa with a baby—seems strange somehow. I always think of her as she was in *Ballerina*—her sublime dancing. . . ."

It was not a good likeness. The dancer's pale hair fell across her face, a thin hand clasped the back of a tiny bundle; they seemed anonymous—not Alexa Rome or Alexa Fairmead and Sandra, Hal's child, but simply "Woman and Infant."

"It's tantalizing, this," she said. "One wants to walk round it —see them from some other angle——"

"What other angle?"

"Her face—her expression—looking at her child."

He repeated slowly, "Her expression . . ." Words stuck in his throat as he recalled the way in which Alexa had looked at the infant Sandra, the clouding of her eyes, the blend of resentment and bewilderment, the fading of the bewilderment, the transference of the resentment—to him.

"Lexa isn't very good with babies," he heard himself say. "Not even with this one. Alexa is a ballerina first and last. If this little baby shows promise of being a dancer, Lexa will understand her —and love her. Sandra's existence will be justified."

His smile was crooked, more sad than cynical, and his eyes were compassionate as he put the snapshot back on the table.

Roxane thought, He is making excuses for Alexa, trying to get into her mind, her way of thinking and feeling, because that is his talent and he uses it all the time. It's what makes him lovable —but is it his strength or his weakness?

"Will Alexa be away long?" she asked.

"I told you. We hope to meet at the Cape. We might even be able to come back together—though that is by no means sure."

"You live on the fringe of her life," Roxane said.

One eyebrow lifted. "I don't do so badly. There's Sandra."

"Yes, there's Sandra. Are you good with babies—better than she is? Do you understand this little one?" She glanced at the snapshot.

"I doubt it. In any case, our Nannie is one of the old school—a dragon. It's hands off for us where Sandra is concerned. What are you thinking—smiling secretly to yourself?"

"I'm thinking of the first time I met you—when you were so kind to little Jannie Krige, the tipsy page, and the way he hung on to your finger—as if it were a lifeline."

"That was long ago—in another incarnation."

"Only five years ago."

"An eternity. We meet at long intervals, you and I. And we part whenever we get to know one another."

Through the open door of his bedroom she saw his light air-mail case already packed. The ticket, she knew, was in his wallet. The parting was very near.

He asked: "What are you going to do when you go back, Roxane?"

She pulled a little face.

"Get married . . . have babies of my own. . . ."

"Have you chosen the fortunate father?"

"Yes, I have chosen him."

Silence entered the room, freezing them both with a slow compelling chill. The clang and clatter of the Embankment rose on the autumn air. In the near-darkness, with her back to the open window, she was moon-pale and the press of unuttered words and thoughts seemed to whirl round them both like the ghost echo of wild starling whistling, drawing them together in its net of invisible sound—the silent discordant song of their quivering nerves.

"*No!*"

All the pent-up strain of the past three weeks, with desire the constant unacknowledged shadow at their heels, burst suddenly through his one protesting cry. The kindness, the lightness and the mockery were gone from him as was her own young helplessness in the face of this new-old foolishness. Scalding defensive anger came racing to her aid.

"Why not? What does it matter to you?"

He took her in his arms, feeling bitter antagonism hold her rigid.

"Not you—not you, my sweet . . . don't marry without love —without the real thing——"

"The real thing—the real thing!" She wrenched herself out of his grasp and stood leaning breathlessly against the high window-sill. "How can one know the real thing? Did you know it? Does anyone know it? There's a man who loves me at home—waiting for me. I'm the one he cares for most in the world. I come first to him! Isn't that enough—to be first to somebody?"

"It's not enough. Not unless he is first to you as well."

"That . . . that . . . to be first to each other . . . to be deep in love, both of you—that would be the wonder-thing—the once in a lifetime thing."

She seemed to rock for an instant like a reed in a high wind, then she buried her face in her hands. The darkness under her palms was shot with red and gold, and the things she wanted to say swarmed up and dispersed unspoken, tiny sparks thrown off by the fire inside her, flying upwards and dying out. To come first to one another, to love equally and without question, to be all in all each to the other—indeed that would be the wonder thing! It had been like that for Hal and Alexa once—maybe it still was. But no, she guessed that now it was he who loved—he who suffered about Alexa as she, Roxane, suffered about him.

The darkness thickened around her, yet she was aware of Hal with every nerve—his light step—he always moved lightly—his nearness, the smoky, leathery smell of him, and his lean sinewy strength as he lifted her off her feet and carried her across the room to the big brocaded couch.

"There now," he said. "And here's your drink."

She tried to smile at him, but her lips were shaking. The room was nearly dark and she was grateful that he could not see her properly. Her mouth and throat were dry and she tasted the sweetish gin and bitter tonic with dislike and relief. Everything seemed mixed—tastes and feelings and the deep, hurt longings inside her.

Then Hal was holding her two cold hands in his.

"What are we going to do, Roxane? Wanting each other so——"

Wanting, not loving. He would never say loving. Love belonged to Alexa. This—to him—was only that other thing—the thing that took no account of heart or soul.

"We are going to say goodbye. Just that. . . ."

Had she said it—or only thought it? The room was full of danger. The magnetism of his touch weakened her and she was shamed at his power over her. Anger was her only weapon.

"Let me go!" But the cry was scarcely above a whisper. "Let me go, Hal! It may be good enough for you to live on the fringe of somebody else's life, never sharing it in full, taking what's left over and being thankful . . . it may be all right for you and Alexa to live that way . . . but I'm not prepared to be the dog on your doorstep—let in and kicked out at will——"

He put his hand over her mouth.

"Don't dare talk like that! It's not like you to be hard and bitter——" My wife, my mother, but not you, Roxane . . .

The sharp explosion of pain and fear had left her spent and trembling. And as the hand that had covered her lips stroked the shadowed hollow of her cheek and smoothed the soft hair back from her brow, she knew that there was no more fight in her.

She waited for his kiss with her head back and her eyes closed. The words "I love you" cried out silently within her, but she knew that they would never be spoken till he had said them first. And she knew also that from him those words were not for her—only for Alexa.

CHAPTER 19

HOME-COMING

It began very early—the day of home-coming.

It began with the dawn and the superb majesty of arrival— the Twelve Apostles with wisps of cloud to halo their gaunt, grey heads, then the massive buttress of Table Mountain coming into view between Devil's Peak and Lion's Head, and the long tawny rump of the lion crouching over the white new flats along the Sea Point shore.

Roxane had wakened at five o'clock and seen the dark outline of the coast through her porthole. She had pulled her coat over her nightgown and slipped out onto the deserted deck to watch the dream-pink of sunrise work its magic on peak and forest and sparkling sea. Mine—she thought—all this is mine! Here is where I belong; not London or Paris, though I love them, but here where I have grown up with so much beauty.

They docked at half-past seven and Thinus was the first on board. Roxane was in the smoking-room waiting to present her passport to the official at his table, and she did not see the familiar figure standing in the doorway.

She's changed, he thought. She's grown up altogether! She's beautiful in her own strange fashion. A young man stood behind her and by the way in which he looked at her Thinus knew that he too found her beautiful. A stab of sheer primitive jealousy shot through him, but as she turned to smile at the young man and talk to him, Thinus relaxed. Her eyes had added nothing to her friendly smile.

The passport official glanced up at her to check the photograph with the living features, and that business-like glance, held for an instant against its will, was not lost upon the watcher. And then she was coming towards him. She had seen him and her face was alight with gladness as she linked her arm through his. He held it tightly to his side and heard her soft laugh of pleasure.

"Thinus—old Thinus—I didn't want to leave England, but it's wonderful to be back."

"Roxie, it's been hell without you—God, how we've missed you—all of us!"

They had breakfast together and he gave her the news.

Grannie Con had gone down hill since Auntie Marthe's death. She missed their rather cantankerous relationship more than people realized. And it infuriated her to see the way in which Krifti had managed to acquire most of his mother-in-law's estate. More vineyards divided, more plots for sale.

"Whenever one of the old ones dies off that happens," he said. "It's the way it goes in the Valley these days—but it still makes Grannie Con mad. She can't face the thought of it happening to Dieu Donné when her turn comes." He frowned and added, "Krifti is thicker than ever with Guy and Merle."

"They want to go to Europe——"

"Ja, so I gather." He changed the subject. "We've had bother with Ben. He's getting hold of dagga. There's more dagga-smoking in the Valley than there has ever been and the police are determined to find the smugglers. I have my own suspicions——"

"Someone at Dieu Donné?"

He admitted that he feared so, and then went on to give her little scraps of local gossip. Aletta Krige was in the family way again, and Jannie had been whacked at school for putting a mole-snake into the teacher's desk. The teacher had made a fool of himself and discipline had suffered. He was an Englishman— new, poor devil—and he hadn't known the difference between a harmless mole-snake and a cobra! Lavinia Fairmead was wrapped up in the baby, she swore she'd never return the child to its parents; Adrian was writing a novel about the Valley and everybody was nervous with him now, for fear he'd put them in it.

Roxane laughed. "Like being put in a cage!"

"And kept on view," grinned Thinus, "not looking your best."

They did not touch on her experiences abroad. That opened up too big a subject. All that could come later. He was content to wait. He is patient, she said to herself. He is good and kind —and I am happy to be with him again. But she said it with too much emphasis.

"Your coffee, Roxie. You haven't touched your coffee. And don't you want your egg and bacon?"

She pushed her plate away and shook her head.

"I'm too excited. If you've had enough, let's go. I want to get home."

He followed her to the customs shed. He had almost forgotten that assured little swing of her hips and the way her shoulders sloped down from the graceful neck. Roxie, when will you give me your answer? Today—tomorrow? I have to know. We must get married soon. But there was a heaviness round his heart— certain dark secret thoughts that he tried to put away from him.

The lush green meadows on the southern flank of Devil's Peak were thickly powdered with little spring flowers, and the buck and wildebeeste of the Nature Reserve grazed low down near the road. Carpets of creamy arums were spread under the oaks; and, at the bottom of Wynberg Hill, they saw the first vineyards, leafless still but pruned and weeded. Here the vines were trellised. The gnarled grey trunks, in contorted attitudes of torment, spread their arms along the wire—each plant the dwarfed semblance of a crucifix. Soon the shoulders would sprout the emerald wings of the first foliage, and in the New Year the heavy bunches of table grapes would depend from those grey limbs. Then the bushy wine vineyards of Constantia came in sight along the sunny slopes of the protecting mountains, and beyond them the breeze ruffled the sombre pine forests of Tokay. Across the Flats sparkled the sea.

"There's a glitter on everything," said Roxane, and suddenly she cried out, "Thinus, you didn't tell me! You've given the homestead a new spring dress!"

Dieu Donné gleamed, new-painted, among the oaks. Not since Merle's wedding had it looked so fine.

"It was a surprise for you. After the stately homes of England we thought we'd better do our best." He beamed. "Anyway, it was necessary."

She thought of the parklands and gracious mansions of the green island she had left, and it seemed to her that, in spite of all their formal charm, they lacked the homely dignity of these old Cape farms. The very word "homestead" carried its own significance.

Grannie Con's wheel-chair was on the high pink stoep, and Ben was waiting to take her luggage. Joshua whistled for Wolf when he saw the car, and the big Alsatian went mad with joy at sight of his young mistress.

"He suffered," said Thinus. "At first he pined—didn't you, boy?"

"If only he could speak!" She laughed and hugged the big dog as she tried to control his wild enthusiasm. And indeed Wolf was speaking to her with whines and whimpers, with tongue and tail and eyes and paws and all the crazy convolutions of his powerful body.

"Lizzie!" Roxane grasped the old cook's hands as she hurried down the steps to meet Miss Roxie come back at last.

"Miss Roxie been away too long! De Oumissus get sick for wanting Miss Roxie home."

And then Roxane was on her knees beside Grannie Con's chair. She had taken off her little blue felt hat, and the old lady's chill hand wandered, with happy disbelief, through the ruffled hair.

"You're back . . . you've come back to us. . . ."

Thinus turned away abruptly and motioned Ben to take the baggage to Roxane's room, and Lizzie's eyes, with their bluish tinge of an old dog going blind, filled with sudden tears.

"Yes, darling, I'm home—did you ever doubt it—wonder if I would come home? This is where I belong."

She took the frail hand, knotted with rheumatism like an old vine, and laid it against her cheek. She's shrunk, thought the girl, she's dwindled. Let me be strong for her when she needs me—strong and faithful!

Impressions permeated her consciousness during the day.

Lizzie, like Grannie Con, seemed smaller than ever as she bustled about her big kitchen, and Joshua too had aged. His grizzled hair was crimped white thatch crowning his moon face. The small eyes had almost disappeared in bags of purplish flesh.

How old they all were! How old! She had forgotten they were so old.

And Ben, the son of Lizzie's heart, the child of her later years —he too had altered. But with him Roxane realized that the change had been gradual and that now, with eyes sharpened by absence, she was seeing the culmination of some evil spell that had been laid upon him by a cruel fate. It had begun years ago when the accident of deafness had forced him into a slow un-willing retreat from normal life—like a young free animal driven into a cage, step by step, before the remorseless whip of a master without pity. Once there had been Saartjie and song in his life, and the leaping glamour of the coon carnivals. What was there now? Saartjie still? She remembered the many times she had seen his eyes fixed on the pretty coloured girl with hungry jealousy. His black eyes had been luminous once, moist liquorice swimming in pure whites. Now those whites were discoloured and inflamed. Red for dagga—red for danger. His features too had coarsened and thickened so that Roxane found it hard to recall the handsome capering coon in his harlequin satin costume.

"How is Saartjie? I haven't seen her yet."

Roxane sat on the well-scrubbed kitchen table and swung her

legs while Lizzie mixed a cake. She ran her finger-tip round the edge of the bowl when Lizzie had poured the mixture into a baking-tin. "This is good," she said.

Lizzie laughed. "Miss Roxie always loved chocolate cake—and licked de bowl!" She slipped the tin into the oven and closed the door. "Saartjie is coming over to press Miss Roxie's dresses and help unpack as soon as she has finished her work at Baas Thinus's place." Lizzie still adhered to the old-fashioned custom of using only the third person in addressing her superiors.

"Yes, but I mean what about the Dramatic Group and her acting and dancing?"

Lizzie's face darkened. It was as if night had gathered on her skin.

"She is crazy, Miss Roxie. She wants to go to England and be famous! What foolishness!"

"There are thousands of coloured people in England now, Lizzie. They all seem to think the streets are paved with gold over there."

"She'd come to no good. Dere's a lot of her mother in dat girl."

And there Saartjie was—standing in the doorway. They had not heard her step and they did not know how long she had been there. She had simply materialized in that odd way of hers.

"Welcome back, Miss Roxie."

"Thank you, Saartjie. It's lovely to be home."

"I can help you unpack now."

"We'll go to my room then."

Roxane watched the girl's hands with the rosy palms and the bluish filbert nails shaking out a skirt or a dress as Saartjie moved lightly about the room in the shafts of morning sunlight. From time to time her blue-black ringlets fell across her dark olive cheek as she leaned over the open trunk. As she unpacked she asked questions, and Roxane realized that her determination to make her fortune on the London stage had not abated.

Had Miss Roxie seen coloured singers and dancers on the London stage? In night clubs or variety theatres? Was it true that brown and white people married over there and nobody thought anything about it?

Roxane tried to answer all the questions fairly and objectively without painting a picture of a coloured girl's Utopia. But it was clear that Saartjie was moving towards her goal and that nothing would deflect her if she could prevent it.

"There is an Engish actor who has been helping us in our Dramatic Group," she said. "He will give me introductions to theatrical agents. I will find work when I go over."

"Have you money for your fare—and to keep you when you get to England?"

"I will work my passage. People always want a girl to help them with their children. And I have saved money. . . ."

Roxane glanced at her sharply. A secret look had blanketed Saartjie's face. She had spoken impulsively to impress Roxane, and had immediately regretted the impulse.

"I will take these to press." She picked up an armful of dresses and the door closed softly behind her.

Roxane heard her high heels click jauntily down the boarded passage. She was a deep one, Saartjie. Literally and figuratively she had made up her mind where she was going. And she could succeed, thought Roxane—with that driving self-confidence and ambition she might well succeed.

When Grannie Con woke from her afternoon siesta in the library she saw Roxane curled up on the couch reading the morning paper.

The old lady smiled and put out her hand with a little gesture of affection and let it fall into her lap. She had been dozing in her favourite high-backed chair, with her wheel-chair—as always —close at hand. By turning her head very slightly she could see the shifting pattern of the oak leaves through the tall windows. The hydrangeas in the big tubs were not yet in bloom, but the many-flowered buds were bursting out among the wealth of healthy foliage. Here and there a squirrel scampered along a bough, and the doves crooned monotonously.

"I'm glad you're awake," said Roxane. "There's so much to say."

"Talk comes in patches when one is catching up." Grannie Con picked up her crochet and examined it as if its design surprised her—as indeed it might, for, like conversation after long parting, it seemed to have developed in patches. "Yes," she said. "Like this lace cloth of mine, there are stitches dropped that can never be retrieved—holes in the pattern that should not be there. . . ." She paused. There was a thought there that refused to be followed up. It was often that way these days—thoughts and words eluded her.

Roxane sat up and leaned forward.

"Grannie Con, I want to talk about my mother—about Maman."

"Of course, child." But the old face had folded down, the eyes were shuttered, and the rusty voice was guarded.

Roxane began to talk—and having begun it was easy to go on. In spite of herself, the old lady's attention was caught and held as she listened to the girl's eager description—of the portrait over Uncle Chris's fireplace, of their visit to Paris—to the place of Maman's birth, and of her death—of the Angelus pealing over the quiet pastures and Uncle Chris standing in the silvery light with his head bowed. She explained Anne's work, and spoke finally of her courage.

"She betrayed no one. Even under torture she said nothing."

The girl's face was flushed and her eyes shone. She was breathless and deeply moved. In retelling Anne's story—what little she had learned of it—she had relived her own experience—the poignant excitement of discovering her own mother. She spoke passionately and it was evident that she had got under the skin of this unknown woman who had given her birth—the skin that had suffered and endured to the end because the spirit was stronger than those who tested the body to destruction.

"I understand her," said Roxane. "I love her for her strength —and for her weakness——"

"Her weakness?"

Roxane went over to Grannie Con and sat on the floor beside her chair. Her head leaned against the old lady's lap. They could talk now without seeing each other's face.

"Her weakness—yes. There are things I know about Maman without having been told. I know now that she was never married." She felt the old lady stiffen, but she went on. "Sometimes I have thought that Uncle Chris is really my father . . . and yet . . . and yet I don't believe he was the man in my mother's life, though I guess she was the woman in his. . . ." She paused, as it came over her again that there was always this unevenness—this one-sidedness—in loving. *Il y a toujours un qui embrasse et l'autre qui tend la joue.* "But I may be wrong. . . ."

"Did you ask him?"

"Yes. He gave me no answer. He said you had a letter Maman had written to you when she sent me to you. That you would give it to me when I was twenty-one."

"That was what she wished. It is what I will do."

"You know the truth?"

"I know the truth."

"Then tell me now. Why must I wait?"

"Because that was the way she wanted it. Don't fight her will. Don't try to persuade me. Remember, Roxie, I too can keep my secrets and not betray a trust."

Silence fell between them as each pursued her own memories. At last Roxane said:

"She must have been very strong. . . . You and Uncle Chris —you accept her decisions and bow to her wishes. . . ."

"She was very strong, my child. *She still is.*"

A strange thing to say, perhaps, thought the old lady. But of late she had felt herself acutely aware of Anne's power—curiously close to the woman whose child had been entrusted to her care. Perhaps because Roxane's twenty-first birthday was drawing near—only a few months now—or perhaps . . .

"Grannie Con—is it such a terrible sin to love where there is not the right to marry?"

The girl's voice was so low that Grannie Con had to strain her ears to catch the words. For a while Roxane thought that she had not heard. She did not repeat the question, just sat with her head leaning back against the chair. She felt the fingers that had been caressing her hair fall away, and the library seemed to grow very still and attentive. Even the doves were silent as the old lady spoke.

"They say that to know all is to forgive all. It is not for us to lay down the law. Only God can explore the whole heart of a human being and give judgment."

"And punish," said Anne's daughter. "God may forgive, but He does not forget to punish."

Mr. Krifti and Louise were announced just before tea, and Roxane thought that Mr. Krifti looked much better than when last she had seen him—less sallow, not so bruised round those pale hooded eyes of his. Fantastically it occurred to her that he had recently bled the estate of Auntie Marthe van der Walt. He was nourished—the Vampire of the Valley!

"We had to come and see you," Louise said. "We know what it means to Grannie Con to get you back."

"We hoped you would bring back an English peer," said Mr. Krifti.

Roxane laughed. "No luck! I did my best. But I couldn't find an English peer who would believe that I was a South African heiress!"

Joshua was beaming in the doorway.

"More visitors for Miss Roxie. Missus Fairmead an' Missus Krige."

Lavinia greeted Roxane with pleased restraint, but Aletta Krige flung her arms round the younger girl's neck and hugged her.

"You're thinner than ever, darling! And just look at me!"

But it was evident that Aletta's increased weight was in a cause that did not distress her. "Probably twins! Oh, Roxie, you must see Lavinia's little Sandra—she's a honey, a rosebud—I told Karl, 'If we haven't made a girl this time I'll never speak to you again.' "

"You must come and make Sandra's acquaintance," put in Lavinia. "And Adrian is clamouring for you to begin typing his new novel."

"The one about the Valley?"

"The one about the Valley. He's just taken out an insurance policy against libel!"

"I'd love to. Typing that will be a thrill!"

"As soon as you've settled down——"

"I have settled. I'm home. Everything is just as if I'd never been away."

But, she thought, that's not true. It's only on the surface that everything seems the same. Really it's all changed because I have changed.

"I'll come tomorrow," she added. "I'm longing to meet Sandra."

There was truth. She wanted and dreaded to see the flesh and blood link that tied Hal and Alexa more closely than ever.

They were all sitting on the stoep when Karl Krige came in to fetch his wife home. How huge he was—how completely a throw-back to his Dutch ancestry—the trekking Boers! Karl was the potential patriarch with that flaxen beard and the great hands that might have been modelled by Rodin—the hands of the thinker rather than of the farmer—the hands of the landowner who ordered others to do the manual labour. Even in Chelsea, thought Roxane, where the unconventional figure was still the commonplace, or in Paris on the Left Bank with its *types* of all sorts, Karl would command attention and respect. Yet we aren't liked abroad, she considered sadly. They'd probably decide he was a beater of oppressed black men if they recognized him for a South African!

As she talked about her trip overseas, the interest in South Africa and the prejudice against it, she caught Lavinia Fairmead's glance.

"It's ignorance," said Lavinia. "The majority of English people only know what they are told about Africa—and that is precious little. And most of it distorted. When they have been to the Union they begin to understand its peculiar problems, and the remarkable work that is being done for the native and coloured population. But so few of them ever do see it for themselves! I wish to goodness Hal would spend some months here and really give his mind to writing about it. Perhaps he will—later on."

Aletta wanted to know about London and Paris—what women were wearing. "We get the fashions six months later—and by the autumn I'll be ready to buy some new dresses. No, don't look like that, Karl, I have a feeling we'll get a bumper crop this season!"

"If Aletta insists on new babies we can't afford new dresses too. I'm always telling her that, but she doesn't believe it. Tell us, Roxie, did you go to the Motor Show? What are the new models like? What do you see most on the road?

As she chattered, the recent past, suddenly vivid, invaded the dappled shadows of Dieu Donné as the Valley had sometimes invaded the little house in Chelsea. Under the talk and laughter she felt wise and mature, profoundly conscious that the essential core of every human being is compounded of experience and memory. Everything that happened to you, everyone who mattered to you, every place you came to know and love, was absorbed into the fabric of your soul. Reminders were always with you. Aletta, here in the Valley, with her wide, sweet face and her happy grandeur, brought to mind Mrs. Maydew's Lucy swaying off towards the shops in the King's Road after the day's chores, her shopping bag over her arm and her shabby coat buttoned taut across the heavy burden of the coming child. And Lavinia Fairmead's attacking grey eyes and high carriage of the head were to Roxane only a stab in the raw, tender wound of her forbidden love. In the end it all came back to Hal. It always did. Perhaps Thinus would unconsciously break that haunted circle of her thinking and feeling.

She looked across at him—blond and sturdy—Thinus whom she knew so well; and suddenly she wondered if he too had hidden places of the heart unguessed at by her who was closer to him than a sister.

He was sitting beside Aletta on the stone *bankie* at the end of the stoep, and the oak leaves moved softly over their two fair heads. The masked side of his face was turned to Roxane, and although she could see the pleasant crease of his smile as he enjoyed some joke with Aletta, she was aware that there was very little to be learned from a blind profile. The eyes were the windows and when the blind was drawn, a part of the inner self was shut away. But perhaps there was no such thing as knowing another person. Even a child could never be wholly known—not from the moment when it gave birth to its first independent thought.

"Roxane is still six thousand miles away——" Mr. Krifti's soft voice recalled her. And then she heard Karl say:

"Come along, Mammie. Time we went home."

He took his wife's hands and drew her to her feet, dwarfing her magnitude with his own.

"*Totsiens*, Grannie Con," he said. "It's fine to have this little *meisie* back. You'll sleep all the better tonight for knowing she's here."

"We'll see you tomorrow then, Roxie," said Lavinia.

"Tomorrow morning."

Their visit had warmed her. She felt wanted, and grateful that this should be so. Thinus saw the guests to their cars and then came back to the stoep.

"It's a great day, Roxie. I'm putting on my dinner jacket this evening! Guy and Merle are coming over to dinner. This is an occasion."

Merle and Guy came early, and they too welcomed Roxane eagerly. But she guessed that in their case it was merely relief that now they could plan their holiday in the certainty that Grannie Con would have her to depend upon in an emergency.

Merle's brilliant blue eyes shone with the flame of some inward excitement such as that which had animated her when they had entered the city of Johannesburg, but Guy's quick near-stammer was more pronounced, and the way in which he glanced at Merle from time to time puzzled Roxane. It was no longer the look of a man physically and masterfully in love with his wife; it held instead a suggestion of appeal, as if he sought to be sustained in some secret project. In a subtle way she sensed that the partners had changed places and that the leadership now lay with Merle where once it had been triumphantly Guy's.

I come home, thought Roxane, and I really *see* people. I don't just take them for granted as part of my life.

Facing her across the dinner table was Grannie Con. How frail she looked! Time and pain had crumpled her features and shrunk her form. For years pity for Grannie Con had been altering the character of Roxane's affection for her guardian, transforming her from the protected into the protector. And tonight the last traces of childhood's awe and girlhood's frequent irritation melted away and left her love pure—all compassion.

Tonight Grannie Con did not rise to carve the joint. Those days had gone with the loss of her leg. It was Thinus who made the first incision in the loin of lamb—the fork held firmly in his left hand with the missing fingers. "I am lucky," he often said. "I have my thumb. A man can do without a couple of fingers." But she knew that he had hated his wounded hand ever since Merle had called it a claw. If she married Thinus he would sit at the head of their table and carve their meat and order their wine, he would say grace, and his yellow-haired children would bow their heads. One day they would leave the Valley of the Vines and go to live in Thinus's share of Tweefontein, and there, in the Free State, Afrikaans would gradually become as much the language of their home as English, and the austerity of the Vos blood and his Dutch Reformed upbringing would prevail. No more wine would be set before them, for surely the spirit of Oom Jacob would descend upon his son. Could she accept these things?

With Grannie Con asleep on the berg, and Merle mistress of Dieu Donné—yes.

Thinus was smiling at her, trying to catch her attention.

"You are the spoilt one tonight, Roxie. I remember you like the brown bits—so I've given you the best crisp brown outside bits."

"That's lovely," she said. "You think of everything."

Behind him Saartjie waited to take the plate. Saartjie was helping Joshua in the dining-room tonight. As she leaned forward her face came into the soft radius of candlelight, and there was a slight smile on her full lips as she murmured in the *taal* so that no one but Thinus could hear.

"You like the brown bits too, Baas Thinus."

He gave no sign that he was aware of her presence, and she took the plate with suddenly impatient fingers.

CHAPTER 20

"I DON'T THINK THAT WE WILL EVER HURT EACH OTHER"

Sandra woke and smiled at Roxane.

Her face had been fat and waxen with sleep, but now the apple-blossom colour came into her cheeks and the lifting of silky lashes revealed a pair of large clear eyes. They might be hazel later or grey, but now they were still the pure pool-dark blue of infancy. The nose was a button and the wide smile showed the pink scallop of gum already hard with the first milk-teeth. The baby made the cooing noise of a young pigeon and her tiny fingers unfurled like fern fronds and reached for the sunbeams that filtered into her pram through the leaves of the big plane-tree. Small bare feet kicked away the pink bunny blanket that covered them and began exercising themselves.

Roxane watched the child entranced. Were these a dancer's feet in miniature with the flexible toes all much the same length?

"Coo-coo-coo," gurgled Sandra through a film of bubbles. Fingers caught toes, tendrils finding an objective.

Roxane leaned over the pram and touched the fair chicken-fluff on the little round head. How soft the texture of the downy curls—how warm the scalp! She stroked the mottled leg—the skin finer than silk—and drew a long breath. This was achieve-ment! Surely the creation of Sandra was worth more than the ephemeral success of a ballerina and the exaltation of applause? This was the only immortality—this new life fashioned from the love of Hal and Alexa. Fashioned and so soon abandoned to the care of others. . . .

She longed to lift the child from the pram and feel all that lively warmth leaping in her arms.

"She's awake then?"

Roxane started at the sound of Lavinia's voice. She had been too absorbed to hear her approach.

"I was on my way to the tower-room," she said. "And I heard her coo. I couldn't resist stopping to look at her. She's lovely, isn't she?"

"Yes," said Lavinia with unusual gentleness. "She's like my daughter, Hilda, was at her age—the one in Washington. She follows our family. There's really very little of Alexa in Sandra."

"But they change. Maybe Sandra will have her mother's dancing feet——"

"I hope sincerely that she will not! I'd rather she grew up to be a happy wife and mother than a famous dancer."

Roxane recognized the quick bite in Lavinia's tone—the dislike of her daughter-in-law no longer dormant.

"Hal told me you would all be united here at Farway for Christmas. You must be very thrilled about that."

"The company is billed to tour the Union," said Lavinia abruptly. "It will suit Alexa's plans—and Simonoff's, no doubt, since he is South African."

"Simonoff? I didn't know he was in the company."

"Oh, yes, my dear. He is their principal male dancer. It was Alexa who persuaded him to go to London. She sponsored him, introduced him to people who could help him make his name quickly. And one has to admit that he has done well—improved quite literally in leaps and bounds." Her high stage laugh had its acid note. Simonoff was no favourite of Lavinia's. "You must surely remember him prancing round here—partnering Alexa when she practised her various rôles. Well, our little Sandra put an end to all that for a time—didn't you, my diddums den, Vee's rosebud, Vee's little pearl?"

She put a grandmaternal palm against the infant's nether end.

"Sopping, my sweet! Roxane, as you go in, sing out to Nannie —tell her baby's wide awake and wet as a fish!"

But, as Roxane went towards the tower, she met Nannie striding across the lawn with a purposeful gait. Roxane recalled Hal's description of her, "one of the old school—a dragon," and thought that Nannie looked a kindly dragon.

"I hope you admire our grand-daughter," Adrian said, when he had exchanged greetings with Roxane.

They stood at the window and looked down upon the shady

patch of lawn where the pram stood. Its occupant was now on hands and knees on a rug spread on the grass.

"Crawling at six months old—not bad, eh?"

"She has beautiful strong limbs like her mother," said Roxane. "She's adorable."

Adrian had been writing when she arrived, and he constantly flexed the cramped fingers of his right hand. "Wish I could use a typewriter," he said. "But it's no good. I can't think on a machine—and I can't dictate either." He had removed his spectacles and his eyes had a weak naked look.

"Did you see much of Hal in London?" he asked suddenly.

"Yes," she said. "After Alexa left—and all of you. It was lonely for him then."

"He has his work—and friends. He needs them, perhaps. How was he looking when you left?"

"Too thin. He flew to the West Indies shortly before I sailed. And soon there'll be Africa. He's looking forward to that assignment. And of course it will be wonderful for him to come here and join up with Alexa at Farway. . . ."

He smothered a sigh. "I hope that goes well—their combined visit to us. Lavinia is so difficult with Alexa. She doesn't make a genuine effort to understand her daughter-in-law."

"Maybe she thinks that Alexa doesn't try to make Hal happy."

Adrian wheeled round in surprise, and stared at Roxane. Her face was curiously without expression, but as she felt his eyes upon her she turned away. He frowned, seeking something—some elusive memory. Somewhere in his receptive writer's mind he had pigeon-holed a note about this girl—and Hal. Long ago. He sought it now, and found it in a strangely vivid recollection of her pale face and clasped hands when Alexa had come up onto the terrace from the garden—here at Farway—on the evening of the cocktail party when Roxane had looked for the first time at Hal's bride. Odd how that poignant expression on the child's face had lingered with him—the hurt and defeat. . . .

"Do you think that?" he asked. "Do you think Alexa doesn't pull her weight in their marriage?"

He saw the curve of her averted cheek mantle with quick colour and pale again, and her fingers had interlaced. It saddened him to discover that he had drawn blood. Poor child, why must she be dragged into this net?

"He very seldom talks of Alexa," she said quietly. "But, if he does, it is always with absolute loyalty. I am sure he loves her——" her throat tightened, but she went on, "is *in love* with her . . . but as to her side of it—who can say? I hardly know Alexa."

"Who indeed? But since it is my profession to analyse situations, emotions, motives—people, if you like—I find myself studying my son and his wife in quite a detached way sometimes. And perhaps the fact that Vee is so intolerant in many ways makes me partisan. I try to see this marriage from Alexa's angle. Naturally Hal fell in love with her." He smiled with the corners of his mouth pulled down, sardonic. "I would have done the same had I been a few years younger. . . . Alexa had everything —glamour, fame, sensitivity and that intangible extra quality that distinguishes genius from mere talent or technical proficiency. But why did she fall for him? Tell me that!"

He did not really expect a reply. For the moment he had forgotten the second butterfly in the net—the insignificant wings beating against the invisible mesh. She was sitting on the edge of his desk while he still leaned against the window-ledge. He looked along his fingers idly, seeing nothing in particular, and then his glance was focused by Roxane's eyes, and she was answering the question he had addressed to the air—that he half thought to answer himself.

"There could be many reasons—even apart from his attraction. You forget that Hal is successful too—remarkably so for his age! He is a fine writer. He has your own gift of looking below the surface. But what makes him lovable is that he looks for the good things—the kind things—and so often he finds them in unexpected places——"

"Damon Runyon," he murmured. "Thomas Burke——"

She continued steadily. "Hal finds the orchid growing in the rubbish heap; he makes you believe in it. It's there, it's real—not just a fool's illusion. That's *his* extra quality—his way of thinking—and living—and loving. . . ."

Her eyes were on his fearlessly. What splendid strange eyes

she had! The slender joints of her clasped hands had whitened. Ah, don't! he wanted to say. Don't give so much away. Don't love this son of mine whose being turns towards Alexa like the needle of the lodestar!

"Those are reasons," he said. "Sound ones. They show penetration on your part. You are very observant, Roxane. You look below the surface, too." He saw her hands fall apart in her lap, and the droop of her neck as she looked down and away from him was child-like and dejected. "But those were not Alexa's reasons. Alexa feels primarily with her nerves and her body. All her life, from early childhood, her body has been dedicated to dancing. Then Hal came. And suddenly her body was out of hand—moon-mad and sick with love. It was the old, old magnetism that betrayed her into marriage—the force none of us can deny or escape."

He moved over to the desk. His long fingers drew the sheets of manuscript towards him.

"But the end of the story, Roxane . . . I don't see the end of the story. How long can the bridge of physical love—even of mutual respect—unite two worlds—two such different worlds?"

"There is another bridge," she said. "There is Sandra."

Grannie Con looked gravely at the girl and the man sitting side by side on the couch in the library.

Here was something she had expected—something which, in other circumstances, she might have welcomed. But she had more than one reason for doubting the wisdom of this match.

She sought in her mind some way of expressing her misgivings that would not hurt either of them, for they were both very dear to her. But these days her thoughts did not assemble easily. The stern will harried them like a faithful sheepdog, but a few were apt to stray. She made a considerable mental effort as she faced Thinus and Roxane. Her eyes were shrewd and her voice had something of its old staccato severity.

"I have guessed that you two would bring me this news," she said. "But I am going to be a difficult old woman and raise a few objections—if only to give you a chance to dispute them."

She sat very erect in the high-backed chair on the opposite side

of the fireplace. In the expression of Thinus she saw a quiet joy
that touched and softened her. Her own dead husband had sometimes looked just so. These staunch, tawny, God-fearing Vos
men could make their women happy. They were not exciting,
perhaps, but they were born to be the fathers of families and the
owners of land. They were accustomed to accepting responsibility and to exerting authority. But there was a look in Roxane's
eyes that caught at the old lady's heart. She read resolve there,
but where was the radiance? Yet peace had settled over the girl's
features. She has come through deep waters that I know nothing
about, thought Grannie Con. Is this her haven?

When Roxane glanced towards Thinus she saw his strong un-
damaged profile, and the hand that touched hers every now and
again was whole. A week had passed since her return and that
week had been full of inner turmoil and strain. She had spent
long hours alone in her secret place by the waterfall, and at night
she had prayed for guidance to the Holy Mother who must
know the inmost heart of every woman. Sometimes the figure
above her bed had assumed the aspect of Maman—Anne, who
had never lacked courage and who had brought a philosophy
of her own to the adventures of living and dying. What would
Anne have advised her to do? Would she have spoken out of her
immense self-sufficiency and said: "You must make your own life
and stand by your decision! The wonder-thing—the all-in-all
each to the other—is not for you. Take your second best and
make of it the best! You are deeply loved. Be grateful, Roxane.
. . ." Would Maman have spoken thus? Roxane thought so.

All week she had fought her private battle. And the forces she
had summoned to defeat the love that was forbidden were self-
esteem and common sense. Pride had taken a hand. Pride had said:
"Never once did Hal tell you he loved you. Hal wanted you as
any lonely man wants a desirable and companionable woman.
Although he hardly ever spoke of Alexa, she was always there
between you—the one he truly loved and could not forget, the
sun that makes the shadow. You were the shadow, Roxane. You
could never be anything but the shadow to Hal. Don't delude
yourself. You have been to the film *Ballerina*, and you have seen
her quality. . . . Well, then . . . ?"

Common sense had spoken too. "You hang on to the hem of his coat, and sometimes he draws you into its folds and holds you against his heart like a little shivering animal. But you are not a pitiable animal, you are a woman with a will of your own, and spirit! If you persist in clinging where you do not belong you will go on suffering the bruises of being shaken off. You have come to the crossroads, Roxane. Go with Thinus and never look back. He will lead you to contentment."

It did not occur to her that she was using Thinus as shelter from an emotional entanglement known only to herself. For her affection for him was never in doubt, and it was her intention to do everything in her power to make him happy.

She heard Grannie Con say:

"Roxie, I know you haven't come to this conclusion lightly. And nor has Thinus. In our family we don't go into marriage hastily. We regard our marriage vows as sacred. If you two marry you will keep yourselves unto each other only until death parts you." The solemnity in the old rusty voice evoked in both of them a picture of Tweefontein and Oom Jacob quoting from the Good Book and the wisdom in it which ruled his life. Grannie Con's next words intensified the image. "But you are not of the same faith. Thinus has been brought up in the Dutch Reformed Church, and you, Roxie, were received into my church as a little child. When you have a family there may be difficulties."

Thinus's slow, mild answer brought her memories of her own long-past problems and their solution.

"Roxie and I have discussed that, Grannie Con. We serve the same God even if we have not worshipped Him in the same church or prayed to Him in the same language. We have decided that, as the mother has the main care of little children, ours will be brought up in Roxie's—and your—faith. After all, we are both Protestants. You and my uncle arranged it so, there was tolerance in your home, and there will be in ours."

"Your parents will not agree with you." She spoke tartly, remembering the years of estrangement between Stephanus and his brother, Jacobus.

He shrugged his broad shoulders. "They have had time to profit by your example."

"I hope you may be right." The old lady frowned as she gathered the difficult straying thoughts and objections that must be expressed. "Have you considered the difference in your ages? Over fourteen years is a good deal."

He grinned. "I am getting out my dancing pumps."

Roxane laughed. "If Thinus is like Oom Jacob at seventy I shall be glad of those fourteen years!"

"I grant that it may be all right—if Thinus is the right man for you, Roxie," said Grannie Con. "But you must be very sure that he is. You must think with your mind as well as your heart, my child."

Roxane answered a little sadly. "I have done that, Grannie Con." There is no sense in my heart, she thought.

But the old lady continued stubbornly.

"You are not without experience. Men have asked you to marry them before. That young naval officer from Simon's Town, and that attractive house surgeon from Groote Schuur Hospital. And there were boys in the Valley making sheep's eyes at you when you were still a schoolgirl—but there was always Thinus. Propinquity is a dangerous thing. When young people are continually thrown together they may believe themselves in love. . . ." She broke off, conscious that she was putting her case lamely.

"We know each other well," said Roxane. But as the words left her lips the voice of Uncle Chris seemed to echo in her brain—"Even with those one knows best there are the waste spaces. . . . Respect them . . . never try to invade the life of another too deeply." There were things Thinus would never guess about her—and no doubt he too had dark corners in his soul. But she added, with the dignity that accorded a little incongruously with her youth, "We respect each other, Grannie Con."

She hesitated, and then she said slowly, smiling gravely at Thinus: "I don't think that we will ever hurt each other."

Something in the way she said it—a sense of dreams relinquished perhaps—brought the tears to Grannie Con's eyes. Those words, "I don't think that we will ever hurt each other," did not express the sentiments of youth.

Thinus's voice fell into the pause.

"I love Roxie with all that is in me. I have loved her since she came here as a child. She is part of me."

Grannie Con had recovered herself. Now she made one stipulation.

"As Roxie's guardian, I must make one request. Wait until she is twenty-one before you announce your engagement. It is October now. Only a few months to April. After that, if you are both still of the same mind, I will make no further difficulties, and you shall have my blessing."

Thinus rose and went to the old lady's side.

"If you wish it we will wait till Roxie's birthday before the announcement is published. It is not important whether other people know or not. It only matters that you should know."

"And your parents?"

"When next I go home Roxie will go with me. We will tell them together. We will go when the pressing season is over—at the end of March."

CHAPTER 21 ~~~~~~~~~~~~~~~~~~~~~~~~~

"YOU'LL PAY FOR THIS, BAAS THINUS!"

Afterwards, whenever he thought about it, the matter and manner of Saartjie's arrest left Thinus with a sick feeling.

He thought about it often. And dreamed of it too.

He could never make up his mind just when he had realized that she was peddling dagga in the Valley—smuggling it from some innocent-seeming cobbler's shop or apparently respectable merchant, hiding it and selling it. And the hiding-place had been his own cottage!

Certainly that night in June while Roxie was still in England he had not guessed what was going on. Suspicion had come much later, and the proof had followed just after Roxane's return from Europe.

But it was the night in June that haunted him. The recollection of it was coiled in the back of his mind like some evil reptile. If only he could drag it out and kill it, fling it away into oblivion! But a man and his acts, and a man and his memories, are inseparable, and Thinus knew that he would never be entirely free of his guilt. Time and again he found himself reliving the experience, hating himself.

The rugger match had been closely contested, and the last try —converted fifty seconds before the end of the game—had been scored by Western Province amid wild excitement from the crowds at Newlands. Afterwards he had gone with some of "the boys" to celebrate the victory of the home side. Then he had driven to Dieu Donné with a slight sensation of muzziness and a mild singing in his ears. He had driven cautiously, for it was raining and the Constantia roads were dark. Moreover, there were always coloured folk about on a Saturday night, many of them the worse for liquor, and Thinus was sensible enough to know that if he should have any form of mishap it might be difficult to persuade a police doctor that he himself was entirely sober.

He had garaged his car and let himself into his cottage after a few moments' preliminary fumbling with the key. The light was on in his bedroom and he cursed Saartjie inwardly for her carelessness in leaving it burning after she had turned his bed down.

He helped himself to a brandy and soda and switched on the wireless. It was ten-fifteen and he hoped to hear an account of the excellent match he had already seen. It would be interesting to know what the sports commentator had to say on the subject. Personally, he considered that the Western Province backs had won the day with their beautiful passing. He rolled a cigarette and attempted to light it. Damn! No fuel in the lighter. He looked round for a match-box. Not one to be seen. That damn girl, Saartjie, never left any in the lounge, and when he complained she invariably said, in that cheeky way of hers, "You put them in your pocket, Baas Thinus—or your friends do!" Well, there were none in his pocket now. He'd have to go and find some in his bedroom.

As he pushed open the door he saw her.

She had her back to him and she was putting out his pyjamas.

"Why so late?" he asked. "You're always clear in here by six o'clock."

She said, "I have been out."

Apart from her presence in his cottage at that hour, something in her manner and appearance startled and annoyed him. She was not wearing her lilac-coloured uniform as usual. She had on a skirt that clung tightly to her rounded hips and a flimsy blouse. Her blue-black ringlets danced on her shoulders with the quick turn of her head. There were raindrops on her hair and the light made tiny crystals of them, while her lustrous black eyes shone with a blend of excitement and some other emotion that might have been fear. She breathed fast, as if she had been running, and her whole body panted. He had a mad impulse to put his hand over her sharp aggressive breast and feel the beating of her heart.

"You're frightened." His voice was hoarse. "What are you scared of?"

She took a step towards him and said softly, "Maybe I am scared of you, my Baasie."

The damp on her skin and hair brought out the scent of vanilla that clung about her—and something else—a muskiness that fired his blood. Thinus saw the gleam of her white teeth between her full parted lips, and with a swift movement she suddenly opened the front of her blouse. Her pale brown breasts—the colour of autumn bracken—thrust themselves at him, and the singing in his ears swelled so that he did not hear the voice of the sports commentator speaking in the next room.

"No!" he cried. "No!"

At this point in his recollections he always covered his face and groaned aloud in an anguish of spirit more desperate than physical pain. Were there any sins, he wondered, that concerned only the sinner? The voice of his father seemed to roll across the miles of empty veld and the high mountain ranges: "She also lieth in wait as for a prey, and increaseth the transgressors among men."

There came other times when he found her in his cottage long after her working hours should have been over—always with that hot excitement about her which, man-like, he had misinterpreted. And then one day he found the trail—the dry dagga leaves spilled on the floor near his bed. He had moved the old four-poster and there, sure enough, was the loose floorboard. So that was her hiding-place for the weed—under the foot of his bed! And someone with a knowledge of carpentry had contrived it cunningly. Ben, of course—Ben who was clever with his hands and used to helping the Malay coopers repair the big casks in the cellar.

His anger at being her dupe was shot with shame and loathing, and in that moment of total revelation and revulsion he could have killed her. He had hardly paused to think. With his rage red in his blood he had gone straight to the police. Yet, even as he laid the charge, he had been oppressed by a sense of guilt, for he too had broken the law of his land and offended against the teachings of his religion. She's young, he told himself. It'll only be the reformatory this time. Not a prison sentence. But he knew that the penalties for dagga-smuggling were heavy.

He had been present when they took her.

"So you want to get rid of me!" she had cried. "Now Miss Roxie is home you want to get rid of me! You wait! You'll pay for this, Baas Thinus!"

The case received a certain amount of publicity. The girl accused was a coloured dancer who had achieved distinction within the well-known Coloured Dramatic Group. The background was the famous wine-farm of Dieu Donné, and the manager's cottage had been used as the place of concealment for the dagga. Thinus came in for some good-humoured teasing among his friends. And then the whole affair was forgotten. It sank into the deep cesspit of Peninsula gossip, and more spectacular scandals bubbled to the surface.

But Roxane was troubled.

"I don't like it, Thinus. Ben has been so sullen since Saartjie went. Brooding really. And when he looks at you—well, somehow his expression frightens me."

They were sitting in the sun on one of the old disused brandy stills. The white stone of the still was mottled with the shadows of magnolia leaves, and near it the blue agapanthus lilies raised their heads from their beds of shining leaves. Arums, regalia and day-lilies and ferns grew beside the little stream that bordered the rose garden, and a pergola of wistaria was sweet scented in the heat of the day.

"Ben has been accustomed to getting his dagga from Saartjie," said Thinus easily. "Now he can't. And I'm responsible because I got the girl arrested. He has some reason to feel sore at me."

"It's more than that." Her thoughtful gaze followed the stream to the willows round the pond. "Call it intuition, if you like, but somehow I feel that it goes deeper."

Thinus knew that she was right. Young Ben had been enslaved by Saartjie all his life. And since he had lost his hearing he had been obsessed with growing jealousy. He had pursued her like a shadow, and she had allowed him to do so, paying as little heed to him as to a dog. He had accepted her attitude with the humility of one aware of his handicap. There was very little that Ben did not know about Saartjie.

Roxane went on, "I'm sorry for Ben, but I'm afraid for you."

He laughed and took her thin sunburned hand in his.

"I can look after myself."

"One person goes wrong and so many get hurt," said Roxane. "There's poor old Lizzie. She has tried so hard to bring Saartjie up the right way, and it wounds her respectability to the quick to have her niece in a reformatory. She has been so quiet since it happened—doesn't even shriek at Joshua these days."

"Then I've done somebody a good turn—Joshua."

She smiled and pressed his hand, but her mind was elsewhere.

"I am very sorry for Saartjie," she said. "You see, I know why she did it."

He looked at her in astonishment. "She did it to get money, of course."

"Yes. But I know why she wanted the money—and I can understand. She's crazy to go to England and make her name on the stage. She's talked to me about it often. She really believes she could make good—and it isn't impossible either. She's got cheek, and glamour—and personality——"

"Ja," he said grimly. "I've noticed that."

This talk of Saartjie troubled him. Roxane was shining the innocent torch of her pity and understanding into a dark room where that which he feared and hated lay hidden. Anger flamed in him. "Why should her mad ambition excuse a thing like dagga-smuggling?"

"Not excuse perhaps—but it explains it. How else—except by stealing—could a girl in her position get the money she needs to buy the clothes and fripperies that would give her a chance to put herself over with agents and managers? One has to see her point of view. Anyway, she wouldn't realize that it was really wicked to smuggle dagga and sell it. The men of her people have always smoked it when they've been able to get hold of it——"

"That's a very sweeping statement!" he interrupted hotly. "And silly into the bargain. Only the riff-raff smoke the stuff."

But Roxane persisted. "At all events she takes it for granted that a great number do. She'd just reckon that if she didn't sell it to them somebody else would. Smuggling is such a common crime. Look at your diamond smugglers in Kimberley and all over the Union—making a fortune out of illicit diamond buying."

"That's a very different kettle of fish," he put in with vehemence. "Buying uncut diamonds—and selling them—doesn't harm or debauch anybody except the fool who gets himself caught and goes to gaol! But dagga is Indian hemp—the drug they gave the Assassins before they did their killings—an infuriator! In America they call it marijuana and even the teenagers get hold of reefers—those damned loaded cigarettes—and our white girls and boys are beginning the same thing in this country. It's got to be stamped out—and the police are going to see that it is!"

She shook her head obstinately, refusing to shift her ground. "*We* know that dagga, and everything to do with it, is evil. But it doesn't seem that way to a lot of the coloured people. To them it is the only channel to a sort of dream state where the poor old *nie-blanke* can be a giant for a night—as good as you in his own estimation, if in nobody else's. Saartjie never thought of it in terms of debauching people——"

"Then she damn well should have! She has seen plenty of the misery caused by dagga, especially when a man has been drinking! She has lived all her life in this Valley with its pockets of vice. She has seen men beat their women insensible when the stuff is in them, and she knows old Klaas's brother killed a man through a dagga-row over a woman. She knows that half the crimes these people commit, like rape and murder, are committed under the influence of drink and dagga. She knows these things, and there is no excuse for her!"

"You declaimed like Oom Jacob then," she said, considering him with wide eyes. "I expected you to quote the Bible any moment."

"Roxie," he said, suddenly cold into the marrow of his bones. "Are we quarrelling—for the first time in our lives?"

"I think so," she said, in a new detached way. "You see, there's something you don't understand, old Thinus. And I do. Saartjie had her dreams—and they were crazy, perhaps, but she believed in them. She did a bad thing to try and help them come true. Well, she failed—and she's in the reformatory—and all those dreams are broken. I don't like seeing dreams broken."

She buried her face in her hands. The little opalescent splinters of shattered dreams seemed to fall like bright dust-motes through the orange darkness behind her closed lids.

She felt Thinus enfold her with his arm and draw her to him.

"Don't!" he begged. "There must never be misunderstandings between you and me. There's intolerance in me. I try to fight it. And with you I will succeed. Upbringing dies hard with some of us."

"It's all right," she said. "I know."

She looked at him with curious maternal kindness. And she knew then that she would always be able to manage this man just at Tante Petronella managed Oom Jacobus. The man believed himself to be the head of the house—and that was as it should be in all practical matters—but in the things that really counted the woman held the reins—gently but with strength. . . . It was so in most Afrikaans homes, and it would be so in hers.

His sigh was almost a groan. "Roxie, Roxie . . . I love you so much . . . too much. . . ."

"I am glad," she whispered. "It is good to be loved—and to love."

Roxane knocked at the door of the tower-studio and went in.

Adrian Fairmead turned from his desk and rose to greet her. She thought that he looked desperately tired—or ill.

"You've been working too hard," she said. "You've strained your eyes."

His eyes were, in fact, more than ordinarily weak and red-rimmed behind his glasses, and his usual smile of welcome was absent.

"Sit down, Roxane," he said. And the weariness was in his voice too. "We have had bad news. I had better tell you."

She put his manuscripts and her typescript on his big walnut desk, and then sat quietly on the wide cushioned window-seat facing into the room. He limped over to her—his limbs dragged as if leaden weights were chained to them—and he stood looking out at the Valley and the sea and the blue enfolding mountains. The fingers of his right hand spread and contracted nervously as he gazed silently at the young green vines glowing in the morning light. The fine transparent leaves of the poplars quivered and sparkled, and yellow and blue lupins and tall pink watsonias spread carpets of colour over the undulating slopes. Great heaps of dry prunings were stacked in the clearings. It was the end of October, the zenith of the growing season.

Adrian's glance took in nothing but beauty, but no pleasure was reflected in it.

"Hal telephoned us from London early this morning. Alexa . . ." He passed his hand across his forehead, and Roxane saw the Adam's apple working in his throat. "Alexa . . . died . . . in New Zealand, in Wellington . . . last night."

She stared at him, the colour ebbing from her face.

"Alexa—dead?" She shook her head slowly. "No . . . not Alexa. . . ."

"She took an overdose of some sleeping-tablets—one of these wretched new drugs that are part of this unnatural age we live in. Why doctors prescribe these dangerous things, God knows."

He spoke like a man in great pain, for, after his own fashion, Adrian Fairmead had loved his son's wife. Or perhaps it was Alexa, the ballerina, he had loved—the dancer who had given life to his favourite character—Olga, the ballerina of his creation—his Galatea.

"Hal is beside himself," he went on. "He sounded quite distracted. For some reason or another he blames himself bitterly. I couldn't make out why—he didn't really say—but he seems to feel himself responsible. . . ."

"But why?" she cried out. "How could Hal possibly be responsible—or in any way to blame?"

He raised his head to look at her. Her face was deathly pale, and her eyes demanded an answer to her question.

He made a helpless movement with his hands.

"Lavinia declares that Alexa had some sort of obsession that bearing a child would ruin her as a dancer. She didn't want Sandra —and Hal did. And in some tragic fashion her fixation was justified. She was thinking wrong, Roxie—thinking herself into failure. . . ." He paused to take off his glasses and polish them as if some mist had formed over his vision. Then in a calmer tone he went on.

"When she arranged to go on this tour it was to give herself a chance to practise—to get back to her old perfection—before audiences not too critical and experienced, audiences unable to compare Alexa now with Alexa as she was before the birth of her child. But even then she didn't make the grade. She received poor notices, and finally she quarrelled with Simonoff—said he wasn't partnering her well—wasn't showing her off, but dancing selfishly to get applause for himself. She couldn't sleep after these disappointing performances—these scenes with Simonoff. And . . . well . . . we know how it ended." He repeated the word "ended" as if to force the fact into his consciousness.

She rose—a straight young woman with the light full on her shocked, incredulous face.

"All that may be so. But it still isn't enough to make Hal feel responsible for her . . . death. There's something else, Adrian— something he hasn't told you. There must be."

CHAPTER 22

CONSTANTIA FÊTE

It was the end of November—the season of charity bazaars and bush-fires.

In the airy kitchen of Dieu Donné Lizzie and Roxane were busy baking cakes for the fête on the following day when Grannie Con would lend the grounds of Dieu Donné for Children's Day. Lizzie was tired and irritable after a sleepless night.

"It's Ben dat worries me, Miss Roxie," she confided. "He gets worse an' worse—always chasing after mountain fires. Dese days I don't seem to know what goes on in his head . . ." Her old eyes filled with sudden tears, and she turned abruptly and thrust a baking tin into the oven.

As she did so, it seemed to Roxane that she read the fear that lurked unspoken at the back of Lizzie's brain. Had the fire-beater become the fire-raiser? Was Ben a "fire-bug"? But she only said gently:

"It was such a terrible thing that Ben, of all people, should get deaf, Lizzie. One has to make allowances for him. He loved music so much. He was always the life and soul of everything."

The old cook sighed. "It's true. He used to call de birds out of de trees. . . . Tomorrow de Constantia Coons will be playing here. It always upsets him to see de coons and not be able to hear dem."

Roxane tried to take Lizzie's mind off Ben. "There'll be some very good side-shows tomorrow. We must hold thumbs for a fine day with no wind. Last year the fête made over a thousand pounds for Our Children. We've got to beat that figure this year."

"Dey say famous aut'ors is going to sign deir books for a half a crown. . . . Will Mr. Fairmead come, Miss Roxie?"

She hesitated. "I think so. After all, it's six weeks' time since——"

Lizzie's button-bright eyes snapped up from a mixing bowl. "Did Miss Lexa take dose pills *on purpose?*"

Even here—thought Roxane—even in this kitchen that question is being asked!

The circumstances of Alexa Rome's death had fed the hungry maw of gossip for weeks. It was a feast. The coroner had given a verdict of Death by Misadventure and added a rider warning the public against the careless use of barbiturate drugs. But the mystery remained. And there were many who professed to know better than the law. The omnipotent THEY of the Valley whispered that Alexa had not been getting along too well with her husband, and, worse still, she had lost her grip as a dancer. Only the top had been good enough for Alexa and marriage and babies didn't fit into that little space on the pinnacle of fame. THEY said that Alexa had no alternative to dancing, that she could never have made a success on the straight stage because she was a dancer first and an actress second. In those parts she had played on the screen her gift for acting had only given point to her performance as a ballerina. THEY said she had no memory for words—that she thought and lived only in terms of music and movement, the world of mime and not of speech. THEY suggested that Alexa—like Olga, in *Ballerina*—had taken her own life—though not for the same reason. Olga had killed herself when she discovered that her lover had left her to marry another woman. She had refused to face life without him. Alexa had turned her back on life when she found that her genius had deserted her.

Roxane said, "Alexa Rome was not sleeping well during the tour. She had got into the habit of taking sleeping-pills. She increased the dose too much. That was all."

"Dere's a lot of talk," said Lizzie.

"There always is," Roxane's tone was sharp. "There now, Lizzie, put these tins in the oven. I'm going for a walk. I'll take a few crusts down to the ducks."

"It's too hot to go outdoors dis time of de morning."

"It's cool enough down by the pool."

"Den put a hat on, Miss Roxie."

"Don't fuss, Lizzie. I can look after myself."

"Only wit' de help of de Lord," said Lizzie sternly. But she handed Roxane a few crusts for the ducks.

The summer heat shimmered on lawns and flower-beds, and the scent of honeysuckle and roses hung heavily in the windless noonday heat. Roxane strolled down to the pond and scattered the scraps of bread to the ducks on the water—decorative birds, like children's toys.

She did not believe that Alexa had committed suicide. It was surely only respite she had wanted—sleep—not death. Yet she could not forget Adrian's words. "Hal is beside himself—he seems to blame himself." Why? For what should Hal blame himself?

She sat on a little rustic bench under the plane-tree. Here Thinus had made her face herself and her future the day after the news had become public property.

He had sat with his blind side to her—inexpressive and stoical. She had known he was suffering and determined not to let her see that this was so.

"Roxie," he had said. "I must know the truth. Does this . . . new situation . . . make any difference between you and me?"

The increasing happiness that had marked his whole demeanour during the past few weeks since she had given him her promise had withered and died.

"Why should Alexa Rome's death change anything between you and me?" she had asked steadily.

"You were in love with Hal Fairmead as a young girl. For all I know, you still are."

"I am engaged to you," she had said. "In any case, Hal was not, at any time, in love with me. He never will be. Alexa was the only person who mattered to him."

She saw a muscle tighten at the corner of his mouth. She had not denied that old infatuation—not even the suggestion that it might still exist.

"Alexa is dead," Thinus had said. "Hal Fairmead is a free man —free to marry you."

She had laughed then with more bitterness than she guessed.

"If Hal had wanted freedom to marry me—or anybody else— he could have had it for the asking. Alexa would never have held him. Of all people on earth, she was the most independent. She had no wish to possess anyone against their will—or to be possessed!"

"Do you know that?"

"I *do* know it—although I can't tell you how or why I do."

Roxane had paused while the thought went through her that if Hal had ever said to her, "I love you" or "I wish I were free to marry you," she would now be answering Thinus differently. She would be saying, "This new situation makes all the difference between you and me, Thinus—the difference between yes and no." Instead she had told him what she believed to be the absolute final truth.

"Hal wanted to find happiness with Alexa more than anything in life. He will be haunted by her always. She is part of him."

"And you are part of me, Roxie," he had answered, turning at last to face her. "You are the part that is good and sound. Without you there is nothing."

The simple sincerity with which he had spoken had stirred her profoundly. She would follow the course she had set for herself. There would be children of her marriage. Her great joy would one day lie in her children.

The morning of the Dieu Donné Fête in aid of Children's Day dawned warm and calm. No leaf moved.

By seven o'clock the farm-produce stalls were already overflowing with fresh fruit and vegetables, poultry, home-made pickles and preserves and Aletta Krige's famous *boer wors*. Louise Krifti brought pails of gladioli and pearly acanthus, and soon after breakfast Merle was decking out her needlework stall.

"These things are lovely," said Roxane, helping her to display her wares. "They'll go before you can turn round."

"All except Grannie Con's efforts," grinned Merle. "I'll probably have to buy those myself!"

Karl Krige had supervised the erection of the side-shows the evening before, and Thinus and Brink, the foreman, had arranged to take conducted tours round the famous Dieu Donné cellars.

By ten o'clock the grounds were already crowded, and when the Bishop of Cape Town, lame and pugnacious, humorous and kind, looked down from the platform to make his opening speech, he looked into the happy upturned faces of a host of children and their parents and grandparents. His heavy old heart lifted. Here was something good! This was going to be a family day, and everybody would have fun—white and coloured. That was as it should be.

Ben, in his white suit, guided Grannie Con's chair here, there and everywhere. And presently they stopped so that she might have a word with old Klaas, the gardener. Klaas cast anxious eyes over the living mosaic of his flower-beds. By this evening many of his blooms would have been trampled under careless little feet or plucked by naughty hands. Klaas did not approve of fêtes at Dieu Donné.

"It's good to share our blessings sometimes, Klaas," said Grannie Con.

"Ja, Oumissus," he agreed. "But children is like young animals in a garden. Dey mus' be put on a lead."

She laughed, but she had a certain sympathy for him. Tomorrow there would be a great deal of tidying up to do in this garden.

Roxane was in charge of the catering, and the old lady could see her slight figure flitting back and forth between the kitchen and the little tables set out under the oaks. And in a secluded corner of the grounds Grannie Con found "Pets' Corner," where Jannie Krige and his friends had assembled a motley collection of fauna. There were rabbits of many varieties, unwanted kittens and puppies, a tiny tame buck, and a roughly contrived aviary of budgerigars.

"And we have some canaries coming later," said Jannie. "And if anybody chooses love-birds from the aviary we will catch them and cage them. All the cages are ready."

Grannie Con kept her distance from Jannie. It was well known that he seldom stirred without his pockets full of tame snakes.

Everybody was busy. There was music over the loudspeaker, interrupted from time to time by announcements, and the air was full of the bird-like shrilling of children's voices. Grannie Con sighed. There should be children of Dieu Donné here today among these others. But Merle still laughed and said, "One of these days—when we've had our trip to Europe—then maybe——"

Grannie Con turned her head and made a gesture to Ben. "Leave me here," her lips said silently. She showed him her watch. "Come back in half an hour."

He nodded, and disappeared among the trees.

The place where she had chosen to remain was in the shade of a big nut-tree looking over the gardens and lawns, but out of range of the cheerful turmoil of the crowd. She could see without being seen.

But Mr. Krifti had observed her progress through the grounds and he now took the trouble to seek her out and talk to her.

"A lovely day, Mrs. de Valois—and successful too, by the look of it. Many hundreds of pounds have already been taken at the gate."

"So I hear, Mr. Krifti. We will do well for the Children's Fund, I hope."

"Unfortunately this sort of thing makes a shambles of the place." He indicated the flower-beds. "The little ones will be helping themselves!"

"I don't think so," she said. "In any case, as I told old Klaas, it is a pleasure to share the beauty of Dieu Donné with others once in a while."

"Why not share it always—at a handsome profit to yourself? The land on which I held a mortgage some months ago—I would like to buy that land. I would make you a very good offer for it."

In the face of his persistence, she felt old and tired. Is the fight going out of me? she wondered. He is always here—always trying to take my vineyards from me—by fair means or foul.

"What do you want it for?" she asked wearily.

"I want to give a great many people a great deal of pleasure—as you are doing today. I should like to put up a hotel on that portion of your property—to be run on the lines of a country club." He balanced himself on the shooting-stick he carried, his hands hung between his knees, and she saw that the ivory chaplet fashioned of miniature skulls was between his fingers. "I would commision Guy to design the place. It would mean a lot to him. . . ."

The pattern of leaves moved across his head. He was nearly bald. Only a few strands of grey hair covered the sallow scalp. He is getting on, she thought. He has to put his schemes into effect soon—or it will be too late. So now he was not only offering her money, but making her promises that would benefit Guy. Suddenly something clicked into place in her mind. When last Merle had talked about the forthcoming trip to Europe she had said, "Guy will soon have some big projects on hand. So we want to travel first. . . ." What big projects could Merle have meant? A fist seem to tighten over her heart and crush it. For a moment the warm green and gold of the morning turned grey and wintry.

She recovered herself.

"Mr. Krifti, I am not selling my vineyards—not any of them." But her voice was weak.

"Is it worth your while to hold them . . . to put off for a time . . . what is inevitable?"

She found it extraordinary—his capacity for instilling fear and doubt—this man whose manner was so gentle, and whose speech was always soft and padded.

"You must explain yourself," she said.

"Do you really want me to?"

She hesitated, dreading what he might say. Then she braced her shoulders.

"Yes, Mr. Krifti, I do."

"Then listen attentively, Mrs. de Valois. Those vineyards on which I held a bond are necessary to my plan for Hotel Constantia. It is a big scheme—it would bring money into the Valley —and trade. You redeemed the bond—and—for the time being —my plan fell through. But I still want to buy that land. Now, as you know, Merle's holding cuts into that portion of your property. If I am to carry out my intentions, I must have her plot too."

Grannie Con smiled thinly.

"I don't imagine my grand-daughter would sell her cottage and grounds without a word to me."

The little skulls were running through Mr. Krifti's fingers, fast now—sands through an hour-glass.

"You are wrong, Mrs. de Valois. Your grand-daughter looks ahead—and she has her husband's future at heart."

She said, with an effort, "What reason have you for thinking that Merle would sell out to you?"

"I hold an option on her property. If you had failed to redeem your bond Merle would have sold me her cottage the moment your vineyards were mine. By now the bulldozers would have been clearing the ground."

Again that cruel fist squeezed her heart. And now her thoughts scattered—the lost sheep of a distressed mind—but she set the dog, Will, to bring them back into the fold.

"Why should you tell me this? What good does it do either you or me?"

"I am trying to impress upon you the absolute futility of holding on to land that must eventually be lost to Dieu Donné."

Krifti knew that he was taking a risk. After his own peculiar fashion, he was a gambler. Before very long the big new arterial road through the southern suburbs of Cape Town would be skirting the Dieu Donné property. And, when that happened, the value of the land would rise steeply. He did not intend to wait for that appreciation if he could buy now. He wanted those vineyards—and he wanted them soon! He realized that the old lady might change her will if she suspected Merle of being ready to sell off Dieu Donné piecemeal as soon as her eyes were closed. But he was prepared to take a chance on that. For he knew that the idea of disinheriting her own flesh and blood would be utterly repugnant and alien to her. The only possible alternative heirs to the estate might—in extreme circumstances—be Grannie Con's nephew by marriage, Thinus Vos, or Roxane, the war-orphan so dear to her heart. But he was relying upon her fetish for keeping the de Valois blood with the de Valois heritage. In any case, he fancied that he could use her affection for Roxane to his own ends.

He said in a tone that was reasonable and persuasive:

"You have welcomed the world here today—and it makes you happy to see the enjoyment you are giving others. Why not shrink your borders by a few morgen and bring this outside world a little closer? What harm would it do? You would still have the core—the very soul of the Valley. Be content with it! Leave Merle that core clear of debt, so that she can do it justice. And bear in mind the fact that if you accept my offer for your land you will be in a position to assure Roxane's future also."

As she sat silent in her wheel-chair with the breath of defeat blowing over her, he made his final point.

"Don't sacrifice the substance of the present to the shadow of the past—the interests of the living to false loyalty to the dead!"

I am old, she thought, I am very old, and I want to do what is best and what is right. Perhaps all these years I have been wrong—too proud and unyielding in my determination to keep my estate intact. But a hotel—tourists—charabancs—native boys seeking women and liquor. . . . She closed her eyes and the picture that rose behind the lids destroyed all peace. She opened them to gaze once more upon the lovely prospect that was her heritage. Gardens and vineyards, mountains and sea. Must the ancient serenity of these be broken by modern buildings elbowing nature out of the way, eating noisily into the quiet undulating vista of the vines? She heard the voices of the children, the shouted commands of parents and the blare of the loudspeaker, and all the joy of the day died on those waves of sound.

As Grannie Con listened, she felt that she was no longer sure of herself, no longer sure of anything. There was a thought somewhere that was important—a black-sheep thought that she did not want to find—but it came unbidden—the sick, sad thought of Merle. All this time, while she had been fighting to preserve Dieu Donné, there had been Merle not caring—the secret enemy within the gates, biding her time to betray the citadel.

Mr. Krifti had risen and the point of his shooting-stick was describing patterns on the gravel. He was standing with his back to her and his shadow fell across her chair—the shadow of the vulture scenting the approach of death.

"Mr. Krifti," she said at last, "I will think about what you have said."

As he turned round she caught the gleam of satisfaction in his eyes. She knew that her words held the seed of capitulation. For the first time he had seriously breached her defences. And the betrayal had come from within Dieu Donné itself—from her own grand-daughter.

The coons had pranced away down the drive in their harlequin satin suits, followed by a band of wide-eyed coloured children singing and dancing with them. The last reluctant merry-makers had piled into their cars and driven away, the stall-holders had sold out and gone home, and Thinus had summoned a gang of boys and told them to begin cleaning up the grounds.

Roxane's helpers had tidied up the kitchen, and she stood with Thinus by the parapet leading down to the rose garden. Westward they could see the golden glow of the Hout Bay Gap. The southeaster had begun to blow—lightly as yet—and the leaves of the oaks were nodding and muttering. Wisps of cloud rolled over the berg—the ragged ends of the great white "table-cloth" that would by now have covered the face of the mountain.

"Lucky the wind didn't get up earlier," said Roxane, with a little yawn. She was tired, but it had been a good day with heavy takings.

"Have you seen Ben?" asked Thinus. "I wanted him to take charge of this cleaning party."

"He's gone off somewhere," she said. "Grannie Con needed him after tea and he was nowhere to be found. Soon after the coons came he disappeared. He can't bear seeing them—and I understand how he feels."

"Ja, my squirrel, you would understand. You walk about other people's minds like Klaas walks about that rose garden. You see the good and the bad, the flowers and the thorns, and the blight that destroys. But I must tell you, I am worried about Ben."

"Any particular reason?"

He looked towards the Tokay forests, soft and blurred in the gathering dusk, tossing a little already, and at the mountain bush behind Dieu Donné, and he said, "When the wind is rising the fires begin. There have been some bad fires round here this season, Roxie—too near Dieu Donné for my liking!"

"I know," she said. "Maybe Ben's gone to fight one. He seems to know of them by instinct. He's always first on the spot."

"Ja, Roxie, he is. And it strikes me that maybe he hasn't gone to fight a fire. Maybe he has gone to raise one."

She looked at him in dismay, and suddenly she recalled Lizzie's troubled face and the tears she had tried to hide. Did Lizzie suspect Ben of being a fire-bug?

"I suppose it is possible," she said slowly. "Ben has driven Lizzie crazy by seeking that particular form of excitement. And it *is* exciting—the sight of a bush-fire—especially at night with the wind fanning it. And Ben depends so much on *seeing and feeling*. . . ."

He laughed and kissed her hair that was blown by the rising wind.

"Will you never stop making excuses for people?"

"It isn't making excuses," she said slowly. "It's just my way of guessing why folk do the things they do."

"And the reasons are such rotten ones, sometimes," he said. "Such wretched reasons can make a fool of a man—or worse—a criminal! A few drinks too many, and he may do things for which he will never forgive himself as long as he lives. . . ."

She was vaguely aware of the unexpected force behind his words. But her mind was still on Ben.

"If Ben gets hold of drink and dagga—and if you are right about his fire-raising, he is dangerous," she said.

And there was the other thing that troubled her—the brutish hate in the boy's face whenever he looked at Thinus. "And he has turned against you in some strange way," she added.

He made a shrugging movement. "He has his motives. I have made it clear to him that if I catch him smoking dagga, or doing anything suspicious in the fire-bug line, I will report him to the police."

"What did he say?"

"He looked a good deal more than he said." Thinus did not tell Roxane that the boy had muttered under his breath, "So you'd like *me* out of the way too, Baas Thinus!" Or that the words had stuck in his mind, eating their way into his consciousness like a grass-seed working its way up his skin.

CHAPTER 23

SOLLY CAINE MAKES A SUGGESTION

Of late Thinus had taken to going to church with Grannie Con and Roxane. The old lady still made the ever-increasing effort required of her to attend divine service, and her wheel-chair in the aisle beside the front pew was as much of an institution as the great jar of flowers at the foot of the pulpit.

Thinus liked to go to church with Roxane. He liked watching her straight back and bowed head as she knelt in prayer, and hearing her pure soprano singing the hymns, but this indulgence had earned him the severe disapproval of his *Predikant*. He did not care. The act of going to the little English church was, in a way, a public avowal of his love for her. It had not passed unnoticed. Krifti said to Louise, "That young man has made up his mind, and he will get what he wants." But she only replied in her detached way, "You can't force love—any more than you can buy it."

Roxane too knew that in making this gesture—to him so important—Thinus was, in effect, tightening the bond between them in a way that laid considerable responsibility upon her. She also recognized that it was a matter for speculation among their friends—that many of them regarded it as a subtle method of announcing an engagement. And, while she was flattered, she was half alarmed. I'm not ready yet, she thought. But what she was not ready for, she hardly knew.

It was on the Sunday before Christmas that Guy and Merle stopped in the porch of the little grey stone church to talk to Grannie Con.

"My mother and Solly are coming to us for Christmas," said Merle. "Mother needs a change of air and a holiday. She has been overdoing things—so I said if she wanted to vegetate for a while there was nowhere to beat the Valley."

Grannie Con said brusquely, "It will be nice for Bella to see something of you for once—especially as you are going to Europe in April. How long will they stay?"

"Solly will be with us for a fortnight, but mother will probably remain on for a month or so."

Louise Krifti had joined them with her husband.

"Kriff and I would like Bella to come to us when she's tired of you, Merle. I'll write and tell her so."

Merle laughed. "Yes, do, Louise! Mother and I soon wear each other out."

Adrian Fairmead limped up to Roxane.

"Can you come in this morning? I have some work ready for you. Or shall I leave it at Dieu Donné?"

"No," she protested. "Don't do that! I'd love to come and fetch it, because then I'll have an excuse for seeing Sandra."

He smiled down at her.

"You women! When Sandra smiles the sun shines——"

"And do you wonder?" put in Lavinia. "Sandra is at the adorable age now. I assure you, she'll be walking and talking before she is a year old!"

"A phenomenon, of course. And every age is the 'adorable age' not to be missed." Adrian's weak eyes regarded his wife with amiable tolerance.

Roxane heard Thinus's slow, warm voice.

"When is her father coming to see Sandra? Will Hal be with you for Christmas?"

"No—unfortunately." Lavinia's tone was keenly disappointed. "His West African assignment has kept him longer than he expected. He will be in Kenya over Christmas and the New Year, and if we see him here in February we will be lucky."

The old familiar stab of pain and disappointment went through Roxane, but with it was a new sense of relief. She thought, Queer how it goes on hurting—even now it's all finished—like poor old Grannie Con's leg! You cut it off, but the phantom is still there. twitching and burning where there is no substance. The old lady's voice recalled her.

"We must be getting along, Roxie. Guy, give Thinus a hand with my chair, there's a dear! Goodbye, Adrian and Lavinia. . . . Yes, Louise, I would like to come to tea next week. Ring up and arrange it with Roxie, you know I hate talking on the telephone. Goodbye, Mr. Krifti."

Krifti was bowing in his over-polite, rather Oriental way. Roxane thought how odd it was that he should be here at all under the pines outside this little stone church. Thinus—yes, that was all right—but Mr. Krifti would surely be more at ease shoeless in a mosque intoning the responses of Islam. His flat, heavy-lidded eyes were on Grannie Con with a conspiratorial look Roxane did not understand. He is up to his tricks again, she thought. What is he up to now?

Christmas at Dieu Donné was less a day for the family than for the *volkies*, but everybody enjoyed it equally.

The Valley, in late December, was at the height of its summer fruitfulness. The wine grapes would not be ready for picking for a few weeks yet, but the trellises of early table grapes were weighted with their luscious burden, while peaches, plums, nectarines and apricots hung on the trees in red and yellow abundance. Outside the farm-stalls piles of great smooth green watermelons lay side by side with little rough-skinned *spanspeks* with firm salmon-coloured flesh and a strong exotic flavour.

The hydrangeas and cannas were at their brilliant best, and bougainvillaea spread its curtains of purple and red on white walls and parapets. Every now and again the emerald carpet of the vineyards was hemmed by the burning opulence of flowering gums or the delicate butterfly beauty of indigenous trees in full blossom; while, behind these, rose the mountains ethereal in the dancing heat. Eastwards the sea called with its dazzle of blue water and crested waves tumbling onto shining beaches that were silken under foot on a fine day but stinging against bare legs when the southeaster set the dunes smoking and the surf flying.

At noon on Christmas Day the vineyard workers and their families came up to the house for their Christmas *sopie* and presents. Their spokesman, a little wizened fellow with the yellow wedge-face of a primitive Hottentot, made a speech in the *taal* to thank the Oumissus for her goodness to them in all things. No *volkies* had a better *baas* than "die Oumissus van Doo Don."

Grannie Con was deeply touched. Each Christmas during the

past few years had seemed to her final—her last at Dieu Donné—
and this year the premonition that she would never receive her
people like this again was stronger than ever before. And the little
yellow man, looking up at his old mistress on her high stoep,
seemed to share her view. He spoke with the naïve candour of his
people.

"Oumissus *is* Doo Don," he said. "And when Oumissus goes the
heart of the Valley will stop beating."

The tears stood in her eyes as she thanked them for the year's
work and gave them her blessing.

Lizzie's midday dinner was superb, and after it everybody
chose somewhere for a siesta. Grannie Con retired to her bedroom
to doze in her favourite armchair. Merle and Guy pulled wicker
chaises-longues into a secluded spot under the oaks. Bella Caine
went to rest on the spare-room four-poster, with the shutters
closed against the heat and light, while Solly made himself comfortable on the canopied garden swing where he could watch
Thinus and Roxane helping to make the final preparations for the
Christmas party that was the year's great event for the coloured
children on the estate.

There was a Christmas tree in the *voorkamer* bright with tinsel
and baubles, and on either side of it were the great bran-tubs full
of lucky dips—one for boys and one for girls. Out of doors the
long trestle-tables were set for tea, and each child's place was
marked by rainbow-bright crackers and a packet of sweets. Later
in the afternoon there would be organized sports and races with
prizes, and the swings and slides that had been used for the fête
had been re-erected for the party.

Solly smiled as the children began to arrive, all neat as dolls in
their best dresses and suits. But soon black ringlets and butterfly
bows were bobbing and frilly skirts were whirling as the little
girls spun on the merry-go-round, and before long the boys'
patent leather shoes had been discarded so that they might run
their races unimpeded on the springy grass.

It was feudal, thought Solly. No wonder the old girl loved it!
She had been Oumissus here for God alone knew how many
years, and this place and these people were her whole reason for
existence.

And Roxie loved it too. Look at her now—getting the children together and making sure that they were all having the time of their lives! She was as much a part of Dieu Donné as if she had been born here, which only went to prove what environment could do for the right sort. Admittedly it hadn't done much for Merle—except antagonize her—but then Merle was very much Bella's daughter, and not at all in sympathy with this dreaming Valley of the Vines. Merle had never liked obligations and responsibilities. She was a taker, not a giver—and an estate like this needed a giver. It needed Roxane.

He could hear the drowsy drone of a big velvet bumble-bee, and the everlasting *werk stadig—werk stadig* of the doves; and now and again there was the quick scamper of a squirrel among the leaves. The children's voices, calling to one another in the *taal*, high and happy, skirled up from the lawns like the distant echo of bagpipes. An idea that had long been in the back of Solly's mind began to take definite shape. While he was here at the Cape he would put it up to Grannie Con. That part would be difficult. He must get everything taped first—talk to Fairmead, discuss the whole plan with Roxane, and then go in to the attack. But Christopher Columbus, that was the part he didn't fancy! How the devil did one ask the little old Queen of the Valley to abdicate?

Solly approached Grannie Con soon after the New Year.

"Talk to her in the morning," Roxane had advised him. "She is always at her best then. As the day goes on she gets tired—and sometimes confused."

So he took a cup of tea with her in the library.

Joshua had half-closed the slatted teak shutters to keep out the intense heat that so often followed the southeaster. The lofty room was cool and dim and smelt pleasantly of beeswax and roses. The old lady sat in her customary high-backed chair with her wheel-chair close at hand. She looked pale as crumpled parchment, but she poured the tea with a steady hand. She was fond of Solly and glad of his company.

He is too good for Bella, she thought. Too kind. One could confide in Solly. There were many things she would like to tell this plump shiny man with the benign, protruding eyes. Sometimes her secrets weighed upon her almost as heavily as her debts, and it seemed to her that the fraying net of her mind was wearing too thin to hold them. When she looked back over her long life the landscape was obscured here and there by mist. Then the sun broke through and the mist melted and what had been hidden came clear again. But these days the mist descended more frequently and the sun was slower to disperse it. If only she could have been sure of Merle—if only she could have trusted Merle— she felt that she would have been stronger to face whatever the future held in store.

She would have liked to tell Solly about the nightmare. Lately it had grown worse. It recurred night after night—Krifti, the surgeon, waiting to amputate her remaining leg, waiting to cut out her heart—first the vineyards, then the homestead—and now Merle assisted him. Merle wore the uniform of a theatre sister, her hard blue eyes stared down from over the white mask and her firm cold fingers held Grannie Con's pulse. "There," she would say to Krifti, the surgeon. "There, she's out! Now we can cut!" All last night Grannie Con had been at the mercy of the dreadful dream, and today she was exhausted.

"It's the heat," she said, when Solly remarked gently that she looked tired. "I feel it more than I did." But he knew that it was not the heat that had made her suffer.

They talked of Dieu Donné and the harvest to come, and presently the conversation found its way to Roxane.

"I worry about her," said the old lady. "I am getting on, and when I go—when Merle has this place—what will happen to Roxie? There is so little I can leave her. Dieu Donné has taken everything—more than I possess. . . ."

"She will marry Thinus," he said.

She sighed. "I worry about that too. Thinus has a nice income to supplement his salary, and one day he will have a good share of Tweefontein, but . . ." She shook her head. "I am not entirely satisfied about Thinus and Roxie."

"Any valid reason for your misgivings?"

But now she drew the blind down over her eyes and pursed up her lips, and he knew that she would say no more.

"You mustn't worry your head about Roxie," he said. "She gets a small legacy from her mother when she is twenty-one, and her godfather is making her a present of a thousand pounds. Apart from that, she is perfectly capable of earning her own living."

"You know a good deal, Solly."

"I make it my business to—on occasions."

"And why—on this occasion?"

"Because I have been working out a plan that concerns you and Dieu Donné—and Roxie."

She thought wearily, There is no plan that can save Dieu Donné with all its debts and mortgages. In a little while it will go the way of so much of this beautiful Valley. It will come under the auctioneer's hammer. God grant that the veil between this side and the other is thick—too thick for the eyes of spirits to penetrate! God grant that spirits no longer feel and suffer!

Solly said, "I am going to ask you to consider a proposition— in principle. As yet I have no details worked out. But if you accept the principle, the rest will follow."

She gave him her attention.

"This estate is limping, Grannie Con. I don't need to tell you that it is limping badly. And the measures that have been taken to keep it going can only be temporary."

Mr. Krifti had told her the same thing on the day of the fête— but Mr. Krifti was her enemy and Solly was her friend. Suddenly she knew who Jimmy Jordaan's anonymous client had been—the man whose loan had redeemed Mr. Krifti's bond. She said nothing —just put out her hand in a little gesture of gratitude. Dear Solly. . . .

He went on: "Dieu Donné could be run as a limited company, consisting of perhaps yourself, Adrian Fairmead, Roxie and me. We are all interested in the fortunes of Dieu Donné, we love it and we want to see it kept intact and running at a profit. You would sell out to the company, keeping only your share in it— a big one. Roxie will have a little money to invest when she is twenty-one—her mother's legacy and her godfather's gift—and I will give her a block of shares for her birthday. I have no children of my own. If I want to make Roxane a present, no one can stop me!" His voice was fired with the spirit of defiance, and Grannie Con smiled, knowing that this was aimed at Bella.

"The creation of a company need make no difference to the running of the estate," he continued. "Except that there will be capital upon which we will be able to draw for improvements; and your autocratic powers, dear Grannie Con, would be whittled down. Thinus, I am sure, would be welcome to remain on as manager, and his salary would no doubt be raised. As for yourself —you would remain here in the homestead for your lifetime, after which it would be the responsibility of the directors to decide who should occupy it and under what conditions. In any event, we will solemnly undertake to preserve it, not only as a private home, but as valuable Africana—the oldest, most historic and loveliest homestead in the first vine-growing valley of the Cape."

The old lady said quietly, "Where does Merle come in?"

Solly sat up and leaned towards her, his hands on his knees, his prominent eyes as hard as Merle's own could sometimes be.

"She doesn't. At least, not at present. That is my only condition in this deal. If you care to bequeathe her your portion of shares there is no reason against it. But she will not be able to sell them in the open market—or to whomsoever she may wish. If she wants to dispose of them, they must be offered to us—the directors—first. If we do not want them, she can sell—with our approval. We will fix a fair price. The same rule will govern the actions of all shareholders in the company."

He had made each point on a plump finger, and when he was done he slapped his hands back on his knees. As he did so Grannie Con began to feel that the burden and confusion of the past few months was lifting. The noonday sun of Solly's presence was diminishing the long evening shadow of Mr. Krifti. *Merle would not be allowed to sell out to Mr. Krifti.* Yet one last regret lingered to embitter this solution to her difficulties.

"The de Valois heritage . . ." she murmured.

Where were the children of Merle's blood—the future that was the continuation of the past?

He said, with kindness in his face once more, "If Merle keeps the share you leave her in your will and bears babies for Dieu Donné—and if she wants to give her life to this place—I cannot conceive of there being any objections."

"But will Merle want those things?"

"Ah, Grannie Con—there you have it! Dieu Donné has never been Merle's paradise. She has chosen always to see it as her prison. Now Roxie—Roxie belongs here with all her great heart! Has that thought no comfort for you?"

She buried her face in her hands, and he saw the pitiful swollen knuckles and the bluish nails, and the smooth thinning white hair of her bowed head. He went over to her and patted her shoulder.

"There now—I didn't mean to upset you. Of course it isn't quite the same. Roxie doesn't belong to your family except by adoption—but it is something."

She looked up at him, her old tearless eyes stern and filled with new courage.

"It is a great deal, Solly. You don't know how much. I am most grateful to you for your plans—and for your understanding. I accept your suggestions . . . in principle . . . and your reservations."

The day before Solly returned to Johannesburg, he and Bella and the Mastersons dined at Dieu Donné.

When Thinus and Roxane said goodnight to them at the foot of the pink stoep steps, Solly took Roxane's hands.

"You'll come and stay with us in Johannesburg just as soon as Bella gets back? Our home will always be open to you."

She answered, "I would love to." But she was aware of Bella Caine stiffening at Solly's side, and the significant silence that followed her response. Bella made no attempt to endorse the invitation, and her voice, as she bade them goodbye, was cold as steel. It cut away the warmth of Solly's offer—sliced off all suggestion of welcome and threw it away.

Back in their bedroom at Merle's cottage, Solly—usually so tolerant and placid—turned on Bella with fury.

"How could you behave like that? How could you be so mean and cruel?"

"You took too much upon yourself. If you want to keep open house for your young women friends I suggest you consult me first."

She was brushing her hair—brassy auburn with the grey showing at the roots. I'm getting careless, she thought, letting myself go. She saw the curl of her own lip, so like that of her daughter, Merle, and the dark circles under her jewel-bright eyes. The tops of her arms were flabby and there was a heavy roll of flesh between her brassière and her belt. It spoilt the set of her expensive close-fitting dress. Getting old was damnable. No compensations anywhere!

"You hate Roxane," he said, staring at the tight-lipped image in the mirror. "You've always hated her—even as a child. It's unaccountable——"

"Perhaps I don't like seeing you make a fool of yourself about a girl young enough to be your daughter. Perhaps all this sugar-daddy stuff sickens me."

He made a contemptuous gesture. "You know I'm not that sort."

"Every man is that sort—given the right circumstances—especially a man whose wife is no longer physically attractive to him."

As if to underline her words, she had begun to "take off" her face, revealing the naked wrinkles of middle age and the sagging signs of the years of self-indulgence. He watched with helpless disgust. Why did Bella have to do these things? She had always been able to attract him—still could if she wanted to! Why otherwise would he have married her—a hard shrewd woman wearing the mask of charm—a mask she stripped off on the slightest provocation? He began to pace up and down the room, hands clasped behind his back.

"Stop that!" she said. "You make me dizzy!"

He stood still.

"Why do you deliberately misconstrue everything?"

His jaw was thrust out, and his eyes seemed to burst from their sockets. She thought that he looked like an angry fish, and a smile crossed her face and faded, as it occurred to her that certain fish could be more ferocious than lions.

"Do I? Are you telling me that you are not in love with Roxane de Valois?"

His fists clenched. "This twisting of a good feeling! Can't you give me credit for a decent affection? Can't you see what Roxie means to me? She is the daughter I have never had—the daughter I would have wanted——"

She swung round from the mirror and called out in a low, choked voice, "So Merle isn't good enough for you!"

"Leave Merle out of it! Merle is *your* daughter through and through."

She had begun to shiver in spite of the heat.

"And Roxane?"

"Roxie is herself—lovable, unselfish, spontaneous, a giver, not a taker——"

"So Merle is a taker?"

"I didn't say so."

She clasped her hands over her ears as if to shut out the meaning of his words—or some echo ringing in her own head.

"Perhaps Roxane is a taker too," she said. "Perhaps she takes love to which she is not entitled——"

For a moment she thought that he would strike her.

"Very well, then," she said, as he turned away from her, mastering himself. "I admit it. I *do* hate Roxane." All the heat had gone out of her. Ice froze over her face and voice. "And I will tell you why. I have been deceived. On every side I have been deceived."

She talked. For a long time she talked. And, as she did so, he saw her soul as naked as her unpainted face—and found it in his heart to pity her. She might cover her predatory hands with diamonds, dye her hair, lift her face and control her figure, but there was nothing she could do to change or preserve her mean and loveless soul.

He put his arms about her.

"My poor Bella—my poor Bella——"

And it was her poverty that touched him—the poverty of soul that even his great fortune could not enrich.

CHAPTER 24

THE CHINESE GAME

The great heat of December and January had ripened the grapes early, and, by the middle of March, the pressing season was over.

Thinus said, "Now at last we can make a plan to go to Twee-fontein, Roxie. We will go for two or three days and receive my old folks' blessing on our engagement. After all, it is only a fort-night now to your birthday."

She caught her breath. Just for a moment it seemed to her that she stood on a high ledge looking straight down the sheer buttress of Table Mountain. Now she must let herself go—or hold back. If she let herself go would she float down like the southeaster "table-cloth"—so far and no farther, safe in the white sunlit cloud rolling over Saddle Face and lifting gently above the wind-tossed gardens of the city? Or would she crash at the foot of the rampart—a broken useless thing?

They were standing at the door of the cellar on the threshold of two worlds—on one side the cool, dim world of old oak casks and young fermenting wine, simmering at this season with the noisy bubbling life of Bacchus; and, on the other, the summer world of the Valley with its leaf-filtered sunshine patterned on white walls and gables. And these two worlds, the one dark and dangerous and the other clear and joyous, were part of the same design—the man-made life cycle of the grape with all its good and evil, its pleasures and its perils.

As she did not answer immediately, Thinus glanced down at her, impatient for her reply.

She looked cool and detached in her linen riding shirt and whip-cord jodhpurs and she tapped one suède veld-boot with a supple quince switch. The mottled light brought out gold and violet glints in her hair, and her downcast lashes were thick and silky, hiding her eyes. He was suddenly aware of insecurity, his whole body invaded by some obscure doubt that left no room for air. He breathed deeply, waiting for her to speak.

"If that is what you want—then, yes," she said at last.

If they accept me, she thought, if Oom Jacob and Tante Pet make me welcome, then the last door will be closed.

"It will be hard for your parents," she added. "They aren't going to want a daughter-in-law who is not of their church."

"They will want you."

"You can't be sure."

"Ja, my little heart—I am sure. I wrote a few days ago to tell them about us, and this morning I received their reply. They understand, and they are content."

She looked up sharply. "But, Thinus, you didn't tell me you had written!"

"I wanted to have the answer first."

"Were you afraid it might hurt me?"

"I suppose so, my squirrel. Roxie—does it please you that they want you?"

I ought to be so glad, she thought. I ought to say so and throw my arms round his neck with gladness. But there was no room in her throat for words, and he saw that there were tears on her lashes. His arm encircled her as she said shakily, "It does please me, dear Thinus. . . . I am . . . very proud. . . ."

When they announced their intention of going to Tweefontein, Grannie Con said, "I am sorry, my children, but you will have to wait a few days. I have just had a wire from Solly Caine. He arrives today by air from Johannesburg. The papers have been drafted forming the Dieu Donné estate into a limited company and they are ready for signing. I must have Roxie here while everything is settled because she is closely concerned. After that you can make your arrangements."

"Then it is going through—this deal?" Roxane's tone was incredulous. Somehow she had never believed that Grannie Con would really relinquish the reins, and when her eyes sought the old lady's face she saw that this had been no easy decision. It is her short face, she said to herself, when she folds it down and shuts it tight.

Thinus, who had been consulted about the plan originally, said, "So the Queen will sign the Deed of Abdication. . . ."

"I have made my decision and I will stand by it," said Grannie Con.

Thinus made a gesture that was part regret and part admiration.

"There is no more to be said. Do you want Joshua to meet the noon plane?"

"No, Solly is going straight in to Cape Town to see Jimmy Jordaan. He will lunch in town and come out by taxi some time this afternoon."

"He never wastes time," smiled Roxane. She glanced at her watch. Half-past ten. Solly would be well on his way.

Grannie Con nodded. "I don't expect he will stay here very long —only a few days—and then you will be free to go up-country." Her eyes had clouded. She was looking at Roxane and thinking that before the girl went to Tweefontein there was something it was her duty to tell her—something she ought to know. She sighed. The loose ends of life . . . the loose ends . . . there were so many . . . and they were hard to collect when one was old and feeble with the fingers of the mind no longer deft and bold. It was strange that Jacob had not frowned upon his son's wish to marry the daughter of a Papist. Perhaps she herself had influenced him by making Stephanus happy all those years ago. How bitter that early feud had been, with Jacobus refusing to speak to his brother because Stephanus had seen fit to marry a woman of the Church of England! But time and the gentle intercession of Petronella had worked their kindly magic, and Jacob had been brought to see that the love of God does not discriminate between the children of one church and those of another. People grew old in different ways. In some, tolerance flowered in the thin dry soil of approaching dissolution—in others, it withered and died. Jacobus was growing old in the better way. She would like to see him again—and Petronella too—dear motherly Pet. She must invite them to stay with her.

Roxane's voice cut through her reflections. "Then after Solly has gone we will make our plans, Thinus." She jumped up from the arm of the chair on which she had been perched. "I'm sorry you can't ride with me this morning, but Rooinek needs a gallop.

And then afterwards I am going over to Farway for a swim before lunch."

She rode alone through the plantations of Tokay—galloping the big chestnut gelding along the wide fire-paths. A few wisps of cloud trailed over the berg, and she knew that by evening the southeaster would be blowing.

The exercise brought colour to her cheeks and the pounding of Rooinek's hooves beat to the rhythm of the question hammering at her brain—"Am-I-doing-*right*? Am-I-doing-*right*? Am-I-doing-*right*?" Later this afternoon, when the heat of the day had subsided, she would go to her secret place to get "smoothed out." It was still her secret place—secret from everybody, even Thinus. Everybody except Hal—Hal had been there with her. . . .

As the big horse slackened his pace to a canter Roxane saw, without really observing, a figure among the trees—a figure that was vaguely familiar and that flattened itself against the trunk of a pine at the approach of horse and rider. But her mind had turned inwards and she gave no thought to that lurking form. It remained a phantom in her consciousness, significant, yet unremarked.

She leaned forward to pat the horse's withers. Sweat foamed on his glossy coat, and her own hair was damp on her forehead. It had been a long hot summer, starting early and establishing breathless noonday records. She turned Rooinek's head towards Farway. It would be wonderful to plunge into the pool! And baby Sandra would go in with her. That infant would be swimming as soon as walking!

One of the Farway boys took Rooinek from her, loosened his girth and led him round to the stable. And there was Elias coming across the lawn to intercept her as she went to the pool. His black face gleamed in the melting heat, but his white tunic and jaunty cap were as crisply starched as ever and his scarlet sash burned in the sun. Elias, like most native house-boys, was a dandy both on and off duty.

"Miss Roxie," he rumbled. "Madam, he is out—but Nannie, he say he bring Missie Sandra for swim."

The water was Lido-blue and invitingly transparent, and Roxane was already standing in the shallow end of the pool when Nannie arrived with the golden baby in a tiny red *bikini*. At eleven months old Sandra was a child of unusual strength and activity—small, neither fat nor thin, but "intensely concentrated," as Lavinia put it. At sight of Roxane the little one crowed and put out her arms, bounding in her nurse's grasp.

"There," said Nannie, leaning down. "There's your water-baby, Miss Roxane. I'll leave her with you."

The tiny dimpled hands were in Roxane's and soon she was trailing the gaily kicking Sandra through the sun-warmed water.

"Time to get out," she said at last. The wet little body was clasped against her breast, the arms wound about her neck, the soft cheek close to her own. She kissed the damp pale curls. "You darling," she said aloud. "You lovely piccaninny!"

"Hand her up to me!"

Roxane's grip tightened on the child, and for an instant it seemed to her that the pool swung right round in space before it returned to normal.

"*You!*" she gasped. "But how can it be you?"

There was elation in his laugh—a wild joy she had never heard in it before.

"If you won't give her up, I will have to come and get her!"

Hal—spare, sun-browned, all muscle, bone and sinew—sprang into the water. His arms, held out for the child, encircled the girl as well.

"Roxane—Roxane! It's so wonderful to see you—you and this little one! Can this really be Sandra?"

She stammered, "But when—but how? Nobody expected you——"

"I couldn't let anybody know I was coming. I didn't even know myself—not till I was given a seat on this morning's plane from Johannesburg. And who do you think was on that plane? Solly Caine!"

"I know," she said. "But you——?"

"I have come from Rhodesia—from Salisbury—I got to Johannesburg last night and slept in the airport. . . . But never mind all that! Elias said Dad and Vee were out and that you were swimming with the infant. So I pulled my bathing trunks out of my suitcase—and here I am——"

"Sandra's getting cold," she said on a laugh that was near tears. "I must dress her."

"Here's Nannie! I haven't seen Nannie since that awful day when they all sailed." He had jumped out of the pool and now he lifted his daughter high above his head till she was helpless with deep-throated chuckles of ecstasy.

"Mr. Fairmead! Elias told me you were here. I couldn't make sense out of it—sometimes he is so incomprehensible—but it's true!"

"It's true all right. And this gorgeous thing is Sandra—the tiny bundle you took away so long ago."

"She *is* beautiful," said Nannie smugly. "But it's high time she was dressed. This is her lunch hour and nothing is allowed to disturb that."

Reluctantly he handed his daughter to her nurse.

"After her nap you may play with her," Nannie conceded. "She is at her sweetest then."

They watched Nannie striding over to the house and the little fair head just visible over her shoulder.

"She's a good soul," said Roxane. "But nothing must ever be allowed to interfere with routine. Not even an earthquake—nor your return."

They sat with their legs dangling in the water.

"I have so much to tell you," he said. "Terribly important things. When can we be alone together?"

"We are alone now."

"For five minutes perhaps! Roxane, I have come here as quickly as possible to see you. . . . I met Simonoff in Salisbury—the ballet touring company is in Rhodesia now—and there are things you and I have to talk about—get straight."

He was vital in a way that amazed her. The shimmering air all round him seemed to vibrate. He looked tough and hard. Older. His wet hair sprang up in vigorous curls all over his head, the scar of Malaya was taut down his cheekbone and the stab wound of Johannesburg had left its small round hollow over his heart. That had been a close call! One slender rib had staved off death.

She wanted to touch his chest—to feel the brave rib that had saved him. She wanted to run her fingers through that springing hair. . . . She must tell him—tell him now—that she was going to marry Thinus. But her lips formed other words.

"I am going for a walk this evening. Meet me at the top of the orchard—the one behind Dieu Donné where we used to meet—at five-thirty."

He nodded—and then sprang to his feet as they saw Lavinia hurrying across the lawn, her sophisticated little head high and silver-bright in the sun. A few paces behind her was Adrian, grey and lame.

Hal ran to meet them with the long loping stride of a natural athlete. Roxane watched him take his mother in his arms, and then she turned away and went into the log cabin to dress.

I should have told him, she thought, as she pulled on her shirt. What madness stopped my telling him? Nothing he could say can change anything now. Oom Jacob and Tante Pet have set their seal on the future—the future of Thinus and me. Hal has come back too late.

She was hurrying along the path at the side of the orchard—a swift little figure with tossing hair and a thin cotton dress blowing about her legs in the first whisper of the southeaster. Wolf, the Alsatian, trotted at her heels.

So often Hal had seen them thus, the girl and the dog, coming to meet him here in the Valley when Alexa had refused him her company. He had wondered, even then, if a man could be in love with two women at the same time—and two so different. Then there had been London, and his loneliness in the knowledge that, emotionally, physically and practically, his marriage had been wrecked by Alexa's other loyalty—her first loyalty—to her career. And at that moment Roxane had entered his life once more —a moment full of tension and peril for both of them.

Now he felt his heart lift at the sight of her, and it was all he could do not to take her and crush her to him there and then. But, as she drew near and looked up at him, he read in her eyes some message that, for an icy instant, suspended all the urgent life in him. He fell into step at her side, and together they followed the course of the stream to the waterfall. Wolf and the Farway lion-dogs trotted ahead of them.

Their talk was impersonal, the prelude to all that must presently be said and made clear to them. He told her of his African tour. He had found it absorbing to witness the growing ferment as the African strove to come to political maturity despite the primitive ingredients still uppermost in him—witchcraft and atavistic superstition, cruelty that was animal because unwitting, and an ancient addiction to slavery.

"He still enslaves his own people—or sells them down the river just as he did in the bad old days when the white man bought 'black ivory' in Africa. Things go on in the dark heart of this continent that you would never believe, young Roxane!"

The Rhodesias, with their varying viewpoints easily corralled in the new Federation with Nyasaland, had been a fascinating study. "There is jealousy between North and South, and an ugly rash of Communism on the Copper Belt. But these things will come right because the Rhodesias are young and progressive—and they have faith in the future."

Rhodesia . . . In Salisbury, the capital of the new Federation, he had met Simonoff. . . .

They had come to the glade. The waterfall was only a trickle now, and the stream was thin. The trees were already wearing the colours of early autumn, and the moss on the sun-baked boulders was dry and shrunken.

They chose a patch of shady grass and sat down to rest. She pushed the damp tendrils of hair off her forehead while he clasped his hands about his knees.

He said, "When I saw you this morning the world stood still. Roxane—darling—will you marry me?"

She trembled violently. And then he saw weariness come into her eyes as she regained control of herself. He thought, But she loves me—I know she loves me—she *must* say yes!

Instead she said, "You don't need to find a mother for Sandra. Lavinia adores her. She never wants to part with her."

"I'm asking you to be my wife." There was hurt and anger in his tone, and his voice shook as he said, "I love you, Roxane—I think I've loved you always——"

He heard her long sigh as he moved to take her hands.

"You have never said that before, Hal."

"How could I? I wasn't free to say it——"

"You never *wanted* to be free to say it!"

"That's not true!"

"It is true. And now it is too late. I am going to marry Thinus."

He felt her hands limp and cold in his—and the curious dead stillness of her. A flame had died in her. There had been a flame and it had died.

"It is all settled," she went on in that lifeless tone he hardly recognized. "There can be no going back——"

"Nonsense!" The anger in him rose above the hurt. "You belong to me. You knew it when you were still a schoolgirl that night at the *braaivleis*—you knew it here the day we parted—and you knew it that night in London at my flat! You know it now! I couldn't come to you sooner. Something stood in the way, something that haunted me—drove me mad. It's only now that the spell has been broken—only now that I really feel free. I had to wait. While that terrible haunt was on me I couldn't come to you and look for happiness . . ."

She had withdrawn her hands quietly from his, and he had let them go. She leaned back on her palms and faced him.

"What haunt, Hal? The haunt of Alexa—of loving her? Because that will be with you forever."

He shook his head. "You don't understand, darling—how can you? Alexa and I have hurt each other to the limit." He paused, and she saw the darkening of his grey eyes.

"The Chinese have a game, Roxane," he said. "Ah, my God, what a cruel game! Lexa and I were the victims of such a game."

"What game?"

"The Chinese are so kind—and so terribly subtly cruel. This game I speak of is one of their cruelties. But it makes them laugh —as maybe the gods laughed at Lexa and me. . . ."

"Tell me, Hal!"

"They snare two wild birds and tie them together. Not closely. The cord that holds the birds is thin, but it is long and strong— so long that, when they are thrown into the air to fly, they believe they are free. It is a matter of seconds before they feel the wrench, the pain and the panic. Then what fun it is for the watchers! Hilarious! The birds, frantic with bewilderment and terror, flutter wildly here and there, the stronger tugging the the weaker. Feathers fly from their bruised wings and damaged bodies, blood drips in the air. Perhaps the cord becomes entangled in the branches of a tree, or it winds itself about the birds, they are mad with fear—trapped by the bond which holds them together. You can see their little hearts beating through the soft torn feathers and hear their cries. They may fight the cord that ties them, or fight each other or batter themselves to pulp among the leaves. But there is no escape. One dies—or both do—before the game is over. . . ."

He covered his face with his hands—the long powerful brown hands she knew so well. Then he said:

"Alexa and I were like those birds in the Chinese game. And it was my fault that we were snared. I insisted that we be tied together—married. And afterwards I believed that it was I who killed her. That was my haunt."

She touched his arm with tentative sympathy.

"Poor Hal. You have never talked to me about Alexa and you. Talk now. Let it all be said."

"You remember the day you brought me here—the last day before Alexa and I left Farway and went back to England—so suddenly?"

"You were sad and troubled that day—but you never told me why."

"That day I had felt the first wrench—the first frightening tug on the cord that bound us. Poor Lexa, it was worse for her . . . she had found that she was going to have a child. To her it was a trap . . . the beginning of death. In a way it was! Poor Lexa. . . . I didn't understand her attitude. I could have been very happy and proud of that baby—about Sandra——" He broke off, and made a helpless movement with his shoulders.

She said softly, "So she went home suddenly because she hoped to find somebody to—help her?"

He nodded.

"She was desperate at first—determined not to go through with it. But it was late already—and she was persuaded that it would be best for her to have the child. She couldn't forgive me."

As Roxane watched him—his face drawn with remembering—she seemed to see two wild white birds dragging at the cord that bound them—fighting on the wing—bleeding and dying.

"That night at the première of *Ballerina*—you remember the tall grey man, the director of the film, standing there on the stage after the show, with Alexa and my father? You remember the speech he made introducing her? He said that Alexa Rome—unlike the ill-fated heroine, Olga—had successfully combined marriage, motherhood and a career. I could have shot him! The travesty of it!"

He turned and faced her. "Roxane, I knew then that it was finished between Lexa and me—but I still refused to admit it. When one is proud it isn't easy to accept defeat. I still hoped that perhaps, after her Australian tour, Alexa might come to love Sandra—that we might find some working basis for our marriage. It was all futile, of course. . . ."

He leaned against the warm trunk of a blighted tree, and this time, when he took her hand she let it lie in his. He touched her fingers as if he were blind—as if he explored their fine tapered shape with the sense of touch alone.

"It was so strange that you should have been there—on the night of the première. Will I ever forget seeing you? The show was over and the stage was empty—and, when I looked round, you were there."

The sun was low over the shoulder of the berg and the shadows were lengthening. The bush was alive with the twittering and calling of birds. A fresh coolness came up from the stream, and he felt her move nearer to him. They were silent, remembering the brief happy period during which she had been his secretary and his constant companion.

She said, "Listen to the birds, Hal."

"Telling their bedtime stories—this is their busy time."

He slipped his arm round her and her head lay back against the curve of his shoulder.

"The starlings," she murmured. "The starlings in Whitehall that evening before you went away—and the gulls wheeling over the river catching the last light on their wings. . . ."

Her words sounded in his ears like a love-song.

"The gulls wheeling over the river——" he echoed, "and you . . . Everything about that night has stayed in my mind—clear—so clear! That was the night I knew I really loved you—only you. After I had taken you home to Chelsea, I went back to that empty flat—God, how empty it seemed with you gone!—and I wrote to Lexa. I told her that I loved you, Roxane, that I wanted my freedom to marry you. I wanted Sandra too—I wanted everything a man could ask of life—my love and my child. . . ."

If she had known—if she had only known!

"It was only afterwards that I realized what bad notices Lexa was getting in Australia and New Zealand. Something had gone out of her dancing—out of herself—and for that she blamed me—and Sandra. The way to the top—so steep, Roxane; a few months lost is a long slide back. Lexa was so afraid of losing ground. And then those bad notices proved that she was disappointing her audiences and her critics."

Suddenly Roxane knew what he was trying to tell her—what his "haunt" had been. She was back at the première of *Ballerina,* she was seeing that tragic final act when Olga had discovered that she had lost her lover to another woman—when she knew that life without him was not worth living. Had Hal's letter reached Alexa in her moment of failure? Had it been the last straw? Had she felt that now there was nothing—neither fame nor love?

Hal went on, "When I got the cable telling me what had happened to Lexa I was certain that I was to blame—that my letter, coming on the heels of all her fears and anxieties, had been the final blow to her confidence. I couldn't bear it—I hated myself for having tried to walk out on her as a woman when she was finished as a dancer."

"It wasn't your fault!" she cried quickly. "No one can tell what really happened—it may have been an accident—they said it was!"

"No one can tell," he agreed. "But all the same, that was my haunt—the conviction that my letter had made her believe herself completely abandoned. . . ."

As she moved her head her hair touched his cheek. How soft it was—how fresh!

"Then in Rhodesia I saw Simonoff—only three days ago, yet it seems years. . . . Roxane, he gave me that letter I had written to Alexa. *It had never been opened—she had never read it!* It had only arrived after her death. Simonoff knew it was from me, and he didn't send it back to me through the post in case it went astray—as it might well have done, because I went on my African assignment very soon after—the news—reached me. I think he guessed what was in that letter. He is a queer half-feminine sort of chap, a creature of strong intuition. We talked . . . for hours we talked about Alexa . . . Simonoff reproached himself bitterly for letting her see that he thought she was slipping. He put it to me in his own way. He said Lexa was finished as a prima ballerina assoluta. The mainspring had gone—less in her dancing than in herself—the source of her inspiration seemed to have dried up, and with it her confidence. If he had helped her to regain her confidence she might have won back to being technically perfect——"

"*Technically* perfect? Alexa! No, Hal, that would never have satisfied her. She had so much more. There is all the difference in the world between technical perfection and the sort of genius Alexa brought to her dancing—the difference between breathing and living!"

As Roxane spoke, the voice of Adrian came back to her, and she saw him again as he had been that day in the tower-room—thoughtful, analytical, trying to explain his daughter-in-law, Alexa— "From early childhood, her body has been dedicated to dancing. Then Hal came. And suddenly . . . her body was moon-mad and sick with love. It was the old, old magnetism that betrayed her into marriage—the force none of us can deny or escape——" And the dancer's body had paid the price of the woman's fulfilment. . . .

"Perhaps you are right," said Hal sadly. "I guess it was just fate playing the Chinese game with Lexa and me—two wild birds tied to each end of one cord and thrown into the air to fly—and Lexa was the one that died."

The sun had gone behind the berg, and the birds called drowsily now like children on the edge of sleep. The sky, framed in the Hout Bay Gap, was wind-brushed by flying clouds, pink-lined like a flock of flamingos rising from the vlei. There was a rustle in the leaves and a murmur in the pines, and the long bell-grasses tinkled faintly and swayed together, dry and pale, in the breath of the rising wind.

"If only I had known," said Roxane. "If only you had told me that you wanted your freedom for my sake—everything might have been different. But now it is too late."

"It is not too late," he said. "You can't fight this, my little love. . . ."

He held her to him, feeling the life flow back into her body, feeling the frozen numbness melt and her tears on his lips as he kissed her eyes. "You know that you are mine, Roxane—only and always mine." She clung to him. So this was it—the wonderthing! This was what it meant to be all in all to each other—to love each other equally, to want each other with body and spirit!

Yet there was no singing in her heart. She saw only the blind, kind face of Thinus waiting to be struck—waiting for the blow that would kill his happiness.

When they came down the berg along the track between Farway and Dieu Donné Wolf bounded away from the two ridgebacks with little whines of pleasure.

Thinus said, "Hullo, jongie," and took the fine head between his hands, rocking it gently. "Come to meet me, have you?"

He saw them approach in the dusk—the way they walked with a rhythm that matched, their faces rapt—two human beings set apart and belonging. His heart drowned and sank in his broad chest, and he found it hard to greet Hal and to drag words and a smile from the ache that had seized his throat.

"So you're back, Hal, man," he made himself say. "I have seen your mother; she is very happy."

Hal's hand grasped his. "It's good to be back in the Valley,

Thinus. I mean to settle down here for a while—perhaps altogether—buy a farm and make this my home."

Thinus walked beside them, and Roxane saw the tightening of his mouth at Hal's words, but his expression was hidden from her, blinkered by the black eye-mask. Usually he walked on her other side, so that they could see one another. What was he thinking? What was he fearing?

"I have been looking for you, Roxie," he said presently. "Solly arrived some time ago and there are many things to discuss. He has been at Farway—and after dinner Adrian is coming over to sign the papers about Dieu Donné." He turned to Hal. "Your father has a big interest in a new plan to farm Dieu Donné as a company. We never believed that Grannie Con would agree to give up control of the estate. But she has aged a great deal since last you saw her. How old she is none of us know—but we do know that she is feeling her years—that she is tired."

They paused at the gap in the fence. The poplars had begun to toss their tall green heads and there was a wailing in their boughs.

"I will come over to Dieu Donné after dinner with Dad," said Hal. "I want to pay my respects to Grannie Con. As a matter of fact, I heard something about the new scheme from Solly Caine. We came from Johannesburg on the same plane."

"Then we'll see you later," said Roxane. Her smile in the fading light was that of one who dreams.

Thinus took her arm as they strolled over to the homestead.

"What time is it?" she asked.

"Nearly half-past seven—dinnertime."

"Too late for me to change."

"Is it too late for you to change? I don't know. Hal comes back, Roxie, and at once you are lost—I look for you—and you are lost . . ."

She heard the deeper meaning in his words, but it brushed past her like the wings of a night-bird—like the cool, ominous breath of the rising wind.

CHAPTER 25

ABDICATION

In the silence that fell when Grannie Con put down her pen they could hear the roaring of the southeaster.

The wind had risen fast during the two hours since sunset, and the great oaks rocked in its fury. On the stoep the hydrangeas—near the end of their season, no longer heavy and fleshy but paper-light—whispered thinly in their tubs; and in the library the heavy damask curtains moved with the gusts that rattled the teak shutters.

Adrian Fairmead found that moment of silence extraordinarily impressive. The atmosphere was loaded. It was charged with more, he felt, than the future of Dieu Donné, though that in itself lent the occasion drama.

Grannie Con sat in her high-backed chair with a light shawl over her lap. She wore her best black afternoon gown and her hair was even more carefully dressed than usual. It shone silver in the light of the bracket lamp, and her face was as pale as the cameo brooch at her throat, fine-drawn, dignified and so old that it was ageless.

She looked up at Solly Caine as he took the papers from her.

"I hope I have done right," she said. "I hope with all my heart that I am doing the best thing for the preservation of Dieu Donné."

He answered gently, "Have no doubts about that! And now we will get Thinus and Hal to witness your signature."

He laid the document on the desk.

Adrian saw the two men move towards it—Thinus sturdy and blond, a faithful-looking fellow with his face rendered oddly inexpressive by that mask, and Hal, taller and much younger, with the arrogant carriage of the head so like his mother's.

"Here," said Solly, "this is where you sign."

Adrian's glance found the sixth figure in the room. Roxane, in the plain summer dress she had worn that afternoon, stood with

her back to the empty fireplace. She had the look of a doe, frozen
into its background, tense, ready to spring away at the first move
the hunter might make. Her hands were behind her rigid back
and he guessed that they were locked. It was said in the Valley
that very soon she would marry Thinus, and so Grannie Con
would keep her at Dieu Donné. And she belonged here—this thin
dark girl with the strange eyes. Adrian saw her catch her lower
lip between her teeth as Hal bent to write his signature, and then
Thinus turned to look at her and smile, and her response came
uncertainly—the answering smile that was on the razor edge of
tears.

Solly blotted the wet ink.

"You will never regret this, Grannie Con," he said. "We promise you that—all of us here who are concerned in this matter."

"Thank you," she said. But her voice was faint.

It was then that Joshua burst into the room, ashen-faced.

"Baas Thinus! Come quick! De Tokay forests is burning an'
de wind is blowing dis way!"

They went out onto the high front stoep. From there they
could see the fire.

The pine plantations to the northwest were already ablaze in a
tongue-shaped wedge driven in the direction of Dieu Donné by
the southeast wind sweeping up the Valley from the sea. The
night was moonless and the fiery belt painted a picture of infernal
beauty against the dark crescent of the mountains. On the peaks
of those mountains, day and night throughout the fire-season, a
lookout was posted ready to report the first sign of smoke or
flame to the nearest headquarters of the Cape Peninsula Fire Protection, and already the battle between man and fire was joined.
Mobile water-tankers were on the spot, with van-loads of experienced fire-fighters in continuous wireless communication with
the Fire Protection headquarters, and the watchers at Dieu Donné
could see the tiny ant-like silhouettes of the beaters attacking the
flanks of the fire.

"Thinus," said Roxane in a strained voice, "I was riding up
there this morning. I could swear I saw Ben."

It returned to her now—the memory of a form glimpsed but
ignored as she had galloped Rooinek up the wide fire-path. The

figure had been familiar. It had been Ben. She ought to have ridden back instantly to warn Thinus. Ben was a suspected fire-raiser, and yet the significance of his presence there had not occurred to her. She had been too preoccupied with her own personal problems and emotions. Yet another thought came to her. Since her return from Europe she had noticed that Wolf no longer accepted Ben as he did the other servants of Dieu Donné. The big Alsatian treated the deaf boy with suspicion, and sometimes, at his approach, Wolf's hackles rose and he snarled in a threatening way. She had mentioned this to Thinus, and he had said, "Wolf recognizes the smell of dagga—and he knows it's bad! When Ben has been smoking the dog mistrusts him." Yesterday Wolf had growled at Ben.

The danger signs had been there for her to read—the growl of a dog, wind-clouds heralding the southeaster and the deaf boy in the plantation—and she had paid no attention. Yet a search would almost certainly have revealed the crude preparations of the fire-bug—the tin with the candle in it—the paraffin. . . .

"I could have guessed it! Damn the boy!" Thinus did not reproach her for failing to warn him. He had more immediate worries. It was horrifying to see the young plantations burn, but the Forestry Department would have every assistance in fighting the blaze, whereas the threat to Dieu Donné was his personal concern.

"That fire is only about three miles away," he said. "In less than half an hour we may be in serious danger here."

He turned to shout at Joshua, who stood at the foot of the steps with Lizzie and a group of farm hands.

"Toll the slave-bell! Get everyone you can up here!"

In a few moments the old bell was clanging its summons across the vineyards, but already the people of the coloured village—men, women and children—had begun to hurry along the paths to Dieu Donné. Most of them carried branches for beating, others had spades or long sticks with sacking tied round the ends. From childhood they had helped to fight bush- and forest-fires and they knew what was required of them.

Adrian Fairmead was well aware that a threat to Dieu Donné included a threat to Farway, for the two estates marched to-

gether, but Dieu Donné was in the direct line of the course of
the fire, standing between it and his own property. He made
no suggestions, accepting, without question, the leadership of
Thinus, who was obviously gauging the situation and considering
the most effective action.

Roxane stood beside Grannie Con's chair, and Hal and Solly
waited to receive their instructions. Brink, the foreman, had come
onto the stoep with Max Immelmann, the wine-maker, and both
were conferring with Thinus.

Roxane heard Thinus say to Immelmann, "You get the pump
down to the pond with the hoses, and I'll keep Brink with me for
the other job."

What other job? Thinus came to Grannie Con. Under the
harsh stoep light Roxane saw his bright hair blown by the wind,
and his strong features set in grim lines of determination. For the
first time she was aware of him as considerably older than herself
—a man in his middle thirties who had given much of his youth
on the battlefield. He is lucky not to be blind, she thought, lucky
not to have been killed! And soon it will be my turn to wound
him. Can I bring myself to do it?

The old lady looked up at him, and a few strands of her thin,
silvery hair escaped the fine net that covered them and blew
across her sunken cheek. The thousand small lines of her face
were mercilessly exposed by the circle of white light, and Roxane
thought, as she had often done before—*the beach* . . . the beach
when the tide is far out and the little birds have criss-crossed the
sands this way and that . . . it would be chill to the touch, that
delicate skin, chill with her great age, and the set of the sun and
the ebb of the tide. The little imprints made by the birds of life—
the gay, lovely birds and the cruel birds—were painfully etched
as her old eyes sought her nephew's face.

"Grannie Con," he said in his slow gentle way. "Immelmann
and a few boys have gone to get the hoses rigged from the pond.
We are going to soak the thatch."

She nodded. "What else?"

"The safest thing is the dangerous thing," he said. "That forest
fire is a bad one and spreading fast before the wind. *We must go
to meet it.*"

"A counter-fire?"

"Ja, Oumissus—a counter-fire. We must start it up there on the rise."

Grannie Con felt a long-forgotten uprush of energy flood her tired veins, and, under the powerful astringent of peril to Dieu Donné, the rents and torn places of her mind seemed to draw together and pulse with a new life.

Her sharp staccato voice had authority and vigour as she said, "In this wind, Thinus? How do you propose to handle your counter-fire? How can you control its course? It may be blown across to us by the wind."

"Brink and I and our helpers will look after that. The big north vineyard will be between the homestead and the fire—and, if it does set alight, it can be handled. Fire doesn't rage through a vineyard. The rise is about a mile away——"

She interrupted sharply. "A spark from that distance could get our thatch!"

"That is a chance we have to take. And the thatch will be well soaked, remember. I shall leave Immelmann and Adrian in charge here. They will take care of the fire-buckets and extinguishers, and fortunately there is still a good deal of water in the pond."

Adrian Fairmead's eyes had brightened behind his glasses, and the crest of grey hair lifted in the wind as he turned to the younger man. The years of menace in London—of roof-top vigils while enemy bombers thrummed over his beloved city—came back to him and the old alertness revived. Here was the emergency, here action.

"I have some experience of fire-fighting," he said mildly, "a hangover from the war." Home Defence—the most active part he had been able to play.

"That's fine." Thinus looked down once more at the old lady in the wheel-chair. "Then we can go ahead with our counter-fire, Oumissus?"

"Go ahead, Thinus!" she said.

Roxane drew a deep breath. So it was to be the bold course, the dangerous course—the one chance that could save Dieu Donné from the flames that even now were racing towards them on the wings of the southeaster! After the flood Grannie Con had taken the big risk—and it had failed. Once again she was taking the big risk. Holy Mother—let her win through this time!

Thinus pressed the frail braced shoulder with a movement of admiration and affection. Then he swung round to Roxane.

"You, Roxie—you must put through two telephone calls! First to Karl Krige. Their place is up-wind and safe. Tell him we are starting a counter-fire here, and we want his help and all the boys he can muster. Second, you must get on to the Mayor of Wynberg, old Jaapie Pienaar. Tell him Dieu Donné is in grave danger and we may need to call on the Fire Brigade. Without his personal permission they dare not lift a hand to help us."

"Wait!" the old lady cut in. "Roxane can get hold of Karl, but I will speak to Mr. Pienaar myself. He will not say No to me. He will not let Dieu Donné burn!"

Roxane knew well that Grannie Con's dislike of talking on the telephone amounted to a phobia. Since the amputation of her leg she had refused to touch the instrument and had always used Roxane or Lizzie as an intermediary. Yet now love had cast out fear—love of Dieu Donné! She knew also that Dieu Donné had no call on any Fire Brigade, for the Valley was outside the municipal area. But Dieu Donné was history, it was the old Cape—and the Mayor of Wynberg was a traditionalist.

"I will get Mr. Pienaar for you, Grannie Con," she said. "And you shall speak to him."

As she wheeled the chair towards the doorway she saw Hal step forward, and her heart contracted. For a moment she had forgotten Hal. Thinus had dominated the scene. And it was to Thinus that the young man addressed himself.

"Tell me how I can help."

Roxane paused. She could not help it. A new tension had sprung into being. She could almost feel the resentment that surged up in Thinus. It was as if, for an instant, she *were* Thinus.

In fact, Hal's quiet voice that must be answered; his presence—both supple and strong—and Roxane's momentary hesitation, all imprinted themselves simultaneously upon Thinus. Rage burned through him, fierce as the fire that imperilled the homestead, for this man threatened all that he held most precious—his love, and with it his whole life—and he knew that between Hal and himself there could be no compromise. One of them would have to leave the Valley with or without Roxane. Words rushed to his lips: You have no place here! Get out and leave us alone to save what is ours! Go back to your English island and your English women and let me keep this one girl who is all my world! But his mind, cold and calculating, assessed another pair of hands to fight for Dieu Donné, a trained soldier who would take his orders and carry them out, a man with initiative and courage. And it was his mind that answered Hal.

"This thing is the work of fire-bugs, and I have reason to believe it is aimed at Dieu Donné. When one fire is at its height a fire-bug will always start another. You must keep a lookout. If you see smoke or flame anywhere take beaters and go there. We will leave a few boys here in case of that emergency. And send Roxane to report to me on the rise at the counter-fire."

His glance swept over the young man's neat grey suit.

"You had better come over to my place with me now, and I'll give you some overalls. It won't be the first time I will have lent you informal togs!" Thinus's smile had a trace of bitterness as he hurried across to his cottage with Hal at his side.

Roxane left Lizzie to take charge of Grannie Con's wheel-chair and ran to her room to change into slacks and an old riding shirt. She pulled a large kerchief out of a drawer to put over her hair should it be necessary.

She was elated by the news Karl Krige had given her over the telephone.

"I know about the fire in the Tokay plantations," he had said, "and I would have been with you at Dieu Donné before now, but Aletta has just presented me with a daughter—half an hour ago! . . . Yes, both splendid. . . . Listen, Roxie, I'll be over at your place in no time. . . ."

Karl's happiness had come over the wire with a sense of invincibility. They had wanted a girl. Roxane knew that Aletta would be overjoyed. Grannie Con's call had been less satisfactory. The Mayor of Wynberg had regretted that the fire engines were already out—Mrs. de Valois knew how it was at this season with fires all over the Peninsula—but he would certainly give his permission for the brigade to go to the assistance of Dieu Donné if it should be needed—providing, of course, that it was back in time.

When she went out again, Roxane found that Merle and Guy and the Kriftis had all come to see if there was anything they could do. They wore rough clothes, and she realized that never before had she seen Mr. Krifti dressed as a countryman, and, even in this hour of confusion and anxiety, she had to smile, thinking that he looked like an elderly actor who has taken a worn shooting jacket from the props cupboard.

Merle's eyes glittered with the unholy excitement that reminded Roxane of the time in Johannesburg when Hal had been stabbed. At last—said Merle's eyes—at last this drowsy old Valley is awake and fighting for its life!

Within a very short time Karl Krige had arrived with a vanload of beaters ready to join Thinus and Brink on the rise, and in the meanwhile the long flat canvas hoses were being run out from the pond to the house. Roxane could see the swell of the water as the pump filled them and soon they were playing on the thatch of the cellar roof.

Up on the rise the flames of the counter-fire were licking at the bush in a wide semicircle as it began to work slowly downwards the raging inferno that was rapidly devouring the young resinous pines of the Tokay forests. Over there men would be fighting a deadly battle in the billowing smoke, losing their way if they lost their heads for an instant, liable to find themselves encircled and cut off—tiny little humans, brown and white, beating at the hem of a monstrous flaming curtain rising some sixty feet into the windy, ash-laden, smoke-blackened air. The dark dome of the sky was lit by a drifting rain of sparks. Any one of those fireflies, borne on the wind, could spell disaster for Dieu Donné. If the cellar should catch fire the great wooden vats with their inflammable contents would go up in a diabolical conflagration and then the homestead adjacent would be doomed.

Roxane could see that Merle was well aware of the danger and profoundly excited by it. What was she thinking—Merle, who had always fought against the claims Dieu Donné made upon her?

In truth, Merle's feelings were mixed. Was the obligation of

her heritage to be destroyed here before her eyes? Was she to be
set free by a catastrophe that would break Grannie Con's heart?
The situation affected her so strongly that it was akin to an over-
whelming sex-thrill—the moment when it became inevitable to
yield. She shuddered and hid her face. It was then that Mr. Krifti
touched her arm and pointed towards the berg.

Against the dark shoulder of the mountain, about half a mile
higher and nearer than the main fire, was a thin gold snake.

Guy and Hal had seen it too, and they came quickly to the
little group standing near Grannie Con's chair.

"We'll take a few beaters over to the new fire," said Guy.
"And Kriff, I suggest you and Merle and Louise begin getting
valuable stuff out of the house. These boys here can help carry
out the heavy furniture."

By now the native house-boys, from Farway, and Merle's cottage, and the Kriftis', had gathered round, and Elias took swift
command of these makeshift porters.

"Guy," said Merle, "I'm coming with you to the fire!"

"You are not!" he snapped. "You will do as I say and stay here!
This is your inheritance at stake, and Grannie Con may need
you."

Defiance lifted her chin, and then, at sight of Guy's mouth and
eyes, she drew back, acknowledging his authority. This was the
lover with the whip-hand in command of his wife. She had forgotten that masterful aspect of Guy and it stirred her to be under
his domination once more. She called out to him. "Don't go without me!" But he was already collecting beaters, and it was Solly
Caine who said to her, "Your duty is here at the homestead."

She spun round. "Solly! What the hell are *you* doing here? I
had no idea——"

"I know you hadn't," he grinned. "I am here on a matter of
business. Now come and help clear the house."

Roxane went a little distance with Hal and Guy, and then she
left them to go towards the counter-fire on the rise and report to
Thinus.

"Darling—you will be careful?" Hal lingered for a moment
behind Guy and the beaters. "I hate to let you out of my sight!"

His arms were round her and his lips pressed down on hers.

"It's all right," she laughed breathlessly, as he released her. "I have been brought up in the Valley and I know as much about this sort of fire-fighting as you do."

He watched her make her way towards the blazing wedge of bush beyond the vineyard and then he turned and hastened up the rough berg track Guy had taken.

Roxane had damped the big kerchief she had been wearing round her neck, and now, as she ran through the vineyard, she put it over her hair as protection against the ceiling of flying sparks.

Her eyes smarted and the acrid fumes of burning vegetation made her gasp. From time to time the rain of ash blinded her. Wolf loped at her heels. He had been trained to fire-rescue, and the roar and heat of the flames did not daunt the big Alsatian. Suddenly a gust of wind blew a pillar of smoke sideways, revealing Karl Krige's huge frame as he beat forcefully at the burning undergrowth.

"Karl!" she called chokingly against the noise of wind and fire, "Where is Thinus? There is a new fire—up on the berg!"

"One of our boys spotted it—Thinus has just left to take some beaters over there." Smoke rolled between them, and when it dispersed once more she was gone.

She tied the damp kerchief more closely about her head as she began to scramble up the hillside with the dog beside her.

She could see the new fire running parallel with the mountain track in a wide wave burning in the direction of the *kloof* and the waterfall—seeking out her secret place! Every now and again a branch or a bush was carried by the wind like a flaming brand and tossed into the night to start yet another fire.

Roxane stopped to draw breath.

As she looked up the berg she realized that this fire had already crossed the track and that the beaters were concentrating only on its lower edge. If the wave followed its present course it would be checked head-on by the stream, and the upper flank would die out on the wide forestry fire-path higher up the mountainside. In the meantime it was clearly the plan to prevent it descending into the pine-woods and orchards behind Dieu Donné.

When the clouds of smoke were torn by the wind she caught

glimpses of the fire-fighters. Hal—that was Hal on the far left, and Guy in the middle—and over on the right, separated by the track from the other beaters, was Thinus.

Then Roxane saw a furtive figure silhouetted against the glare of the flames. It crept out of the green untouched verge towards Thinus. Beside her Wolf stood in his tracks, the hair on his great rough back bristling. Ben was crawling up behind the stalwart form beating at the flames. Suddenly the deaf boy rose and raised an arm. Roxane expected to see the beater's branch descend on the tongues of fire. But there was no branch in the murderously upraised hand—only the short length of lead piping aimed at the smoke-blinded head of Thinus.

Her warning shout went unheard in the furious night as the powerful body of Wolf hurled itself through the air. Dog and boy went down together and Ben felt the teeth of a killer buried in the back of his neck.

Thinus swung round, and Roxane ran forward to meet him, hands outstretched. But, even as she did so, a new and terrifying sound rumbled above the tumult of wind and flames. The bush binding the mountainside had burned away and a loosened avalanche of earth and boulders had begun its deadly descent. Through the wall of flame the landslide thundered—down the track towards the slight form of the girl whose agonized cry of "Thinus!" was lost in the roar of approaching death.

CHAPTER 26

REVELATION

It was past midnight.

In the kitchens of Dieu Donné and Farway Lizzie and Elias were cutting sandwiches and making coffee and tea. The weary beaters would be coming in soon for rest and refreshment while reinforcements took their place.

Outside, at some distance from the house, were piled the most valuable pieces from the homestead, including the great armoire and chest and the family portraits. Mr. Krifti stood over them—a self-appointed guardian assessing their considerable value with interest and respect.

Grannie Con had allowed Merle to bring her a brandy and water, for exhaustion was creeping over her like paralysis. If only she could get about like the others—do something, instead of sitting here helpless and crippled! Where was Roxie?

"Merle," she said. "Have you seen Roxie?"

"Roxie? She's been gone some time. She went up to the counter-fire to find Thinus. She's probably helping the beaters."

Merle spoke enviously. She too would have preferred to be in the thick of things up there on the hillside.

Fear took hold of Grannie Con. God, keep Roxane safe! Her old eyes fastened anxiously on her grand-daughter. "Where is the Bible—our family Bible? Bring it here. Let me hold it in my lap." Let me draw strength and comfort from its weight! The nerves of her missing leg were leaping. The Bible would press upon them and deaden them.

"I will look for it," said Merle.

She found Mr. Krifti hovering over the furniture and rugs, the priceless porcelain and antique silver piled under a big spreading oak still in full leaf. A hurricane lantern stood on the ground.

"Where in this damned junk-heap is the family Bible?" she asked him. "I haven't a clue, and Grannie Con wants it."

He looked at her curiously. Her fair curls were greyed by a light deposit of drifting ash, and the upthrown light of the lantern brought out the brilliance of her eyes and the lovely contours of her face.

He stooped and turned over a Persian carpet thrown haphazard over pictures and rare books. Beneath it lay the portrait of young Sarah de Valois—dark and tender-featured, enigmatic in this strange setting. Next to that was the Bible. Mr. Krifti lifted it, and, as he did so, the heavy leather cover fell open and revealed the fly-leaf with its four seals holding the loose sheet of concealing paper in place.

"Good heavens! What's this?" Merle took it from him and sat

on the stinkwood bench rescued from the *voorkamer*. She read the inscription in her grandmother's angular hand.

These seals are to be broken after my death
by
Maria Merle Masterson and Roxane de Valois
signed
Constance Henrietta Vos de Valois
Dieu Donné
Constantia.

She stared up at Mr. Krifti, puzzled and speculative. "What do you make of that?"

"It might be interesting to know." His voice was soft and insinuating. It came to her through a brief lull in the wind.

"It might indeed," she agreed.

Merle slid the long nail of her forefinger under the edges of the two lower seals and broke them.

"Bring the lantern," she said. "Put it here on this table."

Mr. Krifti did as she asked, and together they examined the page on which were inscribed the births, deaths and marriages of the de Valois' of Dieu Donné.

Adrian Fairmead turned to his wife.

"There is really nothing more we can do here for the present. The thatch is soaked, the best things are safely out of the house, Solly and Kriff are both here, and luckily the wind is going down. So I suggest that you and I go and have a look at the counter-fire."

"But Hal is up at the new fire," she said, her eyes on the ring of flame girdling the berg.

He took her arm gently. "It's too steep for us there. You could never make it, and nor could I with my old game leg. The rise is about as much as we can manage. Come along, Vee!"

They followed the vineyard paths towards the lurid glare of the burning Tokay plantations. The wind had abated and the counter-fire had increased its pace and depth. By making a wide detour they were able to come up on its flank as it strained forward to meet the monstrous sheet of forest flame more than sixty feet high. Adrian drew a handkerchief from his pocket and gave it to Lavinia to tie round her hair to protect it from the pungent canopy of smoke, ash and sparks that drifted over them towards the homestead.

"Here!" he called above the roar of the flames and the crash of falling pines. "We'll wait here!"

She clung to his arm, and he thought that he had not been so close to her in many years. They stood in silent awe as they watched the two fires approach one another—the towering forest-fire raging triumphantly forward to leap the wide protection-path and meet the smaller bush-fire in a blazing elemental embrace. In that moment of infernal consummation it seemed to Adrian that they had looked into the very heart of hell. Then the hungry flames, feeding only upon ashes, cowered and gradually died while the little figures of men beat upon the dwindling vermilion waves that crawled inwards and expired on the blackened earth.

Adrian echoed his wife's long-drawn sigh. How brief and devastating a union—how grievous an end! For years to come only the purple fire-weed would flourish here, where a few hours ago tall trees had tossed in the wind and birds had twittered among flowering shrubs and delicate grasses. Adrian found himself thinking of his son. Thus had been the marriage of Hal and Alexa—one flame mated with another—short, ecstatic and destructive. . . .

He felt Lavinia lean towards him and saw her drawn, upturned face in the glare of the dying flames, and he bent to kiss her lips, moved by some force outside himself, by the majesty and terror of that which they had witnessed.

Merle laid the Bible on her grandmother's lap. She opened it at the page with the broken seals.

"I broke them," she said. "I am glad I did! Does Roxane know?"

Anger darkened the old lady's face.

"You read my wishes on that sealed leaf—*after my death*."

Merle ignored the words. "If you don't tell Roxane, I shall," she said. And added, "I am wondering what difference it makes—to all this—to Dieu Donné—to me——"

"Dieu Donné is no longer mine to bequeath—if that is what you mean. The estate has today been formed into a limited company with directors who will love it and preserve it."

"And this without my knowledge!"

The old eyes flashed. "You were willing enough to dispose of Dieu Donné without *my* knowledge! To Mr. Krifti! I was never to know that, was I?"

"Who told you?"

"Mr. Krifti told me! He wanted forty morgen of my land. He said that it would be his as soon as you inherited Dieu Donné—that it was as good as his already. But he didn't want to wait. He hoped to persuade me to sell it to him myself—and profit from the sale." She paused and grasped the arms of her chair more tightly. *Tock-tock* went her heart, *tock-tock . . . tock. . . .* The hiatus in the beat brought a feeling of faintness and giddiness. She forced herself to go on. "For the first time in my life . . . I was grateful to Mr. Krifti. . . . What I learned from him made my duty clear—to Dieu Donné—to you—and to Roxane." The spasm had passed and she had gathered strength. She went on sternly. "I have altered my will accordingly. You and Roxane will share my possessions equally. But Dieu Donné will never be your sole responsibility, Merle. You will never be in a position to destroy and despoil it as you please!"

Merle recognized the familiar fighting ring in the rusty voice and realized that the old warrior in the wheel-chair was not yet beaten.

"What have you done, Grannie Con?" she asked in a low tone. "What have you done with Dieu Donné?"

"Ask your step-father," said the old lady. "It was his plan—and it is a good one."

"Solly? So his business here was Dieu Donné—to double-cross me! And I'll swear Roxane will profit by his plan. . . ."

A new thought seemed to strike her. "My mother——" she said, half to herself, so that Grannie Con could not catch her words. "No wonder my mother hated Roxie! She must have guessed. Oh, yes, she must have guessed long ago. . . . And Grannie Con knew all the time and never said a thing!"

She turned away in fury. Cheated—cheated by this wise old sorceress who could smell out danger to Dieu Donné like a witch-doctor smelling out his victims!

Danger to Dieu Donné. . . . Her eyes sought the graceful gable above the carved teak fanlight and the open door. The lights were on in the dismantled house, lending it a deceptive air of normal hospitality and homeliness; but, as she looked at it, she saw the slowly smouldering thatch and the first thin tongue of flame breaking through.

"Look!"

She faced the old lady's wheel-chair towards the homestead, and bitter triumph was in her voice. "It's not I who will destroy and despoil Dieu Donné! Look at that thatch!"

"Call Solly—quick! Call Adrian—and Joshua!"

Grannie Con's cry was full of anguish. She put the police whistle on its velvet cord to her dry, shaking lips, and blew it again and again.

The age-old instinct of the primitive hunter, which may still wake to warn a man of an enemy close upon him, had caused Thinus to swing round as Ben raised the length of lead piping with intent to stun him and let the flames do the rest.

In the same instant he saw the leaping body of the big dog bring the boy to the ground. Behind them the slight, loved form of Roxane started towards him with outstretched hands. And then he heard the first fall of loosened rock—uneven and menacing against the bellow of wind and fire—and he knew that the greatest peril of berg fire-fighting was about to overtake them.

He did not stop to think. He flung down the branch with which he had been beating and sprang down the slope to meet the girl, lifting her off her feet and throwing her and himself into the green bushes on the side of the track—the bushes untouched by fire from which Ben had crept. He shielded her light body with his own and felt the hail of stones and sand hammering upon his broad back as the landslide thundered past them. Fortunately the main fall had taken the easy way down the path and only the side spray of lesser pebbles and earth half buried them. Even so, Thinus groaned as a heavy rock splinter crashed through the undergrowth on to his shoulder, crushing flesh and bone.

For a few seconds the force of the blow plunged him into unconsciousness.

Hal and Guy, lost in smoke and dust, were out of range of the full impetus of the landslide, and totally unaware of the human drama that had just been played to a violent conclusion. They knew that Thinus had been on that side of the fire, and they wondered, with sick horror, if the slide had caught him. When the smoke cleared they were able to see that the fall of earth had temporarily blanketed part of the fire, and a lull in the wind allowed them a welcome moment of respite. Guy signalled his coloured beaters to keep on at their job, while he motioned Hal to follow him. They scrambled down through the bush to the track now covered in loose earth and fallen rock, and beyond it, in the red glare that illumined the darkness, they discerned the figure of a man struggling to his feet, aided by a girl. They made their way across the debris and recognized Thinus and Roxane, their clothing torn and their faces grimed and bleeding. Thinus's khaki shirt was soaked with blood on one shoulder and his arm hung limp. His eye-mask had been torn away, and the empty, sunken socket lent him a macabre and deathly look.

"You're hurt, man!" Guy ran to support him, while Hal was already at Roxane's side.

"Are you safe, Roxane? Are you all right?"

"Yes," she said uncertainly. "But Thinus isn't."

Thinus swore a mighty Afrikaans oath as his right hand supported his life arm, which dangled helpless at his side. He had no idea of the extent of his injury and for the present the pain was in abeyance, numbed with shock.

"Never mind me," he said roughly. "Get them out—dig them out—the boy and the dog! They were caught in the slide."

"Ben and Wolf," said Roxane, and began to clamber towards the spot where they were engulfed. "Somewhere here."

Both Hal and Guy had been using spades for beating, and they now began to turn over the mound of earth in the place Roxane indicated. It was not long before they found what they were seeking.

"Oh, my God!"

Guy had uncovered the head and shoulders of both boy and animal. The fangs of the big Alsatian were still buried in the dark skin at the back of the neck, and one dead hand still grasped a short length of lead piping. Gingerly Hal loosened the fingers.

"What was he doing with this?" asked Guy grimly. "This is of more use to a skolly than a fire-fighter!"

For a moment there were only the sounds of the angry night— the crackling of flames and the shouts of one beater to another. The heat was intense, and the smoke billowed straight up into the air that had grown windless.

In a flash of rare perception Thinus saw the black image of Lizzie, who had worshipped this deaf son of hers, and the olive beauty of Saartjie, the girl Ben had loved, and suddenly many things were clear to him. For the space of a heart-beat the true knowledge of good and evil was his, and with it came understanding and compassion. He told the half-truth that would save an old coloured woman's peace of mind.

"The dog attacked Ben," he said. "I saw it. He tried to defend himself with that thing—but there was no time."

"Poor little devil," murmured Hal.

Thinus said, "Get old Klaas to carry him down to Lizzie. He is not heavy."

"What about you?" asked Hal. "Can I give you a hand? You must get to a doctor."

"To hell, man! I have the use of my legs. You and Guy carry on beating up here till we send you a relief party. Roxie can come down with me."

As Thinus and Roxane stumbled through the thick bush at the side of the buried track Roxane heard him moan. Pain was beginning to wake in crushed nerve ends, torn sinews, and shattered bone. Once he stopped for a few minutes.

"Thinus—can you go on?"

"Ja," he muttered. "I can go on. Roxie, you are crying—I know by your voice."

"Yes, I am crying . . . Poor Ben . . . my poor lovely Wolf—the dog you gave me—my friend more than my dog. . . ."

"He saved my life, Roxie."

"You didn't tell them what Ben tried to do to you—I saw it. I know. He tried to kill you!"

"Ja, I saw it too. But, you see, Roxie, I know how he felt. I got his girl gaoled—more than that . . . ja, I know how he felt! Earlier today, I too could have killed a man. I had murder in my heart."

She did not have to ask him what he meant as she stood beside him, silent and spent.

Ash.eddied softly down upon them—the dark, warm counterpart of snow—and round them the bush was quiet with the strange exhaustion of nature that follows the wind. Sadness filled her—aftermath—all aftermath! Dying fires, dying wind, dying love . . .

"I am going away, Roxie," he said. "Back to Tweefontein where I belong. I am not needed here. Brink is as good a manager as I am—he could have taken on years ago, but I wanted to stay— and Hal is a better man——"

"Hush——" she whispered.

"It is so," he said, and winced as Roxane gently touched his limp hand, setting the bells of agony jangling in his shoulder, across the back of his neck and down the length of his injured arm. She felt the shudder pass through him, and drew away in distress.

"I must go back to Tweefontein," he repeated.

A great longing for Tweefontein had risen in him, surmounting the tide of pain. He yearned for the high sky and the open veld and the sweet, clean scent of the golden grasslands. Only there would he escape the taint of that night in June. . . . The Valley seemed to close in upon him with its burned mountains and ruined forests and all their sorrow was his.

"Listen, Roxie." His voice had thickened with the pain throbbing in his shoulder. "I know about you and Hal. You don't have to break it to me. . . . I asked him, when we went over to my place to get rough clothes. . . . I said, 'Do you love her?' and the answer was 'Yes.' I asked if you loved him, and the answer to that was also 'Yes'. . . . So the telling has been done, my little squirrel—the wound is there already—deep down in here. . . ." His hand covered his heart. "But it will heal . . . like the other one . . . this arm. Come, Roxie. . . ."

She followed him blindly with the tears streaming down her cheeks, cutting their salty track through dust and ash and the traces of blood. A bird called to its mate, and called again, but there came no answering call.

At last they emerged into the orchard above the old white house, and there they paused.

"Look!" said Thinus.

They could see the fire-engines and the high ladders and the little figures, and jets playing on the homestead.

"They've come," breathed Roxane. "Oh, Thinus—they've come! Dieu Donné will be saved!"

CHAPTER 27

AFTERMATH

"There," said Merle. "Now you've seen Grannie Con, what did she say to you?"

The cold dawn light filtered into the open window of Roxane's bedroom, and the two young women, bathed and refreshed, sat on the wide cushioned sill and stared out at the berg.

The Hout Bay Fire Protection against bush- and forest-fires had taken charge, and they could hear the last of the Dieu Donné beaters shouting *totsiens* and *dankie* to Lizzie, who had supplied them all with food and coffee. As yet Lizzie and Joshua had no knowledge of the sad burden old Klaas had borne down the mountainside and laid in their little white dwelling. Soon he would tell them.

The main fire, which now no longer threatened Dieu Donné or the Constantia farms, was still burning up towards the Hout Bay Gap, but the Tokay foresters had it well controlled, and, if the wind did not rise again, it would die out harmlessly in a matter of hours.

Grannie Con had bidden the Mayor of Wynberg and the Fire Brigade a grateful farewell, for without their timely help the homestead must have been burned down. And now she lay in her big four-poster and tried to ignore the uneasy beating of her heart and the intermittent pause that from time to time arrested the life-force, bringing its own premonition of approaching death.

Tonight, for the first time in her life, she had sensed in her grand-daughter a sort of sympathy—an emotion born of the quick violent clash between them and of their very dissimilarity. When Merle's first furious resentment had died, respect for Grannie Con's action had taken its place, and with it something very like relief. Merle and I—tonight we knew each other, she thought, we really understood each other. She said that I had done right—she said she was glad. . . .

A sense of peace pervaded Grannie Con, a profound desire to yield to sleep after all that the night had brought forth. Solly Caine and Adrian Fairmead were her partners now in the fortunes of Dieu Donné, and she trusted them both. Money would flow in instead of draining away like life-blood. And Roxane had her share in this new beginning—dear Roxane who loved Dieu Donné as if it were her own. Perhaps it would be one day, for Hal Fairmead intended to settle in the Valley. . . . Grannie Con smiled drowsily. Only a few moments ago Roxane had come to her, looking oddly tall in her long flaring dressing-gown. She had knelt beside this big old bed as she had so often done, and she had bowed her head so that the old lady's hand might stray through her damp hair washed clean of ash and earth.

"It isn't Thinus, darling," she had whispered. "It is Hal I truly love, and always will. I loved him long ago, when first I saw him—and then there was Alexa—now there is only me. . . . Thinus has forgiven me. . . ."

Roxane's pale tired face had lifted, and the old lady had looked into the calm, loving eyes, reddened by the smoke of the night, and she had seen there the great shining joy of a woman deep in love and sure of the future.

"May God bless you, child. Hal is the man for you. I have known it too, and pitied you. I am happy for you—for all of us."

"He wants to live here—to farm and write—here in the Valley. So we will still be near you when we marry."

Grannie Con had shaken her head, but a smile had crossed her lips that was almost mischievous.

"We are near the parting of the ways, my Roxie. But I shall be close to *you* always, wherever you may be. . . ."

"You have been so good to me—everything in the world— mother and father——"

"You are my own."

For a few minutes Roxane had thought that Grannie Con slept. Then the voice had gone on. "Tomorrow you must go to Jimmy Jordaan. Tell him to give you the letter that is in my strong-box. He will know the one. . . . It is the letter your mother wrote to me when she sent you into my care. It was intended for you as well as for me . . . you were to read it on your twenty-first birthday, or, in an emergency, sooner. The emergency is here. . . ."

"I will do as you say."

"One thing more, child. When God gives you a son, call him Dirk—for my sake—for my boy——"

"We will call him Dirk de Valois. God will surely grant us a son for your sake, Grannie Con." Let it be so, Holy Mother!

"Now go, Roxie . . . I am very tired . . . sleep is standing by my bed . . ."

The girl's lips touched the lined forehead, and then she was gone. Grannie Con made a gesture of welcome to the phantom figure that wore the guise of Sleep. Come! said the light cold fingers in a wordless message. You have wings, you have folded wings. Spread them, Sleep!

But, in the faint grey light of the false dawn, the figure did not stir. Grannie Con sighed. *Not my time, but Thine, oh Lord . . .*

She closed her eyes and listened once more to the uneven beat of her weary old heart. *Tock-tock . . . tock-tock . . . tock. . . .*

The long past began to flow through her like an ebb tide bearing away its treasures and flotsam. Images, once loved and cherished, rose and faded. Stephanus—her lips formed his little name, "Fany"—Dirk, whose dust was in the distant desert—but Dirk, my darling, you are near me now . . . and Roxie, who was dearer to her than any living being—Roxie, who loved Dieu Donné, who had helped her fight its battles and who always would. . . .

Tock-tock . . . tock-tock . . . tock. . . .

She raised her heavy lids and sought the open window. The curtains were not drawn, yet the room seemed very dark. That was nature's way—the false dawn, the sinking back into night, and then the glory of the daybreak. The figure in the guise of Sleep drew nearer in the deepening gloom. Grannie Con smiled faintly. Ah, Sleep, you are coming for me now! Your folded wings are spread. Ah, Sleep, how mighty are your wings!

"What did she say?" Merle repeated to Roxane.

The girl drew her gown more closely round her and shivered in the chill of dawn. "Not much. She was very tired."

"Poor old dear—her beloved Dieu Donné so nearly burned down!"

Roxane looked at Merle curiously. "You've changed," she said. "What is it?" In the growing light she discerned the quality of Merle's smile. Almost soft.

"Can one change overnight?"

"Things happen that change one." Thinus—my poor Thinus— Hal, my dear love. . . .

"Maybe," said Merle. "Roxie, did Grannie Con tell you *who you are?*"

"Who I am?" She glanced up, startled. And an old childhood's fear tugged at her nerves. Merle had told her terrible things— *"They killed your mother—shot her as a spy."*

Merle leaned forward and her brilliant gaze rested on Roxane with a queer searching expression that was part resentful and part affectionate.

"Who you are is written in the family Bible," she said. "I took the Bible to Grannie Con last night. She asked for it. Did you know that she had sealed a sheet of paper over the index page— the one with the de Valois records?"

"Yes, I noticed that ages ago. I never bothered about it. She hated the idea of anyone finding out her age."

"*Her age!* It wasn't her age she was trying to conceal, Roxie—

though it might interest you to know that she was nearer ninety
than eighty. Oh, no, my dear, it wasn't her age she was hiding!
I broke those seals myself. And then I took the Bible to her, and
told her what I had done."

"What did you learn, Merle?"

She asked the question in spite of herself, and she waited for
the answer, afraid.

Merle laughed softly, and Roxane saw her fair curly head turn
away as she looked out into the pink fresh light of sunrise. Then
she faced the younger girl with that reluctant liking still in her
eyes.

"You and I, Roxane de Valois, are the daughters of the same
father! We are both the children of Grannie Con's son—Dirk de
Valois. According to the laws of nature, you—as much as I—
belong to Dieu Donné!"

There was a whirling in Roxane's brain. Dirk de Valois? Disbelief and bewilderment chased through her mind on the heels of
intense, incredulous joy. Surely Christopher Williams. . . . She
buried her face in her hands, struggling with this new astounding
revelation. Then, coolly as the first breath of winter, it came to
her that Christopher Williams had loved Maman as Thinus had
loved her—Roxane. He had been the protector, perhaps even the
accepted lover—but never the beloved. Dirk de Valois—yes.
Dirk with the dark deep-set eyes and the poet's mouth—a mouth
shaped so like her own—Dirk had been the forbidden beloved.
Yes, here was truth!

And Bella Caine had guessed that truth long ago. Suddenly
Roxane remembered the night before Merle's wedding—candle-
light and champagne, Grannie Con carving the plump brown
goose, and Bella's eyes disconcertingly upon her, seeking an elusive resemblance—to Anne? To Dirk? And Guy saying suddenly
that she was like the portrait of young eighteenth-century Sarah
de Valois. She remembered the thrill that had passed through her
at his words, for she had often felt a fey affinity with that unknown de Valois bride. Her blood and mine, both de Valois!
thought Roxane now. And Grannie Con truly my grandmother—
and Dieu Donné truly my home! Not in law, perhaps, but in
nature.

"I'm sorry, Merle," she said haltingly. "I believe you—but I don't understand——"

"Grannie Con told me everything," said Merle. And she repeated the story as she had heard it.

"It seems my father and mother were not getting on—and do you wonder? Dirk was sensitive and hot-blooded and my mother is ice. She cares only about herself. Dirk was manager of a farm in Worcester then—getting the experience he needed to take on Dieu Donné—and my mother was bored with Worcester. She decided to go to Europe, that a few months apart would help them to settle their differences. I was three or four then. Mother had always wanted me to be good at languages and she heard of a young French teacher who wanted to come to South Africa. That was how Anne came into our household. She took charge of me and housekept for my father while Mother was away— and Mother spun out her holiday to a year. . . ." Merle shrugged her shoulders and her lip curled. "Do you wonder at the result? If Mother had given a thought to Dirk she would have realized the madness of leaving him for so long—with Anne there—beautiful and attractive. But Mother has never thought about anyone except Bella—Bella de Valois—Bella Caine. . . . I wish I could remember your mother, Roxie, but I can't. I was too small. You can't really remember her either. . . ."

They were silent, trying to conjure the French girl Dirk had loved out of the past.

Presently Merle went on: "She was a secret one, Roxie. Dirk never knew of your existence—nor did Grannie Con—not till the war, when you came here. Anne left that farm in Worcester when my mother returned, and she told no one that she was going to have a child. Only one person knew. Your godfather, Christopher Williams. He had loved her for years and he helped her in every way he could."

"He was married," said Roxane. "His wife was—ill."

"She was in a lunatic asylum," said Merle brutally. "He couldn't marry your mother because both he and she were devout Catholics. But he gave her his name. When the war came he made it possible for her to send you here. It was then that she wrote and told Grannie Con everything. She didn't know Dirk was dead.

She asked Grannie Con to be kind to you—and love you—but to keep the secret of your parentage for the sake of Dirk's marriage —and of his legitimate child—me——"

Merle's voice broke and she covered her face with her hands. At last she said, "Your mother must have been a good woman as well as a brave one . . . I could wish . . . she were mine. . . ."

Roxane touched her hand—deeply moved—but Merle shook it off and rose with a movement of annoyance at her own admission of sentiment.

"Of course she meant you to know the facts when you were old enough to accept them—and understand. And after Dirk was killed and my mother married again, Grannie Con decided to put your birth with the family records. Oh, well, that was all long ago—an old story—a love-affair that didn't work out very well— and there's nothing left of it now—except you, my little sister, and maybe Grannie Con's wish that you, not I, could inherit Dieu Donné!"

"She has never even suggested such a thing!"

"She's wanted it though. And now we know why. But I was the lawful heir, and to her sort that means a great deal. In any case, everything is changed since yesterday—since her deal with Solly and Adrian Fairmead. I don't mind. I'm glad on the whole. I hate the Valley—always have. If I'd inherited this place I would have sold it to Krifti the very next day—and lived in mortal terror of the Oumissus' spook for the rest of my days! As it is I'll get my share in cash and holdings in the company, and no responsibility —nor guilt. It's all fine this way!"

"Mr. Krifti," said Roxane. "He's bad! He'll be furious when he knows he'll never get Dieu Donné—or any part of it."

Merle laughed shortly. "Kriff! He'll be all right. I know Kriff's sort. The Mr. Kriftis of this world don't fight the losing battles— not they! They surrender and go over to the enemy. When Kriff gets wise to the fact that he won't get Dieu Donné at any price, or under any conditions, he will find somewhere else. There are other valleys as lovely as this, other homesteads——"

Roxane's fingers grasped Merle's wrists fiercely. "None so lovely! Don't dare suggest it!"

It was the familiar clash, and they looked at each other in the growing light and smiled.

My half-sister, thought Roxane. How strange!

She said slowly, "So Thinus is my cousin?"

"Yes," said Merle. "Thinus seems to fall for his cousins. He was in love with me once—remember? And Grannie Con doesn't hold with cousins marrying. She wouldn't hear of it for me—and she'll make objections when he asks for you. You wait and see!"

Roxane said, "Thinus saved my life tonight."

"He's tough," said Merle. "They all are—the Vos clan. Oh, Roxie, I forgot to tell you, while you were with Grannie Con, Guy rang up from the hospital. They say that bust shoulder of Thinus's will mend all right. So don't worry about him too much."

But Roxane was thinking—so that was it, so that was why Grannie Con had not really wanted her to marry Thinus, although she loved them both. He was too close—the cousin she had loved more dearly than a brother.

As the morning light gradually flooded the room it seemed to Roxane that the blurred outlines of her own position at Dieu Donné were sharpening. Soon she would go to her secret place— on past the scene of last night's disaster—and there, bit by bit, the picture would come clear.

The southeaster had blown itself out at last, and the hot, still day had drawn to its close.

Roxane stood with Hal on the burned-out rise above Dieu Donné. The Valley of the Vines seemed emptied of life. The vineyards—their harvest yielded and crushed—rested between their wind-breaks of gums and poplars and their sear thinning leaves drifted to the earth where the weeds would soon flourish to bind it against the winter rains. The tower of Farway rose naked beyond the gables of Dieu Donné and its damaged thatch. Up here the blackened bush and forests spoke of the devastation of the night.

Down among the oaks were grief and mourning. In Lizzie's little home a boy lay dead. "Fightin' dose dreadful fires," she

moaned to Joshua; "so brave, our Ben, always fightin' dose fires."
And no one had disillusioned them. In the old four-poster, where
generations of de Valois' had been born and had breathed their
last, Grannie Con still slept; and the thousand furrows of her face
were smoothed but not erased by the white hand of eternal
peace.

The *volkies* of Dieu Donné looked at one another with scared
black eyes. Die Oumissus was gone. It was the end of an era. But
already the tales were unfolding. The old ones, who had known
her in her distant youth, recalled her exploits and her sayings.
They told the children of the wild horses she had ridden, the
floods and fires she had fought, the help and comfort she had
given to her people in distress, and the manner in which she had
faced her own grave misfortunes. They whispered of the spook
who had given warning of Baas Dirk's death, of a ruined harvest
and of the leg she had lost. But, even after they had crippled her,
she had gone about her vineyards in her wheel-chair and to the
little stone church where the people of Constantia worshipped,
whether they were brown or white. They said that the new
houses of Mr. Krifti's building estates might crowd in upon the
wide acres of Dieu Donné, but her spirit would keep them at a
safe distance. It would walk among her cherished vines and bless
them. For this was her home, the home of her ancestors and of
her descendants. It was sad that Miss Merle didn't suit Dieu
Donné, but the Lord had sent Miss Roxie in her place. The Lord
had lifted a little child out of the flames of war and set her in this
green valley where she rightly belonged. Yes, down in the coloured village, over the cooking-pots and on sunny doorsteps, the
legends were growing.

Hal's arm tightened about Roxane's shoulders.

"Darling—the sadness of all this——"

She looked at the scorched earth, and down at the grove of oaks
shading the old homestead with its closed shutters, and her heart
wept silently in her breast. Then she raised her eyes to Karl
Krige's farmhouse higher up the berg. Last night a new life had
been welcomed there. When my turn comes, let me be like Aletta,
she thought, fearless and glad in bearing my babies! Love caught
at her throat and burned her eyes, and all through her body the

young life throbbed, turning her in the arms of her lover so that he bent to take her lips.

The Farway lion-dogs, lonely without Wolf, went bounding through the ruined forest, between the fallen and blighted trees. Somewhere a squirrel showed a cheeky scolding face and quivering tail, and clear in the evening air came the *dee-dee-bee, dee-dee-bee* of the butcher-bird, aggressive and virile. Against the golden glow of the Hout Bay Gap two eagles wheeled, dark and purposeful, creatures of the crags and high places, and from Dieu Donné came the tolling of the old slave-bell to tell of sunset and the end of the long day's labour.